"Please  Maxie Parrish silently prayed.

But she knew no rescue would be coming as her past walked steadily toward her.

She would recognize Kyle Hayden anywhere, anytime. By his stride, the shift of his shoulder... his sexy rocking hips.

"Is this the Wind Dancer Ranch, ma'am?"

"Yes, Kyle. It is."

His head jerked up, his gaze narrow and piercing. His eyes still held the same intensity, making her body talk when she wanted it to be silent.

And unfortunately, after all this time, he knew it.

"Hello, Max."

The sound of his voice, deep as the ocean floor, sent tremors through her bloodstream. It didn't help that he still looked good. The last time she'd seen him, he was cramming his gear into a marine green sea bag, expecting to marry her the next day before he shipped out. Don't panic, she thought. He doesn't know about the last seven years...or *his* daughter.

Dear Reader,

Hectic life? Too much to do, too little time? Well, Silhouette Desire provides you with the perfect emotional getaway with this month's moving stories of men and women finding love and passion. So relax, pick up a Desire novel and let yourself escape, with six wonderful, involving, totally absorbing romances.

Ultratalented author Mary Lynn Baxter kicks off November with her sultry Western style in *Slow Talkin' Texan*, the story of a MAN OF THE MONTH whose strong desires collide with an independent lady—she's silk to his denim, lace to his leather... and doing all she can to resist this *irresistible* tycoon. A small-town lawman who rescues a "lost" beauty might just find his own Christmas bride in Jennifer Greene's heartwarming *Her Holiday Secret*. Ladies, watch closely as a *Thirty-Day Fiancé* is transformed into a forever husband in Leanne Banks's third book in THE RULEBREAKERS miniseries.

Don't dare miss the intensity of an innocent wife trying to seduce her honor-bound husband in *The Oldest Living Married Virgin*, the latest in Maureen Child's spectacular miniseries THE BACHELOR BATTALION. And when a gorgeous ex-marine shows up at his old flame's ranch to round up the "wife who got away," he discovers a daughter he never knew in *The Re-Enlisted Groom* by Amy J. Fetzer. *The Forbidden Bride-to-Be* may be off-limits...but isn't that what makes the beautiful heroine in Kathryn Taylor's scandal-filled novel all the more tempting?

This November, Silhouette Desire is the place to live, love and lose yourself...to sensual romance. Enjoy!

Warm regards,

Joan Marlow Golan
Senior Editor, Silhouette Desire

Please address questions and book requests to:
Silhouette Reader Service
U.S.: 3010 Walden Ave., P.O. Box 1325, Buffalo, NY 14269
Canadian: P.O. Box 609, Fort Erie, Ont. L2A 5X3

THE RE-ENLISTED GROOM

AMY J. FETZER

SILHOUETTE *Desire*®

Published by Silhouette Books

America's Publisher of Contemporary Romance

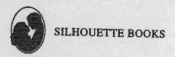

SILHOUETTE BOOKS

ISBN 0-373-76181-3

THE RE-ENLISTED GROOM

Copyright © 1998 by Amy J. Fetzer

Printed in U.S.A.

Books by Amy J. Fetzer

Silhouette Desire

Anybody's Dad #1089
The Unlikely Bodyguard #1132
The Re-Enlisted Groom #1181

AMY J. FETZER

was born in New England and raised all over the world. She uses her experiences, along with bits and pieces of the diverse people she's met, in creating the characters and settings for her novels. "Nobody's safe," she says. "There are heroes and heroines right in front of us, if we just take the time to look." Married nineteen years to a United States Marine, and the mother of two sons, Amy covets the moments when she can curl up with a cup of cappuccino and a good book.

For
Maureen Child
a.k.a.
High Priestess of the Clan of the Plotting Goddesses

To Baileys and coffee and sharing an ashtray.
To skipping PAW just to chat.
To emergency plot sessions
and picking apart a hero's psyche with a surgeon's
precision.
For listening to my whining with patience and sympathy,
then *prodding* me, in your oh-so-gentle way,
to work harder for what I wanted.
For shouting for joy when I finally get it,
and getting mad at me when I didn't.
And mostly, for being the consummate professional and
teaching me
what it really means to write for a living.

Thanks, Moe

Prologue

In five days Kyle and Maxie were going to be married.

In six days he was leaving for Desert Storm.

The possibility that he could lose her, his life and the only sense of belonging he'd felt since he was twelve hit Sergeant Kyle Hayden like a barrage of artillery. He tightened his arms around the woman he loved, knowing nothing could soften the news he'd always expected.

"This is so unfair," she cried, her tears wetting his olive drab T-shirt.

"I know, baby, I know," he soothed, brushing his mouth over her hair, her temple, inhaling and memorizing her lush scent. "But orders are orders." He peppered kisses over her cheeks, tasting her tears, wishing he could erase them, yet even as she sobbed, something tugged hard inside him. No one had ever cried for him before. No one had ever cared enough.

She tipped her head; tortured green eyes filled with doubt gazed up at him. "Oh, Kyle. This isn't one of your thrill-seeking games. This isn't racing a car or a dirt bike where you can stop if you want." Her nails dug into his bare arms. "War is *real*. Real bullets, real danger."

He silenced her with a deep kiss. Yes, it was war, but for five years he'd been training to fight. The need to put himself to the test meshed with nightmarish scenes of battle suddenly flashing in his mind, yet he kept tasting her mouth, kept running his hands familiarly over her plush body, pushing aside the images and focusing on the physical, the tangible…the woman in his arms.

"I'll be okay." His breath rushed with hers, his insatiable craving to get closer to her, get naked with her, right now, raged along his blood. "I'll keep my head down. I swear it."

"You better keep *all* of you down," she said.

He met her gaze, grinning. "Any parts you were particularly worried about?" He wiggled his brows.

Suddenly she shoved out of his arms. "Is everything a joke to you?" she said, swiping at her tears. "My God, Kyle, are you itching to get yourself killed?"

"Come on, baby, don't start this now." He tried to coax her back into his arms, but she wasn't buying it, skating out of his reach.

"Then when, Kyle? When you break your back instead of your leg bungee jumping out of a helicopter?" She flung her hand toward the now forgotten crutches propped against his wall locker. "Or when you take a bullet because you want to experience it ripping through your flesh to see if it compares to one of those ridiculous stunts you've already pulled!" Maxie knew she was nearly yelling, but she was so scared, for him, for their future.

Her temper was amazing, he thought as she paced like an anxious colt, his gaze dropping to her short red shirt and her long muscled legs. He wanted to be between them. "You're overreacting. That stuff never bothered you before. You even came along.'' He looked her over, long and heavy, his mind on the fringes of the conversation. ''And I thought you liked that about me.''

Maxie remembered first meeting him when he raced stock cars in Long Beach. And the collision he was lucky to walk away from alive. ''In a man I was just getting to know, yeah. It was intriguing.'' She paused, leveling him a look. ''But not in a husband.'' The shift in his features told her he was at least listening this time, and she took a step closer. ''I'd like the future father of my children around long enough—''

''Don't,'' he cut in. ''I can't think that far ahead, Max.'' He jammed his fingers into his short dark hair. ''Babies?'' The thought terrified him, and his voice pleaded. ''Why are you bringing this up now?''

Because we've pushed the wedding ahead three months because of the war, and I feel rushed. Because you're not acting at all like a man ready for a wife. Instead she told him her most recent reservation. ''Because I honestly feel you love cheating death more than you love me.''

The fraction of hesitation was far too revealing for Maxie. ''That's not true. I love you, but I have orders.''

''I know that,'' she said impatiently. ''But this is affecting us already, Kyle, and I want you to see beyond it.'' Why did she always have to be the levelheaded one in their relationship?

He straightened, folding his arms over his chest. ''It's affecting you, not me.''

Hurt sprang in her eyes. ''Isn't that enough?''

Kyle knew he was being selfish. But he could be gone for months or a year—or he could get killed and never see her again. He didn't want to talk about kids and a home. He and his older brother, Mitch, had been alone since they were abandoned when he was twelve, and the picture she painted was too foreign to him anyway. He loved her, loved everything about her, yet because he was obligated to the Marine Corps and going into a war, he couldn't give her what she wanted with any kind of certainty. Suddenly Kyle was more afraid of losing her over this than he was of an Iraqi bullet.

He lifted his gaze, hoping she didn't see how scared he was. "I love you, Maxie. This is all we have right now." He held out his hand, waiting.

She hesitated, gazing into his hopeful eyes. Then in a heartbeat, she flew to him, clinging to him.

And he clung back, covering her mouth with his. His kiss was fierce and savage, his lips grinding over hers with his need to draw her into himself, to take part of her with him to Saudi. He needed her, and she gave and gave, and then plowing her fingers through his hair and pressing her hips into his, she gave some more.

And Kyle took, grasping, greedy. He couldn't think that in a few days he was going to leave his new bride alone, that he was trading her smile on their honeymoon for a taste of enemy gunfire. He thought only of Maxie Parrish. Sleek and sexy and here for him. His hunger mounted to unfathomable proportions, his hands driving beneath her blouse, riding roughly up her warm skin. So soft, so Maxie. And when she leaned deeper into him, yanking up his T-shirt, sliding her hands over his flesh, he knew her mind was on the pleasure they would share, knew she ached with the same unrelenting hunger that always raged between them. The anticipation of being inside her nearly undid him as he quickly unfastened her bra, his hands sweeping around to envelop her breasts.

Maxie moaned with dark pleasure, helping him strip off her blouse, her nipples already tight and hard for his questing fingers. He has the most incredible mouth, she thought as he bent her back over his arm and dragged it over her naked flesh, lips tugging, drawing heavier and closer to the center of her breasts. Expectation heightened her nerves.

"Kyle, Kyle," she breathed, hesitating against his kiss, struggling with the swamping sensations to see beyond desire. He was leaving for who knew how long, and apart, they would change. It was inevitable. But how drastically would it affect their new marriage? "Maybe—" She gasped for a breath as his mouth drifted closer to her nipple. "Maybe we should postpone the wedding till you come back."

Suddenly she was upright and he was cupping her jaw in his broad palms, his dark eyes intense with quick fear. "Don't even think it. I need you." He closed his eyes, briefly, tightly. "I love you, Max," he murmured against her mouth, then kissed her again and again. "I need to know you're my wife."

Maxie felt the anxiousness in his kiss, his embrace. "Oh, Kyle. I love you, too, but we have to be realistic," she managed to say, hurriedly peeling his T-shirt over his head.

Abruptly he lifted her against him until her breasts were level with his face. "This is the only reality I want." His lips closed over one nipple, drawing it deeply into the hot suck of his mouth, and Maxie threw her head back, dark auburn hair spilling along her naked spine.

He's putting me off, she thought. He had, every time she'd mentioned waiting. But his touch, his sensual power, overwhelmed her and she surrendered to it, wrapping her legs around his hips as he back-stepped toward the bed. He brought her down with him as he sat on the mattress, his hand already beneath her skirt, pushing aside her panties.

Breathless, Maxie held his gaze as he carefully parted her, her body on some tenuous edge until his fingers plunged into her. Her eyes closed, and she rocked against his hand.

"You're always so warm and wet," he growled, and smiled at the blush racing up her body. "You pulse for me." His fingers moved inside her with deep, deliberate strokes, and he watched her desire escalate, was sure of it as she tore at the button fly of his camouflage trousers. With a look of retribution on her face, she reached inside, enfolding him.

He thrust against her touch. "Oh, Maxie," he groaned in a way that she loved.

"Is this enough reality?" she whispered against his lips as they stroked each other to frantic pitch. "Enough when you're—"

He covered her mouth with his. He didn't want to hear her uncertainties, didn't want to admit he would be alone in the desert, without connection, without family. He needed her here for him, waiting for him. Wanting him.

Like he wanted her now.

"Get naked for me," he told her, easing her off his lap. He bent to remove his combat boots, his gaze hungering over her body as she stood inches from him, skimming out of the rest of her clothes, torturing him with a heavy, bone-racking caress, a thick kiss, before she crawled onto the bed. He stood, shoved down his trousers, then kicked them aside.

Maxie watched him come to her, naked, ropy muscles and darkness, and her body reacted with a rush of liquid. He exuded power and raw sensuality, in his eyes, his walk, and Maxie knew she would never in her life be able to resist him. He was her greatest weakness. Yet the misgivings she was experiencing right now, about her feelings, their uncertain future, were a world apart from the blistering heat that constantly crackled between them.

That heat leaped beyond her anxiety when he ripped away the sheet she'd shielded herself with, his gaze scorching her body, his expression growing hotter by the moment. Defiantly she let her gaze tear over him, his shoulders carved broader and thicker from his recent training, the deep contours of his stomach, the nested maleness, thick and proud for her. Between her thighs she tightened, throbbed.

He's leaving, she thought again, yet knew he wanted to go fight for his country. Maxie would never dream of trying to stop him. The scars still pink from his last skydiving jump and the past year of knowing him told her it was useless to even consider keeping him from the scent of danger. He lived for it.

Kyle pressed his knee to the mattress. "Come here."

She lifted her chin, giving him that "make me" look that drove him wild.

Kneeling, he arched a brow, his gaze lowering to her breasts, watching her nipples tighten the longer he lingered there, before dropping to the dark curls between her thighs. She made a sound, half curse, half pleading, and he chuckled knowingly.

"It's pathetic, this command you have over me," she said, tingling for the moment when he would touch her again.

"Your body maybe—" Suddenly he snatched her by the ankles, and she let out a tiny shriek as he dragged her across the bed to him. "But you?" Slowly he shook his head. "Never." They stared and her lips curved in a sexy smile that robbed Kyle of his next breath. *She's so beautiful,* he thought, pressing his palms to her chest, dragging them over her full breasts, shaping their weight, manipulating her nipples. She growled lushly, covering his hands and arching into the pressure. Her gaze followed his fingers as they slid over her ribs, her hips, stroking her soft thighs before hooking her knees and pulling her closer and closer to his heat.

She lifted her gaze to his. A moment passed, their breathing labored. A dark hunger lingered in the air, bodies and hearts exposed. She caught her lower lip between her teeth.

Then suddenly she was against him, straddling his bare thighs, her arms locked tightly around his neck. Kyle knew without looking that she was crying. He closed his eyes and held her for a long moment, his heart clenching over her soft sobs. The unfairness of their situation increased his frustration and he sank his fingers into her hair, tipping her head and forcing her to look at him. He searched her delicate features, a lump thick in his throat. He was going to miss her. And hoped she'd miss him.

"Make love to me, Kyle. Make it last."

"We have all night. And in a few days, we'll have a lifetime."

Her eyes clouded, and she gripped him back. "No. We won't. Don't you see? You'll be gone. We don't know when you're coming back!" A pause, a whimper of despair and then, "Maybe we should not rush and wait."

In a heartbeat, he dropped her onto her back, covering her

body with his. "I can't," he said, then filled her in one long, hard thrust. "I can't. I need you too much." He withdrew, then surged, again and again, wild and frantic, his mouth crushing hers, each touch, each stroke driving away her misgivings about their future and leaving only the untamed passion they'd shared for over a year.

He was unrelenting, his reality in the here and now and not days away. Not years away. But he felt her slipping from him. He knew he was reckless sometimes, knew he took chances any sane man would shudder at, but even when he felt the hot rush of fear that came with the risk and danger, he always knew Maxie would be here for him. He wanted to make it permanent. He had to. He couldn't lose her, not even a fraction, refusing to believe their lives would change.

He kept making wild love to her, and when she trembled with her explosion, drenching him with her desire, he made love to her again, listening to her cries of passion and ignoring the words he was too terrified to hear.

Maxie sat on the edge of the bed in the cheap hotel room, her hands clenched on her lap. She toyed with her engagement ring until her finger was raw and red, then yanked it off and shoved it into her purse. Tears rained down her cheeks, splashing onto her fists. She didn't bother to wipe them away. She needed them. She deserved them.

She glanced at the clock, the big hand refusing to move past the time of her wedding. Her gaze shifted to her gown, white satin and hand-embroidered lace tossed carelessly in the chair. Once today she'd put it on, if only for a moment to feel like a bride, and she'd almost weakened in her decision. That dress symbolized all she wanted—husband, home, kids. All *she* wanted. Kyle wanted only her. And danger.

Was marriage, right now—before he had to leave for Desert Storm—the wisest move for them? Or was it just fear pushing them to rush their wedding, their lives? Was she in love with the idea of marriage and family, or with Kyle?

She tore her gaze from the gown. She'd asked herself the same questions over and over for the past hour, the urge to race to the chapel and marry Kyle staggering her.

Turmoil and fear held her back, kept her rooted to a lumpy bed in the darkened room. How could she do this to the man she loved? But she knew. Weeks of chaotic thoughts, of preparations for a wedding and for the groom to go to war, of Kyle refusing to discuss postponing their wedding, had brought her to this moment. This horrible, telling moment when she should be walking down the aisle on her father's arm. She squeezed her eyes shut and covered her face with her hands, a deep sorrow tormenting her to the breaking point.

She'd felt it while he was away for desert training six weeks ago. That first-time separation had opened her eyes, scared and confused her. For without the physical passion, she realized they were on the same road, traveling in opposite directions. She loved him deeply, yet they wanted different things, and for a while, she let herself believe she could change him, change his wants to hers. He was thrills and chills, wanting only her and the corps in his life. She wanted a home and fat babies—and stability. The only thing they wanted mutually was each other.

Maxie knew blood-jolting desire wasn't enough.

And it was the sole reason she couldn't face him right now.

One look, one touch and she would never do what she *had* to do. His stare bore too much power, his kisses too much steam, and he knew how to make her forget. Their passion was always so strong, she had trouble seeing beyond it. Until now.

They were afraid and seeking some control in a hopeless situation. He was leaving and wouldn't believe it was best to wait until he came back, that if they really loved, time would be on their side. Marriage in a panic was reckless, and getting unmarried would be much harder.

No, she thought, nothing could be harder than this. Yet

she was willing to risk everything not to make a huge mistake.

Maxie glanced at the clock again and groaned, listlessly crawling onto the bed and curling into a tight ball. She tried not to imagine her groom, what he was thinking, the hurt he was feeling. If only he had listened…if only time wasn't so short…if only there wasn't a war waiting for him…

Clad in his dress blue uniform, Kyle Hayden's spine was straight as a rifle stock, his eyes forward, his gaze on the chapel door. *She'll be here,* he thought. Any minute. Around him, guests and attendants whispered, the tick of the church clock sounding like a gong in his head. His buddies were lined up alongside him, his older brother, Mitch, offering excuses: traffic, a flat or a woman's incredible need to be late for every major function in her life. Yet the longer Kyle waited, the more he imagined her in an accident, bleeding somewhere where he couldn't get to her. He'd already sent two of his pals off to search for her. If she was okay, she would have let him know, he thought. Maxie wouldn't do this to him. Maxie wouldn't make him wonder.

Maxie loved him.

He believed. And he waited.

Waited past the time of the ceremony.

Waited as their guests left, his humiliation hidden beneath the granite expression he'd perfected over the years. His eyes never leaving the door, Kyle let his hurt and anger escalate and even as his heart leaped when a figure slipped into the chapel, he cursed himself for forgiving her so easily in those few seconds. Until he saw her mother and the look on her face. The sympathy and pity Lacy Parrish sent him was enough to kill Kyle where he stood.

He dropped Maxie's wilting bouquet and with his white barracks cover tucked under his arm, he left the church with the measured cadence of a marine going off to war. Which was exactly what he had to do. Married or not.

Less than twenty-four hours later, dressed in desert beige

camouflage utilities, Kyle stood in formation with his platoon, his body weighted down with his pack, bedroll, ammunition and weapons. He didn't speak to anyone, too aware that his buddies knew he wasn't the married man he'd hoped to be today. He tried not to imagine Maxie's face, what she was thinking when she stood him up, what she was doing now. A woman's sob caught him off guard, and his gaze snapped to a fellow marine, his wife in his arms as she cried and told him she would miss him. Kyle's throat tightened, the pain in his chest threatening his breathing. *That should be me,* he thought, tearing his gaze away to scan the crowd of women and children, parents and friends who'd come to see the marines off. He waited for long, dark auburn hair to catch his attention, waited to see her running toward him, begging for his forgiveness and telling him she loved him.

She'll come, he thought. *She won't let me get on this plane without saying goodbye.* Kyle believed and he waited, lagging behind when his platoon filed toward the plane. Still he stalled, back-stepping, searching the mass of people. *She'll come,* he told himself. She might have wanted a wait to marry him, but she loved him. She did.

A sharp command pierced his thoughts, and he faced his first sergeant.

"Move it, marine! The war won't wait."

Kyle obeyed, the last man aboard the aircraft. Yet even as the hydraulics lifted to seal the huge troop carrier, Kyle still hoped, still looked. But as the hatch closed him in with over a hundred other marines, Kyle faced the truth.

And inside, he died.

One

Grand Canyon, Arizona
Seven years later

Maxie paused, the shovel full of soiled hay halfway to the wheelbarrow when she heard the helicopter. The noise vibrated the walls of her barn, disturbing her animals as the pilot made a low-flying sweep of her place before setting down.

"Relax, Elvis," she said to the horse tethered outside his stall. "You ought to be used to that by now." She flung the putrid pile onto the heap, shaking her head. The independent pilots the park service hired when they were shorthanded in bad weather usually had Top Gun envy and were always a little showy. Apparently the pilot she was supposed to board for the next week or two wasn't beyond hotdogging, either.

Since it was likely one of the pilots she'd boarded before, she didn't immediately run out to greet him, estimating it would take him a few minutes to anchor the chopper and walk the hundred yards from the dirt helipad to the barn. If he thought to look for her there. Either way, she didn't want company. Usually the service put the temps up in hotels or at Mrs. Tippin's Bed and Breakfast, but with half the rescue teams out with the flu and the tourist traffic unusually high now for the lack of snow, the overflow boarded with her. The occasions were too rare for her to regret that part of the deal she'd made with the service three years ago. She just hoped this pilot didn't expect her to wait on him. She had too much work to do.

After maneuvering the heavy wheelbarrow down the long corridor of stalls to the truck parked outside the rear entrance, she forced it up the ramp and quickly dumped its odious contents. Maxie hurriedly backtracked, bringing the wheelbarrow back for another load, then hefting the shovel.

Movement at the far end of the barn caught her attention. She froze. The color drained from her face. Her gloved fingers tightened on the handle.

Rescue me. Oh, someone please take me away from here.

But Maxie Parrish knew no rescue would be coming.

Her worst nightmare was walking steadily toward her.

She would recognize him anywhere, anytime. Even with the fleece collar of his butternut suede jacket pulled up against the wind and his face shielded beneath a black cowboy hat, she knew him. By his stride, the shift of his shoulders...his sexy rocking hips.

Seven years' worth of guilt and shame threatened to swallow her whole, and Maxie fought the overpowering urge to run.

Instead, like a sinner anticipating penance, she waited for the moment when he would recognize her.

A duffel slung over his shoulder, his gaze was more on where he was stepping than where he was heading. "This the Wind Dancer Ranch, ma'am?"

"Yes, Kyle. It is."

He stopped short. His head jerked up, his gaze narrow and piercing her straight through to the bone.

He didn't say a word. He just kept staring, whatever he was feeling locked tightly behind an expression harder than ice. His fingers flexed on the duffel strap at his shoulder. His lips tightened. And Maxie felt the hay-strewn floor soften beneath her feet as he moved within a yard of her. His gaze roamed, and she felt heat slowly sketch her face as he searched for changes and absorbed each one. It was hard to believe those eyes still held the same intensity, dark and wicked, making her skin warm in the chilly morning, making her body talk when she wanted it to be silent.

And unfortunately, after all this time, he knew it.

It didn't help that he looked as good as he did when he was a marine, she thought. Oh, he was older, more mature and though there were a few lines around the corners of his eyes and a cynical tightness to his lips that hadn't been there before, he was still essentially the same. Handsome, tanned, sable haired with pebble dark eyes that had always held a glint of mischief. They didn't now, offering nothing. Apparently he didn't think his surprise arrival was any kind of blessing, either.

Kyle was shaking inside. Seven years faded away, and he was a marine, standing on the flight deck, waiting for her, hurting like mad. He couldn't stop the sensations, wishing to God he had never set foot inside the barn, but knew he had to get control, reminding himself that she was his past, not his present.

Damn.

Damn, damn, damn.

It shouldn't be this hard to just look at her, Kyle thought, the agony of losing her and never knowing why clutching at his chest. Yet like a masochist searching for more pain, his gaze moved over her face, her petite features, the lush figure even a shapeless flannel shirt and down vest couldn't hide. She's cut her hair, he thought stupidly. Her auburn waves were evenly trimmed, side parted and skimming her jaw, her long drop earrings emphasizing those great bones. One thing he had to say about Maxie—she had a body that evoked wild fantasies and a face that gave a man sleepless nights.

He ought to know. He'd had his share of them. And he didn't want any more.

He brought his gaze back to hers. "Hello, Max."

The sound of his voice, deep as the ocean floor, coated her, sending tremors through her bloodstream. And with it came a flood of unwanted memories, of heartache and guilt. Oh, Lord, the guilt, Maxie thought. It had never eased completely, and as she stared into his eyes now, it magnified. The last time she'd seen him, he was cramming his gear into a marine green seabag, expecting to marry her before he shipped out to Saudi Arabia. Her gaze wavered. Self-preservation steadied it. *Don't panic,* she thought. *He doesn't know about the past seven years.*

"Why are *you* here?" she finally asked, trembling and trying not to show it.

He arched a brow, his dark gaze boring into hers. "Don't have anything else to say, Max? Like 'I see you survived'? Any bullet holes to show for nine months in the Iraqi desert?'"

She cringed, his bitter tone reminding her that she didn't know what had happened to him after Desert Storm. Only that he'd never wanted to see her again.

Not that she could blame him.

Yet she refused to rise to his bait and acted as casual as she could with him staring at her so intensely. "Hello, Kyle," she said calmly, bracing her gloved hands on the top of the shovel handle and tipping her head. "You look good. Any bullet holes?" He shook his head. "Now...why are you here?"

"Me and my chopper are on loan to the park service."

Disappointment shaped her face. "Helicopters. Surprise, surprise," Maxie muttered, then hefted the shovel, scooping and dumping, relieved that her voice was steadier than her hands. "I should have known you couldn't go far from chasing danger."

Resentment burst through Kyle, that she didn't believe he'd changed—and more so that she appeared unaffected while his heart hadn't made it back to his chest, still sitting in the pit of his stomach. "You mean instead of manning a .50-caliber machine gun in an open chopper during low-flying reconnaissance?" His biting tone grabbed her attention, and she met his gaze. "No," he said, as if mulling over how to solve world peace. "I can't say it's the same." His features sharpened, his eyes penetrating. "Hauling tourists lacks some of that killer adrenaline rush you get under live enemy fire."

His sarcasm wasn't hard to miss, yet she paled at the image anyway. "What?" She focused on hitting the wheelbarrow and not his feet. "Not dangerous enough?"

"Forget about my chopper—" he unzipped his jacket and tipped his hat back "—what the hell are you doing here?" He gestured to the rows of stalls.

She scoffed and kept shoveling. "You don't think I wade in this stuff because I like the fragrance, do you?"

Kyle's lips thinned, his impatience gone. "Look, Max, just point me in the direction of the boss, and I'm outta here."

"I *am* the boss."

"What?"

Maxie glanced up. His disturbed look was almost amusing. If she wasn't doing her level best not to unravel all over the place, she might have smiled. Instead she held on to her frayed nerves, deposited the scoopful in the wheelbarrow, then propped the shovel against the wall. She faced him, brushing her hair off her forehead with the back of her gloved hand and said, "I own this place, Kyle."

Briefly he glanced around, scowling, but her mutinous expression dared him to contradict her.

They stared.

The wind skated along the barn, searching for a spot to

enter and chill them to the bone. The dropping temperature outside didn't compare to the atmosphere inside.

"So. You've been here?" His words dripped ice. "All this time?"

"Not all this time," she answered frostily, bending to move the wheelbarrow farther into the corridor. "And it doesn't matter now, does it?" As she spoke, she pulled a pair of wire cutters from her back pocket and snipped open a hay bale lying outside the stall.

With his free hand, he reached out to pat the horse, anything to keep from shaking some feeling into her. Maxie had never been so...emotionless. "Not that I can see," he said, shrugging.

"Good." She grabbed a pitchfork, quickly spreading hay in the clean stall. "At least we understand each other."

He hitched the duffel higher, shifting his weight to one leg. "Do we?"

Her gaze shot to his, and she shook her head, a warning in her tone. "Don't even go there, Kyle." She told him like it was. Over. "If I'd wanted you in my life, I would have shown up at the church."

He scowled, his gaze raking over her, making her feel as if she'd been scraped raw with a knife. She tried to look away, but couldn't and Maxie told herself it didn't do any good to notice how well the heavy cable-knit sweater clung to him, how well the rich green shade showed off his eyes and dark hair. It would be wiser to notice only one thing about him...the barely checked hostility in his eyes.

"Still heartless, eh, Max?"

She reared back. "Go to hell, Kyle."

A single brow arched, a dark wing over his penetrating eyes. "You're the one prepared for the trip."

She looked down at the pitchfork in her hand. Damn him. Damn him for coming into her life again, for making her see she couldn't escape her mistakes. She was mortally ashamed of how she'd treated him all those years ago, but Maxie had more at risk now than old feelings. She knew what her decision had cost her. And she'd paid for it in more ways than he could ever imagine. But it would be just like a man to want to hear the gory details of how badly she'd suffered, too. And she wasn't about to give him more fodder to feed on.

She met his gaze. "We haven't seen each other in seven years, so don't assume you know me anymore, because you don't." She pulled off her gloves and jammed them in her hip pocket, moving toward the horse.

He rolled the duffel off his shoulder and dumped it on the dirt floor.

Maxie's gaze lowered to his name stenciled on the canvas, and she froze as recognition dawned. It was the same seabag he'd had when she'd last seen him. Her gaze flew to his, and something flickered in his eyes just then. The cold air between them crackled. Her skin flushed. For a moment, they were alone in his barracks room, groping at each other, their wild hunger making them impatient enough not to bother taking off all their clothes.

Kyle's heart did a quick slam in his chest at the familiar heat in her green eyes, vivid enough to create an ache in his groin. Damn. He hated and wanted her all in one breath. It wasn't natural. What was, was his need to shake her, to demand why she'd abandoned him so brutally when he'd needed her the most.

Maxie Parrish had been his biggest heartache and his greatest humiliation.

But he was over her now. If he wasn't, he would have looked her up long before now and certainly before this contracted deal with his chopper put him in her life. Regardless, Kyle's gaze unwillingly lowered over the long slim body he remembered in his dreams. Her faded plaid shirt shaped her torso better than silk, loose shirttail over jeans worn nearly white and fitting her like skin. Her boots were scarred and caked with dirt. The Maxie he remembered was always dressed to kill and never without makeup. This woman had muddy knees and chipped nails.

But she was the same woman who'd deserted him without explanation, he thought as she reached out to unsnap the horse's lead.

He caught her wrist as she passed, and their gazes clashed. "You're wrong, Max. I know you better than any man."

She tugged on his grip. "You're dreaming. Again."

With a jerk, he pulled her against him, hemming her in between his body and the wall as his free hand slipped smoothly inside her down vest. The cold air rushed into her lungs at the contact, then staggered as his fingers found their way beneath her shirttails, touching her bare skin.

Lord. It was as soft as he remembered, satiny, warm, making his body throb for her.

"Kyle, don't." She wiggled her wrist, but he held tight, even as his mind screamed at him to quit torturing himself, that he wasn't prepared for any involvement with her, not again, not after the way she'd humiliated him. Yet without thought, he spread his hand over the small of her back, driving his palm upward, caressing, feeling. She was naked beneath the faded shirt.

"Oh, Maxie," he hissed softly, and her eyes softened, drifting closed, her body gravitating toward him and he remembered...remembered tasting her skin, lying naked with her, being buried deep inside her soft body. His groin thickened painfully, and he pressed her into it. His face neared, his lips a breath from hers. He drank in her startled gasp as his hand swept around to enfold her bare breast, his thumb heavily circling her tight nipple. A moan escaped him, unheeded, like a long-awaited burst of freedom. That this, the passion, the desire neither could fight or understand, hadn't changed, was a complication he hadn't expected. Suddenly it made him feel unreasonably weak.

And he resented it.

Feebly Maxie wrestled against him, but the liquid heat blossoming through her body with every tiny movement of his fingers was hard to ignore. She'd hoped if this moment ever came, that her feelings would be faint, like an old watercolor, yet they were more like a cattle stampede, coming from all directions with a force that defied nature. Her knees softened, and all at once she was hot and hungry, vulnerable for the caress of a man. This man. No one made her feel like she did when Kyle Hayden touched her. The passing years had done nothing to extinguish it; in fact the ache in her was blistering, just waiting to be uncapped. She gripped his jacket lapel to keep from sinking into the floor and waited for more.

"Some things you just can't forget, eh, baby?"

His mocking tone startled her, awakened her, and she knew in an instant he was throwing their past in her face. She focused on his eyes and found shaded indifference, a callous man without sympathy for how the past seven years had treated her.

She wrenched free and stepped back, furious with herself and him. "Yeah, but what we do about it is another," she snapped, embarrassed she was so spineless when he touched her. "That's all we had, Kyle." She leaned a bit closer, her voice low with hot anger. "A little wild sex. Nothing more." The lie rolled too easily off her lips. "At least I was smart enough to see that passion wasn't enough for a lifetime." She started past him.

He caught her, swiftly pressing her up against the wall and covering her mouth with his. He kissed her and kissed her, his tongue plunging between her lips, his hands diving beneath her shirt and molding her bare breasts. His hat tumbled to the ground as she growled against his mouth, teetering on surrender.

This is so good, she thought. He pushed his knee between her thighs, and she instinctively bore down on him, her fingers sinking into his hair and grabbing fistfuls, holding him as she paid him back touch for touch.

Suddenly he jerked back, staring. His lungs worked violently.

Her breath brushed his lips.

He arched a brow. "Not enough, Max?" The malevolence

in his dark eyes was enough to make her see the moment for what it was. A humiliation. A payback.

She shifted past him, ignoring the feel of his eyes on her back as she headed out of the barn.

Kyle remained motionless, grinding his teeth, his gaze on her as she negotiated her way around tack and hay bales. He resented the hell out of it since he couldn't even manage to move without snapping in half. And he was ashamed of himself for what he'd just done. But he'd never had much control around Maxie and knew the instant he'd seen her in the barn, he should have made an about-face and flown right out of there.

He stared at the dirt floor, rubbing the back of his neck.

That was one hell of a reunion, he thought. But ending their relationship years ago was her choice, not his. She'd made the decision for them, excluding him completely and running like a coward. She never gave him the courtesy of having his say in the matter. The humiliation and agony of that day flooded through him again, and he clenched his fist over and over, wishing he'd never laid eyes on her again. He didn't trust her. And the tightness crowding his jeans told him he shouldn't trust himself around her, either. Nor could he board here for the next two weeks. No way. Seeing Maxie for ten minutes was enough to make him consider subcontracting out this flight obligation. That's if he could have afforded it.

He had to make other arrangements. That was all there was to it. Maybe the park service had something else, and he decided he would go check.

Raking his fingers through his hair, he grabbed up his seabag and strode to the entrance, but stopped abruptly when he saw her cross the yard to a horse trailer hitched behind a black Range Rover. She's tucked her shirt in, he thought as she released the trailer door, lowering it to the ground, then disappeared inside, coming out seconds later leading a chestnut mare by the bridle. Her moves were confident as she led the animal into the paddock and out of his sight.

Kyle tried not to crane his neck for a better look and stormed to his chopper. How could he hunger for a glimpse of her and curse the urge at the same time?

Outside, the wind howled around her Range Rover, and Maxie keyed the engine, letting the vehicle warm up. Closing her eyes, she pressed her forehead to the cold steering wheel and warned herself not to cry.

This was the worst, she thought. The absolute worst. That kiss—no—that mauling in the barn warned her not to give Kyle an inch. She smacked the steering wheel, angry with him for taunting her like that and herself for falling for him like a starry-eyed schoolgirl. Being weak-kneed around a man hadn't happened to her...in seven years.

Oh, why did he have to show up now? Her priorities had been screwed up for years, and now that she'd gotten them in order, she didn't want him coming in and fouling everything up. She was happy, for crying out loud. And for whatever reason Kyle was here, other than being a part of the standby rescue team for the park service, was meaningless. He no longer rated a priority in her life. She told herself that over and over, forcing herself to recall the look in his eyes after he'd kissed her, as if disgusted that the desire they'd once shared was stronger than ever. He was a bitter, angry man, and seeing him again only served to bring back the guilty pain. Just being within five feet of him was proof enough that her decision all those years ago had been the correct one. And she wasn't letting him back into her life.

She threw the truck into gear and drove off.

Maybe he wouldn't be needed. Maybe enough of the crew was well enough to work. Maybe the storm predictions were wrong, and he would just disappear again. Yeah, right, a voice pestered. And maybe everything would fall apart just when you got the glue to stick.

Maxie drove, blinking back the tears she refused to shed for him.

Please go away, she prayed as his helicopter passed over-head. Because it was only going to get worse. Worse when he discovered that not only did she leave him at the altar, but he had a six-year-old daughter with a woman he loathed.

Two

In the rescue station, Kyle stared at the men and women relaxing in the worn leather sofas and chairs arranged around a couple of coffee tables.

"Okay, so what are you guys not telling me?" he said after another crew member refused to trade sleeping arrangements with him. He was willing to sleep anywhere if it meant he didn't have to look at Maxie before coffee. Unfortunately no one was cooperating.

"Parrish is a lousy cook," a man finally admitted, sinking back into the body-molding leather chair.

"You know this for a fact?" The idea that half of these men knew Maxie's cooking soured his mood even further.

A few exchanged knowing glances. "Reputations have a way of escalating."

"So don't eat at her place."

"I could say the same to you, Hayden," his temporary boss, Jackson Temple, said on a laugh as he passed the cluster of personnel.

Kyle made a frustrated sound. "Look, I'll make switching worth it." He reached into his back pocket for his wallet.

Hoots and whistles sounded seconds later. Kyle didn't have the sense to be embarrassed. Seeing Maxie on a regular basis was too unpleasant to even consider.

"Watch out, folks, he's desperate," someone said.

A black-haired man frowned curiously. "How much we talking here, Hayden?"

"A hundred?" Good Lord, he sounded pathetic, Kyle thought.

"Food mean that much to you, flyboy?" came from another team member.

"No," he muttered, fisting cash. His sanity did.

"Then why?"

Jackson Temple cleared his throat, then nodded slightly at the doors.

The conversation died a quick, painful death as Kyle looked up, his gaze colliding with a pair of green eyes so aloof he couldn't begin to speculate on what she was thinking. He only knew that she'd heard. Everything.

Then she crossed to the office and murmured smugly, "Bet the back seat of that chopper's looking real good right now," as she passed him.

Kyle closed his eyes briefly, feeling like a heel. He didn't know if it was the smirk on her face she tried to pass off as a smile or the way she brushed aside the discussion he was a jackass for even starting with people he'd just met, but these were her friends. He didn't want to embarrass her. What went on between them had nothing to do with the life she'd made for herself here.

Kyle jammed his cash into his pocket and waved off a crewman who looked guilty enough to concede. He looked up as she shut the office door, closing Jackson in with her. Through the glass, she met his gaze, her expression unreadable. It was hard to believe she was the same woman who'd turned to liquid heat in his arms a couple hours ago, and just the memory, the taste of her still on his lips, made his body tighten. Then she closed the blinds, shutting him out. Nothing new there, he thought, moving to a soda machine and dropping change into the slot, nearly knocking the thing over when he punched his selection. He had to get out of this somehow, he thought, pulling the tab and tipping it to his lips. He drained the soda, trying not to look at the office door, to the room where she was hiding from him. Again.

Inside the office, Maxie paced, not even bothering to take off her parka. On the way over, she'd radioed Jackson and without revealing why, she'd told him she didn't want Kyle at her place. Jackson wasn't cooperating.

"I thought you were my friend, Jackson. Move him to a hotel."

The team chief chuckled, his chair creaking as he leaned back and watched her eat the carpet with her strides. "You've had boarders before, Parrish, what's the deal?" She paused and leveled him a dark look, and the older man cringed dramatically, throwing his hands up. "Okay, okay, I won't pry. Not that you'd ever give details."

"You made the assignment." She slapped her hands down on the desk and loomed. "Change it."

"I can't. There was no other choice." He waved to the charts.

"There has to be." Maxie already recognized the danger of being in the same state with Kyle, let alone seeing him every day, all day until his contract with the rescue team was finished.

"Not for a chopper. Fuel is too expensive to have him land anywhere else. Your ranch is the best place to set one down. Close. Low wind, lots of unobstructed area. You know that." Her expression pleaded for a little understanding, and Jackson frowned. "I've never seen you like this, Maxine. He's got you scared."

She blinked, straightening. Scared? Of Kyle? She peeled off her jacket and tossed it aside before she plopped onto the sofa. Bracing her boots on the scarred table, she folded her arms over her middle and stared at nothing. She was not afraid of him. Just of him touching her. Her mind went blank when he did. And she couldn't afford a single incoherent thought, for her daughter's sake. Mimi depended on her mom keeping it together.

For the ride over here, for the time it took to feed and water the horses and mules on loan here, she'd done nothing but brood and stomp around, having herself a real nice pity party. She was glad Mimi was at her grandma's for the next couple of days or she would be deflecting questions instead of old feelings. Mimi had a talent for seeing to the center of a problem and pestering till she had the entire truth. Or telling Maxie what she *believed* to be the truth, whether her mother wanted to hear it or not. It was one of the things Maxie liked best about her daughter, her candidness.

"I like him," Jackson said.

Only her gaze shifted. "You would."

"Apparently you did, too, at one time."

She looked away. Yes, she'd loved him, or thought she had. Her timing was lousy when she'd wised up and realized it was mostly lust. Good lust, but not enough to base a lifetime on. Yet it was the immature way she'd left him that still haunted her.

Jackson's words came back to her. Kyle had her running scared. She wouldn't, not this time. She'd vanished on her wedding day, only to discover three weeks later that she'd jilted the father of her child. By then he was in Saudi with a broken heart and didn't need to hear from her; he needed to think about staying alive. She had refused to run to him just because she was pregnant, yet knew he had a right to know about Mimi. As soon as his unit had returned, she'd called, left a message and got a terse reply via his big brother: "Don't call back, he doesn't want to see you again."

She'd written him anyway, the hardest letter she'd ever had to pen. And it came back to her, unopened. The message was painfully clear.

But now he was here, and her daughter's happiness was in jeopardy. Mimi was her first and only concern. She'd suffered the "almost my dad" attachment once too often, and Maxie would endure anything, even Kyle's cruel remarks and glares, before she would allow her daughter to be hurt by her mistakes again. Suddenly she lurched off the couch and grabbed her jacket, donning it as she headed to the door.

"Maxine?"

"You need him to move the chopper, right?"

"Yeah," Jackson said, eyeing her warily.

Maxie looked at him. "Then tell him to do it. I'll be out at my place, waiting."

"Are you saying he's stuck with you?"

"I don't have much choice, do I? I agreed in writing to let the rescue service use my land for their choppers. Besides—" she shrugged "—it's a big place. A big house." She could go an entire day without running into him if she tried hard enough. And she would.

Maxie threw the door open and smacked into Kyle's chest. It was like hitting a brick wall, and he caught her shoulders, steadying her, yet keeping her close. Her gaze jerked to his, her hands flattened on his chest. For a long moment neither moved—Maxie lost in the familiar feel of his body molding to hers and the memories that came with it, Kyle wanting to touch more than her shoulders.

Someone cleared his throat. Kyle's lips curved ever so slightly. But it was the self-satisfied twist to them that sent Maxie backpedaling…right into Jackson. From behind, Jackson settled his hands on her shoulders, and Kyle's features tightened.

Even if Temple were in peak physical shape, he was a good dozen years older than Maxine, Kyle thought, then was angry with himself for the need to justify another man touch‚ing her.

"Fire up that bird, flyboy," Jackson said. "Time to move it."

Kyle lowered his gaze to Maxie's and he found only resignation in her expression.

"It appears you're staying at my place."

So she could stick pins in a festering wound? "I'll pass."

The old rebellion he remembered in her rose to the surface.

"I think we can be adults about this."

His eyes darkened and he scoffed. "That's a first."

She smirked, folding her arms. "Being your usual witty self, I see."

Kyle knew she was referring to the ugly remarks he'd made this morning. He regretted that his emotions got the best of him and was determined not to let it happen again. He just wished she still didn't turn him on like a light switch.

Jackson squeezed her shoulders, silencing another dig, and Maxie patted Jackson's fingers, then glanced back at him. "See ya."

Kyle's eyes narrowed as she pushed past, walking briskly to the doors. He watched her go, then brought his gaze back to Jackson. He opened his mouth to say something, but decided against it. If Maxie could appear casual about the arrangements, then so could he.

"Not a room available anywhere, flyboy, so what will it be? Maxine's—" Jackson's lips curved "—or the back seat of your chopper?"

Still Kyle fought the inevitable. "I could sleep here." He'd seen four cots in a small room at the back of the station. And it was a tremendous waste of fuel to head home each night and get here when, and if, they needed him.

Jackson shook his head. "For the team on call, sorry."

Kyle rubbed the back of his neck and muttered a curse. "Not much of a selection left, then, huh?"

Jackson fought a grin and ever the diplomat, gestured inside the office. "Let's get you some gear."

Kyle followed. Jackson Temple was his boss for the next week or two, and although they'd only met earlier this morning, before seeing Maxie, Kyle liked him.

Kyle stood back as Jackson went to the cabinet and threw open the doors, withdrawing coils of nylon rope, extra rigs for mountain climbing, medical kits, a hand radio, a booklet of rules and regulations, authorization passes and stickers and the standard flame orange jacket the crew wore, fur lined and heavy. He stacked the gear on the sofa. "Check the radio—we've had a couple of duds lately."

Kyle did, then started arranging the equipment in a spare duffel bag while Jackson wrote "Hayden" on a plastic tag and slipped it into the clear window above the chest pocket of the orange jacket.

"Thanks for showing up, Hayden," he said, offering the jacket. Kyle looked up, accepting it, frowning. Jackson shrugged, then moved to the coffeemaker and poured a cup. "We're badly shorthanded, with the flu going around. I appreciate your loan of the chopper." He handed the steaming mug to Kyle. "I know this cuts into your paying business."

"Just so you know, no one flies her but me."

Jackson grinned, the corners of his eyes crinkling. "Possessive, huh?"

Kyle sipped. "Yeah, me and the bank are that way about things that aren't paid for." He set the cup aside to load gear.

Jackson chuckled, dropping into the seat behind the desk. He propped his boots on the edge. "So...how long have you known Maxine?"

Kyle stilled, frowning, then jammed ropes into the corner of the duffel. Maxine. He hadn't heard anyone call her that since her father was yelling at her to come home, and she was ignoring him, riding away on the back of Kyle's motorcycle.

"Years."

Jackson frowned. "How many exactly?"

"Eight or so." Kyle shrugged, zipping the bag closed. He met Jackson's gaze. "You?"

"'Bout three, ever since she an—ah...moved up here. And no, we're just friends." He sent Kyle a look that said dating Maxie was robbing the cradle in his eyes. "'Sides. No one gets near Maxine unless she wants it."

Kyle knew that. The woman he'd met today was a shadow of the Maxie he had loved. He insisted he didn't care if she was cold. He just wanted to fulfill his obligation and get out of here. And avoiding her was his preference.

Kyle took up his mug and sank into the sofa, sipping, his gaze on the window. Maxie was climbing behind the wheel of her Range Rover and driving away.

"You two got a serious history, huh?"

Kyle's lips tightened. He wasn't about to let his personal life become the rescue-watch joke of the day. "Just a history. There's got to be a room available somewhere else...?" He was a backup chopper pilot, nothing more. And if he didn't have to be here, he for damn sure wouldn't. He looked to Jackson.

"Sorry, no." Kyle didn't care for the twinkle in Jackson's eyes just then. "Now, get your chopper off my triage pad, Hayden. It stays at the Wind Dancer until you're needed."

Kyle didn't like this, yet stood and hefted the duffel full of gear.

"Have fun."

Kyle glared at Jackson. The man grinned back.

"You're enjoying this."

"Probably more if I knew what it was all about—" he shrugged "—but yeah. I haven't seen any excitement in months. You know, people being cautious. Obeying the rules. Puts me out of a job."

Kyle couldn't fight the smile working out from beneath his scowl. "Call if you need me," he said, holding out his hand. Jackson shook it, and the two men parted.

Kyle took his time and walked outside, shrugging deeper into his jacket and donning his gloves against the cold. The wind whistled softly, but the temperature was dropping. Not any more than when he was near Maxie, he thought, tossing the emergency gear next to his seabag in the chopper, then climbing inside. He stared at the control panel, delaying the inevitable and disgusted with the fates that were screwing with his perfectly ordered life. Checking the dials and his watch, he refitted his sunglasses for the third time before turning over the engine, the blades swiping the air, gaining speed with each turn. Adjusting his radio headset, Kyle waited until he had the ground crewman's signal, then lifted off, tipping the chopper to the right and heading toward Maxie's place. He was anxious and if he had to admit it, fearful. It was too much like Iraq, flying into a hot landing zone. But Kyle had an idea that living under the same roof with the only woman he'd ever wanted to marry would be like living under enemy gunfire. With him unarmed.

A half hour later, Maxie watched his approach from the steps of her front porch. His helicopter was black with a sunrise painted on the side in bright red, orange and metallic gold. His name was stenciled below the pilot's window. Before he was close enough to set the chopper down, she stepped off the porch, walking toward the flattened ground several hundred yards beyond the main buildings. Dread moved through her with every step, and she tipped her cowboy hat low on her forehead and tried to appear as relaxed as possible. But her insides were twisting in tight knots, nauseating her.

This is for Mimi, she reminded herself. If Maxie avoided Kyle, he would just get curious and ask questions, which would inevitably lead to ones concerning Mimi. For the briefest moment, when she'd first seen Kyle after so long, she'd considered stashing Mimi's things, closing off her room and letting her daughter stay longer at her grandmother's to avoid any contact with him. But the thought had died as quickly as it had formed. She couldn't do it. Mimi was everything to her, and she was proud of her little girl. She had had no reason to hide her six years ago and she wouldn't do it now. Besides, Kyle had made it clear by not answering her letters that he'd no interest in what happened to her after their breakup, and if his present attitude was any indication, he still didn't. Nothing had changed.

Suddenly the image of her daughter—dark red hair in braided pigtails and bright, expressive green eyes—burst in her mind, like Mimi always burst into the house. No, she corrected, everything had changed from the moment she'd met her daughter. *I miss her,* she thought, then stiffened her spine, determined to get through the next couple weeks without any more emotional scratches.

Dust and dirt kicked up as the chopper neared, and she admitted she was impressed at how he lowered the craft gracefully to the ground. The noise immediately lessened, the blades beating the air in a slow drone. Maxie stopped, shoving her gloved hands into her jacket pockets, and didn't approach as he flipped switches, then removed the radio headset and a baseball cap. Even from here, she could tell the cap had the Marine Corps emblem on it. He pushed open the door and climbed out, opened the rear hatch and removed his seabag. That faded piece of military luggage was a constant reminder of their last night together. She wanted to burn it, but he hitched it over his shoulder, then reached for a black cowboy hat, donning it as he walked toward her. Her heart jumped in her chest, her gaze moving over him. Even hidden behind sunglasses and beneath the hat, he still had the rugged good looks that made women sigh. She couldn't fight the riot suddenly skipping through her as his thigh muscles flexed with each stride. She remembered what his skin felt like beneath her palms, his body wrapped around hers and what an unselfish lover he'd been. A warm coil of heat curled through her, tightening her breasts, tingling up the back of her thighs. Her knees felt papery, and Maxie jerked her gaze away, staring anywhere except at him. It would not help to think this way, she reminded herself, shoving her sunglasses back up her nose. Kyle was the last person she wanted in her life, not to mention in her bed.

Kyle stopped directly in front of her, and she looked at him as he nudged his hat back. He wanted to see what was going on behind those sunglasses and knew she wore them to shield more than just the sun. He tipped his down, peering, and liked that she tensed. His gaze lowered to her lips, and the intensity of their kiss in the barn ripped through him. He was aching for another taste when the husky sound of her voice made his heart skip.

"Welcome to Wind Dancer, Kyle."

His lips quirked. "*Am* I welcome, Max? Or tolerated?"

"A little of both," she said honestly, not moving a muscle, even when she could feel the heat of his body, see every sinfully long lash surrounding his dark eyes. A brave front, she thought.

Kyle glanced briefly at the ranch house beyond her and imagined what it would be like, living with her. Did she still go nuts over chocolate and hate asparagus? he wondered, looking down at her. Did she still have a wild collection of lingerie that had always made him hot just to look at her and wonder what feminine scrap was beneath her clothes? Even as the enticing thought materialized, he knew he was in for torment. With himself. *Don't let her get to you. Don't. This is one woman you cannot trust.*

The sudden surge of anger made his voice harsh. "Where should I stow my gear?"

She stepped back. "That's all you have?" She nodded to the seabag.

"I travel light."

His tone was clipped and Maxie sighed. Clearly he didn't want to play this beyond the edge of civility. Fine. At least she was making an effort. She spun around, and he followed her to the house, both silent.

But Kyle's gaze was on her back, more so—her backside. And the way it filled those tight jeans enough to fill his mind with nothing but what was beneath and seeing her again without them. Man, oh man, this was tough already, and he forced himself to remember every detail of their wedding day. She was a selfish coward, plain and simple, he thought as he mounted the porch steps behind her. She opened the door, walking briskly inside.

Crossing the threshold, Kyle regained his determination as he removed his sunglasses and hat. His gaze quickly scanned the Southwest decor of beige walls, terra-cotta-hued furniture, the room dotted with blue-and-coral trimmings. The warmth of the decor settled into him instantly, calming the tension he'd felt since he landed on her property. He spotted baskets filled with odd collections of croquet balls, oversize wooden spools of thread and even branding irons. Antique oil cans were tucked here and there, some hidden by plants, others in plain sight like the grouping near a six-foot-wide fireplace dominating the living room. Kyle liked it and thought it suited her. At least this new Maxie.

"Nice place."

"Thank you."

"To hide," he added.

Over the rim of her sunglasses, she slid him a frosty glance as she stripped off her jacket. "I wasn't hiding, Kyle," she defended, removing her shades. "I've been right here."

"But who knew?"

"Anyone who was interested did," she snapped, and was about to add to her defense, then closed her mouth and hung her hat and parka on a peg near the door. She didn't need to provoke questions, she thought, reminding herself to stop responding to his remarks. He had no right to be curious about her life. Crossing the foyer, she turned down a hall. After passing four doors, she stopped near the last on the right, throwing it open.

"In here," she said, leaning back against the frame and folding her arms like a warden outside a jail cell.

Kyle moved past her, his big body brushing hers, and he felt a subtle heat stroke up his body. He stilled, searching her gaze and wondering if she felt it. Wondering if he'd imagined those moments in the barn.

"The bath is next door. Dinner is in—" she checked her watch "—about a half an hour." She turned away.

Summarily dismissed, he thought, but then something made her pause, her hand on the door frame. She looked back, meeting his gaze across the wide brass bed. Kyle felt the world, the room, tighten down on him, focusing on her eyes, green and clear. Wavy dark red hair fell over one eye, partially shielding her face. Her stare was confident, even when he let his meander over her wind-chapped cheeks, her tightly tucked shirt molding to her breasts, defining their fullness. Her nipples tightened, pushing against the fabric, and his gaze flew to her face. Her expression didn't alter a fraction. Lord, she was still so beautiful, he thought, ageless, and for a moment he was twenty-three and so hungry for her he couldn't think straight. So in love with her his arms ached.

Something flickered in her eyes, and the corner of her mouth lifted wistfully. "Make yourself at home, Kyle. The fridge is stocked with snacks...and beer."

He breathed his first normal breath since walking through the door. "Thanks, Max." He dumped the seabag on the bed before he did something stupid like grab her against him.

"Think nothing of it," she said, and by her tone, he knew she meant it. He was immediately on guard again. He was right. This was like waiting for enemy gunfire.

Maxie hastened down the hall, ignoring the heat jumping through her body, ignoring the fact that he could still just look at her and make her crave his arms around her, long for the throb of his kiss again...and force her to relive when she was young and innocent and Kyle was the dangerous man her father didn't want near. And she ignored the fact that he was in the room directly across from hers.

She paused in the hallway, grabbing the edge of the secretary and closing her eyes against her image in the glass. She was a fool to believe she could handle being this close to him. Not when he could peel away her secrets with a look. Memories pelted her like an acid rain without relief, and she longed for Mimi's little arms around her neck, the warmth of her little body snuggled close where she could protect her daughter from the world. From this kind of heart-ache.

Pushing away from the secretary, she walked to the living room and built a fire in the hearth, staring as the blaze roared to life. For a brief moment, her mind wandered, selecting a scene out of their past when they'd gone to Mexico and woken with one hell of a hangover in the back of a vegetable truck in Encinada. With no idea of how they'd got there. At the time, it was fun and funny, but on her wedding day, it had just sounded stupid. The ache of memory caught in her chest. She'd cried for weeks back then. For the decent, trusting man she'd hurt, for leading him to believe she would be there for him when she couldn't and for the innocence she'd left behind.

The pop of burning wood startled her, and she blinked, expecting her eyes to be wet with tears. They weren't, yet her heart felt sore. She stared at the ember just on the edge of the hearth, then quickly kicked it back and replaced the fireplace screen. It reminded her that memories were threatening and she couldn't afford to be this melancholy. Not with her daughter's contentment at stake. Moments later, she donned her jacket and hat, then left the house, slamming the door closed and wishing she could shut Kyle out of her life as easily.

Kyle flinched when he heard the door shut, the vibration rattling the walls. Closing the dresser drawer, he stared out the window, his gaze following her as she crossed the yard to the huge barn. Her steps were angry and quick. He could see her inside the barn, bundled up against the cold, her beige cowboy hat tipped low as she walked down the center aisle, lugging a bucket of feed, he assumed. Did she do everything around here alone? He watched her for a moment until she vanished into a stall, then turned away from the window.

Kyle looked around the room, the soft Southwestern decor carried over in here, too. It didn't soothe him this time, and he shoved his fingers into his hair. A tension he hadn't felt since Saudi radiated through him, and he tried to shake it. He couldn't and sat down on the bed, cradling his head in his hands. He had to get a handle on his emotions. But part of him said to exercise it, get it out, just keep his hands off her and his desire locked away. But he kept remembering the moments in the barn, the hot feel of her skin in the cold air, her ferocious passion unleashing on him and his desperate need to absorb it. It was as if he'd come alive for the first time in seven years and every cell in his body wanted him to know it.

But he made himself recall their past, and he was tucked deep inside it when he heard his name and looked up. His heart slammed against the wall of his chest.

Maxie.

"You okay?" she said, frowning. "Dinner is almost ready, if you're hungry."

He looked away, nodding, anger simmering, the pain of his memories stronger and harder than he thought possible. She was a coward, damn her. She'd made the decision to walk away, alone, never giving him the courtesy of talking with him about what she was feeling. She'd stolen their prospect at happiness, his one chance. And as he turned his head to see her disappear from the doorway, he told himself he wasn't falling for her charm again. He was *not* here to see if her cowardice was a mistake or a godsend.

Three

Kyle held on to his resentment, his only comfort right now, and snapped, "I'm not eating a damn thing you cook. Your reputation precedes you."

"Fine, don't. Starve. See if I care." Pigheaded man, Maxie thought, and didn't spare him a backward glance as she walked briskly down the carpeted hall. Her boot heels clicked on the wood foyer as she crossed it into her tiled kitchen.

Kyle followed, his gaze unwillingly dropping to her behind shifting inside tight jeans. He immediately cursed his preoccupation, even as he noticed that she'd changed into a long-sleeved T-shirt.

"Your compassion astounds me, Max."

"You'll get over it, I'm sure." She moved to the stove, grabbing a mitt to open the oven. Bending to remove a baking tray, she set it on the cutting board, the scent of broiled salmon and Dauphine potatoes making her mouth water. With quick efficiency, she pulled two small salads from the refrigerator, positioning them by the service already set. She served the food onto plates, aware of his gaze following her moves. She didn't have to look to know he was standing near the arched entrance. His eyes had the power of touch, always had, and her frustration mounted as she struggled with opening the soda bottles.

It was only five-thirty, and she wished the day were over. Not that she'd allow his presence in her house to keep her from her routine. She had a living to make. Kyle or no Kyle.

Filling glasses with soda, she placed them precisely ahead of the knife point, and for an instant, Kyle saw the old Maxie, the one who knew which fork to use in a fancy restaurant, who sat beside whom at a banquet, the proper way to greet dignitaries. She would have made a great marine wife, he thought fleetingly. Of course, it wasn't good manners that had attracted him years ago, but the culture and experience he'd hungered for and she had been willing to share without making him feel like the ill-bred kid from the wrong side of town. Then there was the way she kissed. The way she felt in his arms. Naked. Beneath him, over him— he smothered a groan and rubbed the back of his neck, staring at the floor.

Jeez. How could he despise her for abandoning him one minute, then want to hold her so badly the next?

"Earth to Kyle." He jerked a look at her. She was waving in front of his face, and he noticed the faded Pluto oven mitt.

He scowled. "Yeah."

She back-stepped, then gestured to the kitchen table. "Still not interested?"

Briefly his gaze dropped to the elegant supper. "You going to poison me?"

Her lips twisted in a wry smile. "Guess you'll have to take your chances, huh?"

He straightened and moved to the chair, jerking it back. She was already seated and using the remote to turn on the TV.

He sat. "Don't tell me you watch the soaps?"

She scoffed, her lips quirking. "Boy, Hayden, are you out of the loop." He frowned. "Those shows are on at noon, while I'm shoveling stalls." She nodded to the TV. "The weather report."

The Weather Channel was on, and she ate, making notes on a pad of paper and ignoring him completely. Halfway through the meal, he chanced a look at her paper and saw the wind-chill factor, the chances of snow. His brows rose. His gaze dropped to the plate. He'd eaten half of it without realizing how good it was.

"Why do all those guys believe you can't cook?"

She scoffed, glancing around at the table setting. "This isn't cooking. Christmas dinner is cooking. And *I'm* the one who started that rumor." He frowned, and she shifted toward him a little. "I don't need any of the boarders I take in for the rescue team hitting on me. It's happened once too often." She didn't add that bringing men in her house wasn't in her plans, for Mimi's sake. "I like my privacy."

"You forget I know from firsthand experience," he groused.

She looked at him, her green eyes suddenly hard as glass, her voice tight. "I didn't forget a thing, and I told you, Kyle...don't assume you know me anymore. We—" she gestured between them "—were years ago. A lifetime. Nothing is the same. The old Maxine Parrish vanished—"

His expression turned thunderous. "You ran away—!"

"And this Maxie is a stranger to you," she finished without missing a beat. She drained the soda and stood, collecting her dishes and carrying them to the sink. Maxie couldn't deal with him just now, even if she inwardly admitted she was actually glad to see him. Kyle had always possessed a zest for life she'd envied, even if his enthusiasm dragged him into a brush or ten with death. She'd spent her life taking the easy way out. Her lips twisted in a wry smile. Her single moment of defiance cost him so much pain and left her pregnant, single and forced to grow up. Yes, she was different, stronger than before. Jilting him had little to do with the woman she was now, and everything to do with the child he'd given her.

She was running water over the dishes when his deep voice stole across the wide kitchen.

"You're not a stranger, Max, a little different on the outside maybe, but you're the same. You're ten feet from me and still running."

She whirled on him, outrage in her eyes. She'd stopped running the day Mimi was born. "I have a *life* here, and just because you happened upon me after all these years does not mean I've been hiding in Arizona. And certainly not from you." Her expression sharpened, her voice a low rasp. "Don't be so arrogant to believe I've been waiting around for you to come riding up on a charger to save me—I haven't!" Her steam lost its pressure, and she stared at the TV, not seeing the weather report, but envisioning life, after the trauma of Kyle, after her ruined marriage to Carl Davis, which left her daughter sobbing into her pillow and her own heart bruised…because she couldn't be honest with her feelings. Nor could she trust them. They'd failed her once too often. Seconds passed, and she brought her gaze back to his.

"How long are you going to hold a grudge, Kyle?" Her voice fractured and she swallowed. "How long are you going to hang around my ranch and make me pay for a decision I know I was right in making?"

His eyes flared and for a split second, Maxie saw pain there. Dark, aching pain. Then it was replaced with pure rage. "*You* knew it was right? *You* knew?" He rose slowly out of his chair. "What about me, Max?"

"What about you?" She didn't want to get into this discussion, not for a million dollars, and she forced a sneer into her voice she didn't feel. "I called, I wrote. You didn't want to hear my explanations. What difference does it make now? What's changed?"

A pause, everything he ever felt ricocheting through his body, and then, "Nothing." His gaze raked her. "You still think of yourself first."

Hurt flashed in her eyes. "Believe what you want, Kyle. You will anyway." She headed toward the entrance, but he grabbed her arm, forcing her to face him.

"Change my mind."

"No." Her chin came up a fraction. Admitting her mistakes was the one thing she wasn't ready for. "I've worked very hard to make myself a future here, and I refuse to go back to the past." *Please don't make me.*

She'd slammed the door on him again, Kyle thought, but he kicked it open a crack. "I scare you, don't I? The past frightens you." He shifted his stance, bringing his body closer to hers, smothering her. "Why, Max?"

She wrenched her arm free. "The matter is dead, Kyle. Quit trying to revive it," she said, then left, the close of the door a soft click in the big house.

"The discussion is far from over," he said to the kitchen walls. He wasn't going to get a clear explanation from her, and Kyle considered giving up and maintaining a congenial silence. What was the use in dredging up the past? He stared out the kitchen window as she stomped across the yard to the barn, zipping her jacket and adjusting her hat as she went. No, he couldn't let it go, her evasions magnifying his need to know exactly why she'd left him. He had a right to know, didn't he?

Even after you ignored her letters and calls? a voice pestered.

Well, he was here now and he wasn't leaving until he exorcised Maxie from his system. The time was long overdue.

In the barn, Maxie saddled a horse and led it from the stall. She mounted, digging in her heels and letting the impatient beast have its head. Pulling her hat low on her brow, she leaned forward, feeling the power of the animal as it charged across open country, the wind thrashing at her jacket. The thunder of hooves, coupled with her heartbeat, sang hard in her veins. She'd gone two or three miles before the horse tired and she slowed, turning back toward the ranch. And Kyle.

Why did he have to open up this can of worms? He would never understand why she couldn't marry him then. And yet she knew he would keep harping on the subject until he got some answers. She was already weary of his prodding, and he'd only been here a few hours.

As she returned to the barn, the phone extension inside rang. She quickened her pace, riding directly into the barn and leaning out to reach the receiver anchored near the entrance. She heard his voice on the other end.

"Wind Dancer Ranch," Kyle said.

"Who is this?"

Her mom. Great. Now it starts, Maxie thought, listening, then wondered if something was wrong with Mimi.

"Who is *this?*"

"Mrs. Lacy Parrish." The dignity Mom possessed even came through the phone, Maxie thought.

She heard his breath come in a tired sigh. "Hello, Mrs. Parrish," came almost reluctantly. "This is Kyle."

"Hayden?" High-pitched surprise colored her mother's voice.

"Yes, ma'am."

There was a long pause before her mother asked, "What are you doing there, son?"

Mom's compassionate tone annoyed her.

"My chopper's on lease to the rescue association."

"Oh."

Did Mom think she'd actually called him? No, she wouldn't, Maxie thought. Not Mom. She knew everything. Well, almost everything.

"And there were no hotel rooms available?"

Go, Momma.

Kyle chuckled softly. "Don't I wish…?"

"Yes, son, I imagine you would," came softly. "She out with the mounts?"

"Yeah, I guess," he said. "I'll tell her you called."

Her mom said goodbye and hung up. Maxie waited until Kyle had, too, before she did. In twenty minutes, her sister would know who was in town, Dad would have checked out his story with Jackson, considering he was her dad's friend, discreetly of course, since no one but her family knew the identity of Mimi's father.

Maxie briefly closed her eyes.

Her sisters would call, then her dad and, Maxie didn't doubt, her mom would make an "I was just happening by" visit tomorrow. Mom had adored Kyle, a soft spot for a man in uniform, she supposed. But Mom had stood by her when she'd made her decision to have her baby and raise her daughter alone. Again Maxie thanked God for her parents and their understanding. If they had rejected her, her entire life would have been different. Even though her dad had mixed feelings about Kyle, he'd always felt she should have told Kyle about his daughter, returned letters or not. Mom had sided with her. Kyle's ignorance was her and Mimi's bliss.

Dismounting, she drew the horse into a stall, removing the saddle and hefting it over the separation between the enclosures. She curried the hot animal, then went to the next stall and pulled open the gate. One by one she led the mares and geldings into the corral, leaving the docile mules and letting the horses work off some of the anxiousness punctuating the cold air. After she moved several horses to the corral, she exercised each one in turn.

Kyle stood on the threshold of the front door, the screen shielding little of the wind as he watched her ride away for the eighth time that day. She looked good on a horse, and he realized he'd never seen her ride before. Nor work so hard. Even when her father had owned a couple of horses. Maxie had over twenty now, he estimated. Kyle wanted to lend a hand, but after this morning, knew she didn't want him around. Bored, he turned back into the house, and his attention caught on several pictures, each in a different wood frame. He leaned over the foyer table, examining them. They were family shots: her mother, father, sisters and, Kyle assumed, their husbands and children. He smiled, remembering how thunderous her dad could look. There was one of Maxie, a little redheaded girl standing behind her, tiny arms slung around Maxie's neck, their cheeks pressed together. Must be a niece, he thought, then glanced at the other photos. A favorite niece, he decided when he found more shots of the girl.

Kyle had never been around kids much. He and his brother were alone since they were adolescents, running wild when the orphanage counselors couldn't handle them. Or find them. Little kids made him nervous. Kyle looked down at his broad hand, closing it in a fist. He was a big man and was always afraid he would hold them too tight, raise his voice too loud. And he never knew what to say to them. Just as well he wasn't around them, he supposed, looking back at the shots. He envied the togetherness the photos radiated, the love and trust. Kyle and his brother had that between them, but never a family. Not since his mother had abandoned them and their dad split not long after.

His mood darkening too fast, Kyle forced the memory aside and entered the kitchen, did the dishes, wiping the counters before heading to the living room to stoke the fire. He called the rescue station to check in, and although there were no emergencies, he agreed to fly a search team over the canyon before the sun was completely down, to make certain nothing or no one was overlooked.

He checked his watch, calculating the time out and back. He had to leave now to be out of the canyon by dark. Night flying was no problem, but in the blackness of the Grand Canyon, it was dangerous. Kyle thought about leaving Maxie a note, then remembered seeing an intercom by the front door. He walked to it, depressing the Talk button marked Stables and called her name.

She must still be out, he thought when she didn't answer, then grabbed some paper left by the phone, scribbling a note.

He was out the door in less than five minutes, his flight log tucked under his arm and his thoughts wandering over the Disney character toothbrush he'd seen in the bathroom.

Inside the chopper, Kyle traded his cowboy hat for the ball cap and started the engine, flipping on the heat as soon as he could. It was going to snow tonight, he decided, glancing at the low, thick clouds. Lifting off, he veered over the open land, his gaze searching for Maxie, half expecting to find her riding hell-bent for leather. But he found her near the edge of the canyon, the horse gnawing at the grass beside her. She looked up as he passed overhead, and Kyle rocked the craft. She put up her hand, waving. For a moment, he considered flipping on the loudspeaker, then decided against it. The noise would scare the horse and he had nothing to say. He banked on a curve and headed for the horizon.

Still a daredevil, Maxie thought as he maneuvered the chopper to dip and dart through the canyon. Just watching him made her stomach flip. Swinging up onto the saddle, she clicked her tongue and her horse backed away from the rim. She turned toward the ranch. One more mount to exercise before she could call Mimi.

Though she looked forward to talking to her baby, it was her mother's questions she had to answer.

"Grandpa bought me a sled," her daughter said into the phone an hour later.

"Did he?" Maxie tossed her hat aside, ruffling her hair and bracing her back against the kitchen counter.

"Yup, and when it snows we're going to hitch it to Blue Bell and ride behind it."

"Oh, really?" she said in her best "did you ask permission" voice.

"Grandpa says!" came rebelliously, and Maxie could almost see the determination in her daughter, her hand fisted on her skinny hip.

"Hey? Who's the mom here?"

"You are," Mimi said sullenly.

Maxie's heart softened. "We'll see, princess. Let me talk
to Grandma."

Mimi shouted for her grandmother yet forgot to hold the
phone away from her mouth. "Mimi Anne!"

"Sorry, Momma."

"You're forgiven, sweetie."

"Well, you're not," her mother said, a smile in her voice.
"How could you not tell us—?"

"I didn't know until he arrived."

A stretch of silence and then, "How are you with this,
honey?"

"Lousy, but I don't have much choice."

"How's he look?" Pure female fascination lit her
mother's voice.

"Good, Mom, real good." His image blossomed in her
mind, the lines at the corners of his eyes that gave his face
more character, his broad chest and thick arms that called
out to be explored. Yeah, she thought, an exceptional hunk
of man.

"Still dangerous?"

Maxie laughed. "Yeah. How's Dad taking it?" She didn't
think her father would be at all pleased.

"You know him, ready to protect his little girl from heartache."

Maxie sighed and rubbed her forehead. "I don't think he
can this time, Mom. Kyle's different." It saddened her that
his quick smiles and sexy teasing were missing, and for a
moment, she longed for the old Kyle. "Seeing each other
again has only opened up his pain." Maxie pinched the
bridge of her nose. "I feel like such a creep." The backs of
her eyes stung suddenly, and she wondered how long she
could keep her guilt hidden from him. "I never thought it
would last this long."

"That's a man for you, not caring when it counts and
feeling slighted when it shouldn't." In the background, she
heard her father tell his wife she wasn't a man, so how would

she know what one should feel. Her mom ignored her dad, wisest tactic when he was on the defensive.

Her mother asked her several more questions, reminded her that Mimi was sleeping over at her friend Dana's house tonight, then said, "You're a grown woman, Maxine, dear, trust your judgment. I do."

Warmth sprang inside Maxie, and her anxiety eased a little. "Thanks, Mom, love you."

She hung up, grabbed a soda from the fridge, then headed to the bathroom for a long hot shower. A good hour later, she was leaving the bathroom in a wake of steam when she heard Kyle curse. Frowning, Maxie made certain her robe was sashed and wrapped to her throat before she opened the door, peering out. Empty.

An instant later, Kyle jerked open the second bathroom door, a towel wrapped around his hips and something clenched in his hand. Water dripped from his hair, trickled down his chest and for a moment, she let her gaze absorb the carved muscle, the clean, bare skin, the center of his chest sprinkled with dark hair. Oh, this was dangerous, she thought, then lowered her gaze to the Grecian doll dwarfing his palm.

"Oh, good." She crossed the hall, holding out her hand. "I've been looking for that."

He didn't give it to her, arching a sable dark brow. "You play with dolls in the shower?"

"Well, actually…" Her sudden smile was wistful, hitting him in the gut and he gave over the doll. "I collect them—" She adjusted the tiny diaphanous toga, watching her movements. "But this one is Mimi's."

Kyle swallowed tightly. "And Mimi is…?" Kyle had a strong feeling he didn't want to hear this.

She lifted her gaze. "My daughter."

"You have a child!" he roared, looming closer.

Maxie roared back, a mother grizzly protecting her cub. "Yeah. Got a problem with that?"

Four

The betraying little witch.

She'd been pregnant, round with life growing inside her. With another man's child. The redheaded child in the pictures. Yet she wouldn't marry him.

"Didn't take you long, huh?" he sneered, his gaze raking over the thick black velour robe, hunting for changes in her body.

Maxie lifted her chin, clutching the garment at her throat. "Long for what?"

"To hop in bed with another man after I left." No wonder she wrote only once, he thought, unquenchable anger racing over his thoughts.

Her gaze thinned, a shaft of pain driving through her chest. He seriously believed she was that shallow? And why the hell did he care now? He never answered her calls or her letters.

"How long were you going to keep the fact that you had a kid from me?" he said before she could respond.

"Mimi is not a kid. She is a *child* and I wasn't keeping her from you." She leveled him a righteous look, motherhood screaming from every cell and said, "It didn't matter whether *you* knew *or* approved. And by your distasteful reaction, I'm glad she wasn't around to hear it!"

She spun away and ducked into her bedroom, shutting the door in his face.

Kyle blinked, staring at the closed door, her barb hitting its target with deadly accuracy. If Mimi had heard him, Maxie would be soothing the hurt feelings of an innocent little girl. God, he felt lower than dirt.

"Max?" he said to the closed door. "I—ah—"

"Go away, Kyle," she warned. "I'm getting dressed."

Kyle looked down at the wet towel around his hips, then darted into the bathroom to grab his jeans. He couldn't let this drop, he thought, hurriedly hopping into his jeans as he returned to the hallway. He had her trapped, and she couldn't ignore him anymore.

"Max, I'm sorry."

No answer. He yanked up his jeans and managed the zipper before pounding on her door. "Open up."

"Or what? You'll kick it in and insult my intelligence *and* my daughter again?"

He frowned. Her voice sounded funny, strained. "Come on, Maxie. You know I didn't mean it like that. I was caught off guard." That was an understatement! He rapped again, determined to stay here all night if he had to. Yet she was stubborn enough to hold out in there for days. "Maxine Parrish, for once, quit taking the easy way out and talk to me!"

Seconds later, she flung the door wide open. "Damn you, Kyle Hayden," she said, glaring up at him. "You had no right to say those things to me."

Her glassy eyes softened his anger. "We were going to be married. That gives a man—"

She was in his face. "*Were.* Past." She poked his bare chest with every word. "And an engagement seven years ago does not give you any rights—let alone the right to question my life now!''

He caught her fingers, trapping them against his chest. ''I loved you, damn it!''

She inhaled sharply and tried to wrestle free, but he caught her around the waist, slamming her against him, thigh to thigh, hip to hip, their clothing a woefully inadequate barrier between them.

''I loved you,'' he rasped again, his gaze scouring her features.

Maxie's heart skipped to her throat, her body suddenly aware and blistering with untamed sensations. He still said it with conviction, still had the same possessive look in his eyes and she thought of all the hurt he had a right to feel, then and now. ''I know,'' she said sadly, reaching up to brush back a lock of sable hair. ''I thought I loved you, too.''

Thought. Never sure. Hearing her say it, look him in the eye and say it, drove a dagger of pain through his chest and for an instant, Kyle doubted the tangled feelings he'd harbored these years. He didn't know which hurt more—the lie she'd lived then or that he might have been in love alone.

His expression was like an open wound, stripped and bleeding. *Oh, Kyle,* Maxie thought. How much heartache had he wasted on her? His naked emotion made her keenly aware of how easily she could weaken for him again. *Don't trust me.* She wasn't good for him then, and she wasn't now. And for her daughter's sake, she had to make him see they were finished years ago.

Suddenly she pushed out of his arms. ''Have you been celibate since we last shared a bed?''

He scowled and Kyle didn't want to think of the women he'd tried to make into Maxie. Nor how empty he felt right now. ''Of course not.''

''Then don't expect me to have been, either. It's not your business what I did after we broke up, Kyle. Just like it's not mine to know what you did.''

He was eighteen months in a hot desert, not giving a damn

if he got shot, he thought, while she was sliding between the sheets with some stranger. "Yeah, that's right." His lips pulled in a tight, humorless smile, the look offering a parade of women who didn't exist. "It isn't."

She gazed up at him, her brow furrowing before it stretched taut. "This isn't about my daughter or your broken heart," she said in a voice draped with wonder. "It's about your bruised pride. You're still mad because I left you at the altar."

"You're damn right I'm mad," he growled softly, heartache suspended for years rushing forward in a cold wave. "I stood there in that church, in full dress blues, holding some stupid bouquet, with a ring worth two months' pay in my pocket, and I waited for you." He loomed over her, his voice gaining steam. "And then I waited some more." He advanced, forcing her to back-step into her bedroom. "But when your parents arrived without you, I knew something was wrong. God," he rasped, "I felt like an idiot, but love-struck marine that I was...I kept telling myself, no..." He shook his head, still holding her gaze. "Maxie wouldn't do this to me. Maxie wouldn't make me wonder if she was in an accident, bleeding somewhere—" His voice fractured with old misery, striking her in the chest, pulling tears to the surface. "She loved me. I would have sworn on my soul to it!" Briefly, he looked away, shoving his fingers through his hair, simmering an instant before boiling over. "But you didn't give *a damn!*"

"That's not true!" she cried.

He gripped her arms, dragging her up against him. "Isn't it?" His glare was savage. "You were a coward, turning tail, too chicken to even show up and face me...give me the courtesy of a 'nice knowing you, Kyle, don't get shot.' My God, Maxie—" he shook her "—you humiliated me beyond belief! You were self—"

"You're right."

He blinked, choking back his tirade. "What?"

"And I owe you an apology."

He released her, his tone sarcastic. "Say again?"

"I want to apologize." His gaze narrowed, then sharpened with icy calm and Maxie knew it was now or never. "It was cruel and immature, abandoning you like that, especially when you were about to go fight for your country." Mortal shame showered over her, years of repressed guilt unleashing. "I should have done the grown-up thing and come to you." Her vision blurred and she blinked rapidly. "But I wasn't grown-up. I was scared and feeling rushed and I knew if I saw you..." She swallowed back burning tears. "I wouldn't have told you what I needed to say and I would have gone on with the lie."

"It wasn't a lie," came in a soft hiss. "I was in love with you!"

Her gaze locked with his. "If you loved me so much, why didn't you answer my letters? Why didn't you call?"

"I was hurting," he rasped. "You knew I was licking my wounds over there."

"You cut me off. Like that," she said with a snap of her fingers. "You didn't even make an effort when you came back. For all you knew, I could have been dying. Is that how a man treats the woman he claims to love?"

Kyle didn't want to hear the truth of her words, not after all this time. "I was ready to marry you."

"But I wasn't. Not then, not that fast. I'd tried to talk to you days before, Kyle. But every time I mentioned waiting until after you came back, you would kiss me or make love to me or joke, anything but listen." She inhaled a short breath. "Anything but hear me."

Kyle searched his memory and his features tightened. "But we were good together, we could have worked it out."

"We were mismatched and you know it," she said. "I wanted marriage and kids, and all you wanted was to party and to cheat death at every opportunity."

He folded his arms over his chest and stared down at her. "I liked having fun and as I recall, so did you."

"Sure, I did. But you were too irresponsible for a man

who insisted he was ready to settle down." His look defied her, and she said, "You lived in a barracks and ate in the mess hall, but you were always penniless come payday with nothing to show for it." His scowl darkened, and she knew he didn't need his failings thrown in his face, but he had to understand why she left and she needed to say it. "You intentionally risked your life. On a regular basis. It was plain dangerous to be with you sometimes. But you could persuade me into anything."

His lips quirked, wild memories in his dark eyes. "You regret all of it?"

"No, no." Her smile was faint and sad. "But you scared me every time you raced, went skydiving or rock climbing, not to mention that bungee jump that nearly took your leg off. That's not the behavior of a man preparing for stability."

Kyle tried to see her fears, her misgivings. He didn't want to admit he'd been lying to himself for a very long time. "I was willing to give up that life-style. It gets old quick. I was ready then, Max, even if you didn't believe me."

"You're right. I didn't believe you." His face was mapped with hurt, and Maxie tried desperately to explain. "But I didn't show up not because I wasn't certain about you, Kyle," she explained, her tone pleading, "but because I wasn't sure about *me.* I didn't leave you, I left *us.* I was in love with the *idea* of marriage, of having what I wanted. I don't know if we were truly in love then, but I know we lusted more. Or if it would have lasted beyond Desert Storm."

His features tightened, and he broke his gaze. How many times had he thought of how it would have been—where they would be if they'd married then? "Maybe it would have lasted if you'd given us the chance."

"Maybe, maybe not. But those weeks before, we were confused and reaching out." She gripped his bare arms, forcing him to look at her. "You were heading into the middle of war within hours and you wanted someone to miss you."

Her voice softened. "You didn't have any family except Mitch. Married, you'd have a wife who *had* to miss you."

A muscle ticked in his jaw.

She searched his gaze, but when he continued to stare at her, almost in a daze, she shook him and said, "You can rant at me some more, if it will make you feel better."

"No." He let out a long heavy breath. "Then I'd look stupid, and it was better when you did."

She smiled weakly and he reached out, his thumb brushing back a tear moving down her cheek. Her gaze bored into his. She felt better for apologizing, but that didn't mean he'd accepted it. "I'm sorry, Kyle."

"I see that."

Her lip trembled pitifully and he groaned, gathering her into his arms. She rested her cheek on his bare chest, her arms around his waist.

"I didn't want to break your heart." She inhaled raggedly, her voice a sorrowful whisper. "You have to know that." She sobbed helplessly.

Kyle closed his eyes, willing back the burn rising behind them. He never once stopped to think how hard that day must have been for her. "I think I do." He cupped her jaw in his palm, tipping her face. He searched her features. "Does this mean you did miss me?" He still didn't believe she never loved him, masochist that he was.

She smiled tearily, sniffling and thinking of the day Mimi was born, of how badly she'd wanted him with her. "Yes."

He didn't speak for a moment, occupied with pushing her hair off her face, touching her features as if reacquainting himself with them for the first time. "Can we start this reunion over?" he asked softly.

Instantly wary, she eyed him, backing out of his arms and swiping at her cheeks. "I'm not sure what you mean."

Boy, if ever a guard went up fast, he thought dismally, yet remained relaxed as he rested his hand on her shoulder with a gentle weight. "Hiya, Max. It's good to see you again."

She smiled, leftover tears spilling. "Hello, Kyle. Good to see you, too."

His gaze skimmed her gold satin pajamas and the black-and-gold vertical-striped robe. It clung in all the right places. "You look great, baby." His voice was low and husky.

A blush colored her cheeks, her gaze slipping over his bare muscular chest, the jeans unbuttoned against his flat stomach, before lifting to collide with his. "So do you."

"I'm cold."

She laughed shakily. "Considering you're half-naked..."

Suddenly his arm swept around her waist, pulling her hips sharply against his. "Wanna get all the way naked?" He wiggled his brows.

Maxie sputtered, pushing at his chest, trying to muster some anger, but she couldn't. His dark eyes were glittering with irresistible mischief.

"Gotcha," he teased, then kissed her quick and hard, a heady stroke of lips and tongue before releasing her so hard she dropped to the bed.

She blinked, expecting him to take the kiss further, but he was already halfway to the door.

"Kyle." Warning, wary.

"Yeah," he said as if talking to the walls. "That was much better." Then he was gone.

Maxie flopped back onto her bed, her heart pounding as much from his kiss as from the emotional upheaval of the past half hour. She closed her eyes and raked her hair back, holding it there. She'd glimpsed the man she'd known, the fun-loving Kyle Hayden who'd made love to her outdoors or gift wrapped silly little gum-machine toys she still secreted in a box in the top of her closet. The man she'd defied her father to keep seeing. Okay, she thought, they'd cleared the air. Somewhat. But that didn't mean everything was hunky-dory. As long as he was here, she couldn't let her guard down. She couldn't afford to have her secrets exposed.

He was Mimi's biological father and nothing more. He'd never wanted kids. In fact it was one of the issues they'd argued about when he'd first proposed. She'd no reason to believe he was any more receptive to the idea now. He'd refused contact and, as far as she was concerned, he'd lost his chance seven years ago. She was already both mother and father and damn good at it. Mimi was a happy, healthy little girl, and her mother would keep her that way.

It didn't matter that her knees quivered every time he touched her, or that she'd enjoyed their kiss more than any other in the past years. Mimi came first. Maxie didn't trust herself around Kyle, didn't trust her judgment, her feelings. And certainly not him. Whether he was an old flame or not, her daughter's happiness wasn't going to suffer because her mother couldn't be the adult here. She had to stick to the routine, keep more than an emotional distance and act like nothing was wrong. She scoffed. Yeah, right. Act like the father of her child wasn't in the same house with them?

Pushing off the bed, she left her room. Kyle was strangely absent, and she was relieved. After she loaded the washer and turned it on, folded a basket full of laundry, ran the vacuum, then emptied the dishwasher, she headed back to the privacy of her rooms. Sitting on the edge of her bed, she checked the time, then flipped open her address book lying on the nightstand and hurriedly dialed her friend Gina's number. Mimi should be about ready for bed by now.

Gina answered, said hello and they chatted for a few moments before the sound of a high-pitched squeal in the background made her cringe.

"Ready for a couple of tranquilizers?"

Gina laughed tiredly. "It gets a little wild just before bedtime—you know how they are together. Playing dress-up, tons of popcorn and a chic cartoon, then the pillow fight."

"I take it they're at the pillow-fight stage?"

"I've got the cordless phone. Let me check." The giggles got louder. "Bryan's already asleep, the little trouper, and Scott's supposed to be keeping an eye on them, but—"

"Dream on, girlfriend, it's basketball season."

"Yeah, and he's asleep in the recliner, the rat. And it's

not even halftime." Over a squeal, she heard Gina call to Mimi.

"Hi, Mom!" came an answering shout.

Maxie let out her breath, soothed just by the sound of her daughter's voice. "Hey, sweetie, how's it going?"

"A real blast, Mom. Me and Dana had hamburgers and fries and soda and popcorn."

"And you're going to be sick if you don't settle down. You might wake the baby."

"Okay, sure," she said, but Maxie knew when she was being ignored. "Mrs. Trask said we could stay up till ten if it's okay with you."

She's going to be a crab in the morning, Maxie thought, checking the time. "Nine."

"Mom," she whined softly.

"Nine-thirty."

"Yes!" came excitedly, and Maxie grinned.

"But you have to be quiet in the morning. Mrs. Trask needs some rest. Deal?" Mimi promised she and Dana would watch cartoons until Gina was up. "Good night, baby."

"Mom? What's up? You sound…funny."

Mimi was always too insightful for one so young. An old soul, she liked to think. "Funny ha-ha or funny weird?"

"Funny weird."

"I just miss you. It's lonely here, just me and the horses and mules."

"But Grandma said we had a boarder."

Maxie thought of her boarder and the kiss they'd shared earlier. "Yeah, he's an old friend."

"Then why are you lonely?"

"Good question." She tried to sound relaxed.

"I love you, Mommy," her daughter said, and Maxie closed her eyes, thanking God for giving her this little angel.

"I love you, too, princess. G'night."

Gina got on the line. "They're going down for the count."

Maxie smiled, shaking her head. "Girl, you're a saint."

"Yeah." She laughed lightly. "Only you and God know that, though. Hey, is it all right if she stays tomorrow, too, since there's no school on Monday? We're going to the carnival."

Maxie wanted to say no, that she needed Mimi home, needed to feel her arms around her, tuck her in at night, but she had to think of her daughter and a six-year-old's need for friends. "You sure?"

"Oh, yeah," Gina said comfortably. "She's an angel and it's easier, believe it or not, with the pair of them."

Why did children always behave when they were in other people's houses and were holy terrors in their own? Maxie wondered.

"Sure. But you pick the weekend, and it's a slumber party at my place. Bryan, too, of course." Gina protested about adding the baby to the barrage of kids, but Maxie wouldn't hear of it. "You and Scott can have a real date and go out alone."

"Alone? Out? What's that?"

Maxie laughed, said goodbye and hung up.

She rubbed her face, plowing her fingers through her hair. When she lifted her gaze, she found Kyle standing just outside the bedroom door. He'd covered his incredible chest with a faded black sweatshirt emblazoned with the Marine Corps emblem.

"Eavesdropping?" Maxie felt warm beneath the strength of his stare.

Kyle had heard enough to know she'd been talking to her daughter, and that she loved her, deeply. He felt suddenly like a bothersome ant and wondered if she'd deliberately kept her daughter from him. He didn't like that at all.

Maxie stood. "Answer the question."

"No, not intentionally."

She believed him, though she had no reason to right now and tried to decipher the odd look in his eyes.

"Hungry?"

"I can always eat." He was still staring intently.

She advanced, holding his gaze. "What do you say I make us a snack? Hmm?"

He'd like to snack on her, he thought wolfishly as his gaze slipped past her to her room. More specifically the four-poster bed he hadn't noticed before, the rich colors of maroon and pale gray, a complete contrast to the rest of the house. Royal in appearance, yet it was exotic with the majestic draping, the canopy like something out of a harem. He wanted to brush back the fabric, to lie with her on the huge empty bed, stripping those clingy pajamas off slowly and reacquainting himself with every inch of her delectable body. He brought his gaze back to hers as she made to slip past him.

"Nice bed, Max."

She froze at his intimate tone, gazing up at him. "I like it fine," she managed to say with him so close. *I should have dressed in something more defensive,* she thought, brushing her hair back off her cheek and hating that her hand shook.

Kyle noticed and realized that no matter how much she tried to ignore it, the electricity was still there. Something in him wanted her to acknowledge it.

He braced his palm on the frame, blocking her freedom, unable to resist rattling her cage. "Still sleep in the nude?"

She rolled her eyes. "Oh, for heaven's sake," she said, and ducked beneath his arm and headed to the kitchen.

Kyle spared another look into the lavish bedroom. *Now, that's the old Maxie,* he thought, then followed her, trying to forget her bed, her daughter and make the best of the remaining evening, at least.

Maxie could feel his eyes on her back and ignored the sensation as she rummaged in the refrigerator for fruit and cheese, the cabinets for crackers. After preparing a pot of coffee, she switched on the CD player, then carried the filled platter to the living room. Chopin in the background, she set the platter on the desk, gesturing for him to help himself as she slid behind the desk and into the leather chair. She pulled a calculator close and opened her ledgers. The music soothed her frayed nerves as she worked, engrossed with tallying the figures. Tossing the pencil on the desk, she worked a kink out of her shoulders and lifted her gaze. He was near the fireplace, finishing off an apple, watching her.

"What?" she said nervously.

"I don't remember you having an appetite like that."

She glanced down at the near empty platter. "I didn't work as hard as I do now."

"What made you decide to board horses?"

"This place came cheap, and working with horses was the only thing I was really good at." She chuckled softly, sinking back into the chair. "Still *is* the only thing I'm good at."

He scowled. "That's bull." He tossed the core into the fireplace.

"Is it?" she said, arching a brow. "It took me five years to finish college."

"I think I contributed to some of that," he confessed, adding a log to the dying blaze.

She offered a small smile of memory, of her recklessly abandoning her senior classes to be with him. "I suppose. But with sisters who excelled at everything they did, I was mostly a total failure."

Kyle scowled, not liking that she thought of herself that way. "Taking a while to finish college is no crime, Max."

"No, but marrying and divorcing in the space of a year isn't exactly a glowing track record, either."

He tried not to show his shock. Married! Mimi's father, he assumed. "I always knew you were a heartbreaker."

Maxie blanched, wondering what was going on behind his strained smile and wishing she'd delivered that news with a little more tact. "Forget I mentioned it." She hopped up to get coffee.

Kyle watched her go, wisely keeping his mouth shut. They were having a civil conversation, and he wanted the peace to last. Yet he wondered about her marriage, who she'd loved enough to say "I do" and why it had ended.

She returned with a carafe of coffee and two mugs, offering him one, then filling it.

"You were telling me why you board horses...." he prodded, hoping to maintain the easy atmosphere.

She blinked. "Oh. Yeah. Well, Mia and Mariah wouldn't get near Dad's horses, and handling them was something I did better." She took her mug with her as she went back to the desk, curling into the chair. "I have two of Dad's colts, by the way." She watched him as he poked at the fire, stirring it to a crackling blaze. "Anyway, when I had the chance to buy this place, I did. Started out with just a couple of mounts and tack that had seen better days, but—" she shrugged "—now we do all right."

We. She and Mimi, he thought. Alone. "It's a lot of work." He glanced back over his shoulder. "Do you have help?"

Her soft smile caught him square in the chest. "Mimi does sometimes, bless her heart, but as to hiring help—can't afford it. Besides, I'd rather do it alone."

His lips tightened. Running a ranch alone was wearing her down to ten pounds thinner than she ought to be, he thought with a scrutinizing glance, yet didn't comment. It sounded too possessive anyway. Which he was not. He adjusted the screen and faced her.

"I love it. I'm more relaxed working with my hands." She made a pained face. "And my back and legs," she groaned as she shifted in her chair.

"But your daughter can't be that much help."

She shrugged. "It doesn't matter. I just like having her around." *I need it.*

"While I'm here, can I give you a hand?"

"No," she nearly shouted, stiffening, then added more softly, "No, thank you. I don't need it. I can manage."

Like she didn't need me before, Kyle thought, but refrained from saying so. He was tired of fighting with her.

And knew it was his fault for keeping up the tension between them.

Not wanting to discuss Mimi with him, Maxie stood abruptly, gesturing him to follow as she walked into the kitchen. "How's Mitch?" That was a safe enough subject, she thought.

Kyle followed. "Still a marine, still single. Stationed in Camp LeJeune, but he's due for orders soon."

She pulled a covered platter from the fridge, then gathered utensils, plates and napkins on a tray. "Any idea where he's going next?"

His gaze on her satiny behind, it took him a second to answer. "If he told me, he'd have to kill me."

She glanced over her shoulder, a grin spreading slowly across her face. "Ooh, secret stuff, huh?"

"Yeah. He loves it." He nodded to the platter, trying not to salivate over the four layers of cake she was sliding onto a plate. "What's that?"

"Heart failure," she said, bringing the tray into the living room. "Commonly known as chocolate-mocha torte." He followed her heels like an eager puppy, then sat on the sofa, impatient for her to set a plate before him.

Kyle lifted it, fork poised. "Did you make this?"

"Yeah, right. I rarely have time for breathing, let alone playing Julia Childs. Just be thankful for bakeries."

"I am, I am," he said around a huge bite. He never splurged on real desserts, since it was just him alone. It was nice that she remembered his sweet tooth.

Maxie sank onto the sofa and watched him devour the rich cake, offering him more, then grinned when he unabashedly ate another chunk.

"Terrific." He swiped his lips with a napkin and met her gaze. "I needed that."

Her mouth curved slowly. "You always could pack it away."

He grinned back. The fire popped and hissed softly. And the room seemed to close in on them. Maxie avoided acknowledging it by jumping up to gather the dishes, but Kyle stood, catching her hand.

"You cooked dinner. Let me at least do that."

She stared down at his hand on hers and felt the warmth of his fingers, the heat they always generated escalating by the second. For a moment, she couldn't pull away and lifted her gaze to his. Maxie instinctively stepped away, but he didn't let go, looming like a circling hawk to a tender prey before he clamped his arm around her waist and pulled her flush to his body.

"Oh, Kyle, don't do this again," she almost cried, pushing at his chest with her fists.

He didn't let her go, his gaze scoring her face. "I know what you're thinking," he murmured, his hand sliding warmly up her satin-clad back.

"Do you?" Maxie closed her eyes, her fingers unfurling over his chest, flexing deeply into his muscles. It had been so long since she'd been touched like this.

"You're thinking, is this real or just Memorex?" Her lips quirked. "You're wondering if that kiss in the barn was just old anger or feelings that never died."

Her eyes flashed open. "They did."

"Liar, liar," he growled, his mouth descending on hers in a breathless rush. The contact shot straight through her down to her toes, her heels, then rushed along her body with amazing speed.

Oh, Kyle.

She tried to resist it, remaining still, but his kiss was dark and heavy, his mouth grinding over hers, taking in a desperation she'd felt in him only once before. The night he told her he was going to war. The night he'd given her his child. Old memories flooded through her, the anxiety she'd felt, the sorrow of believing she might lose him—the hurt she never wanted to give him. And she clung to him fiercely, her arms around his neck. She couldn't get enough of him and knew he felt the same primal heat as his hand drove up her back, shaping her contours, pressing her closer, his strong, thick arms tightening and making her dizzy. His tongue lushly outlined her lips, then traced her teeth before pushing deeply inside. And Maxie knew she was in deep, deep trouble.

She whimpered softly, arching into him, and Kyle thought he would come apart right there in the living room. His knees felt weak, his body on fire for her. She couldn't ignore this, he thought, and he wanted more. More of this Maxie, the sexy female, naked, uninhibited and driving him to distraction since he laid eyes on her. More of her touching him.

He trembled with the power of it, loved the feel of her, the push and give of her body against his. He wanted to get closer. Wanted to get naked with her. And his hand moved roughly down her spine, cupping her lush bottom and pushing her tighter to the thickness swelling inside his jeans. *Ah, yes.*

This is madness, Maxie thought, feeling his hardness thrust against her, and tried to put some distance between them. But he kept kissing her and kissing her, primitive and carnal, driving away objection and rationalization as he nipped and licked and took again, first her mouth, then raking his teeth along her jaw. His breathing rapid and shaky, she tipped her head to give him better access to her throat.

Kyle groaned at the little shove of her softness to his groin and grasped her hips, rocking her against him. His tongue stroked, his lips savored and he wanted to open his jeans and push into her right now. Right here. He'd lied to himself about not thinking of her over the years. Too many times he'd imagined this moment, her willingly in his arms again, the savage heat bursting to life, the greedy hunger to get closer than humanly possible to each other. Had she thought of him like that since they'd separated? Not likely, he knew, leaning close for another taste. But she was now.

Her robe was open, his hand beneath the satin and covering her bare breast, warm and stroking over her nipple. It's been so long, Maxie thought as his other hand drove beneath the waist of her satin slacks, cupping her bare bottom and pushing. Her body quivered, liquid warmth rushing between her thighs. The ache was unbearable.

"See, Max. It's real, no Memorex," he whispered, then made to kiss her.

Suddenly she jerked back, staring at him for a moment, before pushing out of his arms. "This was wrong, really insane," she said more to herself. She didn't want this—really she didn't.

"Nothing *that* good could be wrong, Max." Straightening, he reached for her, and she put up her hands as if to ward him off.

She held his gaze, blame in her green eyes, and the passion that had escalated to dangerous levels faded rapidly. She couldn't afford to let him get to her like that again. Mimi's future rested on Maxie maintaining control over her emotions. To let him in would invite a whole new area of heartache she knew she wasn't prepared for.

"I knew this would happen with you in my house."

Barely able to stand upright, Kyle folded his arms, aching for another taste of her and knowing she would run screaming. "Want me to leave?"

She blinked, raking her hair back. "Would you?"

He didn't like how excited she was at the possibility. "Yeah, if you can't handle it."

Her gaze sharpened with her posture, a closed look in her eyes. "I can handle anything, Kyle. Including you. Just do me the favor of not touching me. Ever."

Maxie turned and fled, leaving Kyle to stare at the empty room, his body trembling with a fierce urge to either carry her to the nearest bed and make wild jungle love to her until she begged him to stop or pin her against the wall and demand some answers—like why he felt that the only time he was seeing the real Maxie was when she was coming apart in his arms?

Five

Kyle had relived kissing her so many times he'd been in mortal pain till nearly dawn and he was glad she was gone when he entered the kitchen the next morning. Last night, he kept tasting her on his lips, feeling her soft body pressed lushly against his, hearing her moans of pleasure until he was just short of tearing down her door and demanding she ease his agony, since she was the cause. But Kyle still had a few crumbs of good sense left and stayed away. That, however, did nothing for the perpetual crowd in his jeans every time he looked at her, and even the hot shower, the pot of fresh coffee and the massive breakfast Maxie had left him wasn't enough to shake off his lack of sleep.

It galled him to no end that he was falling under her spell again. He couldn't trust her and reminded himself that a promise of love and passion hadn't kept her with him seven years ago, and after last night, he knew it wouldn't again. He wasn't ready for that kind of heartache again, even if she had apologized. Besides, he'd never know if each kiss was just a rebirth of old feelings or something new.

Taking his coffee with him to the phone, Kyle checked in with the rescue team. There was suspicious behavior from a couple of rafters who kept leaving the tour group. Maybe it was better if he was gone, he thought, donning his jacket and hat, then grabbing his flight log. Especially when he could come up with ten reasons not to face her, right off the top of his head. But he wasn't a coward. That was Maxie's forte.

Walking across the yard to the stables, Kyle stepped inside, into the warmth, and found her near a stack of hay bales. It struck him then just how hard she worked. And he wondered if her being up this early on a Sunday was usual or because of him. Undetected, his gaze slipped over her. Like yesterday, she wore a faded flannel shirt, jeans, a sleeveless down vest and heavy work gloves. Her hair hung in her face as she caught a compressed-straw rectangle with a pair of bale hooks and yanked, trying to drag it off the stack.

She would rather die than ask for help, he thought, crossing to her and grabbing the wire. The bale hit the floor and she looked up.

"Thanks," she said, her breath steaming the air. Perspiration trickled at her temples and throat, he couldn't help noticing. She had to have been at this for a good hour to work up such a sweat, he thought. Especially when it looked like snow outside.

"Something you need?"

Kyle ignored the chill in her tone. "Gotta go in. No, it's not an emergency," he added when she looked alarmed. "How many are yours?" He gestured to the row of stalls.

"Exactly half. The horses."

He whistled softly. "Damn, Max, that's great."

Maxie smiled, brushing hair off her forehead with the back of her arm. "Thanks. You're welcome to ride one if you want."

Kyle breathed easier. Okay, this wasn't a bad start. "I might, later. If you'll join me?"

"Afraid you'll get lost?"

He tipped his hat back off his forehead and grinned. "Nah, no one to race."

She rolled her eyes. "Figures." She shook her head. "This need for constant competition must be a man thing."

He laughed softly, and Maxie had almost forgotten how handsome he looked when he did. "But doing all the work yourself is a 'woman thing'?"

"It's an 'I can't afford to hire anyone' thing," she said honestly.

He frowned. "My offer to help still holds."

"No."

"Max—"

She put up her hand to silence him. "Boarders don't work. It's a rule. The park service pays for you to stay here." She peered at him through a curtain of hair, then knocked it back, leaving a smudge of dirt on her cheek. "Can't have you working so hard that you're too tired to fly your chopper when they need you, right?"

"I think you underestimate my stamina."

She barked a short laugh. "Your stamina was never a prob—" Her eyes rounded, her expression mortified. "Oops."

Kyle reddened and laughed, moving closer. She backed away, eyes wary. It was like a territorial line in the sand. He could feel her guarded emotions, as well as see them. In her posture, the way she held the pitchfork across her body. Kyle took the hint, for his own good.

He looked exhausted, Maxie thought. The past twenty-four hours had left her feeling bruised, and if she hadn't been so dog tired last night, she would look as battle weary as he did.

Maxie could never have Kyle again. Not like before, because once he discovered he had a daughter he'd never known, anything they'd start would be destroyed.

"Look, Max. I know it's been rough between us." The sadness in her eyes didn't escape him.

She sighed tiredly. "It has, hasn't it?"

He peered a little. "It was okay there for a while, huh?"

She shrugged. "I suppose. I'll admit up front that you give me a bad case of the hots, Kyle...."

He smiled. "Same here, baby."

She felt the blush warm her cold cheeks. "Yeah, well...I have a daughter to think about and I don't want her to get any ideas about us. You'll be gone and I'd die before I'd break her heart again."

Again—like with her marriage, Kyle thought, yet nodded, understanding. From personal experience, he knew kids saw what they wanted to see. Even at twelve he kept thinking his parents would come for him, take him away from the orphanages and the blur of foster homes. But they hadn't. An impressionable child would read too much into anything beyond friendship. Kyle just didn't know if he could pull it off after all they'd been through and he wasn't looking forward to meeting her daughter. Kids made him nervous.

It was the perfect way to keep him back. A pact for the kid's sake.

A car horn sounded, and she peered around him out the doorway toward the house. "Oh, great."

He arched a brow in her direction.

"Mom."

He cringed sheepishly, then hurried toward the entrance.

"Chicken," she called, and couldn't help but laugh. "You'll never make it."

"Wanna bet?"

Kyle did double-time to the chopper, waving but not stopping. The last person he wanted to see was a member of her family.

Maxie donned her jacket, watching his chopper blades beat the air, lifting the craft as her mother crossed the yard.

"Oh, honey," Lacy Parrish said with feeling. "The years have treated him just *fine.*"

"Mom," she whined. No one needed to tell her how handsome Kyle was, nor how sexy. Especially first thing in the morning, looking a little sleepy and making her think of the passion they'd tested last night.

"Well, I always liked him," her mother was saying, and Maxie knew she'd missed half the conversation with her daydreaming.

"Dad didn't."

"Oh, sure he did. But he was a marine too once and knew where Kyle was coming from. He just wanted to protect his daughter more than he wanted to let him into the family. Besides, you defied him with Kyle, and that hit a sore spot."

More like an open wound, she thought and wasn't going to wake up any more old memories today.

"So, Mom," she said, folding her arms and staring down at the petite gray-haired woman. "Ready to spread some hay, or did you just pop in for a look at Mimi's daddy?"

Max couldn't believe she'd said that until the words left her mouth. She'd never once said that out loud. She paled, and her mom arched a graying brow.

Later that afternoon, Kyle steadied the stick as he brought the chopper out of the canyon and flew over the ground, low, skimming the earth in a rush. Then he saw her, riding fast, almost standing in the stirrups. He got hard just watching her. He followed her, a hundred feet above, his gaze on the woman whose image had distracted him all day. He'd finished his flight a couple hours after he'd left this morning, but offered to check supplies and store gear, giving the other, more experienced team members a break and keeping his mind off Maxie. Hadn't worked much, he thought, then he glanced ahead and swore foully at the telephone wires dangerously close. He yanked back on the stick, bringing the chopper skyward in a violent surge, then tipped to the side, kicking up dirt and nearly shearing off part of her toolshed.

It was an asinine move.

Kyle hovered high in the air and glanced down through

the domed glass near his feet. She'd stopped, shaking her head at him before heading back to the stables. Damn. Now that he looked like a total inept jerk, he had to set the chopper down without killing himself. He managed, shutting off the engine, then securing the craft to the ground. With his arms loaded with groceries, he walked toward the house.

Maxie reined up beside him. "Unusual approach technique, Hayden. Marines teach you that?" she teased, but that little stunt told her he hadn't changed. The rash daredevil was still a part of him.

He glared at her, blaming her for his careless flying. "I'm cooking tonight," he growled, then mounted the steps.

Maxie frowned. "Hey."

He glanced back from the porch. "What?" he snapped.

"You all right?"

He faced her. "Yeah, I'm fine," he lied, and could tell she didn't believe him. *I damn near crashed my chopper to just look at you,* he wanted to tell her. *After tasting you again, I want you so bad I can't concentrate, and working myself into exhaustion hasn't worked.* But he didn't say anything. "Now," he said as if she'd been privy to his silent ranting, "I'm going to cook. And I'll stay out of your way like you want."

She shrugged, wondering what was really eating at him. "Sure, fine," she said, then rose up in the stirrup to peer into the bags. "What'd you have in mind to feed us?"

"Spinach-stuffed manicotti and Sicilian sauce."

"Really?" Her high-pitched surprise and her smile did him in, and his posture softened.

"Yeah." When had her smile affected him this much? he wanted to know. "It takes about an hour or so, though."

She checked her watch. "How fortunate that I won't be finished for about that long."

Kyle smiled faintly and nodded before he marched up the steps. Great. He just put himself in the line of fire again. Stupid. That was the only explanation. He'd contracted a bad case of the stupids around her.

* * *

An hour and a half later, Maxie sank into the sofa, and wished it were her bed. She was stuffed. "Now, *that* was cooking," she muttered through a yawn, and Kyle settled beside her, half turned, his ankle braced on his knee. "Are you more relaxed now?" she asked.

"I wasn't—" She slid him a measured glance that effectively cut off his lie. "Okay, so I was a little tense."

"I like a man who can admit defeat before the battle even starts." She propped her head in her palm and her elbow on the back of the sofa.

Trying to stay awake, Kyle judged. She was still in her work clothes, smelling like leather and sweat and a gust of fresh air.

"Maybe you need to drag race or something."

He scoffed, sipping his coffee and noticing her droopy eyelids. "Nah, just sleep." He was quiet for a moment, staring off into space before he said, "Too old for risks like that."

When she didn't come back with a sharp retort, Kyle glanced to the side. She was out cold, her face on her arm, and she barely stirred when he lifted her in his arms and carried her to her room. Laying her in the center, he unlaced her boots, slipping them off before he tucked her feet under the spread. She sighed and squished the pillow under her cheek, but didn't waken. Kyle squatted, gazing at her face.

All afternoon, he'd picked apart each moment, all they'd said to each other in the past twenty-four hours. And then Kyle had rehashed youthful memories with the seasoned eye of a thirty-year-old man who'd seen too many of his pals die in Iraq, who'd felt the pain of loneliness so deep it choked, and not a passion-struck marine who was living for the moment. His old perspective had hidden the fact that she *had* tried to postpone their wedding, and he recognized that he'd been more afraid of being alone than of losing her. Yes, he was reckless, Kyle admitted easily and mentally cringed at some of the risks he used to take. And she was right about his spending money as if it was never ending. Hell, he'd never had much before enlisting, and the only reason he wasn't dead broke now was because his pay went into the bank while he was in Saudi, where he hadn't needed it. He rubbed the back of his neck and stared at the carpet. If he had loved her so much, why hadn't he come after her? But lasting love was something Kyle had never known. Not even with his own parents. With the exception of his big brother, everyone he'd ever loved had walked out on him.

The phone rang, and he snatched it off the cradle before the chime finished. "What?"

"Is this—is this the Wind Dancer?" came in a tiny voice.

"Yes." Kyle sank to the floor. He knew whom he was talking to without introductions.

"Where's my mom?" The panic in the child's voice drove a lethal dart into Kyle's chest.

"Right here," he assured. "Just a sec."

He covered the receiver and gave Maxie a shake. She blinked blearily.

He pointed to the phone. "Your daughter."

She smiled sleepily, reaching. "Thanks." She tucked the phone close. "Hi, sweetie. How was your day?"

Kyle heard Maxie's half of the conversation, and he couldn't help noticing she perked up a bit. Then suddenly her gaze clashed with his.

"He's big and tall with dark hair and eyes."

Kyle flushed a little, then added in a stage whisper, "You didn't mention an excellent pilot and easy on the eyes." He wiggled his brows.

She rolled her eyes, covering the phone briefly to say, "Excellent pilot? After that stunt today…aren't you stretching it a bit?" Then into the phone, she said, "Yes, you'll get to meet him in the morning if he's around."

Kyle stood, staring down at Maxie, and she held his gaze as she shifted to her back and spoke to her daughter. "I love you, too, princess. See you in the morning."

Kyle experienced a flash of déjà vu. Maxie in his bed, naked, her hair mussed like it was now, the sheet baring her breasts teasingly while he tried getting dressed for work. And what he did seconds later...crawling back into bed, making wild love to her and getting reprimanded for being late.

She held the phone to her chest. "She's eaten way too much cotton candy," she said, then leaned out to replace it in the cradle. She tossed back the spread and sat up. Kyle remained close, and Maxie rubbed her hands over her face.

"It's late. I'll clean up. Go back to sleep, Max."

Max. He was the only one who called her that now.

"I reek."

"Not that I could tell."

She lowered her hands and smiled wanely. He shifted his weight nervously, as if about to do or say something monumental, then turned away.

She frowned at his back. "Thanks for cooking, Kyle."

"No sweat."

He was already out the door, but Kyle kept hearing that tiny voice ask over and over, *Where's my mom?*

It sounded too familiar. Like him, when his mother had walked out.

Just after lunch the following day, Kyle stepped out of the kitchen, then immediately lurched back as a redheaded torpedo shot past him.

"Mom! Mom, I'm home!" She dumped a backpack, pillow and her jacket on the floor.

Maxie flew around the corner, scooping up the little girl and hugging her tightly. She rained wet, smacky kisses over her face, and the little girl repaid in kind, cupping her mother's cheeks in her tiny hands and laying a noisy one on her.

"Miss me?" Maxie said, brushing Mimi's hair from her face.

"Yup." She nodded vigorously, braids bouncing.

"Love me?"

"For-ever!" Mimi squealed, locking her arms around her mother's neck and squeezing.

Kyle leaned against the wall, more for support than to relax. The look on Maxie's face tore through him. Pure, unconditional love.

A mom.

The resemblance in the pair was unmistakable. Red hair, green eyes, petite features.

Maxie set Mimi to her feet with a dramatic groan. "Good grief, you're getting heavy!"

"I ate a lot."

"I'll bet," she said, and bent to kiss the top of her red head. She met Kyle's gaze across the foyer. Panic and worry sped through her. What was he thinking? Did he see himself in Mimi? Did he notice she had his mouth, that she smirked just like him?

She didn't have long to think about it when a horn sounded. Maxie strode to the door and waved goodbye to Gina.

Kyle heard the car leave, but his gaze was on the child. Maxie's daughter. Maxie's flesh and blood was a bundle of energy with red hair in braids, one cockeyed, the ribbons dirty and drooping. She had a dusting of freckles across her nose and vivid green eyes that caught him in the gut like a hammer.

She marched up to him, planted her hands on her skinny hips and craned her neck to gaze into his eyes. "Who are you?"

"Mimi Anne! That's rude," her mother scolded as she closed the front door. "You're supposed to introduce yourself first."

Mimi blushed, looked at the toes of her cowboy boots and muttered, "Yes, Momma." She met his gaze. "Hullo. I'm Mimi Parrish." She thrust out her hand.

Kyle grasped her tiny fingers and shook. "A pleasure, Miss Parrish. I'm Kyle Hayden."

Something flickered in the little girl's eyes just then. "Pleased to meet you, sir." She clasped her hands in front of her and glanced at her mother. "You were right, Mom, he is big."

Maxie smiled, fighting the tears threatening to surface. How many times had she imagined this moment and how many times had she wished it would never come?

Kyle squatted. "This better?"

She looked him over. "Nah. You're still big."

"Do I scare you?" He'd always thought he did that to kids.

"Nah. Elvis is bigger than you, and I'm not afraid of him."

Kyle glanced at Maxie, his brow tightening at the odd glow in her eyes. "Elvis?"

"The horse, silly," Mimi said, and Kyle realized that the little girl was ticked that he hadn't asked her directly.

"Oh, beg your pardon, ma'am."

Mimi grinned, showing a missing tooth, and Kyle smiled back. A heartbreaker, he thought, tugging on her braid.

Maxie thought her composure would shatter any second. To see them together was enough to make her knees weak. "Want to ride, Meem?" She had to get out of here.

"All right! Alone?"

"No way, José. With me." She grabbed her jacket before gathering up Mimi's discards, then tossed her daughter her coat and a look that said not to leave her stuff lying in the hall.

With her hand in her mother's, Mimi was at the door when she paused and glanced back at Kyle.

"Aren't you coming?"

Briefly he glanced up at Maxie as she donned her cowboy hat, trying to read her expression. He couldn't. "Maybe later, short stack."

She giggled, and something broke open inside Kyle's chest.

Mimi looked up at her mother. "But if Kyle rides one, that's one you don't have to exercise later, Mom."

The child's logic was frightening, Kyle thought, straightening.

"Sure," Maxie said, not ready to argue about why she didn't want Kyle along just now. She met his gaze. "I'll saddle the mounts. Bring the hand radio—it's on the desk," she told him. "In case the service needs you."

Kyle nodded and the pair left the house. Standing in the doorway, he watched them go, watched Maxie pause to zip Mimi's jacket and adjust her miniature cowboy hat, then take her hand. Together they ran to the barn, laughing. He couldn't help but notice how alive she was around her daughter, how different than the past two days. The reserve melted, the aloofness vaporizing the instant Mimi ran through the door. It was as if Maxie had been waiting impatiently to unleash the love she hid from him. He'd never seen love like that, and it made him want it.

A half hour later, they were racing across the sun-drenched land, Mimi shouting for her mother to go faster.

Kyle could barely catch his breath. Not from the pace, but from watching Max and Mimi. The little girl was tucked protectively against her mother, holding on to the pommel, but Maxie was nearly standing in the stirrups. Kyle rode abreast of her, and she glanced to the side, smiling unabashedly. Then she focused on the post that was their marker. Kyle dug his heels in and the horse lurched, but Maxie was already overtaking the post. He rounded it, but knew it was useless. She was a better rider than he could ever hope to be.

She was walking the horse, gasping for air when he finally rode up.

"We win!" Mimi whooped, socking the air like a prize-fighter.

Max laid a hand on her shoulder. "Mimi, be a gracious winner."

"Aw, let her have the win, Max. You guys deserve it. Man, you're fast," he said.

"Practice." She shrugged. Maxie asked her daughter

about her weekend, and the child chattered incessantly as they cooled down the mounts. She was still going strong when they rode into the barn and dismounted.

Kyle groaned, stretching his spine and working the tightness from his thigh. One too many bungee jumps, he thought.

"Your butt hurt?"

Maxie sputtered, staring down at her daughter as she removed a saddle.

"Yeah, it does," Kyle admitted, smiling. "Does yours?"

"Nah—"

"Mimi—"

"I mean, no sir. I'm used to it." Mimi grabbed a pail and took off to fill it with water. Kyle watched her, then hefted the second saddle and tossed it over the stall wall.

"She's cute, Max."

"Thanks. I like her."

Kyle chuckled, grabbing a rag and wiping down the horse. "Do all kids talk like that?"

Maxie scoffed softly. "You mean constantly?"

"No, so...adult."

Max shrugged, leading the horse into the stall. She didn't want Kyle to get any ideas about Mimi's age, even though Mimi was little for six. That he'd assumed, through lack of information, that her ex-husband was Mimi's father, was a safety net she needed. He would be gone soon, and she needed to keep Mimi's life normal.

"I haven't been around kids," he was saying, and she heard actual fear in his voice. It more than surprised her.

"You're doing okay. Just don't talk down to her. She's smart and hates being patronized."

He blinked. "Does she even know what it means?"

"Not literally, but verbally she can recognize it. And she has a temper."

"Like mother like daughter, huh?"

"I don't have a temper!"

He arched a brow and she wilted, smiling and shaking her head.

Pail in two hands, Mimi trotted up, splashing water on her boots.

"Got the grub, Mom."

Kyle grinned, his hands on his hips. "Need help, short stack?"

"Na—no, thanks, it's my job." She said that with such pride, he thought.

Then, splashing more water, she hauled the pail to the trough inside the stall and poured, her little tongue sticking farther out the more she tipped the pail. Kyle folded his arms over his chest and leaned against the entrance, watching mother and daughter work. Mimi scooped feed into the wood box and kept judging the level, asking her mom's opinion. Maxie answered while cleaning the horse's hooves with practiced ease. It didn't bother him that they completely ignored him. It was a scene he couldn't recall witnessing before. Parent and child—friends.

Inside, he was a little jealous.

Six

The next morning, Kyle woke to the loudest racket he'd ever experienced since living in a barracks.

Maxie.

At six in the morning. She was singing at the top of her lungs.

The stereo blared, the scent of frying bacon wafted through the house and Mimi was telling her mom to go away. At the top of *her* lungs.

He'd barely had his jeans zipped when he burst into the hall. Maxie was there, outside one of the rooms, a lime green water gun in her hands like a marine ready for assault, her foot tapping and behind swaying to the country music.

She didn't see him. And she looked disgustingly chipper for this hour.

At the end of the chorus, she fired into the room, and Mimi's high-pitched squeal punctured the air.

"Up, girlie, this is call number three."

"Okay, Mom, *okay!* I'm gettin' up," Mimi grumbled, and

Kyle grinned. Maxie glanced to the side and blinked, then shrugged, sheepish.

"She's hard to get up in the morning."

"I would have never guessed." Kyle walked toward her, keeping just out of sight from a little girl who was likely getting dressed and didn't need a stranger seeing her.

He was wrong. Suddenly a stream of water shot out of the room and hit Maxie in the face. She sputtered, then returned fire, backing away as Mimi advanced out of the room, frilly pink nightgown and bare feet flying after her mother.

"I'm gonna murtelize you, Mom!"

"Oh, yeah! Says who?" Maxie shouted, and hosed her daughter.

Mimi shrieked, returned fire and got soaked again by her loving mother.

Kyle simply stayed out of the battle and watched them, a greediness to be a part of it working under his skin.

Then Mimi saw him and doused him with ice-cold water square in the chest.

Maxie gasped.

Mimi let out a soft "Oops" and reddened.

And Kyle threw his hands up in surrender. "You're not supposed to shoot an unarmed man," he told her.

"We have an extra gun," Mimi offered, grinning, water dripping from her nose.

"You wouldn't last a minute, short stack. I was a marine."

She blinked, awed. "Really?"

"I call for a cease-fire," her mom interrupted, giving Kyle a "don't tempt her" look. "And you, little lady, are going to be late for school. Breakfast will be on the table in fifteen minutes."

Mimi made a face, then glanced at Kyle. She put the water gun to her shoulder like a marine before she spun on her heels and marched back to her bedroom. Just before she slipped around the doorjamb, she turned and shot her mom between the eyes, then vanished.

Kyle roared with laughter as Mimi escaped a counterattack. "She'd make a great recon," he said, still chuckling.

Maxie flung water off her face and at him. "Don't give her ideas." She walked to the kitchen and stored the gun under the sink before snatching up a towel to wipe her face.

"Is it like that every morning?"

"Only after the weekend. She loves to sleep."

"And you like waking her."

She glanced over her shoulder, smiling hugely, and Kyle felt the warmth of it down to his toes. "It's a power thing. Breakfast is almost ready...though—" Briefly her gaze fell on the tiny rivers of water winding down the contours of his stomach. Nice. "You might want to go dry off first." Kyle arched a brow, giving her a long velvety look that made her insides jingle before he headed back to his room.

After a shave and a quick shower, he was presentable enough and when he returned to the kitchen, Mimi was chomping into her breakfast to the beat of the music. And Maxie...well, Maxie's sweet behind was swaying back and forth, her snug jeans shaping her bottom, and he wondered at his fascination with that part of her anatomy. She flipped bacon and pancakes, poured juice into a glass, all the while singing off-key and dancing. How could anyone who worked so hard be this cheerful in the morning? And then he knew. Her daughter.

If Max was a grouch, then her daughter would be, too. Kyle couldn't remember his mom ever smiling in the morning and never dancing. Hell, he couldn't remember the last time someone went out of the way to cook for him, for that matter.

This was the old Maxie. This was the side of her he hadn't seen since he'd arrived. The difference stunned him.

Maxie cast a side glance at the clock. "Kyle! Breakfast!" she shouted.

"Gee, Max—"

She spun around, shocked.

"Crank it up another notch, they didn't hear you in California."

Mimi giggled, and Kyle slanted her a quick wink.

Maxie made a face and gestured with the spatula to the vacant chair. "Sit, eat."

He sat, leaning toward Mimi as he said in a stage whisper, "Is she always this bossy?"

"Always," Mimi said, dramatically rolling her eyes.

She did that just like her mom, he thought, smiling.

Maxie plopped a huge plate in front of him.

He looked down, then up at her. "Third Battalion's coming for breakfast, right?"

"Ha-ha," she muttered dryly. "I've seen you pack away twice that much."

"Yeah, but I was twenty-three and trying to impress you."

They exchanged a quick smile. "Were all those wild stunts to impress me, too?"

His gaze slipped over her, quick and thorough, and Maxie felt a warm current follow the path. "Which stunts exactly? Bungee jumping or—" his dark eyes smoldered "—the waterfall in Encinada?"

Maxie inhaled, her cheeks blooming with color at the memory of the two of them—losing all inhibition and making wicked love under a Mexican fall, in broad daylight.

"So," he said on a husky laugh, "I did leave an impression."

Boy, did he, she thought, and it didn't take much to revive it, either. "Must have been the stamina thing," she said, turning back to the counter and heard him nearly choke on his juice.

"When did you know my mom?" Mimi piped up. Maxie glanced and stiffened. Kyle noticed, yet started on his breakfast.

"Way back. She had long hair then."

Mimi looked at her mom, then Kyle. "What else?"

Kyle chewed and swallowed. "Let's see." He sank back

into the chair and sipped his coffee, eyeing Maxie from head to toe. She stilled, halfway to the table, then slid into the chair. He recognized the tense set of her shoulders immediately.

"She had great legs and always wore makeup."

Wide-eyed, Mimi looked at her mother, then Kyle. "Makeup? *My* mom?"

Kyle nodded, watching Maxie squirm and enjoying the hell out of it.

"What else?"

He met Maxie's gaze across the table, his voice intimate. "She liked satin and dark chocolate and lobster dripping in butter." Her eyes softened as he spoke. "And riding on the back of my motorcycle. She has a freckle on her ankle shaped like a tear...and actually purrs when you rub her feet." Maxie's skin pinkened, and Kyle wondered if she was remembering the last time he'd done that. Then he glanced down at the little wide-eyed redhead, suddenly aware they weren't alone. "And she hates bugs."

Mimi smiled, stabbing her pancakes. "Still does, likes caterpillars, though."

"Why is that, you think?"

Mimi was chewing and munching as she talked. "'Cause they turn into butterflies, and butterflies aren't slimy."

Kyle chuckled softly, then focused on his meal.

"Okay, you two, cut the chatter. Mimi, eat with your mouth closed and finish up. Kyle..." He looked up, arching a brow. She blushed. "Just finish," she said lamely.

"Yes, ma'am," he said, grinning behind each bite, having a hard time keeping his eyes off her. Though her worn jeans and the sweater weren't the least bit provocative, they were wreaking havoc on his senses. There was a casual sensuality about Maxie Kyle had never found in other women. Were you looking for it? his mind countered, and Kyle examined his past conquests, none of which had lasted more than a couple months. No one came to mind, but his thoughts were interrupted when Mimi hopped up to go brush her teeth.

And to Kyle, it felt as if a little of the light left the room. Yet he was alone with Max for the first time since Mimi arrived. A frown creased his brows. Now that he thought about it, she'd made a point of having her daughter close, always between them. Was she really that afraid to be alone with him? He didn't think so, then considered the eruption that occurred whenever they got close enough. A defensive move, he decided.

As much as he liked being with both of them, he couldn't shake the nagging image every time he saw them together— of Maxie leaving him at the altar and sliding between the sheets with another man. The nagging persisted. Had she been leading him on seven years ago? Was she seeing this man when she was seeing him? Did she love him? *Had she ever loved him?* That hurt the worst, he thought. And the toughest question, the hardest reality kept seeping into his brain to torture him—*if I had come after Max, would Mimi have been my child?*

Maxie ate, trying to ignore him. It was next to impossible. He smelled great, looked so damn rugged in jeans and a sweatshirt and it didn't help that her daughter liked him. But then, Mimi liked everyone. Maxie thought of what he would do and say if he knew he'd had breakfast with his daughter. And she didn't even want to consider how Mimi would feel if she realized her daddy was in the house. In the past, Mimi had asked a few times where her father was, and Maxie had been as honest as she could be. Her dad wasn't around when she was born, and he didn't know about her. Mimi knew that Maxie had loved him enough to create her, but not enough to stay together. Even as small as she was, her daughter was content to know she wasn't the reason she didn't have a father in her life—that it was her mother he didn't want. It had always been a delicate subject, but with her grandparents, aunts and uncles showering Mimi with love and attention, Maxie didn't think she missed what she'd never had. And her ex-husband, Carl, well, that was three years ago and Mimi's memory of him was fading. She

hoped. But a little part of her resented that he hadn't asked
if Mimi was his. The silence stretched, him watching her,
her finishing breakfast.

Kyle's own thoughts were cut off as he witnessed a parade
of emotion skate across Maxie's face and was about to ask
her about it when she glanced at the clock.

"Oh, she's going to be late."

Maxie was up and calling to her daughter to get the brush
and bands for her hair. Kyle sighed in the seat, munching
on bacon. *I get close and she runs,* he thought. He heard the
pair talking softly and smiled, shaking his head. Mimi was
trying to come up with an excuse to stay home from school.
Maxie had a response for her every suggestion. It was
strange to be in the house with two females and even
stranger that he liked it. A horn sounded, and Mimi dashed
through the house. Maxie stood near the door, holding out
her jacket and backpack, telling her that her lunch was already inside and not to forget her homework this time. Mimi
was wrestling with the zipper when Kyle stepped into the
foyer.

"Are you going to be here when I get home, Mr. Hayden?"

He nodded, not daring a glance at Maxie. "For a couple
weeks, it looks like."

"All right!" Mimi smiled hugely, and a knot yanked in
his chest. She was a heartbreaker, he thought.

The horn sounded again, closer, and Mimi faced her mom
and Max bent to kiss her. "I love you, princess." They
rubbed noses.

"I love you, too, Mommy. Bye." She was at the door.
"See ya, Mister Hayden."

"See ya, short stack."

She giggled and dashed out the door. Maxie stepped onto
the porch as the bus door closed and Mimi waved, then got
busy chatting with her friends.

Maxie glanced back to see him a few feet behind her.

He whistled softly. "She is one ball of energy."

"Hey, she toned it down for you," she said, coming back inside. "I usually can't get her to stop asking questions or sit still long enough to eat breakfast."

The phone rang and after a quick hello, she handed it to Kyle. "It's Jackson."

Kyle took the call, answering in one-word responses, then popped into the kitchen.

She looked up, her hands elbow deep in dishwater.

"Got a flight."

"A rescue?"

"Yeah, rafters are stuck somewhere upriver." He shrugged into his jacket. "I don't know when I'll be back...."

"No problem."

"I'll try to get word if I'm out there long," he said, taking a few steps closer, almost on instinct to kiss her. He stopped just short of doing it, staring into her vivid green eyes, then at her lush mouth. He brought his gaze back to hers and was tempted. But every time he touched her, she shut him out and they were just feeling comfortable around each other again. He wasn't willing to ruin it.

He cleared his throat. "Ah, I guess I'll see you later."

Her gaze slipped quickly over his features, her heart pounding in her ears from his nearness. "I'll be here," she murmured softly. He nodded, then left. Maxie sighed, swishing the soapy water, then went back to scrubbing the pan.

She did not want him to kiss her just then, she thought. Really she didn't.

Kyle's chopper was already on the pad when she returned from the grocery store. She hadn't expected him to be done before Mimi came home from school. With Mimi around, the conversation never lulled and the chatter would keep Kyle from starting something neither of them had a right to pursue.

Why? a voice asked. *Because I'll ruin it. I did seven years ago*, she thought, grabbing a sack and heading into the house. She turned back for another sack, then another, muttering to herself, debating whether she wanted something from him or not, or whether it was just old feelings getting her all hot and bothered when she looked at him. Or when he spoke, bringing up some old memories. Or when his gaze seemed to probe and poke. Like he had this morning in the kitchen. She knew what he was doing—weakening her defenses. What she couldn't understand was why. She'd done the absolute worst to that man, and even though he'd forgiven her for leaving him at the altar, she figured he would stay far away from her and not dredge up any of the sweet erotic memories she'd kept tucked away for years.

Reaching for the last grocery bag, Maxie stilled, frowning at the barn. She set the bag back into the Range Rover, slammed the rear door, then marched across her land to the barn.

She stopped inside. "What the hell do you think you're doing?"

Kyle kept shoveling soiled hay into the wheelbarrow. "Gee, Max, didn't think I'd have to explain this part to you, of all people." He grinned and scooped and dumped.

"You're not supposed to work here, Kyle."

He shrugged. "I'm not supposed to get hungry after that obscene breakfast you served me, but I am."

She moved closer. "Stop right now."

He dumped a shovelful, then paused to look at her, his gloved hands propped on the handle. She was like a hen with wet feathers, he thought. "Make me."

She blinked. "Excuse me?"

"You heard me."

She tipped her head to the side and eyed him. "You're doing this just to start a fight, aren't you?"

"You're the one who's scrapping here, kiddo."

"We've already discussed this."

"Come on, Max." His expression pleaded. "I'm bored out of my mind. Besides, if I help, that gives you more time to spend with your daughter when she gets home."

He had her there, the skunk.

Kyle laid the shovel aside, then grasped the wheelbarrow handles, maneuvering it to the rear of the barn, up the ramp he'd seen her use days earlier. Finishing that, he removed his gloves and went to the open sink, washing his hands and face. He reached blindly for the towel, and Maxie walked to his side, shoving one in his hand.

She was irritated. He'd cleaned all the stalls and yes, though she would have more time with Mimi, that didn't give her anything to occupy herself with in the meantime. Not really. And idle hands got her into trouble around Kyle.

She turned away.

"Running?"

"I have groceries to take in."

"Chicken."

She whirled on him, anger in her eyes. "I *have* groceries."

He simply grinned, swiping his jaw dry. "In this weather? They'll stay cold."

"My vegetables will freeze."

He stared, his expression even.

"What?" she said nervously.

"I'm waiting for the next excuse you'll give me for not being wherever I am."

"I'm not making excuses."

Like hell. She looked ready to bolt any second, Kyle thought. "You're not a good liar, either, Max."

She fumed.

"Then come closer."

She took a couple steps.

He shook his head.

Maxie marched right up to him, staring him down. She felt like a kid confronting a bully, except the two-foot stretch between them did nothing to stop the heat racing through her blood. Or the anticipation of more as he moved nearer.

He stared down at her. "You're trembling."

Her chin lifted. "Am not."

He chuckled softly, his gaze holding hers. Stubborn woman.

"So...what does this prove?"

"That you're hiding behind chores to avoid me."

Her gaze narrowed dangerously.

"If you're not, then let's go riding."

"You don't like riding."

His warm gaze swept heavily over her, telling her exactly whom he wanted to ride. "That was in the past."

What was he saying? she wondered, feeling flushed under his steamy look. Was he willing to shed everything they'd had before, for something new now? Just as the warm thought blossomed in her brain, it died. Her deception about Mimi was enough to keep Maxie from getting her hopes up. She couldn't take it if she hurt him again.

Suddenly he tipped his head and kissed her, light and warm. Kyle felt her jolt of surprise, yet kept kissing her, unhurried, coaxing, until she responded to him, pressing her mouth harder and inching closer. Then he drew back enough to look her in the eyes.

He liked that it took her a second to open them.

"Kyle. Please don't start this." The plea in her voice wasn't hard to recognize, and Kyle's brows drew down.

"We never finished, Max. I can't just ignore it. And neither can you."

Yes, she could. But ignoring the pangs of feelings was an hourly struggle, Maxie thought. Her defenses were weak to his smiles and gentleness, but the consequences were too great. Letting him into her heart meant revealing her secrets, and not hurting him was suddenly as important as not hurting her daughter. Frustrated, she rubbed her hands over her face and muttered, "Jeez. Do I have to worry about you, too?"

He scowled. There was a lot more behind that statement than words, Kyle thought. "I'm a big boy, Max. I can handle anything you've got."

She looked at him. He was fooling himself, Maxie

thought. "I'm not alone anymore, Kyle. When I make a choice, it's not just for me."

His scowl deepened, and he caught her shoulders. "I'm not looking for some casual sex while I'm here, Max. So get that right out of your head." His expression softened, and he slid his hands up the sides of her throat, cupping her jaw and sinking his fingers into her hair. He gazed deeply into her eyes. "Mimi is a great kid, but she has nothing to do with us."

Oh, yes, she does, Maxie thought. Maintaining Mimi's happiness was what had kept her levelheaded and emotionally distant from him since he'd arrived. And it was fast becoming the only thread left.

She looked exhausted, Kyle thought, and wondered what was going on behind those pretty green eyes. "When was the last time you thought of yourself?" he asked in a sympathetic tone.

Her gaze sharpened. "As I recall, your first insult was that I was selfish and only considered my own feelings."

"So I was a jerk," he admitted, and her lips curved. "I'm better now." He tipped her head and pressed his lips to hers, gently. She accepted it for about two seconds, then backed out of his touch.

"What are you so afraid of?" he said. He could almost feel her distance herself.

She glanced away, and he noticed the quick gloss in her eyes. Her expression was suddenly so defeated it caught him in the chest.

"Of making mistakes. Of ruining my life and Mimi's—" she looked at him "—and yours."

She's more than a little gun-shy, he thought, trying to see beneath the wall she'd thrown up around herself. "Is that why you close yourself off from everyone?" She was about to deny the charge when he cut in with, "I've been here a few days, Max. You've isolated yourself out here."

"I like privacy."

He sent her a disgusted look. "You're practically a hermit."

"Fine!" She threw her hands up. "I'm a hermit." She grabbed a broom and entered a stall, sweeping. "If that's what it takes to protect my daughter, then I'll keep it that way."

"She's not here."

She stilled, meeting his gaze. "She's always here, Kyle. She's everything to me." *She's part of you,* she thought with a jolt of unchecked longing.

Kyle stepped into the stall, holding her gaze. "Is there room in there for me?"

She groaned. *That* she did not need to hear. "You don't want me, Kyle. You just think you do. That's hormones talking." She swept furiously around her feet.

Then he was suddenly inches from her, advancing, forcing her to let go of the broom as he backed her up against the wall. He braced his hands on the surface on either side of her head, hemming her in.

Maxie flattened her hands on the slats to keep from reaching out to him.

"That's the second time in our history that you've assumed you know what *I* want, Max," he growled, a hint of anger coloring his tone as he shifted his body closer to hers. "And you're not taking the choice away from me this time."

That sounded too much like a challenge, and she tilted her head back, meeting his gaze head-on. "I'm not giving you one."

"I don't need your permission." He shifted his knee between her thighs, and Maxie's heart shot to her throat.

"You can't have me."

His arms stretched above her, he gave her a long appraising look. "Having your body was never a problem, baby. But years ago, I was young and foolishly thought your heart went with it." He ground a sudden kiss to the bend of her throat, then whispered close to her ear, "I'm wiser now."

She closed her eyes, her senses clawing for more. "But

I'm not," she murmured, gasping for breath after breath as he kissed her throat, nipped her lobe. "I'm not."

"Risk it," he growled, covering her mouth with his, his kiss strong yet unhurried, dark with promise yet restrained. The pull was unlike any other. He didn't touch her, didn't sweep her into his arms, but simply kissed and kissed her, his body a layer of heat away from hers.

Maxie was losing ground fast. The quiet determination in him scared her, the patient way he kissed her tearing through her resistance like a blade through paper. And still he didn't touch her. She could duck and run, go hide in the house till she regained control, but his mouth was rolling heavily over hers—knocking the fight out of her. Then his tongue came into play. She whimpered, greedy for more, for the feel of him against her, and when he pulled back slightly, her mouth sought to keep contact.

She reached, her hands hovering near his jaw, but not touching. And still, they kissed, only their lips touching. There was a tenuous shield between them, and Kyle waited, his body on fire for hers, his patience stretched thin. But he wanted her to come to him, to touch him and admit that there was more than desire between them.

To risk more than a kiss with him.

A little sound worked in her throat, a pain, a plea.

Then Maxie caught his jaw in her hands, pressing him harder to her mouth.

Kyle lost it. He sandwiched her against the wall, wrapping his arms around her. She moaned with pleasure, clamping his thigh between hers.

The well-stoked blaze flared hotly, and she moaned, digging her fingers into his hair and holding him. His hand slid downward, cupping her bottom, squeezing and pushing her to the hardness growing between them. She arched against it.

Kyle felt the smoke of passion curl through his blood, rushing his breath and his heartbeat. He grasped her hips, rocking her. She licked his lips, and his kiss grew stronger.

And stronger. His hands found their way beneath her shirt, then under her bra. He groaned at the delicious warmth of her skin, his fingertips working her nipples into tight peaks, still kissing her, still rubbing against her. And like all the times before, she gave and gave.

And Maxie wanted more. She felt sexy and adored when Kyle touched her—cherished and needed as a woman, not just a rancher or a mom. It drew her tighter to him, sent her hands to the band of his jeans. She wanted to touch him. And her fingers molded familiarly over the tight ridge fighting against the fabric of his jeans.

"Oh, yes," he groaned darkly, driving his body against her.

Then her jacket was open, her shirt seconds after, and his lips were on her bare breast, drawing her nipple into the heat of his mouth. Maxie dropped her head back, holding him there, guiding him from one breast to the other, and Kyle suckled and licked until she was moaning like a wild creature. Then he captured the sounds with his lips.

Before he peeled open her jeans, his hand slipping inside. Anticipation made her shift for him. His fingers slid along the skin of her stomach. Her flesh quivered. He hooked the edge of her panties and sank deeper inside.

His fingers found her, and she gasped, answering the push.

Kyle moaned against the curve of her throat. "You're so hot and wet for me."

"I always am," she rasped, and he stroked. Her breathing shuddered, her hips rocking harder and Kyle thrust and withdrew.

But he knew Maxie. Knew her body. He felt her excitement, reveled in the rush of her passion along her skin and drew back enough to look at her. Her face darkened, but she didn't look away, her lips parted, her eyes glazed. He loved her panting, her bold stare and her hurried movements over him.

He pushed and withdrew. "Maxie, baby."

"Kyle...I—" He could feel it, the clench of feminine

muscles, the way she kissed him so frantically, grabbed his hips and pulled.

He stared into her eyes. "Don't fight it, baby, let me see it."

"But—"

"I don't have any protection...and you can't wait."

"I know!" she cried, and he chuckled darkly.

Kyle watched her passion unfold, felt it strain through her body and onto his fingers wrapped tightly inside her. "I want this to be me, baby. *Me*," he chanted in her ear, then told her he would, how much pleasure he had feeling her release drench him. Then he told her what else he wanted to do with her. And Maxie dropped over the threshold, clawing him, her body tightly drawn around his. He watched it and got harder.

"Kyle."

"I love it when you say my name like that," he said against the curve of her throat. His thumb swept across the tight bead of her sex, and she flinched, grabbing his hair and kissing him hard, riding the threads of her desire in his arms.

He removed his hand and dragged her to the fresh hay pile with him, wrapping himself around her. "I always enjoyed watching you do that," he said into her mouth.

"Kyle—"

He heard the unease in her tone and tightened his hold. "Shh. Don't." Kyle stared at the wood ceiling, snuggling her close. "Right now, I'm so hard for you I could forget about protection and just take the consequences. So please, baby, not a word." Gallantry was hell, he thought, waiting until she relaxed in his embrace.

Maxie worked her hands inside his jacket, feeling sheltered and warm and relaxed for the first time in years. She didn't want to think of the problems this seduction would cause now, and the cocoon of silence kept sour thoughts at bay just a little longer. Maxie reveled in the simple peace of satisfaction.

The wind whistled through the cracks in the barn, cooling them.

A horse nickered and stomped softly.

Then the distinct sound of a school-bus horn shattered their contentment. Maxie sat up sharply, glanced at her watch and hopped to her feet. Kyle just lay there, his hands propped behind his head, watching her finger-comb bits of straw from her hair, then adjust her clothing. She had to shower and she was thankful now that Kyle had done half her work for her. Since she'd wasted the afternoon. She sent him an impatient look.

"Aren't you getting up?"

"Nah." Kyle saw that her lips were swollen, her hair a mess and she had that freshly ravished look he'd always loved giving her.

"I can't let Mimi see me like this."

His brows knitted.

"Or you like that." She nodded to the very prominent bulge still in his jeans.

"Max—" He sat up, groaning, but there was something other than passion making her tremble like that.

"No, don't argue. She's a sharp little girl, Kyle. And she comes first."

Despite his discomfort, Kyle climbed to his feet, catching her before she fled.

Her gaze locked with his.

"I'm not arguing. Of course I don't want her to know what we did in here, either." He pulled a piece of straw from her hair, then flicked it aside. "I just don't want her mother to forget."

She gazed deeply into his dark eyes. "Oh, Kyle." Her voice fractured with a misery he couldn't understand. "I couldn't seven years ago." She cupped his jaw, her fingers trembling. "I can't now." She brushed her mouth over his, then moved quickly away, snatching up her hat before she left.

Kyle had a sinking feeling that he'd just made everything worse.

Maxie walked easily toward the Range Rover to get the last bag of groceries, using the cold blast of air and brisk steps to shrug off the haze of passion. Her daughter hopped off the bus, bolting into her arms. And Maxie's heart twisted in her chest when the first words out of her mouth were, "Hi, Mom, where's Mr. Hayden?"

Seven

In the shower, Maxie sighed against the cool tile, hot water sliding luxuriously over her body. She closed her eyes and pushed wet hair from her forehead. Bathing did not wash away the afternoon, and she recalled...everything—the heat in his eyes, his hardness pressing against her and how much she'd wanted to feel him inside her. Kyle had more than just sexual power over her. He was fast clamping a vise on her heart. She admitted that she *wanted* to be in his arms, despite what it would do to her control. She was honest with herself that if they'd had protection, the whole situation would have escalated to the inevitable, and the emotional consequences would have been harder to accept. She was thankful now for small favors.

She couldn't finish what they'd started. Her future was already mapped out. If he knew she'd had his child and kept the news from him, any relationship they began now would be destroyed. He was going to jump to conclusions, she thought, letting the hot spray rinse away the last of the soap and shampoo. He was going to think today would change everything. And sadly, it wouldn't.

She didn't know what to expect as she stepped from the shower, but hearing Mimi's and Kyle's laughter was not it. For an instant, she let the pleasurable sound seep through her. Towel-drying her hair, she quickly dressed in fresh clothes, then left her bedroom, heading toward the music and voices. She found Kyle in the kitchen, wearing an apron and standing alongside Mimi, trying to do the tush-push.

Mimi was a pro. Kyle was hopeless.

Just the same, her heart did a fierce jump in her chest as she watched them sidestep, wiggle hips, sidestep.

"Nah, like this," Mimi said, reaching up to grab his hips and give them motion.

"Face it, short stack. I don't have any rhythm."

"Duh," she said, rolling her eyes.

Kyle sent her a crestfallen look. She giggled. And a smile burst across his face. He pinched her nose, and she laughed harder.

"Okay, okay. I think I've got it this time," Kyle said when the chorus started again. In synch they danced, Kyle still with the sauté fork in one hand and her best apron flapping at his knees. And Mimi whacking her hair out of her face to watch his feet with an intensity that scrunched her face up so adorably, Maxie's smile widened.

When the song ended, Mimi clapped for him and Kyle curtsied, thanking her with a dainty kiss on her hand. Her daughter giggled and blushed, then Kyle ordered her back to work. Maxie backed out of the kitchen without being noticed, leaning against the outside wall. She sighed, pushing damp curls off her face. Her heart ached so bad it hurt to swallow.

How could she keep them apart? she thought. Was she doing the right thing by keeping Kyle's identity a secret from Mimi? Then in the next breath she knew she was caught in her own trap. What will happen to Mimi when he leaves?

It's you you're worried about. Mimi could spring back

from most anything, and Max knew it. It was Maxie who wasn't ready for more heartache than she'd already had.

She lingered out of sight, listening to them chat, Mimi telling him about her pet turtles, Kyle cooking something heavenly while Maxie gathered her courage to face him. When she entered the kitchen, he looked up and a smile lit his features. Her heartbeat tripped. Oh, to see that smile every day, she thought. It was so much like his daughter's.

"Where ya been? Trying to cut out on K.P. duty?"

"That means kitchen police, Mom. But not like cops or detectives," Mimi said while setting the table. "*Policing* means cleaning up."

Maxie bit the inside of her mouth as Mimi carefully laid out the utensils. "Oh, does it?"

"Yup. Mr. Hayden said he got K.P. duty a couple times when he was a marine. For being late for work."

Because he spent time with me, Maxie thought, her gaze flashing to Kyle's. He sent her a long hungry look that brought this afternoon to the surface with amazing clarity. She felt her skin warm, and her lips curved without thought. He sucked air in through clenched teeth and started toward her. Immediately she stepped back, shaking her head. He stilled, his expression wilting. Maxie glanced meaningfully at Mimi.

His lips tightened, and he turned back to the counter.

Maxie felt rotten, but pushed it aside. She couldn't let Mimi know there was more than just a boarder in her house. If she got a clue, she would seize it and hold it out for inspection with questions. Questions Maxie wasn't prepared to answer. Not that she would know how.

"What's cooking?" she said brightly.

"Lemon chicken, fettucine Alfredo and steamed broccoli."

"Broccoli, yuck," Mimi said sourly, pouring drinks.

"With cheese sauce, short stack."

She glanced at Kyle. "No, thank you, Mr. Hayden," Mimi muttered, trying not to be rude, and the adults exchanged a silent message to get her to at least try it. Kyle ladled food into serving platters, and Maxie took one. Over a steaming pot, he met her gaze, his expression so tender her emotions sank to a dangerous level.

"You okay?" he said softly.

"Shouldn't I be?"

He shrugged, holding up streamers of fettucine, then swirling them onto a platter. "The way you rushed off out there, I was wondering if you'd forgotten about me."

That wounded-little-boy look wasn't cutting it with her, and she jerked the platter from his hands. "Like hell you were wondering." She carried it to the table. He chuckled lowly, and Maxie knew she was in for a tough night.

Mimi was already in a chair and doing what she did best—talking.

Bless her heart, she kept the conversation going through dinner, and Kyle even convinced her to try the broccoli and cheese sauce. She was on her third helping when the phone rang.

Kyle's gaze followed Maxie as she answered it. "The rescue station," she mouthed, then went to the window, peering into the dark. A light snow was falling.

"You sure it can't wait till morning? No, I understand, Jackson. Give me about an hour." She hung up. "I've got to bring in a couple of fresh mounts," she said to Kyle, then looked at Mimi. "Let's get going, princess."

"Max," Kyle ventured as he brought dishes to the counter. He met her gaze. "Let me help take the horses in."

"It's no big deal, Kyle. We've done it before." Maxie winked at Mimi.

"Yeah, I help," Mimi piped up.

"But it's late and dark and snowing." Maxie's look said she was aware of that. "Okay," he conceded. "I tell you what. You get the horses ready while Mimi and I finish up here. Then I'll give you a hand hitching the trailer. That okay with you, short stack?"

Mimi shrugged, oblivious to the tension between the adults. "Sure."

Maxie's lips pulled into a tight line. She walked straight up to Kyle. "I know what you're doing."

"Do you?"

"Ganging up." Her gaze swept briefly to Mimi. Including her in the decision gave him a shot at tagging along.

He'd been found out, Kyle thought, and the corner of his mouth quirked. Just as well. He was enjoying the family atmosphere way too much, anyway. "Okay, fine. I could stay here, see that she does whatever little girls do before bed." He looked apprehensive just then.

"The same thing as boys, except they wash behind their ears." Yet Maxie considered one fact: Mimi might like him, but she wasn't ready to have him as a sitter.

"Come on, Mom, we'll get done faster and I'll get to bed on time." Kyle and Maxie looked down at Mimi, her sweet face tilted up, but Maxie recognized the devious glint in her daughter's eyes. She was hoping she would get to stay up late.

"All right. But you'd better be finished with K.P. duty by the time I get the mounts. And wear your gloves, Meem."

Kyle turned his attention to rinsing and loading the dishes with record speed. Mimi was bundled up and out the door a good ten minutes before him. When he left the house to help Maxie hook up the trailer, Mimi was standing by, holding the horses' leads, her tiny cowboy hat tilted against the wind. Maxie lowered the gate, and Mimi led the horses into the mobile stall. Kyle watched the little girl secure the leads and run bracing straps under the mounts without a shred of fear.

"Careful, short stack."

"I'm fine, Mr. Hayden, honest."

Maxie glanced at Kyle and had to smile at the concern on his face. "She's my partner, Kyle. Ease up." Maxie closed the gate as Kyle and Mimi climbed into the already warmed-up Range Rover.

Two hours later, after Jackson filled Mimi with far too many treats and Kyle and Max with hot coffee, they were headed back.

"So much for getting her to bed on time," Kyle said, and Maxie spared him a glance. Her breath caught. Mimi was snuggled trustingly against his side, sound asleep.

"I knew she wouldn't last," she managed to say casually.

Kyle toyed with a bright red curl. "But you weren't ready to leave her alone with me."

"No, Kyle," she said. "*She* wasn't ready."

His features tightened. "You think she's afraid of me?" He didn't like that, not at all.

"Hardly." In fact she'd never known Mimi to be so trusting of any man who'd been at the ranch. "But getting ready for bed is sometimes a drama for a little girl. They like their privacy and are shy about anyone coming within fifty yards while they bathe." Maxie laughed shortly, shaking her head. "Sometimes...even their moms."

She looked out of sorts just then, and where Kyle had thought she knew everything about kids, he realized she didn't. It was comforting to know since he was just getting the hang of being a *real* adult. But then, Max had always wanted children, a house full, she'd told him once. Kyle's gaze slid over her as she drove. Still beautiful, he thought, even without makeup and chic clothes. And she turned him on like no other woman ever had. He just wished she would quit hiding behind parenthood.

When Maxie pulled up in front of the house and shut off the engine, Kyle reached for her, cupping the back of her head and bringing her mouth to his. She resisted for about two seconds, then sank into his kiss with a hungry moan. Kyle had felt her pulling away from him since dinner. He hated that she could do it so easily when he was nothing but confusion and mush inside. And he got to her the only way he knew how just then and kept kissing her, nipping at her lips and drinking her soft shudder.

"I can't stop thinking about this afternoon," he whispered in her ear. "I get hard just remembering how you—"

"Kyle, shh," she said, yet accepted another deep kiss, although she'd spent the past hours convincing herself she didn't want this.

Between them, Mimi stirred and they jerked apart. Maxie's damning look was enough to cool his passion for her, and sighing, Kyle carried Mimi inside, laying her on her bed. She woke immediately, sitting up and folding her arms over her flat chest. Her gaze shot between the adults, ending with a damning look on Kyle.

"You kissed my mom."

Kyle blinked, then glanced briefly at Maxie. "Yes, I did."

Mimi looked at her mother. "Did you like it?"

Maxie sputtered.

"You sounded like you did."

Maxie reddened. "You shouldn't have been eavesdropping, young lady." She stood. "It's way past your bedtime."

Kyle took his cue and headed for the door, but Mimi's words stopped him. "Do you like my mom, Mr. Hayden?"

Kyle's gaze clashed with Maxie's. "Yes, I do." *I always have,* he thought as he left, stepping into his room. He dropped onto the bed, folding his arms beneath his head, and stared at the ceiling. In those moments in Mimi's room, Kyle realized how much a simple kiss could affect Mimi. He liked Maxie's daughter. She was lively and sweet tempered, and Kyle felt an odd companionship with the little redhead. But Maxie was right. Choices included more than just them. And he debated whether or not he was prepared for what that entailed and if he could handle it. He sat up, swinging his legs over the side of the bed and rubbing the back of his neck.

In her bedroom, Mimi sleepily slipped out of her clothes and into her nightie. Mother and daughter chatted about school, decided what she'd wear tomorrow and how nice it was that Kyle cooked tonight.

AMY J. FETZER

113

"Do you think Mr. Hayden likes me?"

Maxie met her gaze and tugged on her ruffles. "Hey, what's not to like, princess?" Mimi shrugged her narrow shoulders. "I'm sure he does. *I* could never get him to dance."

Mimi smiled, and Maxie crawled into bed with her daughter, sitting behind her and braiding her hair.

"You know he's going to be gone in a week or so, honey." How was she going to deal with this?

Mimi yawned hugely. "Yeah. I know."

Maxie scooted off the bed and tucked Mimi under the covers. She was half-asleep.

"Is he a good kisser, Mom?" she said softly.

"That's none of your business, madame."

Mimi opened one kelly green eye and let it rake over her mother. "He is—I can tell."

Maxie had the irresistible urge to straighten her clothes. "Kissed many boys, have you?"

"Yuck," she said with feeling and a sour face. "But you haven't kissed a man in a *loonngg* time."

Maxie didn't need to be reminded of that. Especially by a six-year-old. "Go to sleep, child. Before I ground you for playing possum in the truck."

Mimi squeezed her eyes tightly shut, and Maxie turned off the lights, backing out of the room, closing the door. She turned and stopped short.

Kyle was leaning against the frame of his bedroom door, his gaze moving over her with positive intent. He'd discovered a few things about himself in the past few moments. The least of which was that he felt like an outsider and he didn't want to, that he liked being with them both. Yet as much as he wanted to remain unbiased, he wanted to know—no, needed to know—whom she'd betrayed him with, enough to get Mimi and still be single after all these years. That she'd been married was still a bit of a shock, especially since she couldn't manage the feat with him. But why didn't she have her ex's name? Hell. Why didn't Mimi have her father's last name, at least? And neither female mentioned Mimi's dad, so what was the big mystery? He'd rehashed the question so much in the past few minutes, his brain was smoking.

But one thing he needed to prove to both of them right now was that old passion and new were one and the same. Seven years or seven hours and a lot of soul searching wouldn't change it.

Before she could react, he crossed the hall, slipping his arm around her waist with gentle purpose. She didn't back away and the instant she tipped her face up, he covered her mouth with his. His kiss was brief and hard, a liquid slide of lips and tongue, utterly savage.

"Good night, Max." He liked that her breathing quickened and her eyes were still closed. He stepped back and slipped into his room, closing the door.

Maxie sighed against the wall, brushing her hair off her face. *Okay,* she thought. *What were you expecting? For him to lift you in his arms and carry you off to his bed?*

As Maxie moved through the house, switching off lights and locking doors, she realized that was exactly what she was hoping. And she was hoping that in the morning everything would be fine, no heartache, no deceptions or recrimination—no secrets that threatened their feeling for each other. Damn, she thought as she walked past his bedroom and into hers. She couldn't get the flicker of hope out of her mind. *Don't want,* she told herself. *It will never work.* She'd screwed up—everything—again. And they still had another week to go. Her past, she thought, had definitely come back to haunt her.

Two days later, Maxie held on to the leads of the horse she'd been training, staring across the paddock to the pair just beyond the fence. "A ride in your chopper? I don't know," Maxie said uneasily, eyeing her daughter and the man beside her. Since Mimi met Kyle, she'd been waiting for this moment.

"C'mon, Mom," Mimi said, climbing onto the lower rail, then swinging her leg over to straddle it.

"No daredevil tricks, I swear." Kyle crossed his heart convincingly, aware this was one past flaw she was having trouble getting over. But he was suffering from having his own chaotic thoughts for company and terminal boredom. And since Maxie stopped him from his latest try at ranch work—something he would discuss with her later—he thought he could help out by keeping an eye on Mimi. "A short ride, fifteen minutes' air time tops. Nowhere near the canyon."

"Oh, rats," Mimi said, huffing. "I wanted to see the river from the air."

Kyle leaned toward her and whispered out of the side of his mouth. "Cool it, short stack. Let's not push our luck." Mimi grinned and winked.

Kyle climbed up onto the rail beside Mimi, and they looked at Maxie with innocent expressions. She wasn't fooled. That they were becoming fast friends unnerved her, yet seeing them together, or rather Kyle willingly in her daughter's company again, created a wealth of hope Maxie didn't have a right to feel. She couldn't keep them apart without Kyle becoming suspicious. Although Mimi seemed to accept that Kyle wasn't sticking around, Maxie wasn't satisfied.

But Mimi appeared as if her world depended on this one ride. And if truth be told, she'd been more underfoot than help since she came home from school.

"So what'll it be, Max?"

"Yeah, what'll it be, Mom?" Mimi piped up, her hands on her thighs like Kyle, her head cocked to one side like Kyle's.

Seeing the resemblance drove a hard punch to Maxie's chest and she swallowed. Individually they were hard to resist; together, she was sunk. "All right. One ride, a short one."

Mimi squealed, bouncing up and down on the rail.

Kyle grinned, hopping off the fence and crossing the distance to Maxie. He held her gaze and could tell she was scared. "I won't let anything happen to her, Max," he said softly. "Trust me."

Maxie searched his features, the sincerity in his dark eyes, then glanced past him to her daughter before bringing her gaze back to his. "I already am, Kyle." Her vision blurred a little. "She's all I have."

His eyes softened, and he helped the wind brush her hair off her cheek, his fingers lightly stroking her cool jaw. Immediately he recognized the shuttered look in her eyes, her stiff posture. She'd been giving it to him since that afternoon in the barn. "You're wrong, Max." Before she could respond to that, he spun on his heels toward Mimi. "Let's get in the air, short stack." He vaulted the fence, then helped Mimi down. "We're losing good flying time."

"Yeah, good flying time," Mimi mimicked, and they raced across the field toward the chopper.

Maxie watched them until they lifted off, heading away from the canyon, as promised. It was really hard to see them together, she thought, and though Mimi didn't miss what she never had, Maxie recognized their growing attachment. It didn't surprise her. Father and daughter were more alike than she cared to admit. Maxie dreaded Kyle's inevitable departure.

For who, a voice asked. *You or Mimi?*

Maxie dismissed the notion. She would be fine. Although every hour was a struggle to be near him, she couldn't give in. It had to be this way, she silently insisted. It had to. She would just hurt him again, and Mimi would get caught in the middle. She glanced at the clock, then went back to work, determined to be finished before they landed.

Inside the chopper, Kyle belted Mimi in, gave her his ball cap and adjusted the headset around her thick braids.

"Ready?" he said into the mike.

She gave him a thumbs-up. "You bet!" Her wide eyes scanned the dials and switches before she looked at him.

That smile was going to split her face in half, Kyle thought, turning over the engine. The blade rotated faster, and she crooked her head to watch, then looked downward as they lifted off.

"Cool!"

She wasn't the least bit afraid, and he admired that, but then, kids didn't know what real fear was at that age. Hell, he didn't until he'd felt his first enemy bullet whiz past his ear, miss him and kill the man beside him. Still, Kyle didn't know what to think of Mimi. Yet every time she spoke, every time she grabbed his hand and dragged him along to show him her doll collection or her turtles, Christine and Louise, his heart smiled. He was fascinated by her, the adult way she talked, her uncanny logic and blunt speech. Yet when he looked at this little girl, in the recesses of his mind, he wanted her to be his—even thought about it a half dozen times but Maxie had used birth control and all his mind could muster was seeing her and the faceless man she'd given herself to after abandoning him.

He shook off the thought and let the chopper gain altitude. Mimi shrieked happily.

"You okay, short stack? Too high?"

"Nah. Go higher!" He did, smiling at her bubbling description of the ground below. "How does it work, Mr. Hayden?"

Kyle glanced at his gauges, checking altitude and airspeed before looking at her. "How does what work?"

She rolled her eyes. "The helicopter, silly. How does it get off the ground, straight up?"

Inwardly Kyle groaned and spent the next twenty minutes fielding questions on aerodynamics so a child could understand.

Twenty minutes later, Maxie was standing in the field when the chopper landed, and she could see Kyle hurrying to unstrap Mimi before she busted out of the chopper. The door opened, and her daughter raced toward her, launching into her arms.

Her excitement was contagious. "That was so cool! You shoulda come along, Mom. Everything looks like toys! People waved to us, and Mr. Hayden rocked the chopper. That's saying hello in chopper talk."

Maxie's lips twitched. "Chopper talk, huh?" Maxie set her down.

"Yeah. And guess what?"

"What?" She tried to sound excited when Kyle was standing a few feet away, his gaze boring into her.

"Mr. Hayden let me fly the chopper! Wait'll I tell Dana!"

Maxie's gaze flew to Kyle's. "You did what!"

"Now, hold on, Max—"

"When can I do it again, Mom? When?"

Maxie looked down at Mimi and didn't want to crush the happiness in her eyes. "We'll talk about it later, okay?" Mimi's lips curled down, and Maxie smoothed her bangs back, touching her under her chin. "Why don't you go call Dana and tell her all about it?"

Mimi nodded and looked back at Kyle. "Thanks, Mr. Hayden."

He winked at her. "You're welcome, short stack. You make a great copilot."

She beamed, then took off toward the house in a dead run.

And Kyle knew he was a dead man. He could tell by the look on Maxie's face.

"You let her fly?"

He stopped inches from her, his hands on his hips, his expression sour. "Give me some credit, Max. I had control all the time. I'm not a complete fool, you know." Though why he didn't just grab this woman and kiss the anger right out of him was beyond him. "I let her put her hands on the stick for a couple minutes, that's all."

Her skin colored. "Oh."

"You really think I'd do something that stupid?"

"Well, no—"

"But you're not convinced."

Her chin lifted, her gaze clashing with his. "I know you. You love danger."

Resentment rose to the surface. "No," he snapped. "You don't know me, Max. Seven years changed you, and it changed me, too. Eighteen months overseas showed me more danger and death than I needed for a lifetime." And the past few days showed him all he'd really lost.

Her features tightened. Maxie couldn't imagine what he'd been through in the desert, but from the look in his eyes, it had scared him. "I'm sorry. I don't know what got into me. I know you'd never do anything to hurt her."

He touched his finger along her jaw, and for an instant, her eyes flared. "Or you, Max."

But you did hurt me, she thought, stepping back. *You stopped loving me when all I wanted was to slow down.* Instantly she called herself a whining pansy for even thinking that and stiffened her posture. He had to see she wasn't good for him. "Don't make promises you can't keep, Kyle. And what about you? Aren't you afraid of getting hurt? I did it to you once." She shrugged. "Hey, I could do it again."

"Yeah." He rocked back on his heels. "I suppose you could." With this coldhearted Maxie, it was almost expected, Kyle thought.

His blasé attitude annoyed her. "And that fact doesn't bother you? Warn you off?"

He took a step closer. "This isn't a war to see who can hurt the other first, you know." His brows knitted. "I know you're thinking of Mimi all the time, and now so am I, but come on, Max, when are you going to step out from behind her and let your feelings go?"

She wasn't going to deny the truth of his words. "I can't."

"Why?" he asked, his gaze searching hers.

Her shoulders drooped. "Because it's pointless."

His anger flared. "Well, thanks a heap, Max. I can see I still mean nothing to you, except for maybe a little distraction in the back of a barn."

She slapped him, hard.

His gaze darkened.

"How could you believe that?" Her voice broke.

He threw his hands up. "For crying out loud, I can't believe anything else around you. One minute you're so wild in my arms it's as if time stood still, and the next, it's like talking to a wall."

Maxie shored up the crack in her emotions. "Then don't try anymore. Okay?" She headed toward the barn. Kyle met her stride, and she could feel his gaze raking over her. She wasn't going to get into this with him. She couldn't, not after seeing him with Mimi. All afternoon she'd been remembering how much of his daughter's life he'd missed—her birth, her first steps, first words. Maxie never once questioned her decision not to go hunt him down and tell him about their child. In refusing her letters, her calls, he'd told her that she wasn't worth the effort anymore, that his love had quickly died, and she saw no reason to reopen a wound then. Loving her daughter had gotten Maxie through the worst pain of her life. Yet seeing them together made her question her choices. Why was she dredging this up now, she thought, reaching for a bridle. It was too far gone to revive.

From close behind her, she heard his soft whisper. "Mimi is six, I asked her."

Maxie bowed her head, refusing to face him. "Damn you for questioning her!"

"You know what that means to me?" Maxie's heart jerked up to her throat. "For a split second I thought she was mine. But she couldn't be. We'd been making love for over a year, and you were on the Pill then," Kyle said. She heard him inhale a shaky breath. "The hard truth is that while I was knee-deep in sand and dodging bullets, you were giving to a stranger what you promised to only me." His voice wavered and his hoarse whisper revealed every fraction of his pain. "And for the rest of my life, Max, I'll wish it wasn't true."

He brushed past her, out of the barn, and Maxie stared, brushing the tears from her cheeks. *Oh, Kyle. What have I done?*

Eight

Kyle had taken about twenty steps when he stopped, turning and covering the distance to where she stood on the threshold of the barn's open double doors.

Maxie back-stepped, and Kyle drew on sheer will to ignore her tears, her stricken look, and ask, "You married this Davis guy because you were pregnant." It was more of a statement than a question.

Lord, how it stung that he thought she'd turned into a bed-hopping tramp after leaving him. Maxie wanted to wound him back. "My daughter was two when I married Carl."

His eyes rounded. Davis wasn't Mimi's father! Good God, she'd been unmarried until four years ago. Kyle yanked her inside the privacy of the barn. "Why did you let me believe otherwise?"

"Gee, Kyle," came acidly. "I don't know—maybe because you were so receptive to the idea that I even *had* a child!"

Kyle flushed, ashamed. He'd kept her from telling him the truth with his attitude.

"You were on the Pill," he said.

"I forgot to take one! It happens."

"Why'd the marriage end?" he said softly.

Still steaming, Maxie folded her arms over her middle and glared at him. The chill radiating from her was worse than the one outside. "He cheated on me three weeks after the wedding. I kicked him out. Satisfied?"

His brows tightened. "You think I *like* that you got hurt?"

"Would be justice, wouldn't it? I hurt you, then I get hurt." She shrugged, bitterness in her tone. "Actually I wasn't that upset for myself, but for Mimi."

Kyle hated to think of sweet Mimi being hurt like that and he wanted to smash something. "Did you love him?"

"No."

His scowl deepened. "You say that so easily." And coldly, he thought.

"It's the truth. He was nonthreatening. I don't even know *why* I married him." Her gaze thinned on him. "Maybe because I thought it was my last chance at what I wanted. Or he was the first man to accept my daughter without a ton of questions and accusations." Her shoulders moved restlessly, and her voice softened. "I still don't know what he had in mind, keeping me and a mistress, but I think I married more for comfort than emotion."

"You couldn't marry me for love and passion, but this jerk," he exploded, "you married for simple companionship!"

"Don't you dare yell at me, Kyle Hayden," she snapped. "And why do you want to know all this—why are you prying into my past?"

His voice was a dark growl. "Because I still have feelings for you, Max, and I feel betrayed every time I look at you and your daughter together."

Her eyes narrowed. She knew there was nothing left for them if he couldn't accept her past. "Too bad. Get over it."

His expression fell. "God knows I'm trying, but damn, Max." He moved away and paced, rubbing the back of his neck. "It still tears at me to know you got over me so quickly—" he paused and faced her down "—when it took months for me to even think of you without feeling pain."

She went incredibly still. How could he believe that? How could he stare her in the eye and not see that she *never* got over him? It hurt deeply that he thought her so shallow. But he needed to see her life from her perspective, without revealing her secrets.

"How I got over you isn't the problem, Kyle. It's whose genes Mimi has that upsets you," she said up in his face. "Don't sweat it. She's mine. Her father doesn't know Mimi exists. I tried to tell him, but he wasn't interested in anything to do with me. *Ever again.* He chose to cut me out. And he cut his child out of his life, too." Her voice wavered, the agony of needing him then, of loving him so much and knowing he'd never come back, rushed through her with a force that threatened her breathing, yet bravely she held his gaze. "So I had my baby alone, and we made it work together. We were better off without him, anyway."

"Are you, Max?" Her gaze narrowed. "Are you better off?" She looked away, and he caught her chin, forcing her to meet his gaze. "Have you closed yourself off to everyone, or is it just me?" She stared blandly back, her lips pressed tight, and Kyle felt helpless. So what held her back? What kept her from just telling him what she was even feeling? For one horrible second, he thought that it was him she was talking about. An instant later he dismissed it. She wouldn't lie about a thing like that. "Living like a recluse isn't protecting your little girl, Max—it's protecting you. And this closed-hearted attitude is going to affect her."

She jerked from his grasp. "Don't tell me what's good for my daughter, Kyle." Her eyes flashed with outrage. "You have no idea what it's like to be a parent. Let alone a single one."

His lips thinned, and he felt again like the orphaned kid

from the wrong side of the tracks—not good enough to love. "You mean I have no reference to pull from, huh? That's what you're saying."

She poked at his chest. "Don't put words in my mouth. You don't want to hear what I really have to say to you."

He stared down at her, his hands on his hips. "Take your best shot, baby."

She couldn't. It would be like unleashing a dam of emotion she wasn't ready—didn't think she would ever be ready—to face. She tipped her chin up. "It would just be wasted ammunition."

Kyle made a frustrated sound and wanted to shake her. She was so closemouthed about her feelings, had them buried so deep it would take a shovel to dig her out. He knew how to get emotion from her, emotion the old Maxie gave freely, but Kyle didn't believe for a second that wild jungle sex was going to solve any of this. Yet like a sadist he asked the one question that had been ripping through his brain since he discovered she was a mother.

"Just tell me one thing, Max." Her gaze swung up to meet his. "This guy who gave you Mimi, did you love him?"

Maxie stared into his dark eyes. The feelings she had for him, the ones forced into hiding in a private lonely part of herself for the past seven years, suddenly swelled to the surface.

Kyle clenched his fists, waiting.

Her vision blurred. And the truth came easily from her lips. "Yes. Desperately."

Kyle stared at the book and didn't see the words. He kept picturing the look in Maxie's eyes two days ago when she'd told him she'd loved another man. *Desperately,* she'd said and he knew the truth. It felt like a poison moving through his veins. He didn't think anything could hurt more than hearing her say it.

It was enough to bring him to his knees.

That she'd blithely broken his heart and turned her attention to another, let him love her beautiful body only weeks after, left him raw inside. A knot swelled in his throat as he looked across the living room where she was setting up a game board with Mimi. He tried to imagine the Maxie he once knew, the Maxie he'd adored and how she could coldly turn her back on all they'd meant to each other. He couldn't. There was more to this. And it was the single reason he hadn't taken up residence on Jackson's office couch. Kyle knew if he walked out the door, he would never see Max again. Leaving would be the simplest route. Hell, he thought, rubbing his aching thigh. Nothing with Max was simple.

He watched them, their red heads bowed together, talking softly, and he wished he were a part of the conversation. In the past days he'd been a part of their lives, the family, and he didn't like being the outsider just now. He wanted in. He wasn't ready to give up. But he wasn't sure if he was ready to fight for the right, either. Did he even have one? When his time was up with the rescue team, would Maxie just say goodbye and dismiss him from her mind? Kyle had come here to do a job, and when he'd found Max here, he swore to himself that he wasn't going to repeat the past. And here he was, looking at what she'd offered him in the past and wanting it.

A frown knitted his brows, and he stared at the carpet beyond his outstretched leg. He was jumping between berating himself for his choices, Maxie for hers and cursing life in general when feminine voices brought his gaze up.

His lips curved as Mimi leaped on her mom, pushing Max into the sofa cushions and tickling her wildly. Maxie shrieked, tickling back, and Mimi's laughter staked a claim on his heart.

Maxie staked one on his soul.

What he wouldn't have given for his mom to have shown him attention like that when he was a kid. Even just a little. But she never did, walking straight out of his and Mitch's life forever. And his father right behind her. How different would his life have been if he'd been part of a real family, he thought. Any family. Maxie had everything she'd ever wanted or needed from her parents: love, clothes, food, security. But he and his brother…they'd had to work just to survive. Kyle wasn't holding that against her and knew she was more likely drawn to him because of his recklessness back then, but Kyle realized he'd wanted to feel that love himself, give it back and know when it got tough, there would be someone to back him up, no matter what he did.

He still wanted it. His sour feelings weren't about what she had, but what he was afraid he might never find. Or didn't know how to keep.

Hell. What did he know about family? Without constant guidance in the foster homes and orphanages, he and Mitch were trouble waiting to happen, and the less restrictions, the more they were willing to risk for a rush of excitement. It was to get attention; he understood that now, but after he'd joined the marines, the wild behavior had magnified, skating along the edge of danger. And he foolishly dragged Maxie into it. Yet it had been like running with a wolf pack—free, untamed fun.

And lonely, a voice reminded, and Kyle closed the book, his gaze on his fingers as he shaped the spine. Half the reason he'd joined the marines was so he wouldn't be alone anymore. And he'd known that in marrying Max, he would never have had to feel that ache again. Or was he trying to grasp something tangible and lasting in an otherwise dismal existence before the war?

Hell, that was then and this was now, he thought, rubbing his thigh, his fingers digging into the still-tender scar tissue.

"Your leg hurt, Mr. Hayden?"

His gaze jerked up, and he couldn't help but smile at her gap-tooth grin.

"Yeah, bothers me sometimes when it gets really cold."

She tilted her head. "How come?"

Boy, she's cute, he thought. "I jumped out of a helicopter with a giant rubber band tied to my ankles. And when it sprang up, I got tangled and nearly lost my leg."

Mimi's eyes had widened as he told her the story and now were as big as coins.

"Bungee jumping?" she squeaked, and he nodded. "That was a *really* stupid thing to do, Mr. Hayden."

Kyle flushed with embarrassment.

Beyond her, Maxie snickered.

With sheer willpower, Kyle kept his gaze on Mimi. "Yeah, I know. But I did a lot of stupid things back then." *Like let your momma go,* his conscience whispered.

"Wanna play with us?"

Kyle's gaze shifted past her to Maxie and the game board. Being across the room from Max was bad enough, inhaling her scent, seeing what he couldn't have would be torturing himself. "I don't think so."

"Please," she said.

"Mimi," Max said, her gaze on the board as she arranged game pieces, "if Mr. Hayden doesn't want to play, then don't bug him."

That sounded too much like a challenge to him. "Afraid you'll lose, Max?"

Her head jerked up. It was the first time he'd spoken to her in two days beyond the essentials of good manners, and across the room, their eyes locked. Maxie thought she would come apart right there. She didn't realize how much she'd missed talking with him, having his attention. It was like being released from the bottom of a cold pool. She could breathe again. She knew she shouldn't have said what she did in the barn the other day. It gave him a distorted and ugly view of her. But she couldn't let him know her feelings, since she wasn't sure herself.

How much deeper a hole could she dig? she wondered. Would she ever escape her feelings for him? Or was she destined to be haunted by her mistakes?

"So...you're admitting you're chicken?"

Mimi folded her arms over her flat chest. "My mom isn't afraid. Are you, Mom?"

Maxie blinked, realizing she was staring at him. And he

was staring back. "Put your money where your mouth is, Hayden." She set a tiny metal race car on the board. Mimi hopped up and down, grabbing his hand, pulling him out of the chair and leading him to the coffee table to play.

An hour later, he was getting smoked. By a six-year-old.

Mimi owned most of the avenues, and the last roll of the dice decided the game.

"Well, I'm busted." He handed Mimi the last of his cash, then looked at her mother. "How about you, Max?"

She could barely look him in the eye all evening, he noticed. She would smile and laugh with Mimi, join in the conversation during dinner and the teasing as they hovered over the game board, yet she hardly spoke directly to him. He didn't really blame her, and if he weren't swimming in emotional sewage, he might have apologized for how he'd treated her in the barn the other day.

"Penniless. Totally wiped out," Max said as she gave over her measly one-hundred-dollar assets to Mimi, who grinned and made a show of stacking it neatly.

"Thank you," Mimi said politely. "Can we play one more game? Please?"

"No way," Maxie said as if she were asking for the moon. Two games was her limit. "You've got Nature Girls in the morning, so git, princess." She cocked her head toward the hallway. "Six o'clock will come mighty early."

Mimi rolled her eyes, since her mother said that every night. "Oh, all right," she groused, and wiggled out from her spot at the coffee table. "Night, Momma." They hugged and kissed, and Mimi started toward the hall, then stopped short, running back and stopping beside him.

Kyle was still as glass.

"Thanks for the second helicopter ride, Mr. Hayden," she said, even though she'd already said so. The two rides were about the most fun she'd had all year.

"You're welcome. You're the best copilot I've ever had."

Mimi grinned proudly, then leaned out and pecked a quick kiss to his cheek.

Kyle blinked, then smiled gently, tugging on her braid. He was a sucker for redheads, he thought, a wrenching warmth curling through his chest. She looked so cute in her flannel pj's, robe and Tasmanian Devil slippers. Downright squeezable. "G'night, short stack. Sleep well." She took off to bed, and Kyle's gaze followed her.

Maxie felt the tightness in her chest pull harder when Mimi kissed him. The look of pure longing in his eyes drove a bolt of guilt through her and made her feel she was wrong in keeping fatherhood from him. Biology had little to do with being a father, she told herself. Any man could be a father, make a child, but there was only one mother. She knew it was sexist, but he hadn't been willing to take her calls years ago and when she had just managed to get her life together, he was worming his way into it as if he had the right. He didn't. He'd given that up years ago.

"Mimi's a great kid—child." He brought his gaze back to hers.

"Thank you." Maxie gripped the coffee cup resting on her lap and could feel the instant change in the atmosphere. "I had help from my parents." In more ways than he could imagine, she thought.

"Yeah, I don't doubt it."

Deep envy tinted his voice, and Maxie's heart cracked a little as she left the sofa, moving to the fireplace to stir the blaze that didn't need stirring. *Leave the room,* a voice said. *Don't open this wound again or it will never heal.*

"You have great parents, Max." Kyle'd known from the first moment he met Lacy and Dan Parrish that they were committed to each other, that they loved, deeply, and loved their children even more. And Mimi knew her mother would die for her. Kyle realized suddenly, that even though he'd known the little redhead only a short time, he would, too.

Kyle watched her, wanting her in his arms, wanting to be inside her life instead of on the edge. He just didn't know how to go about smashing that wall she'd built. Or if he wanted the pain that would come with it. He gazed at her profile as she poked at the fire, then noticed the wet path of tears on her cheeks. The sight tore through him like an unsharpened blade. "Max?"

She looked at him, her eyes burning with emotion he couldn't name. "Please, don't say anything, Kyle." Her voice broke, and the tears she'd been fighting flowed free. "At least until Mimi leaves for her Nature Girls."

She rushed past him and into the hall, but not before she covered her mouth with her hands, smothering a sob as she passed her daughter's room.

Kyle sank deeper into the chair and rubbed the back of his neck.

She looked like a wounded animal just then. It made him realize she was hiding more from him than he imagined, that if she was finished with him, if she was really so ready to have him out of her life—then why wasn't she happy he'd soon be leaving?

The next morning, Mimi stood on the porch, her pack beside her and her little body bundled up to her green eyeballs. She looked like a cowboy elf in Santa's workshop with her red hair, freckled cheeks, boots and hat.

Kyle winked at her, and her red nose grew redder. They were waiting for her bus ride to Nature Girls, a two day outing to look for animal tracks. Kyle didn't think she was old enough to go—guides, group leaders or not. Maxie often went with them, they'd said. But it wasn't her turn on the schedule. And then there was the threat of another snowfall and the rescue teams' need for more fresh mounts. And then, of course, there was the boarder, as Max put it.

Kyle looked at Max, who stood several feet away from him, a regular occurrence since the day in the barn. Yet it was her somber expression, the way she folded her arms over her middle and tipped her hat down, that made him want to shake her. Or hold her.

Mimi Anne Parrish glanced worriedly at her mom.

Kyle looked down at the crimson-haired cherub. She was

craning her neck so hard to look up, he stooped. But not before he chanced another look over Mimi's shoulder at Max as she hitched her hip on the porch rail and stared out onto her land. He met Mimi's gaze.

Her little forehead was furrowed tightly.

"What's up, short stack?"

Mimi felt a strange tickle in her tummy when he called her that. She liked Mr. Hayden. He smiled a lot and didn't yell and gave her helicopter rides even when Momma didn't want him to. And Mom liked him. A lot. Mimi could tell by the way she looked at him. Except right now. Right now was different. And Mimi figured it was 'cause of the argument they'd had in the barn. She'd come back to ask if she could have a snack and even though she hadn't heard the words, she understood the sound of their voices and left before they saw her. What she couldn't understand was how they could kiss one day and be so mad later. Adults were strange, she thought quickly.

No one knew it, but she'd heard Grandma and Mom whisper about him a few times, too, when they thought she was asleep. It was a long time ago, when she was just a kid, and she never knew what it was all about. But even after the whispers, Mom was always sad like she was now. And she always cried. Like she had last night. Mom hardly ever cried, even when a horse stepped on her foot last Halloween and turned it purple, so Mimi knew she wasn't feeling good right now. And she knew Mr. Hayden was the one who made her sad.

"Can you do something for me, Mr. Hayden?"

The seriousness in her voice made him uneasy. "Sure."

"Don't make my mommy cry again."

Kyle blinked, a fierce pain catching him in the chest. Oh, God. She'd heard her mother cry after their fight in the barn. He glanced at Maxie, but Mimi cupped his face in her gloved hands and made him look at her. The brim of her cowboy hat touched his.

"Promise?"

"I'll try not to," he said. This child was far too old for her britches, he thought.

"You gotta promise."

"I do." He would die before breaking his word to her, but Kyle didn't think it was possible.

The bus horn tooted.

Maxie took a step away from the rail and froze, frowning at the pair. "Mimi, the bus."

Mimi let go of Kyle, and he stood.

"Have a good time, short stack."

Mimi tried to wink at him. "You, too, Mr. Hayden."

He smiled to himself as she went to her mother, took her hand and lifted her pack.

Kyle stayed on the porch. The bus was rocking from a good two dozen little girls bouncing in their seats, singing loud enough to make him cringe.

Maxie kissed her daughter, and Mimi was about to step on the bus when she suddenly bolted from her mother's grasp, racing back up the porch. Kyle knelt and she slammed into him, her little arms locking around his neck. "I like you, Mr. Hayden."

Kyle felt his heart shatter and come together in one hard breath. "I like you, too."

She didn't meet his gaze as she tore away and ran to the bus, climbing in and dropping into her seat. She kissed her mom through the glass, and the door closed.

Kyle moved beside Max as the bus drove away.

"Are you sure she'll be all right? I mean it's snowing."

"Sure, she will. They're going to search for deer tracks in the snow, and they need the white stuff to do it."

Kyle continued to watch the retreating bus. "Yeah, I guess. She's just so little."

His concern touched off a warm spark she'd suppressed for days. "It's only overnight, and they stay in cabins." The bus vanished at the turnoff, and she shifted her gaze to his profile. "What did she say to you?"

He arched a brow in her direction, his gaze taking in her

eager expression. "Nothing. Copilot stuff." Let her stew, he thought, then almost relented when she stormed into the house. Kyle stared at her retreating back, then her retreating behind, and followed her into the house.

He had the urge to check for land mines before stepping into the war zone.

It was going to be a long two days.

Nine

Kyle stilled as he passed Mimi's room, then peered inside. He'd never actually been in here, but the fact that Maxie was on her hands and knees, rooting under the bed with her sweet behind up in the air, had a lot to do with his hanging close. He let his gaze briefly scan the frilly room, pink and white, elaborately dressed dolls lining shelves and assorted toys scattered everywhere. Kyle brought his gaze to Maxie as she muttered to herself about her daughter's habits and that she honestly didn't have time for this. Yet just the same, she sat back on her haunches and dressed a naked doll, even hunted down the lost shoes and hat before setting it on the shelf. She loved her daughter so much, he thought, jealous not of Mimi, but that he'd been denied that kind of devotion.

Kyle watched her for a few more minutes and was about to turn away when she plucked a black ball cap from a spot on the shelf. It was his. He'd given it to Mimi on their last flight together. He never expected it to garner so high a position in her collection. Nor did he expect Maxie to fold to the floor on her knees, bending over to sob into her hands.

Kyle swallowed hard, the sound driving through him and shredding his composure. It was such a helpless sound, strained and muffled, and his arms ached to comfort her. Yet he couldn't move.

His features tightened, and a niggling suspicion darted through his brain.

He moved away from the door unnoticed, but the rest of the morning he was haunted by the sound of her cries. And the questions racing through his brain without answers.

"You don't have to do that."

"I know." Kyle slammed the hammer down on the nail. He could feel her eyes on his back as he lifted a plank and fitted it into place under the porch eaves. Tapping it into position, he scooped a few nails from the pail and secured the wood.

He'd fixed the back windows, the two stall doors coming off their hinges, hauled horse manure to the nearest farmer who wanted it and still they weren't talking. Oh, they made conversation, idle, non threatening, "dancing around their feelings" talk. But the heart of the matter hovered just on the edge of explosion. Kyle wasn't sure he wanted it to ignite. Not after seeing her cry this morning. He only knew he couldn't take much more of this artificial calm.

"Lunch is ready. If you're hungry."

He was, for more than food, he thought, straightening and letting his gaze move over her. She was on the threshold, a dishrag in her hand, a little spot of flour on her cheek. He knew it was old-fashioned to consider the homey picture she presented, but the hard tugging in his chest came anyway.

"Thanks," he managed to say, setting the hammer aside. The radio perched on the rail squawked with his call letters. Kyle frowned, reaching for it, responding. Seconds later, he collapsed the antenna and said, "Chow will have to wait. I have to go." He quickly collected the tools, leaving her on

the porch as he stowed them in the shed. She was there when
he returned, standing in the frigid cold. Kyle met her gaze,
then looked down at her outstretched hand. She held out his
log book and Marine Corps ball cap. He took the book.

"That's Mimi's," he said, nodding to the cap.

"No, hers—the one you gave her—is in her room."
Maxie swallowed hard and took a step forward. "This is the
one you gave me."

Kyle's features went taut and he reached out, taking the
ball cap, turning it over in his hands. He'd put it on her head
the day before their wedding. It was new then, yet now
looked as worn as the one he'd given her daughter. How
often had she worn this for it to be so faded and frayed?
And mostly, *why*...if she was adamant about not letting him
into her life? He met her gaze. Her green eyes watered, and
he wondered if it was from emotion or the sting of the wind.

"You kept it?"

"I kept everything, Kyle." Her gaze shifted over his features, a wistful smile ghosting across her lips. "Even the
gum-machine junk."

A dull red crept up from his neck. "That was so juve-
nile."

"I thought it was terribly sweet."

Kyle scoffed, then rubbed the back of his neck, staring at
his boots. He wanted desperately to say something, to
change the way they'd been tiptoeing around each other. But
he had to leave, and he didn't want to start what he couldn't
finish.

"Be careful," she said, and wanted to touch him.

His head jerked up. "Do you care, Max?"

Her expression was infinitely sad. "Never doubt that,
Kyle. Never."

She sounded on the verge of tears, and Kyle stepped
closer, reaching, cupping the curve of her jaw and sinking
his fingers into her hair. Her entire body trembled, and he
realized by the look in her eyes, she was afraid. What had
her so worked up that she couldn't come to him?

"Baby, we have to talk. I can't go on like this."

Maxie bit her lower lip. "Me, either."

"But I gotta go."

"I know." Yet he didn't move.

"Can I kiss you?"

Her lips curved softly, and she laid a hand over his heart. "That's the first time you've ever asked."

Trapped in each other's gaze, Kyle bent, Maxie rose and his mouth brushed over hers, a whisper at first, back and forth. He trembled, his need for her making his throat tight, his knees weak. A tiny sound escaped her, almost a sob. And Kyle pressed his mouth harder to hers. Maxie gripped his jacket, hanging on as he kissed her tenderly, slowly, his tongue moistening her lips. Their breath rushed, and when he drew back, she still held him close, staring into his dark eyes.

A tear spilled and Kyle's expression crumbled. "Don't cry, Max. Please. I'm sorry for what I said the other day. I had no right—"

"Shh," she hushed. "No more, not now."

Later, she was saying. How could he leave now? The radio crackled, and she let go, stepping back and taking the decision away from him. Kyle stared at her for a moment, then looked at the snow-dusted porch.

"You'd better get in the air," she said. "They need you."

He looked up, studying her. "All I want to know is do you need me, Max? 'Cause I know I need you."

He was always so up front, Maxie thought, staring into his dark eyes. She reached out to brush the melting snow from his shoulder, touch his jaw. "Yes, Kyle." Her gaze shifted rapidly over his chiseled features, as if memorizing them. "More than I realized." The next moment felt suspended in wintry air, crisp and sharp with unanswered emotion.

Maxie wanted to change things...her life...maybe his...but she wasn't certain she could risk so much at once.

There is always a price, she thought, then put distance between them. "Go. I'll be waiting."

"I'll hurry." Kyle forced himself to turn away from her and march down the steps. Yet he could feel her watching him and resisted the urge to look over his shoulder. He would never leave on the flight, if he did. Apprehension slithered through him as he climbed into the chopper and turned over the engine. *This isn't going to be good,* he thought, although clearing the air was what he wanted. Kyle just didn't think he was going to come out the winner.

Maxie watched him lift off, swoop past her, then hover and rock the craft before gaining altitude and veering off toward the morning sun.

Chopper talk, Mimi called it, and the muscles in her chest squeezed down on her heart as she remembered Kyle and Mimi, their heads together, their profiles nearly the same. At first it had bothered her that they'd struck a friendship, then it pleased her. Yet she still had tremendous reservations about it. But their closeness was as natural as loving Kyle was to her.

Loving Kyle. It was a hard fact to admit. In the past years she'd buried it, found ways around it, like seeing herself in her daughter instead of Kyle's features. Like refusing to discuss him with her parents, sisters, even herself. His return brought those feelings to life. Not rekindled them, but released them from hiding. She'd never stopped loving him. Never. But her secret held her back.

She turned back into the house, finishing up the last of her morning chores before heading to the barn. She was tired of always being on guard around Kyle, around her family. Even around Mimi. Yet Mimi was the sole reason she hadn't confronted her emotions, until she'd seen them together. Until she saw the cap he'd given her baby.

She didn't know what she was going to say to him, still wasn't sure if she could admit to being such a fool. But neither did she feel completely to blame.

* * *

Kyle lowered the chopper to the pad and cut the engine then once the blades stopped, he gave the signal for the hikers to leave the craft. They thanked him, dripping melting snow in his chopper, and he resisted the urge to shout at them to get the hell out so he could go home.

Home. He stared out the frosting glass at nothing in particular. Ironic that the one place he hadn't felt welcome at was the one place he wanted to be. The hardest part was admitting that seven years ago, Maxie was ready to give him a home and family and he'd let it go. *He had*, not her. Years of feeling mostly angry and sorry for himself were his own damn fault. But the past weeks with Max and Mimi showed Kyle just how much he'd lost. Not just the companionship the togetherness, but that family he'd hungered for as a kid and still did. And regardless of what had passed between him and Max, Kyle had turned his back on his feelings for her. Regret tore through him, and Kyle removed his sun glasses and pinched the bridge of his nose with thumb and forefinger.

Everyone he'd ever loved left him, he thought. Yet Maxie—he could have gone after her, could have hunted her down. Hell, he hadn't even read the letters she'd sent him What he wouldn't give to be able to read them now. His pride was a nasty thing. And he was going to have to swallow some of it today.

Get on with it, then, his conscience prodded. *Crank over the engine and go home.*

Inside his gloves, his palms sweated. What he would find at the ranch was anyone's guess. He accepted that he was scared to see her. As much as he wanted to talk, he didn't want her to greet him at the door with his bags and tell him to take a hike, either. Kyle only had days left with the team—maybe even less. In fact one of the regular pilots was in the offices earlier, still looking pale and drawn, but available. His time was over.

He jolted when something smacked his door, and glared at Jackson. Jackson grinned back and pulled open the hatch

"Man, who are you sore at?"

Myself, he thought, *for not seeing what an idiot I've been lately.*

"Got another run?" Kyle asked.

Jackson frowned softly. "No. All's quiet, so far." He glanced at the gray sky. "Be on alert though. We're trying to discourage as many people as we can from going into the canyon today. But you know tourists."

"Yeah, I do. They keep me in business."

Jackson scoffed. "It's a wonder with the fees you charge, Hayden. You'll be raking in the bucks in a few more days and won't feel the dent this meagerly state-funded contract made to your pocket." Jackson smiled. "Did I say thanks for that yet?"

"So much it's getting pathetic."

"Good, I like being pathetic." He grinned. "Attracts the women." He eyed Kyle. "Speaking of women...how's life at the Wind Dancer?"

"Fine." Tense, he thought. And so fragile.

"What do you think of Mimi?"

Kyle smiled for the first time in hours. It almost hurt. "She's great. Smart as a whip."

"Those eyes will steal your heart, huh?"

Kyle scoffed, thinking of what a marshmallow he was around the little redhead. "Already have."

The crew chief laughed. "How many rides did she talk you into so far?"

"Two or so. She declared that being a chopper pilot was her life's ambition."

"Bet that went over with Maxine real well."

Kyle's lips quirked. "Mimi promised not to tell her until she was at least sixteen."

"Wise move. Don't imagine you got her mother up in this, did you?" Jackson said, with a nod to the chopper.

"She never asked."

"Figures. She's afraid of heights."

Kyle arched a brow. This was news to him.

"Don't tell her I told you," Jackson said, backing away from the craft. "I'll radio if I need you. Phones have a tendency to go out sometimes. Now get this crate off my triage pad, flyboy." He shut the door and ran back to the warmth of the offices as Kyle turned over the engine.

He lifted off, taking a sweep of the canyon to see if he could spot Mimi's group before heading to the Wind Dancer. To fight for his life.

Maxie stood at the edge of the canyon and managed to look down for a brief instant before moving back several yards and sitting on a boulder. It was a feeble attempt to get over her fears and it rarely worked. She did it almost daily and never got used to the rushing vertigo. Bracing her elbows on her knees, she bowed her head. At a distance behind her, her horse pawed the ground for something to nibble. The wind kicked out of the canyon, biting through her jacket. She didn't care. The cold numbed her body.

Over and over in her mind, she played out what she would say to Kyle. Nothing worked to where either of them didn't come out wounded. She knew she couldn't tell him about Mimi. Not yet. It wasn't a decision she came by lightly. And she wasn't looking for a way to ease her guilt. It was just too much to dump on him just yet. She wanted to come clean with him—and herself.

I'm getting too old for this, she thought, and imagined herself in a few years, alone, Mimi gone off with boyfriends or on to college. She didn't want to be this way, more mentally alone. But she'd buried her feelings for so long, she didn't think she had it in her to admit them to another living soul.

She squeezed her eyes shut, oblivious to the cold and wind or the nickering horse, her thoughts in the past. On the moment she sat in the hotel room and waited past her wedding ceremony, the awful crushing sensation working through her blood. Maxie swallowed hard, biting back old tears. Whom was she fooling then? What purpose did it serve to leave him like that? Neither of them had been happy since.

I've ruined more than my life.

Then she remembered his face the first moment she saw him again, the anger and distaste. But the memory was overshadowed by his smile, his kisses, the incredible way he looked at her, the heat they shared in the barn. The tightness in her throat increased, and Maxie huddled on the rock, snow sprinkling her hat and back. She tried to think of how this would affect Mimi. But his words came back to her.

When are you going to step out from behind her and let your feelings go?

With her head bowed and arms huddled against the wind, Maxie didn't hear the noise until it was too late. Her head jerked up and her eyes widened as the helicopter rose out of the canyon right in front of her like a black specter from hell. Her horse bolted as she scrambled off the rock and back-stepped, glaring at the man at the controls. She turned and ran after the horse, but it was too late. The chestnut mare was already a mile away. Slowing to a walk, she headed toward the barn, her breath steaming the air. Anger spread through her with every step, and she ignored the chopper hovering overhead and kicking up fresh powder. Damn it, she was miles from the barn, on foot. Cold feet. She would have to take the main roads instead of the forest. It was good that Mimi was on her field trip, because Maxie knew she wouldn't have made it back in time.

"Want a lift?" came over the loudspeaker, startling her.

She glared up at him. He smiled down through the bubble of glass.

Kyle lowered the chopper to the ground, cut off the engine and before the blades slowed, he left the craft. Maxie glanced over her shoulder and ran. He chased, catching her arm. Immediately she spun around, punching his shoulder, then punching again.

"Don't do that again. You scared the life out of me!"

"You seem pretty alive right now. Ow," he said when she caught him on the chin.

But she wasn't letting up and shoved at his chest with both hands, making him stumble back. "Damn you, Kyle Hayden! You always do stupid things like that! You like scaring me. You liked being scared more than you loved me!"

He took a step forward. "That's not true and you know it."

"Isn't it? You never cared what happened to me, never bothered to see that when you took all those risks, you were risking our future!"

"I wasn't thinking of the future then. I was gung-ho. Young. Stupid."

"And ready to die. God, how I hated that about you sometimes," she hissed, and the frost of her breath hazed the air. "I hated that you were a marine and a war rushed us." She advanced, in his face with each word. "I hated that I wasn't worth it to you to let me know you were alive! And I hated you when you sent back my letters and told your brother to talk to me instead of doing it yourself!" With her last word, she shoved him again.

He caught her against him, and she tried wiggling free. He wouldn't let her go. "What else did you hate, baby?"

She tipped her head and stared into his eyes. Hers were filled with unshed tears. "That I put faith in my love for you and I lost."

His expression crumbled. "You left *me*, Max, not the other way around."

"What do you call turning your back on me? I wanted to slow down, not stop completely. Never that. But you never came back, never called. You couldn't be bothered..." Her voice fractured. Her lip trembled.

Kyle steeled himself against the heart-wrenching sight of it. "Damn it, Max. Don't dump this all on me. You ran, you took the easy way out. You always do."

"*You* said you loved me, and I trusted it!"

"I did love you." *I still do*, he thought, yet wasn't sure she was ready to hear it.

"Not enough to come to me!" She broke free.

"Because I was sure you didn't want me. I didn't want to admit that I had any part in it. It was better to blame you." He threw his arms wide. "Hell, I even told a few guys that I dumped you. My pride was in ruins, Max. I couldn't face what I'd done to bring it on. I was alone before." He shrugged. "I could do it again."

He was quiet for a long moment, looking anywhere but at her. When he finally did, her knees turned to water at the desolation in his eyes.

"But I couldn't understand what made me so incapable of keeping anyone from walking out on me. What was so repulsive about me that no one wanted to love me?"

She moaned in sympathy, and his expression grew more miserable.

"I know it's pathetic and childish. But God, Max, until we met, I didn't belong anywhere...except with you."

Maxie's expression crumbled, and she took a step. "Oh, Kyle—"

"Don't. I don't deserve it. I've had to face a lot in the last few days, and recognizing that my selfishness cost me a future isn't something I could easily admit, so let me get this out."

She nodded, silent, tears falling.

"I ignored what you were feeling, didn't want to listen, because I was terrified that you didn't love me, that I wasn't good enough to be your husband."

She shook her head wildly, brushing at her tears.

"Chasing danger wasn't for the rush of excitement, but for the look on your face when I did it. The way you ran to me and held me so *damn* tight." He clenched his fists in front of him, shaking them. "Like you never wanted to let go. And I needed that, Max. Danger tested us. But ve loving me, even when I was in the hospital an were mad about the bungee jump, eve know you'd keep loving me, no matter what stupid risk I took." He wet his lips and swallowed. "So you see…I tried so hard to hold on, but I couldn't do it right." His shoulders moved. "I didn't know how."

"It's all right," she said.

"No. It's not!" He yanked off his hat and raked his hair back. "I could have taken a chance. I could have dined on my pride and grown some guts to come after you. But the truth is…*I* let you go." His features tightened. "You don't know how much I regret that," he said, closing his eyes briefly. "And I didn't come after you because…I was terrified if I opened that door again—" he looked at her "—you'd just slam it in my face." He shook his head, holding her gaze. "I couldn't take that. Not when I loved you so damn much."

"I would have opened the door."

He groaned, regret sluicing through him. "Aw, baby, I'm sorry. You don't know how much."

"Yes, I do." She took two steps and stopped, glancing to the side, and Kyle recognized the apprehension in her.

"I love you, baby."

Her gaze flew to his.

"I love you and I'm not leaving." He bore down on her, snow crunching beneath his boots. She stepped away. "I want you and Mimi and the family we can be and—" He stopped inches from her.

"And?" she said on a breathless gasp.

"And you close me off because it's easier than facing me and what you're feeling. You hide out here in the damn wilderness—" he waved to the open terrain "—because you think it protects your daughter, but it's you you're smothering. You're scared to love me."

"Yes!" she cried, hugging herself. "Yes. I'm afraid I'll hurt you again. You have no idea what it cost me to go on, Kyle. You don't know what I've done—"

"And I don't want to," he cut in, a hand up. "No." He

shook his head when she tried to speak. "One step at a time."

Numbly she nodded, willing to push her secrets aside for the moment.

"But what about you, Max? Aren't you afraid I'll turn my back again?"

"No," came small and weary as she stared at his chest. *Not yet.*

"Why?"

She toyed with her jacket snap. "Because I've been a royal pain in the butt and you're still here."

"Look at me, Max." She did, and he let his gaze roam her wind-chapped features, the tears dried on her cheeks, the fresh ones still filling her eyes. Lord, how he loved this woman, he thought, his Adam's apple bobbing in his throat like cut glass. "Then take a little risk." He yanked off his glove and held out his hand. "Come to me, baby. Give me another chance to love you right."

Maxie stared at his bare, callused palm, then his face—his handsome, vulnerable face. And her heart opened wide.

"I love you, Kyle Hayden," she said, and his features tightened. "I always have."

Kyle's insides melted. His gaze sketched her. His voice was a trembling rasp when he said, "Then trust me—I'll keep it safe this time."

Maxie flew to him, slamming against him, and Kyle clamped his arms around her, squeezing and squeezing. She buried her face in the curve of his throat and sobbed. Kyle closed his eyes tightly shut and held her, breathing in her scent, feeling all he'd wanted to feel for years.

Thank you, God, he thought. *Thank you.*

"Say it again," he whispered close to her ear.

And she gripped him tighter and whispered, "I love you. I love you."

Kyle's eyes burned, and he rocked her in his arms, content to hold her.

A light snow dusted them, coating their shoulders, pillowing on their hats. Icy wind skated gently over the white powder. The horse trotted close and stopped, pawing the ground, almost in shame for deserting her.

Kyle brushed his mouth over her throat, then whispered in her ear.

Maxie leaned back, blinking. "Kyle!" Her cheeks reddened. "Is that all you can think about right now?"

"Well, we do have twenty-four hours alone. We're *real* good at it—" he wiggled his brows "—and I can't think of anything, in the past seven years—" his expression softened "—that I've wanted to do more."

"Doesn't hurt that you're ah—already prepared, huh?" She pressed her hips to his, feeling his hardness between them.

"That should tell you something, since it's damn freezing out here."

She smiled, loving that he wanted her so bad. "I'll race you." She nodded to the horse, clicking her tongue to call the skittish mount closer, and he glanced briefly, then grinned at her.

"I'll win."

She touched his jaw with a tenderness that bordered on reverence. "Fat chance, flyboy." She patted his cheek, hard. "And the first one home gets naked." She tore out of his arms. Kyle simply stood there, watching as she caught the horse's leads and swung onto the saddle. She bolted in a quick gallop.

She loved him, he thought, and his smile widened. She'd always loved him.

Kyle's brows drew down slightly as he turned toward the chopper. Conflicting thoughts stirred in the back of his mind, just out of reach. For about two seconds, he tried to remember their recent conversations, then quit, his thoughts on beating her home so he could strip her naked—himself.

Ten

The door jolted on its hinges as Kyle backed her up against it. Urgency cloaked his movements as his tongue pushed between her lips, his big body mashing her to the door. And she urged him on, plowing her fingers into his hair, knocking his hat to the floor somewhere near hers. She didn't care. She didn't care about anything except Kyle and showing him how much she loved him, how much she wanted him. She didn't waste a second, unleashing on him like a rainstorm, yanking at the snaps of his jacket, shoving it down off his shoulders. He did the same to her, but it wasn't enough.

There were still too many clothes between him and the skin he'd been aching to taste so badly that he had dreams about it. He urged her away from the door, peeling off layers of thermal clothing as they moved toward the hall, leaving a trail with their heat.

Maxie yanked his shirt from his trousers, driving her hands beneath the fabric and feeling the warmth of his skin. "Kyle," she chanted over and over, tasting his mouth, his throat. They toed off boots and socks, Maxie yanking his shirt off over his head, groping, kissing anything exposed. He hurriedly unbuttoned her shirt, opening it, pausing in the middle of the hall to push her bra up and take one nipple deeply into his mouth. She moaned, sinking her fingers into his hair, bending back, then urging his mouth to hers. Her breasts brushed his naked chest, his hands fumbling with the bra clasp.

Suddenly Kyle pushed her up against the wall again, opening her jeans with frantic moves. "I need to touch you," he said on a rush, shoving her zipper down. She gasped as his hand found its way inside her panties, stroking her, pushing a finger between the damp folds. Maxie closed her eyes and tipped her head back, and Kyle watched the play of desire on her face. It made him harder.

"Kyle…" She rocked and inhaled, looking into his eyes. "We—I don't have protection."

He smiled, slow and deliberate. "I do."

"Get it. Now."

He kissed her deeply, then pulled away and darted into his room. Seconds later, he came back, his trousers open to relieve some of the strain, a fistful of foil squares in his hand. She took them, grabbed him by the waistband and pulled him into her bedroom.

Immediately she was on him, kissing him, unzipping his jeans. He stripped off her shirt, her bra, covering her breasts with his palms, his mouth rolling frantically over hers. His hands rode lower, shoving her jeans and panties downward, and Maxie slipped her hand inside his trousers, wrapping her fingers around his hardness.

Kyle groaned darkly. "Don't, baby," he murmured against the curve of her throat, even as he thrust into her touch. "I won't make it."

"Losing stamina in your old age?" Her fingertips glided over the tip of him as her tongue slicked his lips.

"If you keep that up, yeah."

With her teeth, Maxie tore open a foil square, rolled the

condom into place. She took immense pleasure in his still-ness, his short, rapid breaths.

His eyes opened. "I'm going to explode." His fingers flexed on her waist.

"I know."

"I want to do it inside you."

Maxie's legs wobbled, and she licked her lips. "When?"

His gaze darkened with promise. "Now."

He shucked his jeans in one motion, then attacked hers, leaving them in a heap before gathering her in his arms. Naked flesh to naked flesh, they kissed and groped, stagger-ing toward the bed. Maxie held him in her hand, pushing him down to tease him against her softness.

With a growl, he drove her back onto the bed, pushing open her thighs. He met her gaze. She guided him to her.

Kyle stilled, his chest heaving, his body trembling. He could feel the heat of her surround him. Then he shoved, filling her at once, pressing her deeper into the mattress. Maxie cried out his name, a breathless rush on her lips.

Kyle rose up, lacing his fingers with her, braced above her, her body exposed. For an instant they stared, bodies shuddering, hearts open. His gaze slicked over her to where they joined before meeting her gaze. His face lined with strain, he withdrew and pressed home. She arched, her feet digging into the mattress, her body like a sleek, pulsing cat. Meeting him, matching him, faster, harder.

"Oh, baby, you're so hot." He felt her feminine muscles clench and flex around him.

She thrust her hips, meeting his tempo. "Give me more," she breathed. "Hurry."

Suddenly he lowered onto her, his hips rocking, his gaze locked tight with hers. He watched her passion fracture, felt the wet heat of her ripple through him and just the feel of her delicate body flexing around him sent him over the edge. He lost a part of his soul, the eruption a hard grind through his body, and Kyle succumbed, stiffening, thrusting.

"I love you," she whispered against his mouth, gasping

and gasping as he pushed deeper, harder. And still they strained for more, to linger and cling to the rapture. The fade of passion was slow, the trembling linking them like an unbreakable chain.

His lungs still working hard, Kyle gazed into her eyes, smoothing her hair from her cheek. "I love you, baby." It was intense and frightening, how hard they climaxed, how deep it drove into his blood. He was marked as well as if she'd carved her name on his chest. He tried easing his weight off her, but she wouldn't let him go, keeping him close, bodies still joined, hearts still pounding erratically.

"Don't leave," she said sleepily, burying her face in the warmth of his throat.

"Never," he whispered against her temple. "I'm home." Kyle sank into the pillows, smoothing his hands over her bare back until he fell asleep, well loved.

They slept hard, and it was after midnight when Maxie stirred awake. She blinked sleepily and stared into his soulful brown eyes.

"Years of frustration is hell on the body, huh?" Kyle said, and her lips curved. He was kneeling between her legs, stroking her thighs and the fire, barely touched, flamed. "I knew we were good together, but to pass out?"

She smiled. "Call it years of sexual frustration coming to an end."

"Nah," he said, leaning forward and sliding his hands along her legs. "We're just getting started." He caressed the flare of her hips, let his thumbs meet and press into the sweet bud of her need. She made a little sound, spreading her knees a little, and his fingers slicked over the sensitive bud, loving the way she caught her lip in her teeth to keep from moaning. He was going to make her scream tonight, he thought, enfolding her breasts in his palms. He brushed his thumbs over her nipples, circled them, watching them peak as his tongue snaked out to lick one pink tip.

He smiled against her flesh as she arched and breathed

deeply, and he met her gaze, hands prowling over her skin, pushing her arms above her head. He hooked her hands over the edge of the carved headboard.

"Stay just like that," he said, nose to nose, his body a breath over hers.

Her expression questioned, her breathing quick. "What do you have in mind, Kyle?"

He laughed, a sinister sound laced with mischief. He kissed her, a long drugging play of lips and tongue. "Promise me you won't touch me."

"But I want to do more than touch you."

He smiled as his hands grazed down her arms, over her breasts. "But I want this to last, and if you touch me..."

She smiled, stretching languidly, aware of his gaze raking over her. "So. Old age has taken its toll, huh?"

He knelt between her feet, hands caressing again. "We'll see." He lifted her leg, his mouth on her calf as he propped her heel on his shoulder. He tasted her flesh, his free hand smoothing upward in slow deliberation, coming nearer and nearer to the source of her need. He nibbled at the inside of her knee, her thigh, smoothed her flesh. His breath was hot and moist on her skin, and she squirmed, whimpering, thrusting her hips.

"Kyle. This isn't fair."

He chuckled lowly, dipping his hands beneath her and squeezing her buttocks. His fingers rubbed near, but not near enough, his mouth toyed and taunted, yet denied her his kiss.

She couldn't stand it. "Touch me, please."

"Ah, that's what I like, Max begging for me." He splayed his hands high on her thighs, thumbs rubbing lightly over the join of her leg, hovering on the edge of the dark curls.

Maxie felt a rush of liquid drench her, and he met her gaze across the length of her body.

His dark eyes raked hungrily over her nakedness. "You look exceptionally lickable right now." He bent to drag his velvety tongue across her stomach, dipping into the contours, over the curve of her hip.

The headboard creaked, her arm muscles straining to bring him closer to her aching softness.

Suddenly he spread her thighs wide and ducked his head, laving her with his tongue. She shrieked and choked, lifting her hips as he ground his mouth against the slick wet heat. Cupping her buttocks in his palms, he held her to him when she squirmed, his tongue probing. She chanted his name, nearly snapped the headboard from its posts and Kyle parted her, thrusting two fingers inside.

Maxie came apart at the seams, shuddering, begging for him to stop and join her. But he refused and pushed her knee up, exposing her more.

"Stop, oh, please." He lifted his head, easing her leg off his shoulder, and she leaped on him, shoving him back onto the bed and straddling his legs.

"I ought to tie you up and do the same to you," she said.

"Oh?" he chuckled smugly, then grew still and silent as she bent and took him into her mouth. He growled, flexing on the bed and watched her.

The torture had its effect, and he reached for her, dragging her over him. Maxie spread her thighs, her body open for his touch. She held his arousal against her dewy softness, letting him feel the heat of her.

"Baby, oh jeez." He was reaching for the foil packets, and Maxie didn't care. She felt wild and reckless, and the thought of having his baby, another of his babies, wouldn't stop her. But he did, quickly donning protection. Yet she was already inching up, then she was sliding down over him. Kyle sat up sharply and they stared, his body buried to the hilt inside her. He could feel her heart beating there.

"You still have power over me," she said.

"And I still love you, Max." He brushed her hair from her cheek. "This is how it should have been." He gripped her hips, giving them motion. She rose and fell with sweet cadence, tucking her hips to feel every inch of him. His body shuddered.

"Maxie—baby. I—"

She felt him flex and throb and she leaned back. Instantly Kyle pushed her into the mattress and withdrew, then thrust into her, once, twice. She laughed at his eagerness, his wild, frantic pushing. Then he left her, turning her sharply on her stomach, sliding an arm beneath her hips and lifting her. She glanced back over her shoulder, gripping the headboard. He entered her smoothly from behind. She moaned, wiggling against him.

Kyle stroked her, his arousal thick and heavy between her soft thighs. Reaching around, he touched the heart of her. She slammed back into him and called his name, telling him to hold nothing back. He didn't, taking their lovemaking to new and inventive levels. And Maxie met him and matched him at each one.

Hours later she was limp in his arms when they fell to the jumble of sheets.

"Remind me to tease you like that more often."

He gazed into her eyes. "Just looking at you is enough."

A warm tingling spread over her.

Her body draping his, she folded her arms on his chest. "I love you, Kyle." She sighed. "And as much as I want to make love with you again, I'm hungry and we're out of condoms."

His grin was slow. "No. We're not."

Food was a priority with Maxie—an all-out grazing. He sat across from her at the kitchen table, watching her eat leftovers, which constituted desserts, fettucine and chicken. In that order.

"Where do you put it?" he said, propping his feet on the extra chair. "'Cause I know every inch of that delectable body."

"I know you do," she said, swiping her finger in a mound of chocolate. "But I think you missed a spot." She opened her robe and smeared the fudge frosting over the swell of her breast. Kyle grinned, then pulled her from the chair and onto his lap, laving at her breast, sliding his hand between

her thighs. He found her, warm and wet, and she spread her
legs a touch wider.

"I love it when you get hot for me."

"I always am."

"You hid it well."

"Years of practice." Maxie couldn't think of the reasons
why they'd been apart, of the pain that would come when
she fully exposed her secrets. She just wanted to indulge in
Kyle.

"Not anymore. Give me everything, Max." His grip
around her waist tightened, his face buried in the bend of
her throat. "We've wasted so much time."

His fingers manipulated her, and she clung to him, cupping his face and kissing him as he brought her again and
again to a shattering climax. She sagged in his arms, and he
lifted her, carrying her to the living room.

"I'll get you more food later." He laid her on the carpet,
dragging a blanket from a nearby chair. He made love to
her, again. Yet no matter how much she gave to him, how
uninhibited she was with him, Kyle felt she was holding
something back.

Maxie stepped from the shower, drying quickly and slipping into a terry-cloth robe. She left the bathroom and stilled.
Kyle was asleep in her bed. He looked so big and ferocious
in the draped four-poster bed. Settling in a chair, she watched
him sleep, tempted to touch him, to run her fingers delicately
over his muscles. He was on his stomach, his arm dangling
off the bed, his body bare and languid in repose. Her gaze
strayed to the scar marking him from ankle to midthigh, the
redness long since gone, but she knew it caused him pain.
It reminded her of watching him jump from the helicopter,
springing up, then the horror as he got tangled.

That was the old Kyle, she reminded herself again. The
danger-loving Kyle. The man who wanted her back but was
afraid to ask.

But was he ready to hear what she had to say? Was he

ready to know what loving her, *really* loving her meant? Maxie closed her eyes and sank into the chair. She couldn't spend another moment with him without telling him. She was sure of her love for him, just as she knew she would have to risk it to be happy.

"Baby?"

His whiskey-rough voice curled through her before she opened her eyes. She smiled. "Hey, flyboy." Her gaze slid briefly over his bare body. "Nice butt."

His arm still dangling over the edge of the bed, he tugged on the hem of her robe. "Wanna get naked with me?"

"Not satisfied yet?"

"Never."

"Never say never, Kyle."

His gaze moved over her with undisguised possession. "Marry me, Max."

She inhaled sharply, her eyes wide.

"Marry me, tonight."

"Kyle. Let's not rush things."

He propped his torso on one elbow. "Rush things? Jeez, Max, don't you think we're long overdue?"

"Yeah, we are," she said shakily. She glanced at the closet, and Kyle's frown deepened. He sat up and swung his legs over the side of the bed.

"Max. Don't do this. I can feel you leaving me. You married the wrong man for the wrong reasons. Marry me for the right ones. The same ones we had years ago."

She met his gaze. "I'm not running, Kyle. I'm facing us, head-on. This time, the choice will be yours." He frowned, opening his mouth to speak, but she leaned close to press two fingers to his lips. "Why don't you shower and I'll get you some coffee. Then we'll talk."

He nodded, impatient to make her his wife, to start living like the family they all should be. He sure as hell didn't think they had anything left to discuss. He loved her. She loved him. The past didn't matter.

Kyle stood, recognizing the worry on her face. He gathered her close and kissed her deeply, loving that she drove her fingers into his hair and held him tighter to her mouth. He moaned, growing hard, then stepped back and headed into the bathroom.

Maxie moved to the closet, drawing down a large box before leaving the room.

He was sitting on the edge of the bed, toweling his hair dry when she returned, a cup of steaming coffee in one hand, an envelope in the other. She handed him the coffee.

He took a sip, sighing with pleasure as the warmth simmered down to his stomach.

"What's that?" He nodded to the letter clutched in her hands.

"My—our future."

Kyle frowned, carefully setting aside his coffee. An uneasy feeling swept through him as she held out the crumpled, yellowed envelope. Her hand trembled. "We'll talk after you've read it."

He took it, turning it over to read the address.

A painful chill raced over his spine, his blood going cold.

It was addressed to him, from her, seven years ago.

It was marked "Return to sender, delivery refused."

And it was unopened.

Be careful what you wish for, he thought.

Eleven

Dear Kyle,

Well, now, at least, I know that you did as you promised and kept your head down during Desert Storm, since your name didn't show up on the KIA or wounded lists. I wished you'd let me know, but I understand why you didn't. I know I've hurt you and I'm so sorry. I didn't want to. Though I guess it means nothing to you now, huh? Your heartache won't heal with words. And neither will mine, but I do love you. I always have and unfortunately for me, I think I always will.

Oh, for weeks I'd lay awake wishing you would call, wishing you could find the love we'd shared, enough to let me know you survived. I let it go for a while, and when your unit returned, I tried calling, but I got your brother. His attitude tells me he's taken sides. A shame, I liked him. Rather than become an annoyance to you, I've decided to try one last time in this letter.

I'm not begging you to come back when it's obvious you don't want to. You've already proved that you didn't love me as I imagined. But I feel you have the right to know that you're a father.

Kyle's eyes widened, and he reread the line over and over. Mimi.

I guess I forgot to take one of those pills, call it pre-wedding stress. It doesn't matter now.

He swallowed, his suspicions unfolding, memories rising. The moments in the barn… *Mimi's father turned his back on us. He chose to cut us out.*

This guy who gave you Mimi, did you love him?

Yes. Desperately.

You don't know what I've had to do to go on….

Kyle felt a barrage of emotions, regret, sadness, joy—utter joy. Then came anger. He stood, leaving the room, calling her name. It didn't take him long to discover he was alone. He strode to the door, flinging it open and shouting for her just as horse and rider bolted from the barn. Kyle clenched his fists, ignorant of the icy wind and falling snow as she rode away in a hard gallop. He stayed there, on the porch, barefoot and shirtless until the figures were a dark slash against the white snow.

Damn her for not trying harder. Damn her for not coming to him and demanding he listen. Kyle groaned miserably, returning to the house, to the bedroom. He'd turned his back on her and couldn't blame her. It was a choice he'd made with a broken heart. He chose not to answer her letters, her calls.

God. He'd been a complete and total pigheaded fool.

And he'd missed everything. She'd carried his child,

alone. She'd suffered ailments and labor, questions and likely some gossip—alone.

He sank to the floor, moaning. Tears burned the back of his eyes. And he forced himself to finish reading the letter.

I know you don't want to have anything to do with me, but your child deserves to know her father, at least in some small way. Our daughter is eight months old, by the way. I would never have kept you from her, Kyle, if you wanted to be with her. If you do not call or write in a few days, I will know your answer and although it will be difficult, I will accept it.

It's okay, my parents are handling this great. They're supportive and happy over their grandchild. Your child will know I loved you and at the time we created her, we loved.

Kyle felt a tear roll down his cheek. He smeared it across his face, then pinched the bridge of his nose with thumb and forefinger. "Oh, God."

The anger was gone, replaced with regret so deep it was hard to breathe. His chest clenched down on his heart, squeezing and squeezing. He dug the heels of his palms into his eyes and thought of Maxie—pregnant and alone. Of her going through labor knowing he'd abandoned her—of holding their child for the first time, seeing Mimi walk and talk and sharing it with her parents, her sisters. But not him.

No wonder she was so cold to him, not forthcoming with her past, making him pry it out of her. She didn't want him in her life, because she'd let him in before and he'd turned tail. Anger at himself spirited through him. He should have recognized his suspicions for what they were: a thinly disguised truth. He was afraid to see it. Afraid to confront it. And he was ashamed that he'd even thought Maxie could have jumped into bed with anyone. It was never in her. My God, how could she forgive him for being so cruel and self-

ish? How had she gotten past her pain to love him again?
He didn't have half the strength she did.

He dropped his head back on the edge of the mattress,
flinging his arm out. His knuckles hit a box and he sat up.

The note read

You've missed a lot, baby. And I'm sorry. Start with
the video.

Kyle grabbed it and scrambled across the room to the TV,
jamming it in the VCR and pushing Play. His heart pounded
violently as the picture came into view, jiggled, then focused.

Maxie.

She was on a hospital bed, her knees bent. She was
breathing through her mouth. Rapidly. She was in the throes
of labor, he realized and watched, enthralled as she bore
down, forcing the child, *his* child, from her body. Her mother
and sisters were there, encouraging her, giving her water and
drying her face between contractions. Then he heard the doctor tell her this was it. Maxie groaned and bore down, and
Kyle clenched his fists, his body sweating with her, his face
contorted with hers. "It's a girl," he heard, and felt dizzy,
sinking back onto his haunches. He touched the screen, his
gaze scanning every detail as the doctor placed the blood-
cloaked child in her arms. Everyone laughed and applauded,
cooed and smiled.

Maxie sobbed and sobbed, and faintly he heard her say,
"Oh, Kyle, look what we did." She looked at her father,
who was holding the camera. "I wish he was here to see
this, Dad."

"I know you do, poppet. I know."

Kyle's heart shattered, for the sadness in her voice, for
the moment he'd missed, for the time he'd wasted. Then he
noticed she wore the ball cap he'd given her years ago. The
faded, worn one she'd offered him this morning. She'd loved

him then. She'd loved him when she should have hated him, cursed him.

The video stopped, and he punched the button, rewinding it, watching it again and again and each time catching something new. Then he looked at the box, carefully lifting out a smaller one, opening it to find tiny shoes, white and a little worn. He brought them to his nose, smelling musty leather and baby powder. He put them carefully aside, reaching for a rattle, then the tiniest bonnet he'd ever seen. He tried to imagine Mimi wearing it, her red curls sticking out, her green eyes staring trustingly up at him. *My baby,* he thought. *My daughter.* His hands shook as he reached for the albums. There were photos of him and Maxie, at the Marine Corps ball, in Encinada, the marketplace in Coronado. Then there was a photo of Maxie, a wedding photo taken for the newspapers.

Kyle had never seen her wedding gown, and she looked incredible, sexy and innocent, a sparkle in her eyes the photographer caught so clearly. It hurt to see it. And in the next photo, it was gone. It was a picture of Maxie, round with his child. He ran his fingertip over her belly. Her smile didn't quite reach her eyes, although everyone around her was beaming. It looked like a family barbecue or something, he thought, flipping the page. Maxie at about six months, Maxie at eight. He frowned and noticed she was rarely smiling in any photo and in most of them, she was wearing that old black ball cap.

Other than gum-machine junk and an engagement ring, it was the only thing he'd ever given her. Except a child. He found articles about Desert Storm, his unit and the KIA list. Oh, Lord.

"Kyle?"

His head jerked up, and the desolation in his eyes was palatable.

"I didn't give you much of a choice, did I?" he said softly.

"Oh, honey, don't," she moaned, stepping into the room. "Don't beat yourself up."

"What you went through. God, I was stupid and selfish."

He climbed to his feet, letting the photos and memorabilia fall to the floor. He moved to her. And she looked away.

"Max?"

When she looked back, her eyes were glossy with tears. Her lip trembled. "I missed you so much, Kyle." Her voice broke and wavered pitifully.

"Aw, baby, me too." He clenched his fists.

"I wanted to hate you."

"You had the right."

"I couldn't and it hurt so bad to keep loving you when you didn't want me." Her expression grew more miserable. "I didn't want you back if you were coming just for the baby."

"So when my letter came back, you just quit trying."

She nodded, fighting tears. "Mimi gave me the strength I needed. Mom and Dad were great, still are, but it was you I needed."

"I wish I was. How I wish I'd swallowed my pride and come after you. The time I wasted."

"Don't. It's useless."

He nodded shakily, holding her gaze. "Need me now?"

"Yes," she whispered quickly. "Yes."

"You gonna let me hold you again?"

She nodded, looking small and forlorn. They stepped, bodies impacting, arms around each other, tight and warm.

"I'm sorry, I'm sorry. God, I keep saying that."

She sobbed in his arms, clinging to him. "Don't, not anymore."

Kyle closed his eyes tightly, rocking her in his arms. She cupped his face in her hands and kissed him. "I need you, Kyle."

"I need you, too."

"No, I *need* you," she said against his lips. Her teeth

scraped over his jaw, his throat. She rubbed his chest, then flipped the button of his jeans.

Kyle could feel it. The energy. The rush. She wanted to master and take. Start again and relive. Kyle hurriedly peeled off her clothes, taking her to the bed, covering her body with his.

"Now, Kyle. Now." She spread for him, guiding him.

Kyle grappled for the nightstand, tearing open the foil packet. "Max, hold on. Hold on."

"I've waited long enough."

He barely got it on before she caught his hips and pulled him down onto her. He filled her completely and he groaned, loud and harsh.

Maxie couldn't get enough of him, her mouth anywhere she could reach, her hands roaming roughly over his big body. The back of her throat burned. She needed to feel him, deeper, needed to make a permanent link with him. All the secrets were out, and they were still together. They were loving and Maxie let herself go, inhibition set free.

"I love you. I love you," she cried, and he kept making love to her. Wild jungle love. They tasted and nibbled, suckled and kissed and Maxie cried for years lost and Kyle held her, loving her until she rejoiced in the new feeling of peace.

Then she ate hordes of chocolate.

"I need more than a sugar rush," he said, sliding from the bed and pulling on his jeans.

Maxie watched him; she couldn't help it. He looked so sexy all sleep tousled and bare chested. And when he yanked up the zipper and left the button unfastened, she thought she'd come apart again and drag him back into the bed. And her expression said as much.

Kyle took a slow, steady breath, calming himself. "Food. Food," he chanted as if to keep his mind off his body's reaction as he turned away and headed to the kitchen. He slapped together an obscenely large sandwich, added fruit and cheese to the plate, in case Max somehow lost her appetite for chocolate and returned to the bedroom. He stopped short when he saw her reclined on the mound of pillows, her legs curled to the side as she sucked chocolate from her fingertips, empty candy wrappers scattered on the spread.

She'd slipped on a skimpy nightgown that gave him immediate fantasies of taking it off her, and Kyle didn't think he'd seen anything as erotic and beautiful as Maxie waiting for him. His gaze shifted to the box on the floor, the baby things and photos sticking out, then back to her.

"Sustenance," he said, hefting the plate a little higher as he moved to the side of the bed.

She balled up a wrapper and aimed for the trash can. "You're going to need more than that before the night's over," she said, innuendo in her tone as she tossed and missed.

His gaze slid over her like liquid silk. "So are you, baby."

Maxie couldn't respond, her insides gone to jelly under his heated look.

Smiling, Kyle set the plate on the nightstand and bent for the wrapper, his hand straying to the baby shoes, the photos, his fingers lightly touching. Look at all he'd missed, he thought, all he'd nearly lost. He sat on the bed and pulled the box to his lap.

"These," he said, dangling the tiny shoes from his fingertip, "go in my chopper."

Maxie smiled tenderly, watching him poke and pluck through her past. Then suddenly, he stilled, digging deep, and she didn't see what he took out. She frowned curiously as he laid the box on the floor and turned to her.

"You look strange." Her gaze dropped to his fist. "What is it?"

Kyle shifted closer, his thigh pressing along hers, his gaze skimming her features over and over, as if memorizing each one. The intensity of it trapped her, held her heart in midbeat. Then she heard a soft creak and looked down. Her breath caught, memories flooding back at the sight of her engagement ring nestled in the tiny black velvet box. Images flickered in her mind—Kyle in his uniform, on one knee, proposing with so much doubt in his eyes and hesitation in his voice she'd almost said no then. Her gaze flew to his.

And she saw only his faith and their love mirrored in his eyes, his expression, his determination, his surety growing as he took her hand, the ring poised at the tip of her finger.

He stared at it for a moment, marveling at his own calm and he lifted his gaze. "We love each other."

"Yes," she said in a fractured voice. "We do."

"This time, it's forever, baby."

Her smile sent a tear down her cheek. "Forever, Kyle."

He slid the ring onto her finger, then brought her hand to his lips. He kissed her knuckles, holding her gaze, and her hand unfurled, sliding to his nape. She brought him down to her on a soft kiss. He slipped his arms around her, shifting over her, molding her to him, and made slow, delicate love to her, with her, supple movement and soft breaths, binding their new love in time's oldest dance.

When they stirred again, they ate a decent meal. They rode horses and she soothed his aching leg. Kyle listened to her "I told you that bungee jump was stupid" speech as he lay back on the couch, loving her for still feeling afraid for him, for her tender touch on an old injury.

That afternoon, Kyle called his brother and told him he was going to finally marry Max and he was already a father, a funny smile on his face. They talked for a good hour, and Mitch apologized for his part in screwing up Kyle's life.

"I'm a dad," he said, hanging up the phone, sinking into the sofa cushions.

"Yeah, you are." She patted his full stomach.

"Let's go get her."

She shifted, meeting his gaze. "No."

"Max," he warned, frowning.

"She doesn't know. Though I know she likes you—" Kyle beamed "—we have to ease into this."

Kyle mulled that over for a few minutes. Mimi would be more than traumatized if she discovered he was her father.

But that couldn't stop him from wanting to hold her in his arms, look at her with new eyes.

"Is marrying me the first step?"

She smiled, spinning the ring on her finger. "Yeah, it is."

A little frown marred his brow. "I don't have to adopt my daughter, do I?"

"No. Your name is on her birth certificate."

She never hid it. He just didn't want to see. She'd dropped crumbs for him to follow, but Kyle was too caught in his own misery and need to see what was there. He questioned her for hours, found out her prewedding jitters made her forget to take a couple of her birth-control pills, then told her he loved her and would do his best to make up for the past years.

"Don't bother. I hate it when you're trying to suck up to me."

He laughed, kissing her, pushing her into the cushions. She was just getting started on stripping off her clothes when the radio crackled. They listened, frozen. Then Kyle realized they were his call letters. Maxie sighed and thrust him off. He crossed the room to answer.

Jackson's voice barked over the radio.

"Got a problem, an individual wandered off the path. Now she's stuck on a shelf, too scared to move."

"She must be freezing!" Maxie glanced at the windows. The snow was falling in a light dust, but she knew how different it would be in the canyon.

"On my way," Kyle said.

"Roger. Tell Maxine to come, too."

Kyle frowned, glancing at her and her brow furrowed. "Why? Need horses?"

"Possible."

Kyle frowned, rubbing his knuckles over beard stubble.

Jackson clicked on. "Kyle. It's Mimi."

Kyle's eyes flared, and he snapped a look at Maxie. She was already grabbing their coats and cold-weather gear. "On our way."

"Hurry!" Maxie shouted.

"Maxie—baby, don't panic."

She whirled on him. "Don't panic? She's in the canyon, caught somewhere, cold, freezing—"

He grabbed her arms, giving her a quick shake. "And we don't need to scare her."

"This is our daughter, Kyle."

Hard emotion played across his face. "We'll find her, Max. I swear it."

Or die trying, he thought. His little girl needed him to be calm, and Kyle focused on gathering his equipment. He knew if the wind was high and the snow was falling, he would have trouble with the chopper. The blades could freeze. He warmed Maxie's truck engine, and helped her load two mules into the trailer.

"I'll follow overhead," he told her, kissing her hard, then pushing her into the driver's seat. "Drive carefully," he warned. She nodded, grasping his hand and squeezing. "I'll get her out, I swear."

"I know you will."

When they entered the rescue station, the Nature Girls were being picked up by their parents. But most lingered, wanting to help. Maxie was in a state of absolute panic when she confronted the guide.

"Why did you leave her?"

"Max—"

She shrugged off his touch, bearing down on the guide like a cougar protecting her cub.

"I had to get the other girls out first. They were all panicking. The team spotted her, but she wouldn't let them help her."

"I'll get her."

Kyle nodded to Jackson and Maxie grabbed his arm. "Not without me."

"Let me take the chopper up first. She'll recognize it. Know that we're here. I can lower a rope."

He was off the ground in minutes, circling to spot her. The wind was high and hard, and Kyle fought to steady the chopper. He'd done a lot of stupid, dangerous things in his life, he thought, but never one with good enough reason as saving his baby. Then he saw her. He rocked the craft and she tried lifting her hand to wave. It was worse than he thought. She was on the edge of a shelf. How she got there, he couldn't wonder. But when she tried to wave, she slipped. He couldn't lower a rope. Damn. Kyle couldn't leave without talking to her, easing the fear on her tiny face. He flipped on the loudspeaker.

"Hey, short stack. I'm coming down for you, okay?"

She nodded, her cowboy hat gone, her hair whipping in the wind. He rose out of the canyon and landed quickly. Maxie was on the pad and ducked, racing to the craft. He told her the situation. She already had the mules saddled. Horses were too skittish for the narrow trails.

Jackson was ready to mount up.

"No, I'm going," she insisted.

"Max, you're not trained."

"Yes, I am. She's my daughter, and I know the trails and ruts better than anyone. I'm going in!"

Kyle grabbed her against him, holding her tight. "It's okay, it's okay." He met Jackson's gaze over the top of her head, a plea in his eyes. Jackson looked ready to deny them, then nodded sharply. "Come on."

She moved the mules to the trail entrance, loaded with extra thermal blankets and a jacket. They put on bright orange parkas. Kyle had to crush the urge to race to Mimi. His features were mapped with worry, and when he met Maxie's gaze, he offered her a reassuring smile.

He would succeed. He wasn't ready to lose when he just got his life back.

Twelve

Kyle found her first and quickly slipped from the saddle, his gaze darting to where his daughter sat, twenty yards above him. "It's amazing that she got up there in the first place."

"The guide said she was a little sad during the outing," Maxie said guiltily.

"She heard us arguing the other day, heard you cry. In fact she made me promise not to make you cry again." His face creased deeper. "One I quickly broke."

"Oh, Kyle—"

"Now, what I want to know is," he interrupted, "if you're going to wear white when you marry me."

She blinked, taken aback.

"Well, after the past two days—" he wiggled his brows suggestively "—I'd say you were on your way to scarlet."

She smiled, nudging him, loving him more for recognizing her fear. He'd been talking casually to her the whole way down, forcing her to make plans for their future rather than linger on the terror both of them were feeling.

As he stood beside the mules, Maxie watched his quick, practiced moves as he stepped into the climbing harness, checked waist straps, his boots, his supply of pitons, the coil of nylon rope. Then he turned to her.

"Let's get her." He helped Maxie into her equipment, though he doubted she would need it. Mimi wasn't that far up, but Kyle wanted the assurance of pitons locked into the canyon wall and Maxie nearer to the ground to steady ropes.

He hoped Mimi wasn't injured.

Kyle started climbing, his razor-point boot tips sticking into the softer granite, his gloved fingers grappling for purchase. He ascended quickly, getting closer and closer to her, yet forced himself to set pitons in the wall, run cord through the metal loops. Then he climbed higher and saw the fear in his daughter's face.

"Hi, short stack."

"Hullo, Mr. Hayden."

He longed for the moment when she'd call him Daddy.

"Ready to go to Mom?"

She nodded shakily.

"You'll have to come to me, Mimi." The ground was too delicate around her, and he was afraid his added weight would disrupt her already precarious position. "Jump into my arms."

She shook her head wildly.

He tried once more and she refused. Kyle plucked the radio from inside his jacket and spoke to Maxie. "She won't come to me."

Maxie stared up at them and spoke into the handset. "Mimi, baby. Do what Mr. Hayden says. He loves you sweetie—he won't let anything happen to you."

Kyle met Mimi's gaze, praying his love for her, the love that had come without thought or reason, showed enough for her to see. He held out his arms. "Come on, short stack, come to me. I promise you won't fall."

Mimi bit her lower lip, indecisive, then nodded, leaning out, teetering for balance. Then she leaped into his arms. The impact made him slip a little, and Kyle clutched her, the locked piton jerking them to a stop.

Kyle closed his eyes and thanked God. He held her a moment longer, then smoothed her hair back. She tipped her head, staring trustingly into his eyes.

"Thank you," she whispered, and clutched her arms around his neck.

Kyle felt like a king.

He radioed Maxie, and she tightened the rope, hooking it on the mule's pommel. They started down. Kyle worked slowly, speaking gently, yet Mimi kept apologizing for causing trouble, for getting stuck up here and telling him she was really, really cold.

Maxie was there, reaching for her, grabbing her tight, raining kisses over her chilled face. She reached for Kyle, bringing him close, and his arms surrounded his family.

"Can we go home now?" Mimi asked, glancing between the two and ending on Kyle.

"Yeah, short stack. We have to. I'm hungry." She giggled and fell into Kyle's arms. Maxie smiled, letting him put her on the mule and talking to them both while he removed the equipment and stored it. Then he swung up into the saddle and led them out.

Kyle glanced over his shoulder at Maxie and Mimi. They were nuzzled tight, and he wanted to hold them, wanted to ease the worry in Maxie's eyes that Mimi might get sick now.

They were out of the canyon in a couple of hours, the paramedics checking Mimi, then letting her mother take her home. Kyle rode with them, leaving the chopper, not willing to spare a moment apart from them.

Once inside the house, they rushed to get Mimi warm, her mother forcing her into a bath, drying her hair and dressing her in tons of flannel. Mimi ate a quick sandwich, but

Kyle made her a mug of hot chocolate laced with vanilla. His daughter grinned up at him, thanking him sleepily from a mountain of comforters, and he could see she was sleepy.

He stood in the doorway, the empty mug in his hand, and Kyle felt a little left out when Maxie tucked Mimi in, then sat to read her a story.

"G'night, Mr. Hayden."

"Night, short stack." *I love you.*

Maxie glanced over her shoulder and smiled at Kyle, then turned back to the book. Mimi stared between the two, ending on her mom.

"You're different."

Maxie looked up from the book. Her daughter was a sharp cookie, and it didn't surprise her that she recognized the change between her and Kyle.

"Why do you say that?"

Mimi grinned hugely. "You look at each other different. Smilin' a lot." She tilted her head. "You love him, don't you, Mom?"

Maxie inhaled and tried to hide it. "Yes, I do."

Something in Mimi burst and she looked down thoughtfully at her hands. After a moment, she looked up and her eyes bored into Maxie's, as if she knew her mom was hiding something from her. Suddenly, with a yawn, Mimi sank into the soft comforter and closed her eyes.

"That's nice, Momma."

Maxie smiled tenderly, tucking the covers around her before leaving the bed. Kyle stood at the door, his arms folded over his chest, his back braced against the jamb. She came to him, sliding her arms around his waist and laying her head on his chest. His arms enfolded.

"I'm so glad you're here."

He rubbed her back. "So am I."

She tilted her head to look at him. "I think she knows."

"I want her to."

"Come on." She jerked on him. "Let's get something to eat, and we'll talk about our strategy."

Kyle smiled down at her, straightening, his hands lowering to the sweet curve of her buttocks. "Don't I get a reward
for rescuing her?"

Maxie brushed her mouth over his, lightly, hungrily. "Oh,
yes, a big one."

He pulled her from the doorway, gently closing it after
them, then returning to leave it open a crack.

They talked and ate and played with each other, and Kyle
made warm, slow love to her in the living room, before a
roaring fire, giving her more and more of his heart and she
held it gently. She'd been waiting years to hold it this gently.

In the morning, Kyle stood in the kitchen, staring at the
drawings, the school papers tacked to the fridge with mag-
nets shaped like vegetables. He wanted to be around when
she presented them proudly, be there to pick her up when
she fell, to protect her from under-the-bed monsters and too
fresh boys. But he wouldn't be, not yet, at least. He wished
Maxie would trust him more, to believe what he felt, that
delaying would be worse.

Half the night they'd talked about how to handle telling
Mimi he was her father. Kyle wanted to do it right away
and get on with any problems they might encounter. He
knew one thing—the news had to come from him. But Kyle
was the new guy, and Maxie knew their daughter better than
him, a point that gnawed on his guilt. It was his fault he
hadn't been there, and he was trying to get over it. Not
telling Mimi the truth was stopping him.

But he was out of time, for the next day or two at least.
He had a business to run. A business he'd let stand still for
almost two weeks while he discovered what it was like to
really live again.

Maxie entered the kitchen, sliding smoothly into his arms.

"She still sleeping?"

"Like a rock."

His lips curved. The only time his daughter was still, he
thought.

He pressed a kiss to the top of her head, then her mouth. "I know you want to take it slow—"

"Please, Kyle, give it just a couple of days."

"A couple days, Max, that's it."

She smiled gently. His determination was heartwarming. He wanted them both and quickly. "What I'd really like is for you to move in so I could wake up to you every morning." But they couldn't. It wouldn't set a good example for Mimi.

His hands smoothed over her behind, his fascination with that part of her body making him hard with just touching it. "I love you, baby."

"I know. I live for it."

Maxie kissed him, her heart aching a little. He moved with her toward the door, his arm wrapped around her waist. It was going to be dull without him for the next couple of days or so.

Kyle kissed her once more, then stepped away, striding quickly down the steps to his chopper. The rescue team had kindly brought it to him. *So much for my rule that no one flies her but me,* he thought, forcing himself not to look back. He was in the air before he chanced a look at her. She was on the porch, leaning again the post, watching him leave her again.

Later, Maxie was working in the barn when Mimi burst in.

"Where is he?" she demanded, hands on her hips.

Maxie ignored her daughter's sharp tone, sensing she was still overtired and needed more sleep. "Good morning, sweetie, you shouldn't be outside."

"Where did he go? What did you say to him to make him leave?"

Frowning, Maxie faced her daughter, the currycomb in her hand. She'd had tantrums before, like any kid, but never so vicious. "What are you talking about?"

"He's my daddy!"

Maxie's eyes widened. Oh, God.

"I heard Grandma and you talk about my daddy. I heard you call his name when you cried. He's my daddy, and you made him go away again!"

"Mimi, honey, calm down. You don't understand." This was too much, too soon.

"I hate you!" Mimi shouted, tears in her eyes.

"Wait a minute, young lady," her mother warned. "That attitude is going to get you grounded big-time."

"I don't care. You made him go. I hate you!" She stomped her foot, then whirled about, racing back to the house. Maxie started to follow, then stopped. She needed to cool down, she thought, plopping down onto a hay bale and covering her face with her hands.

A half hour later, Maxie returned to the house, bracing herself for another fight with a six-year-old. What she found was an empty house.

Kyle entered his offices, a clipboard in his hand as he scanned the next week's appointments. Too few, he thought. "Randy?" Kyle called to his assistant and bookkeeper. "Is this all?"

"Yeah. But I got six calls this morning. Two coming just to see what your choppers look like. Oh, you have a guest."

Kyle's gaze jerked up and pinned Randy. The younger man nodded to the closed office door.

"A female. Real looker, too."

Maxie. He strode to the office, shoving open the door. He froze at the sight of Mimi behind his desk. How did she get all the way here? He glanced around. Alone apparently. This was not good, he thought and tried for calm. He popped back out of the office, scribbling Maxie's number on a pad and telling Randy to call and let her know where her daughter was.

"Hey, short stack."

Mimi looked up, and Kyle felt as if hit by a sledgehammer at her teary eyes.

"Hullo," came sullenly.

"What are you doing here?" He tossed the clipboard on the sofa and came to sit on the edge of the desk. "Where's your mom?"

"I don't care." Mimi pouted, folding her arms over her chest. "I hate her."

His brows shot up and he straightened a bit. "Whoa, little lady. Is that a nice thing to say about your mom?"

"I don't care. She made you go."

"What makes you say that?"

"You left," she said plainly.

"I had to go to work."

Her lower lip curled down.

It was clear she wasn't seeing the logic. "Mimi," he said, rubbing the back of his neck. "How did you get here?"

"I walked."

Good God, that wasn't possible, and the alternative made his gut clench. "All the way?"

"No." She looked at her hands, then glanced up. "A lady gave me a ride."

Kyle came off the desk, looming like a taunted bear. "And you took it!"

Mimi cringed. "Yes," she said in a small voice.

"Sweet mother of God, Mimi. You could have been kidnapped, or worse! Do you realize that?"

"But I wanted to see you!"

"That's no excuse. You have to think before you risk things like that." He mashed his hand over his face, at a total loss as to how to handle this.

"You left."

His next words died on his lips. "Huh?" he said stupidly.

"You left us."

"I have a business to run—"

She shook her head wildly, crawling out of the big leather chair and standing before him. He stared down. She stared up.

"You're my daddy, aren't you?"

Kyle felt his legs give out and he sagged onto the desk. "Did your mom tell you that?"

"No." She told him about overhearing her grandmother and mom talk about him. "You're *that* Kyle." He nodded and half expected a smile. What he got was the blackest little-girl scowl he'd ever seen. "Why did you leave my mommy?"

Boy, this was hard. "Aw, Mimi, baby..." He reached for her, and his heart leaped when she went to him. He lifted her in his arms and sat her on his lap. "I was stupid, I didn't think of anything, except what I was feeling. I wanted to hurt your mom, 'cause she hurt me."

"Like me when I ran away and when I took that ride?"

"Yeah. It was a big mistake." He sighed heavily, then eyed her. "But I didn't risk my life."

Fat tears welled in her eyes and she sniffled. "I'm in big trouble, huh?"

"Oh, I'd say that was definite."

"You're mad at me, aren't you?"

"No, I'm just a little disappointed." Her expression crumbled, and Kyle knew he'd hit a nerve. "I know your mom taught you better," he said softly. "Did you think about what she's feeling right now, looking for you, worried that you're hurt and she can't help you?"

Mimi looked ashamed and remorseful, and Kyle figured that her mother would have a few things to say to her and that was about as much as a kid could take right now. He set her down, pointing to the chair. "Get your butt there and stay put. Understood?"

She nodded, flipping her braids over her shoulder as she scrambled into the chair.

Her eyes watery, her mouth turned down, she about broke his heart right there. Kyle stiffened against going soft on her. She'd risked more than he wanted to consider by running to him. But she *had* run to *him*.

"Do you love my mom?"

"Yes, very much."

Mimi grinned. "Are you going to get married?"

"Is that okay with you?"

"Yes."

"Good. 'Cause she said yes."

He was about to leave his office to call Maxie in private, when she burst in.

She looked to Kyle, then to the child curled in the chair. She opened her mouth.

"Max." Kyle caught her arm before she unleashed on her daughter. "Let's get you two home, and we can discuss this."

Maxie nodded, and Kyle gestured to Mimi. She left the chair, following her parents outside. "Where's your truck?" he said after a glance around.

"Jackson dropped me off. I couldn't drive. I was too scared to concentrate." She looked down at her daughter, and Mimi fairly hid behind Kyle.

He rubbed the top of her head, his lips curving gently before he nudged her forward to face her mother's angry stare. "I'll give you a lift."

"In the chopper?" Max squeaked.

She was afraid of heights, he recalled. "Got to trust me sometime, Max."

"I trust you."

"Yeah, sure." He opened the chopper door, and Mimi climbed in the back, glancing between her parents like a squirrel perched in a tree.

"Who didn't bother to tell me he lived on the other side of the canyon?" Max said, waving the business card he'd left her.

He arched a brow. "Who didn't bother to ask?"

She flushed red. True enough, she thought. "I do trust you, Kyle." Still Maxie didn't move.

"Then let me in, Max." He stepped closer. "All the way in," he said in a dark voice. "You have to let me be a part of everything. Not just what you pick and choose until she gets used to the idea that I'm her dad. Neither of us can help what happened in the past. But this—" he nodded to Mimi, her face tucked between the two seat backs "—this could have been avoided."

Maxie's eyes lit with green fire. "That was a chance—"

"She knows who I am," he interrupted. "And there's no getting around it this time."

"I know," Maxie muttered.

"She just wants us to be honest with her," he said. "And you need to get used to the idea that you are not alone anymore." He pressed his lips to her forehead. "Trust me on this." Kyle took a step back, then came around the front of the chopper to his side and climbed in. "Aren't you coming?" he said through the open passenger's side.

A chopper. High up, too high.

He put the headset on, one on Mimi and leaned out, extending his hand to her. "Come on, Max."

"Yeah, come on, Mom. It's fun."

She was still as a rock, her hands clenched, her gaze darting all around the chopper. He knew she was terrified to get in and worse, lift off.

"Hey, I'm willing to bend, but you have to start first."

She would, she knew it, and trusting him to put her safely back on the ground was something she'd easily give. It was the trip in between she was scared about. "I'm bending, I'm bending," she said, climbing in before she lost her nerve. "I've been in love with you for years and I'm trusting it now. And your skill as a pilot." He lifted off quickly.

"I'm proud of you, Max."

"Me too, Mom."

"Okay. I'm taking the risk." She couldn't look at the ground and looked at him instead. "Now, get on the ground and marry me, Kyle. Please."

"Yeah. Marry us...Dad."

Kyle's eyes watered, and he twisted in the seat, brushing his fingers along Mimi's jaw, then looking at Maxie. These women were his life, he thought. His hands on the control stick faltered, and the helicopter wobbled as they hovered over flight-legal canyon airspace.

Maxie inhaled, gripping the seat edge till her knuckles turned white. "You'd better hurry," she said. "Before I decorate the windshield!"

"Go ahead, if you feel the need."

"Kyle!"

He didn't want to laugh at what was obviously a horrifying experience and instead bit the inside of his mouth to keep from smiling. She wouldn't appreciate that right now. It was a long enough ride back now as it was. "I have to get you to a preacher before you change your mind." He swooped quickly, lowering the craft to the ground.

"Not this time." She let out a lungful of air and sighed back into the seat. Then she looked at him, her heart in her eyes. "My mind hasn't changed in seven years. I just wasn't listening very well."

He pried her fingers from the seat cushion and pulled her across the seat and into his arms. He kissed her, deeply, powerfully.

"You guys," came from the rear seat, followed by a soft giggle.

They pulled back and looked at their daughter. Kyle reached around Maxie and twisted the lock, then shoved open the door. "Get into the house and into your room, short stack. You're grounded."

Mimi looked wide-eyed at him, then at her mother, and Maxie knew she was weighing her options, the little devil. But Maxie wasn't about to let her daughter start their new life with playing them against each other—now that she had big-gun backup.

"You heard your dad." God, it felt good to say that aloud. "Beat it."

Mimi climbed out, sulking as she walked toward the house, a tiny smile working at her lips.

Maxie and Kyle watched her go.

"Kyle?"

"Hmm?" He dragged his gaze from Mimi's hunched form to her.

Her gaze sketched his features as she brushed a lock of hair off his forehead, letting it sift through her fingers. Oh, how she loved this man. He'd given her more than his love, his child—he'd given her freedom. She'd been trapped for so long.

"Thanks."

His forehead knitted slightly. "For loving you?"

"That—" she rubbed her thumb over the pad of her lips "—and for rescuing me from my own loneliness."

"Aw, baby," he said, the back of his eyes burning. "I'm the one who needed rescuing. You and Mimi, you brought me back from my own prison."

She leaned closer, brushing her mouth over his, teasing him, making him squirm in the seat. "Think about that when we're stuck in the house all day, with a child who's grounded. Talk about a prison sentence."

Kyle chuckled softy and covered her mouth with his, not thinking about disciplining a spirited little redheaded daughter, but of thanking God for the chance to love them both. Ah, he thought, sinking into her kiss. Life was suddenly very, very good.

Epilogue

Ten years later

Kyle came around the side of the barn and stopped short at the sight of his oldest daughter talking with a young man who looked far too dangerous to be even in the same state with her.

"Kyle, honey, will you put it into gear?"

He looked at his wife and his three other daughters impatiently waiting for their mounts.

"Yeah, Dad, get it into gear," Christa repeated, bouncing on the fence rail.

"What's zat mean?" came from his youngest, Brianne, as she climbed onto the fence beside her sister.

"Means Dad's being too slow." Kate, nine, folded her arms over her flat chest and wondered if her parents were going to kiss in public again. Gross.

Brianne looked at her dad, then her sister. "But he's not even moving."

"I know, silly." Christa rolled her eyes, and Maxie told them to behave as she crossed the paddock, hopped the fence and came to stand beside her husband.

"Hey, what fog has you captive?"

He looked down at her, smiling and inching closer. Every time he was near her, touched her, slept his nights away in her arms, he loved her more. Each day he realized a man didn't get this lucky and live to enjoy it. So he wasn't wasting a moment.

"Who's the guy?" He nodded to Mimi and the kid clad in way too much leather, his hair dangling over one eye and his butt hitched on the motorcycle seat.

"That's Jackson's nephew."

Kyle cast another look at the kid. "Well, I don't like him."

She laughed softly. "You don't even know him."

"I know *how* he's looking at my daughter, and that's all I need."

"Ooh—judgmental *and* a tyrant."

"Well, look at him, Max." He snapped his hand in the kid's direction. "He's got trouble written all over him."

"Careful, honey, that's exactly what *my* father said about *you.*"

He met her gaze, the protectiveness of a father melting into soft memories. He hadn't thought about the years they'd spent apart much and saw only the new ones mesh together and erase the wasted pain.

"Your dad likes me now."

A devilish glint brightened her eyes. "Yeah, but that's a marine thing, you know, old corps, buddies forever. You're still on probation."

"Gonna send me packing?"

"We could work out a deal." Out of anyone's view her hand slipped between them, shaping the hardness straining his jeans. Kyle groaned and swept his arm around her waist, pulling her tightly to his body. Four children, and she was still slim and sexy as hell. Ten years of marriage, and he still got hot for her on a regular basis and was continuously fascinated with the shape of her bottom in tight jeans. He cupped the spot, squeezing gently and pushing her to him.

"Oh, Kyle," she whispered.

"God, I love it when you say my name like that."

"It won't come out any other way when you touch me like that."

Christa and Brianne giggled. Kate rolled her eyes and stomped off, muttering something about her parents and how weird they were.

Kyle bent and kissed Maxie, his mouth riding lushly over the warm curves, his tongue pushing deep inside.

"I love you, baby."

Her heart skipped every time he said it. "I love you, too, Kyle."

"Way to go, Dad!" Mimi hollered, and Kyle looked up, winking at her. The boyfriend of the week snickered, and Mimi socked him in the arm for it. His *short stack* was a dead ringer for her mother, tall and leggy, and Kyle knew she could take care of herself. Especially since he'd trained her in marine hand-to-hand combat.

But that didn't mean he wouldn't be there for all the women in his life if they ever needed rescuing. Because their mother, he thought, staring down at Max and kissing her again and again—had rescued him.

And he was still loving every minute of being saved.

* * * * *

SILHOUETTE® *Desire*®

THE RULE BREAKERS

an exciting new series by
Leanne Banks

Meet The Rulebreakers: A millionaire, a bad boy, a protector. Three strong, sexy men who take on the ultimate challenge—love!

Coming in September 1998—MILLIONAIRE DAD

Joe Caruthers had it all. Who would have thought that a brainy beauty like Marley Fuller—pregnant with his child—would cause this bachelor with everything to take the plunge?

Coming in October 1998—
THE LONE RIDER TAKES A BRIDE

Bad boy Ben Palmer had rebelled against falling in love, until he took the lovely, sad-eyed Amelia Russell on a moonlit ride.

Coming in November 1998—THIRTY-DAY FIANCÉ

Nick Nolan had to pretend to be engaged to his childhood friend Olivia Polnecek. Why was Nick noticing how perfect a wife she could be—for real!

Available at your favorite retail outlet.

Silhouette®

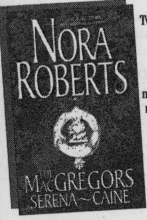
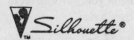

MEN at WORK

All work and no play?
Not these men!

October 1998
SOUND OF SUMMER by *Annette Broadrick*

Secret agent Adam Conroy's seductive gaze
could hypnotize a woman's heart. But it was
Selena Stanford's body that needed saving—
when she stumbled into the middle of an
espionage ring and forced Adam out of
hiding....

November 1998
GLASS HOUSES by *Anne Stuart*

Billionaire Michael Dubrovnik never lost a
negotiation—until Laura de Kelsey Winston
changed the boardroom rules. He might
acquire her business...but a kiss would cost
him his heart....

December 1998
FIT TO BE TIED by *Joan Johnston*

Matthew Benson had a way with words
and women—but he refused to be tied
down. Could Jennifer Smith get him to
retract his scathing review of her art by
trying another tactic: tying him *up*?

Available at your favorite retail outlet!

MEN AT WORK™

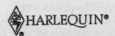 

SILHOUETTE®
Desire

COMING NEXT MONTH

#1183 THE PERFECT FIT—Cait London
The Tallchiefs
Corporate cowboy Nick Palladin, December's *Man of the Month*, would never exchange his sacred bachelorhood for a bride, especially not for saucy Silver Tallchief. His matchmaking family might force him to work, live and *sleep* beside the exquisite virgin, but this rugged loner would keep his distance, the best he could....

#1184 THE SHERIFF AND THE IMPOSTOR BRIDE
—Elizabeth Bevarly
Follow That Baby!
Sheriff Riley Hunter had tracked down the wrong woman—but Rachel Jensen wasn't about to tell this temptation in a taut tan uniform that he'd mistaken her for her pregnant twin sister. He'd see soon enough she wasn't showing. But by then would *he* be showing...his newfound love?

#1185 MARRIAGE, OUTLAW STYLE—Cindy Gerard
Outlaw Hearts
When sworn enemies sultry Maddie Brannigan and surly Clay James woke up naked in the same bed, they didn't know whether to make love or war. Could a surprise baby on the way have this sparring couple calling a truce...and each other Mr. and Mrs.?

#1186 HIS ULTIMATE TEMPTATION—Susan Crosby
Lone Wolves
He was fiercely protective of everyone he loved. And that need to safe-guard his family had caused millionaire Ben O'Keefe to lose the only woman he'd ever wanted. Yet now he was stranded with his ultimate temptation, and Ben vowed to make the lovely Leslie his...for always.

#1187 THE MILLIONAIRE'S CHRISTMAS WISH
—Shawna Delacorte
This millionaire bachelor had one Christmas wish: to remain a fancy-free playboy. And Chance Fowler couldn't help but pucker up and plant one on sweet, sensible Marcie Roper. But delivering wayward kisses could have this Prince Charming granting *her* greatest holiday hope: a husband!

#1188 JUST A LITTLE BIT MARRIED?—Eileen Wilks
Beautiful Sara Grace never imagined that she'd still be single on her hon-eymoon! And she never dreamed she'd be nervously searching for the words to invite her groom—a dangerous, enigmatic stranger named Raz Rasmussin—to stay with her on their wedding night...and forever.

"There's a [...] **other, Anni** [...] **already a c** [...] **sure about."** [...]

"Such as?" Annie knew she was going to hate herself in the morning for asking that question.

Putting his hands on her shoulders, he turned her to face him, and with one index finger he pushed her hair behind her ear. "Well, we know we probably won't agree on the future of the mill."

Her heart was hammering in her throat. "That's true."

"And we know our lives and backgrounds are totally different."

"That's true too." There seemed to be less and less air in the room, and his face seemed to be getting closer and closer.

"We know there might not be a lot of time for us," he said.

She nodded. Speech seemed impossible.

"You know I want you, and I know you want me."

"I know," she said softly. Then, unable to stand the suspense any longer, she closed the distance between their lips. Without a thought in her head or a warning in her heart, she leaned into the strong, lean contours of his body. She hadn't realized how much she wanted him to kiss her until that moment. He may not have gone to college or seen much of the world, but the man really knew how to kiss. . . .

WHAT ARE *LOVESWEPT* ROMANCES?

They are stories of true romance and touching emotion. We believe those two very important ingredients are constants in our highly sensual and very believable stories in the *LOVESWEPT* line. Our goal is to give you, the reader, stories of consistently high quality that may sometimes make you laugh, sometimes make you cry, but are always fresh and creative and contain many delightful surprises within their pages.

Most romance fans read an enormous number of books. Those they truly love, they keep. Others may be traded with friends and soon forgotten. We hope that each *LOVESWEPT* romance will be a treasure—a "keeper." We will always try to publish

LOVE STORIES YOU'LL NEVER FORGET
BY AUTHORS YOU'LL ALWAYS REMEMBER

The Editors

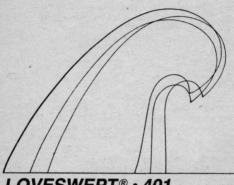

LOVESWEPT® • 401

Mary Kay McComas
Lovin' a Good
Ol' Boy

BANTAM BOOKS
NEW YORK • TORONTO • LONDON • SYDNEY • AUCKLAND

LOVIN' A GOOD OL' BOY

A Bantam Book / May 1990

LOVESWEPT® and the wave device are registered
trademarks of Bantam Books, a division of
Bantam Doubleday Dell Publishing Group, Inc.
Registered in U.S. Patent
and Trademark Office and elsewhere.

If you would be interested in receiving protective vinyl
covers for your Loveswept books, please write to this address
for information:

Loveswept
Bantam Books
P.O. Box 985
Hicksville, NY 11802

ISBN 0-553-44027-6

Published simultaneously in the United States and Canada

Bantam Books are published by Bantam Books, a division
of Bantam Doubleday Dell Publishing Group, Inc. Its trademark, consisting of the words "Bantam Books" and the
portrayal of a rooster, is Registered in U.S. Patent and
Trademark Office and in other countries. Marca Registrada.
Bantam Books, 666 Fifth Avenue, New York, New York 10103.

PRINTED IN THE UNITED STATES OF AMERICA

OPM   0 9 8 7 6 5 4 3 2 1

This book is dedicated to
the good ol' boy I married.

Yankee: Anyone who is not from Kentucky, Virginia, Tennessee, North Carolina, South Carolina, Georgia, Florida, Alabama, Mississippi, Louisiana, Arkansas, Texas and possibly Oklahoma and West-by-God-Virginia. A Yankee may become an honorary Southerner, but a Southerner can not become a Yankee, assuming any Southerner wanted to.

Good ol' boy: Any Southern male between the ages of 16 and 60 who has an amiable disposition and is fond of boon companions, strong drink, hound dawgs, fishin', huntin' and good-lookin' women, but not necessarily in that order.

Steve Mitchell and Sam C. Rawls
How to Speak Southern
BANTAM BOOKS

One

AMBITIOUS, UP-AND-COMING YOUNG CORPORATE EXECUTIVE WITH PROMISING FUTURE . . .

"No," Anne Hunnicut said aloud, deciding that the newspaper headline she was fantasizing about didn't describe her well enough. She started over. FAIRLY ATTRACTIVE COLUMBIA GRADUATE; COMPUTER-LITERATE CORPORATE EXECUTIVE WITH PROMISING FUTURE; OWNER OF MIDTOWN APARTMENT AND REALLY NICE CHINESE ART COLLECTION, FOUND DEAD ON A DESERTED ROAD EARLY THURSDAY EVENING, IN THE BACKWOODS OF KENTUCKY.

"Details on page thirty-two," she added, giving in to her drooping spirits. She hoped her boss, Calvin Schwab, would read it and feel never-ending guilt over the lengths he'd driven her to.

Standing beside a useless, smoke-belching rental car in the middle of nowhere, Anne wondered whether exposing herself to any number of perilous situations was mentioned in her job description.

"This isn't all that scary, Anne," she told herself, trying to bolster her courage. She kept her voice low to avoid disturbing the wildlife that lurked in the nearby underbrush. She hadn't actually *seen* any wild animals yet, but it hadn't been hard for her fearful imagination to convince her that they were there, watching her, waiting to attack her when she was most vulnerable.

"This isn't any worse than standing all alone, totally defenseless in the middle of Central Park," she said, casting a wary glance at the tall, deciduous trees lining both sides of the road. They looked like not-so-friendly green giants.

The nightmare she was presently participating in was probably just as much her own fault as anyone else's, she admitted. Other job opportunities had been open to her over the past few years. But she'd been at Harriman Industries for so long, it had become one of life's little challenges to her to prove that she was as capable as any man there.

The textile industry was run primarily by men. It was notoriously chauvinistic. From the top of the line to the bottom of the barrel, every mother's son of them had the innate belief that a woman had no place in the industry, aside from being a manual laborer or a clerical worker, of course. It was a man's profession. It always had been and it always would be. Amen.

Anne had heard it all before. And she wasn't impressed. She had cut her teeth on trying to keep up with three older brothers. Comparatively speaking, proving herself in a corporation was like child's play. Closing down a textile mill couldn't possibly be any harder than learning how to slam dunk at the age of ten had been.

For years now, all the big projects and really juicy jobs had gone to the men in the office. Time after time she had been passed over because she "lacked the specific skills needed for the task." She knew as well as they did that the only thing she lacked was an overabundance of androgens. She was as competent as any man at Harriman, except that she couldn't handle a fifth of scotch as well and she didn't have any sordid sexual conquests to boast about.

When the problems developed at Webster Textiles, she had all but begged Calvin Schwab to let her handle them. He had hemmed and hawed for so long that she hadn't thought he'd let her. But in the end she had prevailed. She'd told him that if she couldn't settle the dispute successfully, she'd come back, chain herself to her computer, and fade quietly into the woodwork. Now look at her. She gave the rental car a swift kick in the tire.

That was when she heard it. The moment she had been hoping for and dreading at the same time had arrived. A car was coming down the road.

She heard it, and she turned expectantly, waiting for Lord only knew what to come around the bend in the road.

Having lived her entire life north of Philadelphia and east of Chicago, Anne wasn't sure what to expect in Kentucky. But she'd seen movies and heard stories about southerners and was of the general opinion that she wasn't going to have a whole lot in common with them. Well, she could probably learn how to drink mint juleps with the belles or swap corn recipes, but chewing and spitting tobacco was out of the question, and she'd rather die than call a hog.

A big, shiny black Ford pickup truck came barreling around the corner, then slowed immediately. She had envisioned something a little older and spotted with paint primer, but at this point she was far more interested in the condition of the driver and whether or not he'd stop to help her.

When he came to a stop several yards behind her car, she breathed a sigh of relief, and when he looked to be normal in appearance, she breathed another.

She didn't like making automatic judgments

about people, but she'd had no experience with the people who lived in these mountains. She was scared spitless that she'd hear dueling banjo music. It was an irrational fear, of course, but so was hydrophobia. Fear was fear, whether it made sense or not. She wanted to be open-minded. She had a tendency to believe that most people were pretty much the same. But then again, it was always better to be safe than sorry.

The first thing she noticed when the man got out of his truck was that he wasn't carrying a banjo or a shotgun. He was tall and lean with very broad shoulders and a slow, loose gait that gave her the impression that he thought he had all day to waste getting from his truck to her car. Taking brisk city steps, she met him halfway.

"Thank heaven you stopped," she said. "I was beginning to wonder if I'd ever see another human. I feel as if I've been stranded here for days."

"Afternoon, ma'am," he said, his voice low and soft; his smile amiable. "Car trouble?"

Given that the hood was up, the doors were open, and the car was billowing steam and smoke all over the road, his question seemed slightly redundant to Anne, but she answered anyway.

"Oh, the stupid thing. First its little red lights were flashing, and then it started smoking, and then finally it just stopped dead," she said, knowing it was usually wise to give the impression of being the reputed dumb blonde in situations like this. Her hair was auburn, but that didn't matter. It was the innocuous stupidity that always got to the male ego in these instances and encouraged them to be helpful. Besides, she always had been pretty stupid where cars were concerned. "If—if it had a flat tire, I'd know what to do. My father made a point of showing me how to change a tire. But he never said anything about smoke."

As he came closer, she got a better look at her

rescuer. Normal didn't do him justice. As a matter of fact, he was very nice looking in an earthy, rugged way. Under a cap with an emblem that said MADE IN AMERICA, his dark hair was brushed back away from his face. He had a square jaw and broad cheekbones. His nose was straight and his lips were full. He had rather a nice mouth, actually. She couldn't see his eyes behind the dark glasses he wore.

There wasn't anything extraordinary about him; there was just something about his face that impressed her. Character, maybe. Or the unique quality that distinguishes one person from another, which appears even in the faces of identical twins and makes them individuals. She wasn't sure why, but she liked his face instantly.

He ambled past her to the open hood of the car and peered in. He seemed to know just what he was looking for, because he turned his head toward her and said, "Your fan belt's gone."

"Gone?" She'd heard about fan belts. They were usually broken not gone.

"Must've broke a ways back, and you lost it. I've got an extra, but it won't fit your car. Gotta go to town for one."

What did that mean, she wondered. In New York it would have meant that it was time to find a phone and call her auto club. She had exhausted that possibility two hours earlier and she now prayed it meant something entirely different in Kentucky. She was casually taking in his long legs and very nice tush, when he turned and pressed them up against the car. He leaned back and crossed his arms over his chest as if he were waiting to see what she was going to do about the situation.

"Is the town very far from here?" she asked. "I'm not even too sure of where I am. I was heading for Webster."

"It's down that way, toward Knott County, about ten miles," he said, tilting his head in the direction she had been driving before the car died.

"You visitin'?"

"Ah. No. Not really. I'm here on business." She didn't want to say too much about why she was there for fear he wouldn't help her. She had a feeling that the people of Webster were not going to welcome her with open arms.

She could tell that he wanted to ask what her business was, but he didn't. Instead, he took off his glasses. Anne fought an urge to rush up and put them back over his eyes. Added to the rest of his features, his eyes made all the difference in the world in his appearance. They were green, or maybe hazel. But it wasn't the color so much as their expression that threw her for a loop.

His eyes were keen and intense, making a mockery of his loose, lazy stance. They revealed a confidence in the man that was staggering. They all but shouted, "I'm-an-all-American-man-and-I-wouldn't-have-it-any-other-way." Anne had never seen anyone like him before. His confidence went beyond bold and cocky to something so ingrained that he quite obviously took his membership in the Superior Gender Club as something ordained by God and therefore unquestionable.

Oh, Anne had seen arrogant men before. She'd grown up with three of them—her brothers. Later, she had come to know men with an overabundance of pride, men full of self-conceit, and others with a great deal of impertinence. But this one was a dilly. This man was so blatantly male and so secure in his manhood that he could probably make a bull blush, she decided.

And there he was, boldly assessing her as if she were a side of prime grade A beef. The merriment in his hazel eyes was irritating, and his audacity was making her madder by the minute. She tried to ignore his behavior, but she grew warm under his prolonged scrutiny, all too aware of her circumstances.

Tolerance had its limits though. And rude was just plain rude.

"I really wish you'd stop staring at me," she said bluntly.

"Why?"

"Because pound per pound I'm more expensive than any other piece of meat in this whole damned state, mister. And you just plain can't afford it," she told him when his impertinent staring had finally gnawed her nerves in half. His eyebrows shot up as if he were surprised by this bit of news, and amusement settled into his expression.

Anne didn't need this. She really didn't. It was proving to be one of the longest, most nerve-racking days she'd ever experienced. Lord, what a face he had, she thought to herself, and great buns too. Maybe walking to Webster and getting someone there to help her wasn't such a bad idea after all. This man was making her as jumpy and nervous as a cat in a fiddle factory—so to speak.

"Hey. Where you goin'?" he called as she snatched her purse out of her car and started to walk away.

"To Webster. To find someone who'll be gentleman enough to help me without staring at me. I don't like being stared at," she said without looking back at him.

"You'll never make it in those shoes," he said, laughter ringing in his voice.

Anne stopped and looked at her high-heeled shoes. Then she looked back at him. He was still lounging against the rental car as though he hadn't a care in the world, a late May breeze rustling the sleeves of his shirt. Balancing on one foot at a time, she took her shoes off and moved on.

She'd taken several yards off her journey before she heard rapid steps coming up behind her. Images of the mentally deranged southerners she'd seen in the movies flashed through her mind. For all she knew, his family tree could look like a bamboo shoot, straight up with no branches, insanity flowing through its hollow center. She almost started running, except there hadn't been anything crazy in the man's eyes. There had been too much certainty, too much amusement, and too much awareness, but no craziness. Intuitively, she knew it would be wiser to stand up to him than run from him.

She stiffened indignantly when she felt his fingers wrap around her upper arm. She turned to face him.

"Jeez, you Yankee gals sure are prickly," he said, grinning. Unfortunately, he had the sexiest smile she'd ever seen. Full, malleable lips spread across even white teeth, crinkling the skin around his eyes and forming deep oversize dimples in his cheeks. "I was just lookin' at ya. Do they have a law against lookin' at pretty women where you're from?"

Anne wasn't going to dignify that with an answer. She looked down her nose at the sun-darkened hand on her arm, refusing to acknowledge the strange fluttering in her stomach and the way her heart raced when he touched her.

"Okay. I'm sorry," he said, releasing her. Anne saw the humor fade from his face, replaced by a sincerely contrite expression. "I was rude."

"Yes, you were." Sheepishness wasn't something that came naturally to him, and Anne found it hard to resist. She smiled. "Do you stare at all *Yankee* women like that? Is it something I ought to get used to while I'm here?"

He laughed. It was a soft, rumbling chuckle in his chest that Anne found very appealing. "Well, yes, ma'am. I do think you should get used to it. But it's not because you're a Yankee."

This time his admiring gaze made Anne blush. He'd tempered it with a little more respect and a lot more goodwill, and it was nothing but complimentary. Self-conscious and suddenly feeling awkward, Anne smiled and glanced away.

"Look. I was just goin' into town anyway. If you don't mind hangin' around till I finish the stuff I have to do, you can go with me. We can pick up a belt, and I'll fix your car on my way home. How's that?"

Any other time his suggestion might have made all the hair on the back of her neck stand up in alarm. But any other time she wouldn't have had a long wait on a desolate mountain road ahead of her either. She agreed to go with him.

He took the keys out of the ignition and moved her luggage from the back seat of the car, where she had put it for convenience, into the trunk for safekeeping. Then he led the way back to his truck and held the door open for her.

Even though the truck was only about two and a half feet off the ground, it could have been a couple of stories high for all the trouble Anne had getting into it. Her straight, tailored skirt had not been designed with trucking in mind. She tried several different leg maneuvers until she finally yanked her skirt up around her thighs in frustration and tried it again. When this also proved hopeless, and her only alternative was to crawl in head first, she reluctantly turned to her companion for assistance. She found him standing close behind her, still holding the door open and watching her with great relish.

The man was impossible.

Unaccustomed to feeling so miserably helpless, Anne put her hands on her hips and fought to maintain what was left of her shattered dignity, while she watched him make a huge production of drawing on a straight face. He released the door, clicked his heels, gave her a small graceful bow, and then very politely said, "May I?"

Anne's backbone sagged a little bit; she sighed and closed her eyes. But before she had time to reopen them or to think of how he planned to get her into the truck, he stepped forward and removed her hands from her hips. He placed his own hands where hers had been, and then lifted her up into the air, plopping her down on the seat. He could just as easily have shaken her like a rattle and set her on her head for the effect it had on her, she was so surprised.

It all happened so quickly. Her eyes came open. Somehow, her hands had come to rest on his shoulders, and with his fingers remaining at her waist, they came face to face with mere inches separating them. The brim of his cap shaded the sun from his eyes and made them seem darker and more intense. Anne swallowed hard, trying to control the erratic skipping and thumping of her heart. She was only vaguely aware that her hands were trembling at his shoulders, but it didn't seem important to remove them just then.

He was wearing such a strange expression that Anne's focus on the world narrowed to the circumference of his face as she tried to decipher it. It was almost as if he'd come to a decision of some kind. His face was full of determination and that confidence she'd seen before. Odd thing was, she also had a feeling that his resolve had something to do with her.

"You know, my granny used to grow pansies in a flower box on her front porch. Your eyes are that same shade of purple." His speech had gentle southern inflections that were as smooth and intoxicating as Kentucky bourbon.

"What?" Anne liked his voice and the odd way

he spoke. She could have listened to him talk all afternoon.

"Your eyes. They're as pretty as my granny's pansies."

His granny's pansies? That was exactly the sort of corn syrup stuff her brothers and the guys in the office had warned her about. They'd been teasing her for days, telling her to beware of all the charming southern gentlemen she would meet on her first official business trip. She wanted to brush the remark off as hokum, but for some odd reason she was terribly flattered. Maybe it was the soft way he said it—and the way he kept looking at her.

"My eyes," she said, trying to sound unaffected, wanting him to say more.

"Mm. They're real pretty." He ought to know, he was looking at them hard enough, she thought, growing warm under his intense inspection.

He looked deeply into her eyes as if he were looking for her soul. And then, suddenly, he seemed to reach in and wrench something away from her. That scared her, and she immediately pulled away.

He didn't try to hold her. He stepped back and waited for her to move her legs inside so he could close the door. Shaken to the core, Anne took several deep breaths in an effort to calm herself and tried to find something else to think about. While he walked around to the driver's side she took note of the truck's black interior, the cooler over the lump in the middle of the floor, and the rifle racked in the rear window.

She found nothing else to ease her distress or relieve her mind by the time he slid effortlessly into the cab beside her. She was immediately aware of the smell of lilacs, warm, musky lilacs, and knew it was his aftershave or the soap he used.

"It must help to have long legs. Getting in. To

the truck, I mean. It must help to have long legs," she stammered, extremely ill at ease, acutely aware of everything about him—including his long legs.

He glanced down at her legs, his gaze lingering a trifle too long before he looked up and said, "Yep."

He put his dark glasses back on, turned the key in the ignition, and put the truck in gear. The silence between them was thicker than the dense green forest that hung over the road and cupped it on both sides like a tunnel. Anne began to feel claustrophobic. The man seem to fill the whole cab with his presence, leaving so little room for her that she could hardly breathe.

What had happened back there, she wondered, trying to shake the strange, possessed feeling she was having. It was as if he'd said something very important to her in a foreign language, and now it was imperative that she learn the language in order to understand him. Or it was as if he'd planted a seed in her brain and it would be weeks before it sprouted and became identifiable.

Maybe it was voodoo. Did people practice that sort of stuff in this part of the South, she wondered. Mountain people had spells and potions, too, didn't they? It seemed to her that Granny Clampet was always doing strange things like that on the *Beverly Hillbillies*. And that sort of thing was usually based on fact. Anne's mind began to run amok with the possibilities.

"How long are you stayin'?"

"What?" she yelped, startled from her eerie thoughts.

"Will you be here long?" He repeated his question and gave her a quizzical look.

"I'm not sure," she told him honestly. *I hope not*, she added mentally, watching the scenery flash by. "You know, I think I can honestly say that I have never in all my life seen so many trees before," she said, pondering the vast expanse of wooded knolls and valleys that spread out before them as they topped a steep hill and started down the other side. "It's really beautiful here."

He nodded, and she saw him look out at the land with tremendous pride and something that looked very much like reverence. She could tell that she'd said the right thing, that her words had pleased him. Remarkably, that pleased her.

Less than an hour earlier, she'd found the woods frightening. But she felt relatively safe now. Nothing could creep out from behind a tree to harm her. She felt secure enough to take a really good look at the incredible beauty around her. It was lush and green and looked healthier than any place she'd ever seen before.

Healthy. It was a strange word to use to describe scenery, but it was a true description. The land was strong and vibrant and full of life.

Birds flapped their wings through clear, fresh air. The leaves on the trees rustled in a gentle breeze. Spring flowers bloomed in abundance, and their fragrance filled Anne with a sense of well-being. The contrast to the concrete and asphalt she was used to was like the difference between natural spring water and the water that came chemically treated, distilled, carbonated, and bottled from the corner grocery.

"Have you lived here all your life?" she asked, thinking that he suited the environment he lived in, wondering if she looked as well suited to hers.

"Sure. My kin moved down here from Letcher County during the Depression to work in the factory. We've been here ever since."

"Do you ever think of leaving?" she asked, knowing that in a few short weeks he might have to do just that to earn a living.

"Leave Kentucky?"

Anne nodded.

"I'd rather cut off my legs," he said shortly and with such conviction that it startled Anne, though the underlying anger she heard in his voice was to be expected. If he worked at the mill in Webster, as most of the people in the area did, he knew it was about to be closed. She decided that it might be best for her to let the subject drop for now.

She kept her eyes trained on the roadside as they entered the town of Webster. The closer they got to the town the more houses there were, until the residences lined the street one right after another. Some were brick, some were wooden. Some were tidy and well kept, others looked like garbage dumps. Most were about the same size and style; none were too elaborate. Factory towns were factory towns, she guessed, whether they were located in Pennsylvania, New York, or Kentucky. But wherever they were, it was always plain to see that it wasn't the people who lived in the town who were getting rich off the factory they worked in.

"Will we be going past McKee's Motel?" she asked.

"Yes, ma'am. It's just a ways up the road."

"Well, if you could drop me off there, I could go ahead and check into my room, and then you wouldn't have to drag me all over town with you while you did your errands. You could come back for me later."

"Yes, ma'am." He wasn't much of a talker. Yes, ma'am. No, ma'am. She wished he'd stop calling her that. It made her feel ninety-two years old.

"My name's Anne," she said, giving him an alternative.

"Buck," he said.

Instead of letting her out in front of the motel, he pulled in and parked in front of the office. He got out while Anne slid to the ground on her side of the truck.

"Makin' it okay?" he asked from the front of the truck.

"Oh, yes. It's a lot easier getting out." She smiled at him for his thoughtfulness.

"Sorry to hear that," he muttered, letting his disappointment show.

Anne rolled her eyes heavenward and gave a weary sigh. How could anyone be so aggravating and so appealing at the same time? She had a feeling her visit to Webster was going to be very, very long, no matter how many days she stayed.

He was holding the office door open for her, but she didn't pass through. "If you know about how long you'll be, I can be waiting out front when you come back," she said, not wanting to cause him any extra inconvenience.

"A couple of hours, maybe."

"Fine. I'll be waiting." She walked into the office simply assuming that the man would go about his own business. She was dumbfounded when he stepped up to the desk and slapped the palm of his hand down over the little bell for assistance.

Before she could tell him that she didn't need any help checking into a motel, a short, gray-haired man with a moustache and black horn-rimmed glasses came through a door behind the desk and saw him.

"Buck, you hound dog. Don't tell me you and Bryce got your nights mixed up again," he said in greeting, laughter crackling in his voice.

The man at her side laughed and cleared his throat at the same time, looking a little self-conscious. "Not this time, Jimmy. This is an all-night customer," he said, motioning to Anne with his head. She wondered if she was supposed to be flattered or grateful for the general announcement that she wasn't a woman who'd only be spending *part* of the night at the motel. She felt an embarrassed heat moving up into her cheeks.

"Well, where'd an ol' boy like you find somethin'
as pretty as this little gal?" the motel keeper asked,
already passing a friendly, speculative glance in
her direction. He must have liked what he saw,
because he moved up and leaned on the counter in
front of her without looking away.

"Picked her up off the road into town."

Anne gasped. He made it sound as though she
were a stray dog.

"Literally," she said, with a straight face as she
turned to stare blankly at the man who had rescued her, and then back at Jimmy McKee. "But
that was after my car broke down."

"Car trouble, eh?" the older man said. This led
to a very long conversation between the two men
about what exactly had happened to her car, who
had the best supply of fan belts in town, and the
time the exact same thing happened to the older
man somewhere outside Lexington.

Anne wasn't an impatient person. In fact, she'd
always thought of herself as being exceedingly
tolerant. Hadn't she put up with Harriman Industries longer than she should have just to prove a
point? Hadn't she tried to forbear the man's inso-
lence back on the road? Wasn't she being good
just standing there while they talked on and on as
if she weren't there at all? How much more was
she supposed to put up with?

"Excuse me," she broke in as politely as she
could. "I'd really like a room, please. I have a
reservation."

"Ms. Hunnicut," the old man said, looking surprised to see her.

"You know my name?"

"Well, we don't get many reservations. Mostly
drop-ins, travelers. And occasionally a mixed-up
brother," he said, winking at Buck.

"A mixed-up brother?" she asked, looking from
one to the other.

"They take turns at—"

"Just give the lady her key, Jimmy," her rescuer broke in with a chuckle. "She doesn't need to hear that story."

The motel owner grinned at them but didn't finish his explanation. Instead he gave a card to Anne, asking her to fill it out, and then he turned to get a room key from a rack behind him.

"Anne Hunnicut," the man said, reading the card over her shoulder. "Nice name."

"Thanks. My father gave it to me."

"My last name's LaSalle. Buck LaSalle."

"Buck LaSalle?" she repeated. Her heart sank into her shoes.

TWO

Anne's room wasn't even kissin' kin to a room at the Ritz, but it was clean and adequate. She washed her face and hands and then reapplied what little makeup she wore, trying to pretend it would make her feel better. It didn't.

She stretched out on top of the bed with her hands behind her head and began to plan her strategy against Buck LaSalle.

"The first person I meet in Webster would be him," she complained, bemoaning her misfortune out loud. LaSalle and his younger brother were the ringleaders, or spokesmen, as they called themselves, for a large group of workers who were refusing to comply with corporate headquarters in New York to prepare for the closing of the mill. They had demanded that a company representative be sent to hear their grievances, and they indicated that if the company executives wanted the factory closed, the company executives would have to close it. As far as they were concerned, business would go on as usual until certain of their demands were met.

It had all been pretty impressive coming from what Calvin Schwab had referred to as "a bunch of hillbillies." More often than not, when a factory closed, it closed quietly. The only reason Mr. Harriman had bothered to concern himself with the Webster mill was because he didn't want news of this closing to go slamming into the newspapers. He wanted it handled quietly.

That was Anne's job. As an assistant controller, she was also there to go over the financial records and to make sure that everything was in order. One of the main reasons she had been allowed to come was that she would be able to explain to the workers why it was economically impossible for Harriman Industries to keep the factory open and what financial arrangements had been made to compensate the workers.

Somewhere in the back of her mind she'd been hoping that it was an accident that Buck LaSalle could write an intelligent, forceful letter, that he was one of those people who sounded smart if he had a dictionary in front of him but was actually quite dense in person.

Needless to say, Buck LaSalle wasn't anything like what she had expected him to be. No banjo. No gun—except for the rifle in his truck, and it hadn't been permanently attached to his shoulder. No beer belly. His clothes were clean. He didn't chew or spit anything black and disgusting. He even had teeth. Worst of all, she decided, thinking of his sharp, intuitive green eyes, he didn't look stupid. Cocky and rude, maybe, but not stupid.

Perhaps the crux of her uneasiness lay in the fact that as obnoxious as he was at times, she liked him. There was something very solid and basically trustworthy about him. Oh, he was a brassy one all right. But underneath it all, she instinctively sensed a core of gold.

However, she decided, sitting up on her bed with a new resolve, she couldn't let her personal feelings for Buck LaSalle sway her. So he was a little brighter and bolder than she had antici-pated. *So what?* she asked herself. She had a job to do. Nothing and no one was going to stand in her way. Long ago she had learned that determination could eventually overpower height, skill, and experience in nearly every sport she had ever pursued. It could overcome Buck LaSalle as well.

She repeated this over and over, steeling herself to succeed. The two hours Buck had planned to be busy elsewhere were almost over. He'd come looking for her soon, and then she could make the situation perfectly clear to him. She'd needed time to regroup her resources when she'd first discovered who he was. She'd given him fifty dollars for a fan belt and had practically run all the way to her room before he could see how confused she was. But she was okay now. She'd arranged for her car to be repaired on her own. She could handle him. She'd close that damn mill come hell, high water, or Buck LaSalle.

As if on cue, there was a knock on her door. She socked the mattress with her fist to psych herself up, and then she scrambled off the bed to answer it.

He was braced against the doorjamb with his hands, his glasses dangling from his fingers. For the first time she took in the blue-and-gray plaid shirt worn open at the neck to reveal a stark white T-shirt, jeans that were snug, well worn, and that outlined the lower half of his body with undeniable accuracy, and she swallowed hard. Then she looked at the happy grin on his face and felt a light lifting sensation in her stomach.

That he was extremely male was not a sudden revelation to Anne. But it was certainly something she was becoming increasingly uncomfortable with. It was a weird perception for her. She spent most of her time with men. She was used to coming into close proximity with men. She was comfortable with the idea that some people were men and some were women. But she'd never, ever felt as soft, as . . . female as she did standing toe to toe with Buck LaSalle.

"Ready?" he asked in a cheerful voice, unaware that everything had changed between them in the past two hours. His gaze gave her a quick once-over, coming up to meet hers full of lurid questions and possibilities. His smile was now a smirk.

Anne frowned in confusion and looked down at her feet. She'd forgotten to put her shoes back on. Her suit was rumpled and her blouse was hanging out suggestively. No, she sure didn't look ready to go anywhere.

She straightened her spine and looked out past his left shoulder before addressing the situation.

"Mr. LaSalle—"

"Buck."

"Buck. Umm. I wanted to thank you for helping me today. It was very nice of you, and I'm sorry I put you to all that trouble. But the car's been taken care of."

It was his turn to frown and be confused. "I don't understand."

"While you were gone, I asked Mr. McKee to call the garage. They'll put a new belt in it and drive it into town for me."

"But why?" Now he looked hurt and confused. Anne sighed. She was making a mess of this.

"Well, it's not because I didn't appreciate what you did. I was scared to death out there all alone," she blurted out. "I—I simply think it's better that I don't put myself too deeply into a position of being indebted to you for anything else."

"Indebted?"

"Beholden to you."

Now his frown was stormy and angry. Great. She'd hurt him and insulted him in less than sixty seconds. She was pretty sure this wasn't listed under How to Have Good Labor Relations.

"I never had any intention of askin' for anything for helpin' you. If you're still mad about the way I was lookin' at you back there, that didn't have anything to do with it. I'd'a helped you even if ya looked like a cow."

"Oh, I'm sure you would have. I'm not doing this very well, Buck. I . . . maybe I should tell you who I am. Then you'll understand what I'm trying to say here."

His anger subsided, but just a little, as he put the hand with the glasses on his hip and leaned impatiently on the other, waiting for her to explain.

"I'm an assistant controller at Harriman Industries, and I've come to shut the mill down." She wasn't a beat-around-the-bush person. She liked to get unpleasant things over with. She braced herself for his reaction to the news.

He just stood there. Completely unimpressed.

"So now you see," she said, wondering if he did, in fact, understand.

He shook his head. "I don't see what it's got to do with my fixin' your fan belt."

"Well, maybe it doesn't," she said, feeling a little foolish. "It's just that I thought that maybe if you knew who I was, you wouldn't want to help me."

"Oh. That's rich. And you called *me* rude?" He looked back over his shoulder as if looking at her was revolting. Anne's heart grew tight and painful. When he finally turned back to her, she could see that he was very angry. "I'm not some fancy-pants city person who doesn't give a damn about anybody but himself. I'm somebody who, when he sees somebody in need of a hand, lends one. How many Yankees you reckon come here to Webster on business, Annie?"

He very obviously wanted her to answer.

She shrugged. "I don't know."

"Hardly any." And with that he turned to leave.

"You knew who I was?" she asked, reaching out to touch his arm and keep him from going away.

"You knew what I'd come here to do, and you helped me anyway?"

He didn't answer her. His expression told her that what he'd done was perfectly clear.

Anne felt like a wad of tissue paper stuck to a rest-room floor. She found it very hard to look him in the eye, but she did. "Buck, I'm very ashamed and very sorry. I shouldn't have assumed you'd be so petty and spiteful."

"No, you shouldn't have," he said, and then he walked away.

Anne watched him go around the corner of the low building, toward the street. She turned back into her room, closed the door, and sank down onto the bed. She released a huge sigh through loose lips and let her shoulders hang in dejection. She hadn't meant to hurt him. She'd only been trying to keep things between them on a professional level.

What if she just kept making one mistake after another while she was there? If she kept judging people on the only standards she knew, she'd have the whole town in a rage. Buck's act of kindness was even bigger now that she knew he'd done it despite knowing who she was. She'd never felt so small in her life.

She jumped, startled by the sound of another knock on the door.

Her heart rate zoomed to Mach 1 when she opened the door and found Buck standing there once again. It went into a tailspin when she saw what he had in his hand. He wordlessly held out the fan belt and the change from the fifty-dollar bill. His face was stony and cold.

Anne took the fan belt and then closed his fingers around the money. "Please, you keep that for your trouble."

"I don't need charity . . . yet."

"It's not charity. You saved my life out there

and—and you went out of your way to get this fan belt and all. . . ."

He stepped past her into the room and smacked the money down on the little table just inside the door. Then he stepped back out.

"I'm no redneck. You don't need to pay me for that," he said.

"But I'd like to repay your kindness somehow. And I'd like to make up for thinking all those terrible things about you. I—I just don't know how."

The look he gave her was thoughtful.

"You could have supper with me."

"No," she said too abruptly. "Thanks. But I don't think that's such a hot idea."

"Why not?"

"Well, I don't think we ought to compromise our positions by seeing each other informally."

Buck's dark brows gathered in confusion. "Supper. That's all I'm offerin', Annie."

"My name is Anne."

"Unless, of course, you didn't really mean what you just said and you're really thinkin' I'll tie a bunch of strings to it."

Anne hesitated. She wasn't sure what she was thinking anymore.

"Maybe that's not it at all," he said, responding to her silence as he watched her closely. "Maybe you're thinkin' I'm just some jerkwater hillbilly with a pea for a brain who can't spit straight and walk at the same time. Is that it?"

"No!"

"Maybe you're thinkin' that I'm not good enough to go to supper with."

"That's not true either," she said, feeling indignant and a little guilty at the same time. "I admit that I wasn't sure what the people here would be like. And I do have this thing about banjo music. But I've always thought that—"

"You were a little better than most people anyway?" he said, rudely finishing her sentence before she could.

"Stop that." The man was infuriating. "I've always thought ·that people were pretty much the same no matter where they lived. Except for you, of course. I think you're rude, conceited, and mean."

"Who me?" he asked, astounded. Something twinkled in his eyes. "I haven't got a mean bone in my body."

He stood, arms out to the side, and displayed himself for her inspection. She didn't want them to, but her eyes roved slowly down the strong lean lines of his torso and slowly back up to his face again. A shiver of pure unadulterated lust passed through her as their gazes met and held once more.

"You do admit to being rude and conceited, though, I take it."

"Oh, sure," he said shamelessly. "But I'm a good ol' boy, and it's part of my charm."

"That's hardly what I'd call it." She could see the light in his eyes flicker with humor. He had purposefully baited her, tested her, and he was pleased with her reaction.

"That's just because you don't know me very well . . . yet."

She heaved an exasperated sigh that seemed to come all the way up from her toes, before she shifted her hips impatiently and gave him a stony stare. "I really don't like being toyed with, Mr. LaSalle. I don't have time for this sort of nonsense. If you're such a good ol' boy, why don't you give me a break? I meant what I said before. I'm sorry I offended you. And I would like to make it up to you." She took a deep breath. "But if going out to dinner with you means an evening of being heckled and ridiculed because of my job and where I come from, then you can forget it. Tomorrow morning, at the mill, we'll sit down and discuss whatever problems you have with the mill closing.

We'll iron out the differences, and then I can go on about my business."

"Annie. Annie," he said, throwing his hands up in the air as if she'd completely missed his point. "That's all well and fine for you. But what sort of business will I go about if you close down the mill?" His brows rose, then lowered again. "Be that as it may, the mill's got nothin' to do with our supper."

"It doesn't?" She couldn't help but sound suspicious. The man might drop most of the g's in his vocabulary when he spoke, but in his mind he didn't miss a trick.

"No, ma'am," he said. "Supper's personal. For woundin' me so mortally." He tried looking pathetic but couldn't quite carry it off.

"All right. All right. I'll go," she said, chuckling. "You're not going to bleed all over the restaurant are you?"

"Oh, no, ma'am," he said, grinning. Anne turned her back on his smile to keep her knees from melting and hurriedly set about making herself presentable.

When she came out of the bathroom, Anne noticed that he'd stepped into the room and closed the door. She felt dumb for not having invited him in earlier. But being in a room with him was even more flustering. The cab of the truck was smaller, but somehow this was far more intimate. It didn't seem to bother him a bit that they were in the same room with only a bed separating the distance between them.

"That's more like it," he said, smiling that smile again. He extended his hand to her, and as he was leading her out the door he said, "We'll have supper together tonight and we can . . . compromise our positions some other night."

Anne stumbled. Could he really have misunderstood the term compromised positions? She shuddered inwardly and began to wonder what kind of evening lay ahead. She looked up to see him glance over his shoulder at her, his eyes full of laughter, and a teasing grin looking very at home on his lips.

"Had you worried for a minute there, didn't I?"

"Of course not."

He graciously overlooked her blatant lie and moved on good-naturedly. "We've got lots of time for feudin' over the mill, Annie. Tonight, we'll just be a couple of Harriman employees, havin' supper together."

"Fair enough," she said. Her mind was riveted on the warmth generated by the easy clasp of his fingers with hers. He seemed to think it was the most natural thing in the world to be walking hand in hand with a perfect stranger, but she didn't. She was very uncomfortable, yet she didn't pull away.

With laughing good humor he communicated his pleasure at having to help her into the cab of his truck again. Even she had to laugh at their ridiculous routine.

"Stay put. I'll go in and tell Jimmy to watch for your car and to take care of your things for you," he said through the open window.

"Oh, he doesn't need to do that. If he could just get the keys from the mechanic, I can take care of my luggage later."

Buck shook his head. "Jimmy's a good ol' boy. He won't mind helpin' you out some."

Before she could say more, he was inside the office. Anne took the opportunity to catch her breath and to remind herself of who she was and what she wanted out of life.

There was no denying that Buck LaSalle was a handsome, earthy man or that he appealed to a few of her baser instincts. Being attracted to someone like him was understandable, when she had time to give it more thought, but getting involved with him would be something else entirely. Insanity. The last thing she needed in her life was a—what had he called himself?—a good ol' boy?

"Heaven help me," she muttered, once again wondering what she'd gotten herself into.

Her caution served only to increase the feeling of being confined and close when Buck finally climbed into the cab beside her. "Okay. We got an I-talian place," he said, pronouncing the first vowel with a long *i* sound. "Or we got an American place. Your choice."

Anne smiled. "What's that? Pizza or hamburgers?"

He looked over at her, a little surprised. He recovered quickly and smiled. "I'm goin' to be part of the unemployed pretty soon. I'm sure as hell not goin' to blow a wad of money on fancy food for the lady who's fixin' to put me out of work."

"Well, I can understand that. Either one is fine with me," she said.

"That's what I like," he said with a smirk. "An easy woman."

Not as easy as you think, buster, she thought as the engine came powerfully to life. Anne found herself enjoying the moment. She derived a certain comfort from what was consistent and obvious. Like Buck LaSalle. With the superior attitude of someone who was used to dealing with people who had considerably more finesse, she began to think that handling somebody like Buck might not be all that hard. He was about as subtle as a wart on the end of a nose.

"Is your brother very much like you, by any chance?" she had to ask, ignoring his "easy woman" remark, wondering if she could handle two LaSalles. The report Anne had received hadn't mentioned much about the younger brother, Bryce. Only that he existed and worked at the mill too.

"Bryce?" He was thoughtful for a minute. "Maybe,

I guess. He's quieter than I am, but he's a pretty good ol' boy."

Quieter?

"I understand that the two of you are very close, almost inseparable."

Buck laughed. "We work together sometimes and live in the same house. But aside from that, we're very . . . separable. We're scoutin' around for a good woman for him to marry. Then he'll have to move out and find a place of his own."

"Don't the two of you get along?" She would have sworn that she'd understood them to be very close.

"We get along fine. Always have. But two grown men livin' together is a bit of a strain." A pregnant pause. "He cramps my style, if you get my drift."

She got it but it wasn't worth commenting on.

"How old are you?" he asked out of the blue, as if she might be a good candidate for his brother.

Knowing that she wouldn't be, she answered, "I'll be twenty-eight in a few weeks."

"How many kids do you have?"

"None."

He cast her a curious glance. "Haven't you ever been married?"

"No."

He frowned but kept his eyes on the road ahead of them. Anne could almost hear the gears in his brain grinding away on her answer.

"Why not?" he asked, ignoring the fact that it wasn't any of his business.

"Haven't met the right man yet."

His brows shot up, and she could tell that he was surprised, that it didn't seem to be a good enough reason for a halfway decent-looking woman of nearly thirty to be unmarried and childless. Still, he didn't comment on it.

"What about you?" she asked, feeling bold and entitled to be just as nosey as he was. "Shouldn't you have called your wife and let her know you wouldn't be home for dinner tonight?"

"No."

"Don't tell me you're not married either," she said, feigning incredible shock. She grinned at him playfully.

He executed a sharp turn in the road and then glanced over at her, wearing that smile that made the muscles in her belly quiver. "Not anymore, I'm not."

"Sorry."

He shrugged. "It was a long time ago." He didn't appear to be overly affected by the loss of his wife or feel a need to elaborate. He simply changed the subject again. "Where'd you go to school?"

"What do you want, my résumé?"

"Well, you have my personnel file. And my brother's. I'm just curious as to what we've come up against, is all."

"Penn State. I got my M.B.A. at Columbia."

He released a long low whistle. "And you been workin' for Harriman ever since?"

Anne nodded. It had been a long, frustrating six years with Harriman Industries. But that was about to come to an end. Once she proved to everyone that she could handle any job previously considered to be a man's, she might just go out and find herself a new job. It was a principle she was dealing with here.

"I noticed on your employment record that you've been with Harriman for considerably longer than that," she said conversationally.

"Off and on, but mostly on, since I was fifteen."

She quickly did some mental arithmetic and came up with seventeen. Seventeen years with the same company was impressive for this day and age. He'd done well for himself, moving quickly up to day-shift supervisor and union representative. She knew that there were men at the factory who had been there twice as long, but still, it seemed like a very long time. It certainly explained at least part of their resistance to the closing of the mill.

As if reading her thoughts, he said, "Around here, gettin' a job at the mill is as good as it gets—unless you're the banker's boy. Then you go off to college and never come back."

Anne thought she heard a note of bitterness in his voice, but his facial expression was bland until he glanced her way. Then he grinned and added, " 'Course if you leave town, you automatically lose your spot at all the best fishin' holes."

"A grave consequence, I take it?"

"The gravest." His smirk told her it was a penalty that far exceeded the deed.

They passed several chain restaurants on their way through town, and Anne was prepared to pull into any one of them on Buck's whim. However, he passed them all by for a quaint little eatery in the business district of downtown. It came complete with red-and-white checkered tablecloths and candles stuck in wine bottles.

"This is a wonderful place, but fast food would have done just as well," she said, even as she deeply inhaled the perfume of garlic, yeast, and oregano. It made her mouth water.

"Not for me." Buck shook his head and recited his life's creed. "I believe in fast cars, hot women, slow sex, and real food."

"In that order?" she asked, not surprised.

He had to think it over. "Usually. Cars generally stay fast longer than women stay hot, or I'd reverse the order there. But I do get real hungry after sex." He paused thoughtfully and grinned. "Do you?"

Caught up in mentally elaborating on the cause of his post-coital hunger, Anne didn't hear the question. "Do I what?"

"Work up an appetite durin' sex."

"For food?"

"Yeah," he said, grinning at her confusion.

Her mind went blank. She couldn't remember if she was hungry after sex or not. In fact she could hardly remember her own name as she sat staring into a pair of green eyes that seemed to twinkle and dance like exotic jewels, gripping her mind and hypnotizing her senses.

Buck allowed the question to fade away as the silence and tension between them grew thick and oppressive. Anne could feel her heart beating in her throat and tried to swallow it, to no avail. She was holding her breath too. She began to feel as if she were suffocating.

In a desperate attempt to save her own life, she released a gust of pent-up air by saying the first thing that came to mind.

"My brother Charles is a priest."

Buck looked startled. He laughed. And then he laughed harder. It was a wonderfully clean, pure sound, but it served only to make Anne feel more foolish. Boy, did she hate feeling foolish.

Why on earth had she told him about Charles? He wasn't exactly the family talisman. Although, come to think of it, in this particular situation his name and occupation had effectively broken Buck's spell over her.

"Look, Mr. LaSalle—"

"Buck."

"Look, Buck. How I feel after sex isn't any of your business."

"You're right. I'm sorry," he said, looking not the least bit contrite. "I just thought I might need to bring in extra provisions, just in case."

"No need to worry. I'm not going to be here that long," she said, refusing to allow his arrogance to get to her.

"It only takes a couple of minutes."

Lord, did the man ever give up?

"Not if you like it slow, Buck," she said, her voice and smile dripping with saccharine sweetness.

Buck was saved a reply by the waitress who came to take their order. But before he looked away, Anne caught a glint of approval—or was it challenge—in his eyes? It might have been both. Either way, she was glad the discussion was over. She felt as rattled as a bat in daylight.

Anne's manicotti was delicious, her companion docile, as the sun disappeared behind the tree-lined mountaintops that circled the valley. She carefully avoided conversational topics of an intimate nature, and he seemed to be steering clear of subjects that had anything to do with the factory.

Ordinarily, Anne would have thought that there was little else for them to talk about. It was her understanding that men of the southern rural working class had few interests beyond their cars, their jobs, their women, and their favorite sport. Yet Buck seemed well informed on a variety of subjects, from farming to folklore to foreign and local history and politics.

"Actually we were one of the border states," he told her as they drove along in the darkness toward her motel. "We are a southern state, and slavery was legal here. But there were a whole lot of abolitionists here, too, and we never did break away from the Union. We fought on both sides, with brothers fightin' brothers on the field."

The small cab of the pickup truck was warm and cozy even as the late May night grew chilly. The delicious food, the two glasses of wine at dinner, and Buck's euphonious voice had lulled Anne into a relaxed state of contentment. And Buck's failure to mention even once anything about fishing, hunting, or football made her realize she was reluctant to see the evening end. Who would have thought that someone as rusticated as Buck could be such a pleasant companion, Anne marveled to herself. Loath though she was to admit it, she was beginning to like him . . . a lot.

"Course ya know Lincoln and Davis were both born here. Less than a year and a hundred miles apart. I always thought that was real interestin'," he said, contemplating it once again.

"Mm. It certainly is," Anne agreed, but to tell the truth, Anne could have cared less about the one-hundred-mile coincidence. She was too beguiled by this man. To say that she'd never met anyone like him would be a huge understatement. To say that he puzzled and intrigued her would be another. One minute he was the "spittin' image" of a classic American rube. The next minute, he was an intelligent, charming, and fascinating man.

Anne saw the motel lights in the distance, and her heart gave a little lurch. She wasn't ready for this night to end. Tomorrow they'd still be just a couple of Harriman employees, but with one major difference—he'd be labor and she'd be management. They'd be separated by a battle line that was chasm deep and as long . . . well, as long as it needed to be. And she just wasn't ready to start fighting with him. Not yet. Not after their past few hours together.

In a way, she wished she hadn't gone out to dinner with him. Their upcoming dispute over the closing of the factory would be so much easier if she could have gone on thinking of him as a none-too-bright country yokel. Knowing him as a person, as someone real and very human, was going to make it a thousand times harder.

"Annie?" he said, as he drove across the parking lot past the office toward her room at the rear of the building.

"Hmm?" Annie, she thought. No one had ever called her that before.

"About tomorrow night. . . . There's a union

meetin' scheduled. We thought it might be better if we aired all our complaints out in the open, all at one time. Fewer rumors are passed around that way," he said, faltering as if he, too, were beginning to realize that the evening they'd shared was simply a lull before the storm and that everything between them would be different the next day. "I think I ought to warn you that the workers . . . well, folks are feelin' pretty desperate. They're likely to get nasty. All they really want, though, is for someone to listen to them."

Already she could feel him crossing back over the invisible line that separated them as far as if they were standing on opposite sides of the Grand Canyon.

"I'll listen, Buck, but it won't make any difference," she told him honestly. "Harriman wants this factory closed down."

"That's what we really need here, Annie. An open mind." He cast her a disapproving glance that told her he'd been hoping she'd have a better attitude. She didn't like disappointing him, but he knew the facts as well as she did.

The truck came to a stop several feet in front of the door to her room. He took it out of gear but didn't turn the engine off.

"I'm sorry, Buck. I really am. But I have a job to do, and I have every intention of doing it."

He turned toward her on the seat, the overhead lamps that flooded the parking lot revealed his thoughtful expression. His eyes were dark and solemn. "Your job stinks, Annie."

"I agree," she said. She found no joy in putting thousands of people out of work.

Silently they acknowledged that their short-lived friendship had come to an end, that the truce was over. When next they met, they'd be enemies. "Look, Annie, I—"

She held up her hand to stop whatever it was

he was going to say. She felt that it was important to say what she had to say first. "Whatever happens in the next few days, Buck, I want you to know that I wish you well."

"I know. You too," he said.

Anne watched as he moved slowly toward her. She swallowed hard several times, trying to suck air into lungs that were tight and tense. Her heart fluttered in a panic of anxiety and anticipation.

"Maybe . . . maybe we shouldn't do . . . this," she said, breathless and wanting him to kiss her more than anything.

"Maybe we should," he said, his lips mere millimeters from hers, his breath warm against her face. "We might not get another chance."

"Well, yes, but—"

He silenced her by pressing his lips to hers. He drew back and scanned her face. He must have been able to see that the kiss hadn't been enough to satisfy her curiosity, that she wanted him to do it again, and that she needed him to really kiss her this time. Because suddenly he took her face in his hands and placed his mouth over hers.

Urgently, his tongue swept across her lips requesting entrance. It teased the soft inner tissue of her lips, skipped across her teeth, then darted inside. With the skill of a great hunter, he drew her out into the open, by coaxing, enticing. He let her grow confident and bold within her surroundings, reveling in the pleasures and intoxicating sensations he offered her. Then, when her joy was peaking, he moved in for the kill, sapping her strength, drugging her senseless, drawing out her life's breath until she was too weak to beg for mercy.

They parted, panting and tense. Needing more. The passion in his eyes overwhelmed her. She could lose herself inside this man, and the world would never see her again, she thought, struggling to squelch the emotions.

"Buck. I—"

"I know," he said, cutting her off. If curiosity killed cats, then kissing someone you shouldn't be kissing with the same fascination was just as deadly. "Come on. I'll walk you to the door."

Reluctantly, she got out of the truck and walked through a hazy cloud of exhaust fumes to meet him at her door. She slipped the key into the lock but didn't open the door. "Thank you for the nice evening," she said. "And thank you for all you did this afternoon."

"You're welcome."

"And I'm sorry . . . about before."

"Hush now." He reached out, gently cupping her face with his hands and turning his whisper into a light tender kiss that made her whole body tingle. They were slow to part and even after they had, he continued to stroke her cheek with the pad of his thumb, as if her face were the most incredible thing he'd ever seen.

"I guess . . . I'll see you tomorrow night then," she said, placing the mill firmly between them again.

Buck just nodded. She could tell by his expression that he wasn't looking forward to the workers' meeting anymore than she was.

"Well, good night then," she said, turning to the door. She felt his work-roughened hands, hands that had been so amazingly gentle moments before, slip away from her face.

"Bye, Annie," she heard him say. She stepped inside her room and closed the door. She stood in the darkness, her heart heavy and pounding, her breath coming in short gasps, until she heard him drive away.

Three

Over a thousand pairs of eyes watched as Anne arrived at Webster Textiles the next morning. Everyone seemed to know who she was and why she was there.

She shouldn't have looked at the faces of the workers as she drove through the huge parking lot on her way to the main office. They were angry and resentful. The few remarks she heard when she got out of her car were bitter and snide. If the people were trying to make her feel like the villain in this drama, they were succeeding.

She climbed the metal stairs to the office door and looked out over the lot below. Even though most of the vehicles were pickup trucks, she picked out Buck's with an uncanny certainty. The man himself, of course, was who she was looking for, but he was nowhere to be seen. She would have liked to have seen a friendly face that morning. At least she was hoping it would still be friendly.

Anne introduced herself to Drake Edwards, the mill superintendent, who in turn introduced her to his secretary. Edwards was of medium height with a large abdomen and a friendly smile. He looked to be very near retirement age, which explained how he could afford to be nicer to her than the people she'd encountered in the parking lot.

Anne spent part of the morning familiarizing herself with the office and financial records. Drake Edwards's secretary, Lily, an older woman who was quite obviously an asset to management, was of great assistance. She explained the billing and crediting of materials, salaries, and a thousand other details that had kept the mill running smoothly for almost a hundred years.

There were pictures on the wall of the original mill when the looms had been wooden and far more complicated to operate than the huge mechanical looms that had replaced them. There were several pictures of new ones, too, the day they had arrived all bright and shiny. It made Anne a little sick to think that very soon the safety awards and the company picnic pictures would fade on the walls, meaning nothing to anyone once the mill closed.

Then Drake Edwards escorted her over to the mill where an unexpected tour of the factory had been arranged for her. She wasn't exactly treated like a welcome dignitary. There were no cheers or smiling faces or friendly waves. On the contrary, the workers either ignored her and went on with their work, or they scowled at her and muttered things that were covered by the din of the machinery.

It wasn't long before Drake introduced her to a man by the name of Buck LaSalle, a mill supervisor who shook her hand as if they'd never met before, and then winked and smiled at her.

She was glad that he wasn't going to shun her, too. She knew they couldn't be friends, not like they had been the previous night, but at least he was going to be cordial. Anne's smile must have shown all the relief she was feeling.

"Ooo. Kinda chilly in here since you walked in," he said with a droll expression as they walked away from Edwards, who had turned her over to Buck for the tour.

"You noticed that, did you? And here it was such a fine day, I didn't think I'd be needing my coat."

"They been givin' you a rough time of it?" He sounded concerned, and it touched Anne.

"Not unexpectedly. I'd probably feel the same way if I were in their shoes."

Buck looked down at her with the strangest expression on his face. It was both gentle and calculating. His smile showed his pleasure at her words, and his eyes searched her face with something that looked very much like a mixture of hope and pride.

He started the tour in a very businesslike fashion. Thankfully, he made no sexual remarks or innuendoes on the sly. He did, however, seem to be going to a lot of trouble to make sure she saw everything and that she understood how things operated. He reminded her of a real estate agent trying to sell a fixer-upper, even going so far as to point out what small and large improvements could be made with little effort.

She only half-listened to his speech. In her mind, she wasn't being discourteous. As a matter of fact, it was damned big of her to listen at all. He was pitching pipe dreams at her, and she was letting him. The truth was, there were to be no more improvements or repairs made on the factory. There was no point in discussing the mill's future, because it didn't have one.

The only reason Anne didn't stop him and tell him this flat out was purely personal. She liked listening to the soft drawl of his voice, and since the mill was a very noisy place, it had the added benefit of forcing a physical closeness between them, so he could be heard.

The way he looked down into her face when he spoke, his eyes bright and his face animated, was very titillating. The marginal space between them grew heavy with the smell of her wintergreen breath mints, whatever kind of soap he'd used in his shower, and a muskiness that was a mingling of their unique male and female scents.

She had flashes of his strong, calloused hands entwined with her soft, pale fingers. She was acutely aware that his chest and shoulders were wide, hard, and powerful, while hers were smaller, softer, and basically functional. She even considered the fact that his legs were longer and stronger than her own. But if they were supine . . . well, then it wouldn't make any difference, would it?

"Did you have a question?" he asked, a note of interest lowering his voice, disturbing the other notions about the innate differences between men and women that were bouncing about in Anne's head. "You're lookin' a little lost."

"No. No. You're painting a very clear picture for me. Please go on." Anne smirked as he stepped in front of her to lead her through a narrow passage between two industrial looms, and her gaze dropped to his trim waist and cute little tush. She shook her head. Half the rear ends in New York were male, and she estimated that she'd probably seen just about every variation possible. But to her, Buck's was a winner; it left all others in the dust.

The mill was set up in four huge warehouselike structures, open and connected at the sides. The first was filled with gigantic looms that wove huge spools of nylon or cotton-blend threads into fabric. This was not Anne's first visit to a textile mill. She knew about the warp and filling, or weft, and stood to watch the interlacing for several minutes. It never failed to amaze her.

Buck lead her through the next stage, which was a series of huge vats that contained several thousand gallons of aniline dye and mordant to color and fix the cloth. This was also where the Webster mill specialty took place. This particular factory produced a variety of synthetic materials that were flame retardant. Some were still in the experimental stages and, hopefully, would someday be used in draperies, upholstery, and other materials to replace those now in homes and businesses that easily burst into flame when exposed to the heat of a fire.

The printshop was Anne's favorite. She didn't think she'd ever tire of watching the big rollers put prints on a solid-color cloth. But then again she didn't have to stand there and watch it all the time either, did she? As frustrating as her own job was, she was sure she wouldn't want to trade it for the tedium of factory work.

The pressing, folding, and bolting of the fabric took place in the last chamber. And it was there that Anne was approached by a woman who felt compelled to overcome her anger and resentment to speak her fears.

The woman was thin and blond and younger than she, but Anne knew intuitively that she was older than she looked. Anne could see the pain and hardships the woman had endured in her life in the depths of her eyes and by the calluses on her hands.

As the young woman approached her, Anne could almost feel the terror, courage, and strength it took for her to do so.

"I can't come to the meetin' tonight cuz I ain't got no one to watch over my kids if I did," she said, when Buck suggested she save her complaint till then, so that everyone could benefit from the answer. "And I need to know what will happen to my middle boy if the mill closes down. He's hard sick and needs medicine. Will the company still pay?"

Anne stepped out from under Buck's protective shadow and addressed the woman as straightforwardly as she could. "What's the matter with your little boy, Ms.—"

"My name is Mrs. Dillard Evans. I'm Liddy," she said. "My Teddy has diabetes. If he don't go to his doctor and take his medicine . . ." She choked on her words as her eyes welled with tears. "I come close to losin' him twice already, ma'am."

"Can the state help?"

"Yes, ma'am. But they don't pay as much, and there's a waitin' period once the insurance stops. And I do have two other boys to feed, ma'am."

"Have you and your husband tried to find other jobs? The company has opened as many positions as possible in some of the other mills."

"It's just me, ma'am. And I don't see how I can afford to move. We live pretty thin as it is," the woman broke in, not offensively, but simply to stop the whole relocation pitch which she'd probably heard before.

Anne was silent for a moment as a germ of an idea began to form in her mind. "The insurance will pay your son's medical expenses for two or three months after the mill closes, Mrs. Evans. After that, you'll have to make other arrangements. But . . . well, try not to worry about that right now. I'd like to look into something else that might help. Right now, I think your best bet is to concentrate on finding a new job."

She promised the woman she'd get back to her before the end of the week if her idea panned out, and she and Buck walked away.

There wasn't much of the facility left to see. Anne wasn't in the mood to look anyway. She was finding it very hard to convince herself that the town of Webster wasn't her responsibility.

"Thanks for the tour, Buck," she said rather absently as he led her down off the loading dock and back into the May sunshine. "You'll be at the meeting tonight, I suppose."

He nodded, his expression grave.

A long uncomfortable silence stretched out between them. Nothing was going to change for them. The mill was too important to them both, for different reasons.

"I'll see you there, then."

Again Buck nodded. Anne started to walk back to the office.

"Annie?" She turned to look at him. His expression hadn't altered; if anything, it was even more serious. He reached out and, taking her by the shoulders, drew her closer to him. She felt his fingers gently brush against her cheek as he played with a strand of her dark hair, the look in his eyes softening. He placed a tender, heart-twisting kiss on her lips before murmuring, "Look after yourself, Annie." And he left her.

If she didn't look after herself, who would, she wanted to know, as the earth vibrated under her feet from the kiss she'd just received. The only reason she'd come to Webster was to close the mill, and whatever happened after that wasn't any of her concern, right? Walking between cars on her way through the parking lot, she wasn't so sure. If it was her job to close the mill, then didn't that make at least part of what happened to the jobless people of Webster her responsibility?"

If she were one of the guys from her office, would she still feel rotten about putting all those people out of work? In all fairness, she had to admit that she probably would feel just as awful. That left her wondering what it took to do the job.

Maybe Calvin was right. Maybe this was tearing her apart simply because she was a woman. Maybe there was something to that androgen theory. Maybe men felt just as badly but had that little something extra that they relied on to get the job done.

She growled and shuddered trying to dispel every lamenting feeling and weak thought she was having. Buck LaSalle was getting to her. Come to think of it, that's probably why she'd gotten the unrequested grand tour. He knew she wasn't made of stone, and he was playing on her sympathies. He was exposing her to the people whose lives she was destroying by shutting down the mill. He was making her look into their faces and see their anguish.

He wasn't playing fair, and the more she thought about it, the angrier she got—but not at Buck. Pages of her memory flipped back to a time when she had felt that the odds were so stacked against her that she, too, had found it necessary to bend the rules of fair play to get what she wanted.

"Anne. Honey. Why are you doing this to yourself?" she heard her father say years ago. "Do you know what time it is?"

"No," she said, weeping silently as she bent over the engine of her very first car, her pride and joy, her tears rolling off the grease that covered the distributor. Looking back, she realized she'd spent most of her sixteenth year either in tears or in ecstacy about something or other.

"It's two-thirty in the morning, and you have school tomorrow. Come in and go to bed."

"I can't. I have to fix this thing."

"Tom'll do it for you tomorrow. Come in now."

"No, Daddy. I don't want Tom to do it. I can do it myself. It's just that . . . well, it's confusing. I've taken this apart three times already," she said, holding up the filthy distributor to show him with a loud sniff. "When I put it back together, I'm either missing parts, or I have all sorts of nuts and screws left over—and it never works any better than before."

Her father was frowning at her, as if he'd never seen her before. "Why is it so important to you to do this yourself, Anne. No one expects you to be able to do everything. Maybe you just weren't cut out to be a mechanic."

"Tom, Charles, and Kevin fix their cars. I should be able to fix mine. You always said there wasn't anything I couldn't do if I set my mind to it. I've got my mind set on this, Daddy. I just can't do it," she said, hating that sinking, failing sensation in her chest.

Her father's face, aged with wisdom, softened with love and understanding, was filled with regret. "Tom's flunking algebra. Chuck couldn't swim to save his own life, and Kevin's a lousy cook. But Tom's one hell of a basketball player. Chuck is the kindest, most compassionate kid I've ever met, and Kevin can remember damned near everything he's ever read. Everybody has a special talent, sweetheart, but nobody's perfect," he said, taking the distributor out of her blackened hands and tossing it haphazardly into the exposed engine. Then, wrapping an arm around her shoulders, he lead her out of the garage saying, "Remember that, Anne. Trying is what's important. Try everything. Do your best at it. Then, if it's something you're just not suited to, let it go."

"They'll laugh at me."

"Who will?"

"The boys."

"Let 'em. You did your best. That's all that counts."

"What's special about me, Daddy?" she couldn't help asking as they walked along in silence.

"I'd have to say it's your determination. You never learned how to walk. You started out running to keep up with your brothers, to be included as one of them. And for the most part, I'd have to say, too, I was right about one thing." She turned her face upward to look into his. "There hasn't been anything you haven't been able to do, once you set your mind to it. Except—" he kissed her temple slowly, "you ain't no mechanic, honey."

The next day she'd called a mechanic. He had come to the house to fix her car, her first car, her pride and joy, while her brothers were still at school. When her brothers, all of whom knew of her aversion to failure, had expressed their amazement at her skills, and she was just about to confess the truth to them, her father had stepped in once more.

"Seems to me that Anne set her mind on getting the damned thing fixed, and that's what she did."

Anne had every intention of closing down the mill so fast, it would make Buck LaSalle's head spin. She'd show all the guys back in the office— Calvin Schwab and even Joel Harriman himself— that she could do anything she set her mind to. All the cards were stacked in her favor this time. She couldn't fail.

The anger she felt was *for* Buck, not at Buck. She knew what an impossible task he was facing and what it would mean if he failed. She also knew how unqualified he was to undertake it and that he would, indeed, not succeed.

When it occurred to her that she had just walked past the tailgate of Buck's truck, she purposely walked back to it. With the bottom of her rolled up fist she smacked it good. She didn't like being put in the middle of hopeless situations. She didn't like having such a clear view of Buck's perspective. She didn't like knowing what he was going through. She just wanted to do her job.

"Don't take any crap off them, Anne," Calvin Schwab was telling her a short while later over the phone. She'd returned to her motel room because everything at the mill kept preying on her conscience, confusing her, and weakening her resolve. She'd taken a shower to help her relax, and then called the office in New York to check in and report on the progress she'd made. She didn't have much to tell. "You go to that meeting tonight. You state the facts, clear and simple. And then you give them the sixty days' notice and leave."

"What? No discussion period afterward?" she asked, the sarcasm in her voice sounding sharp and biting even to her own ears.

"If that's the way you want to play it, fine. Stay for cookies and coffee too, while you're at it, if that's what you want. Just get the job done."

"I will, Calvin. Don't worry."

"Anne?" he said, sounding as if he were reconsidering his earlier words.

"Yes?"

"Be careful. Don't push them too far. Be firm but gentle. Be diplomatic. Promise them anything within reason. Just don't let them blow this whole thing out of proportion. Know what I'm saying?"

"Yes. I hear you," she said. *Keep it quiet*, she translated mentally.

"Good girl. You'll do fine." The line went dead.

Yes, she would, she decided firmly. How could she not?

She put a lot of consideration into the proper attire for a Textile Workers of America union meeting. It was one of those things Emily Post simply forgot to mention in her book.

Anne didn't want to appear too frilly, for fear the men would see her only as a woman and eat her alive. She didn't want to wear slacks, because they might think she was trying to imitate them —in which case they'd get angry and eat her alive.

She settled on another skirt and jacket in navy blue and white, hoping that they'd see her only as the messenger and curb their desire to eat her alive.

Her image in the mirror looked professional and reasonable, but there was no avoiding the fact that she was the person Harriman had sent to shut down the mill. Her sex and what she wore wasn't going to make a bit of difference. Those workers were going to have her for dinner, and she knew it.

It was with this deep-seated conviction of impending disaster that Anne introduced herself to the local's president, a balding, overweight gentleman in his fifties by the name of Leroy Spencer.

"Why in the world did Harriman send a woman?" he bellowed, more to himself than at Anne. She had arrived well in advance of the meeting to make his acquaintance and found him making coffee in a huge electric coffee maker.

"Well," he said, turning to her with not unkind brown eyes. "I hope you're a lot tougher than you look, Anne Hunnicut. Folks are pretty riled up. They're gonna try to eat you alive."

"That's pretty much how I had it figured too," she muttered fatalistically under her breath as she watched him walk off into another room.

"Then again," he said, returning a few moments later with long tubes of Styrofoam cups in each hand, "Buck says you're not stupid, so maybe it'll turn out okay."

"Buck LaSalle?"

"The same. Says you're quick in the head and fair-minded. Said you'd know a good thing when you saw it—woman or not."

Anne could hear her teeth grinding as she stood giving him what she felt certain must have been a very stupid smile. She was at a complete loss for polite words. How dare that man, that insufferable, pigheaded man, Buck LaSalle, talk about her in public like that, she blustered indignantly in the darkening recesses of her mind.

Although, she cautioned herself with a second thought, "quick in the head and fair minded" wasn't so bad, especially coming from someone who believed a woman had no mind at all, according to her sources of information.

She took a seat at the small table in the front of the room, putting off her decision to be angry with Buck until later. The workers were beginning to arrive, and she needed to focus all her attention on them.

She did, however, start looking for Buck a short time later, as the men and women streamed in steadily just before the meeting began. She wanted to see one familiar face in the crowd. The faces she saw were of strangers, angry, worried, and looking at her with great hostility. He wasn't there.

Leroy Spencer called the meeting to order. He waved the reading of the minutes, skimmed over the old business, and came directly to Anne.

Where were earthquakes, tornadoes, and other acts of God when you needed them, Anne wondered as she stood and walked to the podium. She looked out over the crowd, her gaze coming to rest on Buck's face. When had he come in? And what a sight he was for sore eyes.

Not that his countenance was of any comfort, mind you. His nod of recognition was reserved and noncommittal, an acknowledgment that they had met. That was all. But she took a certain amount of gratification in seeing him standing tall and strong in the back of the room and knowing deep in her heart that he wouldn't let the gathering crowd stone her to death.

Beside him stood a younger man she instantly realized was Bryce, his brother. Not as tall, but built lean like Buck, he had the same color hair and light eyes. A quick glance between the brothers told her that Bryce didn't have Buck's quietly forceful personality, for lack of a better description. He looked much less imposing.

She looked down at her hands to clear her mind of the LaSalles. She had a job to do.

"Good evening," she started.

"What the hell is so good about it?" someone in the crowd called out. Anne's heart sank. After only two words out of her mouth, they already were showing their fangs.

Leroy Spencer was on his feet immediately. He came back to the podium and nudged Anne out of the way to get to the microphone.

"Listen up," he ordered. "If you have somethin' to say, you wait your turn and wait for me to recognize ya. We're here to see if anythin' can be done to keep the mill open, not to badmouth this little girl."

She gave Leroy a small appreciative smile—even though she hadn't cared much for the term "little girl"—and moved back to the podium.

"You're right," she said, looking at the man who had spoken out of turn. "This really isn't such a good evening. I know that all of you have come here tonight because you're concerned about your jobs and the futures of your families. I . . . am very well aware of what the mill means to the town of Webster. No one more than I regrets that it has to be closed." A disbelieving rumble broke out near the center of the hall.

"Harriman Industries has done all it can to keep this mill open," she said, her voice calm but loud enough to be heard. "It just isn't feasible for us anymore. We've also tried to be as fair about this as possible. Those close to retirement will be compensated. And we've opened up as many other positions at our other factories and spinning mills as we could, to those willing to relocate. There's nothing more we can do."

"Sure there is. You just can't see it through all them dollar signs in your eyes," a large angry-looking man said as he stepped out into the aisle to be recognized. He hadn't been noted by Leroy, however, who stood to reprimand the disorderly gentleman. Anne waved him away. She had an answer for him.

"All right. Look at it this way then," she started honestly and without resentment for the man's outburst and hostile demeanor. "Consider the facts. First, Webster is only one of four mills owned by Harriman Industries. Second, the textile industry in America has become increasingly precarious because it's cheaper to import. And lastly, from the company's financial standpoint, in order to keep three of the mills open to capacity, one has got to be closed down. Then it becomes simple to pick the oldest and the one most in need of repair, and sacrifice it for the good of the other three."

"Well, it's sure as hell easy for you to talk about sacrifices and things being simple, now ain't it?" the man said, turning to gain support from his fellow workers who were agreeing.

Anne watched as the bodies in the audience grew restless and turned away from her to focus their attention on the man standing in the aisle.

"That's not what I meant. I was trying to explain it from the company's point of view." She had to shout to be heard, even with the microphone. "I—I was sent here to talk with you, so that perhaps we could come to some sort of understanding in this situation. The mill is closing. And Mr. Harriman and I would like it to be as painless as possible—for everyone involved."

The man gave a short loud laugh but only half his attention seemed directed on the conversation. The rest he used on the crowd around him. "I bet you would," he shouted. "Then again, you ain't the ones losin' your jobs, now are ya?"

"No," she said. "But we're not doing this to you and your friends personally. It wasn't an easy decision. If I could, I'd leave the mill open and give everyone a raise. But I can't. No one can. This wasn't an instant decision on Mr. Harriman's part either. He's seen it coming for years now. He put it off for as long as he could. He just can't put it off any longer."

"Well, I hate to pop your bubble, honey, but it ain't goin' to happen," he said, taking several menacing steps closer to the podium. "Least ways, not if I can help it."

Suddenly the crowd of concerned workers looked more like a lynch mob. They were yelling their approval and cheering the angry, spiteful man on in his defiance. He all but took a bow as he turned toward his supporters.

Anne had taken just about all she could from him. She was prepared to give them their sixty days' notice and make a mad dash for the door when a loud, shrill whistle rose up and split the air in the back of the room. It could just as easily have been a blast from an UZI for the effect it had on the crowd.

The room was silent almost immediately. People slowly returned to their chairs. Even the rabble-rouser stepped aside as Buck walked up to take his place in the center of the crowd.

"Looks to me like we're a little off the track here," he said. "So far, the company's been pretty good 'bout meetin' our requests. Attackin' the rep isn't goin' to get us anywhere. Let's just do what we planned to do and take it from there."

They all seemed to be in general agreement, and when they grew quiet once again, Buck turned to Anne and said, "We've been talkin' about it. And we've decided to buy the mill from Harriman and become an employee-owned business."

Anne felt as if she had just survived a blizzard to get hit and buried by an avalanche of snow.

"You want to what?"

"Buy the factory. We can get a small business loan from—"

"No, no, no," she broke in, waving her hands. "Do you have any idea what's involved in becoming an employee-owned operation? You can't just walk blindly into something like this and think it's going to work out for the best. At the very most, you'll only be postponing the inevitable."

"We don't see it that way," Buck said. "And we've been doin' our homework. We're not goin' into this half-cocked."

Damn. Damn. And double damn, Anne mentally expostulated as she stared at Buck's determined expression, one she recognized all too easily. She saw the same resolve in the faces of his co-workers as she scanned the room. Then she thought of Joel Harriman and Calvin Schwab. She knew exactly what they'd say about this new development.

"There's no way," she said, perhaps a little too pointedly. "This mill can't carry its own weight, and Harriman wants it shut down."

"Then he should have sent a bigger man than you to do it," the large man jumped up once more to say. And again, even more swiftly this time, the crowd was behind him.

"Don't underestimate me, Mr. . . . ?"

"Shanks. Roy Shanks." He supplied his name proudly, boastfully, to show the gathering how fearless he was of the company's power over him. Since the mill was closing, he didn't have anything to lose by his act of bravado, but this obviously hadn't occurred to his cohorts. They cheered him on.

"If you and the other workers refuse to cooperate, I'll get a court order to shut the mill down, and I'll have it enforced by the National Guard, if that's what I have to do. Now, if there's some way we can all come to some amicable settlement, Mr. Harriman is more than willing to meet you half-way. But the mill will close down."

Pandemonium broke loose in the hall. Everyone was talking and yelling at once. Leroy Spencer whacked the table several times with his mallet to regain order, but no one paid the slightest heed. Anne, answering a thin wiry woman who had a child by each hand and hatred in her eyes, was only partially aware that a few people were advancing toward the front of the room and that Buck had stopped them with his outstretched arms.

"You can't close the mill," the woman yelled at her. "Don't we have any say? No rights? Where do you get off just marching in here and shuttin' down the mill?"

"We are within our rights to close down this facility. Your union was notified. And your rights come in the form of sixty days' notice, as of Monday next," Anne said, shouting but trying not to sound cruel.

The announcement of the sixty days' notice had a horrible effect on the crowd. Voices rose several octaves and decibels. Chairs scraped on the floor. The knot of people at the center of the room thinned out, broke off into groups, and moved along the outer edges toward her.

Suddenly Anne was grabbed from behind. Strong hands clasped her shoulders and pulled her backward.

"Let go of me," she said, gasping, frightened and outraged. She twisted her body around, wanting to identify her attacker. Staggering sideways and back toward the rear of the union building, they were in a short, isolated hallway before she could get a good look at the man's face. "You!"

"Hush. Buck told me to get you outta here, if anythin' like this was ta happen," Bryce LaSalle said in a quiet voice. "I didn't mean ta scare you, but I was in a hurry. I didn't want to have to waste time on introductions and explanations."

"You look a little like your brother," she said, breathless in her anxiety, indicating that this was introduction enough. Somehow she had transferred the trust she had in Buck to his brother, as she automatically followed Bryce out the rear exit saying, "But I'd still like an explanation."

"Buck didn't want you hurt."

That stopped her dead in her tracks. "That's ridiculous," she said, wondering what she was doing out in the middle of the gravel parking lot. If she were a man, would she be running away? "I can handle them. A few angry words and some accusations never hurt anyone. This is my job, and I'll take care of it."

She turned to go back into the union hall, but Bryce's grip on her arm impeded her progress.

"It wasn't a shouting match he was worried about. Said you could probably hold your own if that's all it was. But he said to get you the hell outta there if things started gettin' ugly, and that's what I'm goin' ta do, even if I have to knock you out to do it."

"I beg your pardon?"

"I got Buck's permission, ma'am. He said I was ta knock ya out if you put up a fuss." Then Bryce added a heartfelt plea, "Please don't."

Anne just stood and stared at him with her mouth open before the full impact of his words hit her.

"Well, of all the . . ." she sputtered, frustrated, angry, and indignant. How dare he? If she were a man, she'd punch Bryce's lights out, march right back into the hall, and then punch out Buck's. As it was, she let her would-be protector drag her across the parking lot and put her into her car.

"I'll follow ya back to the motel," he said, and then assuming that she would comply with Buck's wishes just as he had, he left her to find his own vehicle.

It did enter her mind to disobey. However, the idea of being knocked out notwithstanding, she didn't relish the thought of facing that angry mob again either. What if things did get out of control? What if the police were called and didn't get there in time to help her? What if they wouldn't come at all? What if the incident got into the newspapers?

Prudently she waited for Bryce's headlights to appear in her rearview mirror, and then she drove back to her motel room.

"Are you going back to help Buck now?" she asked through the open window of Bryce's small pickup truck. The night was warmer than the night before, almost balmy. Spring didn't seem to be able to make up its mind, she thought absently, recalling the coat she'd left behind at the union hall.

"No, ma'am. I'm to stay here with you."

"But what if something happens? What if someone tries to hurt him? I don't want him fighting my fights for me. And I certainly don't want him getting hurt on my account."

"He won't get hurt, ma'am."

"Don't call me ma'am. We're practically the same age," she said testily, hating the idea that Buck was doing the job she'd been sent there to do. She'd botched the meeting somehow, and now he was cleaning up her mess.

"Yes, ma— Okay," he said, following her into her room.

Four

Bryce sat in a chair opposite the television set and flicked the channels back and forth until he found a rerun of *Three's Company*. He half-watched the program and half-watched Anne as she anxiously paced back and forth between the bed and the window.

Her first assumption about Bryce had been correct. He had even less to say than his older brother and had a much less commanding personality. Anne felt instantly at ease with him and didn't feel obligated to make small talk while they waited to hear from Buck.

It was this sense of easy uneasiness that was disturbed when Bryce startled her by saying, "Jimmy's gonna charge ya extra if ya wear out his rug there." She looked at him, and she smiled his understanding. "You don't need to worry about him. Buck can take care of himself," he added. Quiet though he was, he didn't lack intelligence or a sharp sense of perception.

"I can't help it. What if something's happened? It would be all my fault. It was my responsibility."

"Well, ya didn't give us much of a chance to tell ya about our plan," he admitted, agreeing that it was her fault that the meeting had gone askew. "Buck thinks we can do it."

"Buck's wrong. There's a lot more to it than just buying the mill. You need sales reps and marketing people, all sorts of professionals to get the fabric to market, not to mention setting up a network of thread suppliers, coal distributors—and Lord only knows what else to stay alive in this business. Who in Webster is trained to do those things?"

He shrugged carelessly. "Buck'll think of some way to work all that out."

Bryce's faith in Buck was carrying brotherly devotion a bit too far in Anne's estimation. There had been times in her life when she had turned to her own brother Charles for answers to complicated questions. But he was a priest after all and was expected to have a few more of the answers than everyone else. And heaven knew, Buck was no priest.

"Well, for your sake, I hope so." There's still Harriman to convince, she thought as she watched out the window for Buck. She couldn't help the little smirk of humor that came to her lips as she envisioned the man of few words, Buck LaSalle, trying to talk fast enough to get Harriman to sell the mill. Turning back to Bryce, she said, "You seem to think Buck can manage just about anything."

Again he shrugged. "He always has. Can't see somethin' like that changin' now."

"How long have you been at the mill, Bryce?"

"Eight years."

His eight to Buck's seventeen meant that he'd started at an older age than his brother, since she knew Buck was thirteen years older. Anne was curious. "You got to finish school then."

"Had to. Buck wouldn't let me work, 'cept for odd jobs, till after I finished high school."

"Even though he started when he was fifteen."

"He worked the swing shift back then. Went to

school durin' the day. They let him come a few minutes late all the time cuz they all knew he was savin' to go off to college."

"What happened? Why didn't he go?" Anne recalled the tiny breath of bitterness she thought she'd heard when she and Buck had discussed college the night before. Now she knew she hadn't been mistaken. "They go off to college and never come back," he'd said. Had he wanted to get away from Webster and never come back, only to lose that dream somehow?

"He did go. For a while anyway. Him and Momma had this scheme, see, where they'd use his savin's and the money we got from the company when daddy died, and Buck'd go to college. Then when it was my turn, he'd pay my way."

"What happened?"

"Momma died. Buck came home to take care of me. I was seven."

"How sad. So you both missed out." Her heart ached for Buck. It wasn't hard for her to picture the proud, arrogant young man full of hopes and visions. Nor was it hard for her to see him with his dreams suddenly dashed to the ground.

"Actually, I never took to books the way Buck did. I'm happy at the mill." His reference to the mill brought back her concern for Buck's present well-being. Hours had passed since Bryce had taken her away. What was keeping him?

"I hope nothing's happened to him," she said peering through the window once again. She let the curtain fall back into place and turned to Bryce. "That—that Mr. Shanks wouldn't do anything to hurt him, would he?"

"Nah. Everybody knows Buck's a good ol' boy. They'd never hurt him." He seemed very sure of this.

"Are you a good ol' boy also, Bryce?" she asked impulsively, her cheeks beginning to burn the

moment the last word was out of her mouth. It
was a natural question for someone who couldn't
tell the difference, but it somehow felt very rude
to ask.

"Yes, ma'am. I am," he said proudly, and then
recalling that he'd called her ma'am again, he
apologized.

"Bryce? Would you mind answering a very stupid question for me?"

"No, ma— No. I wouldn't mind."

"Could you explain to me the difference between
a redneck and a good ol' boy? I know they're not
the same as a hillbilly, but I'm not sure what the
difference between the two are."

He laughed. "You Yankees. Always gotta have a
nice little niche for everythin'."

"But you call yourselves and each other red-
necks and good ol' boys. I'd just like to know the
difference so I don't insult anyone."

Bryce was still grinning as he began to answer.
"If ya got to pick and choose your friends, you'd
want to pick a good ol' boy. He don't care what
color your skin is or what church ya go to or who
ya vote for, so long as you're a good ol' boy too. And
if you were in trouble, say your car was to break
down. Well, you'd want a good ol' boy to help ya,
cuz he'd probably feed ya the lunch his wife packed
for him while ya sat and watched him fix your
car. Now a redneck, if he stopped at all, would
probably charge ya for his efforts."

A seed of suspicion began to grow in Anne's
mind. "Did Buck tell you how we met?"

He nodded, but his expression told her that he
thought it a very strange question. "Said he gave
you a tour of the mill today, why?" he asked
guilelessly.

She lifted one shoulder. "I was just wondering."

Buck hadn't told his brother about their meeting the day before or the rotten way in which

she'd treated him *or* about their dinner and the kisses they'd shared. And yet Bryce didn't seem to think it the least bit strange that his brother had asked him to protect someone who was a total stranger. She was beginning to like the good ol' boy concept and wished there were a few more of them where she came from. They weren't as smooth and polished as some of the northern men she knew, but then again, how many real diamonds were found that way? Frankly, she had to admit that she'd rather have a raw, uncut natural gem than one that was shaped and buffed to look like a thousand others—and was possibly synthetic to boot.

After waiting in companionable silence for twenty minutes, they heard a truck pull up outside the door.

Buck looked both worried and relieved as he burst into the room without knocking. "Get your stuff together," he ordered her without preamble.

"Why?"

"I don't want you stayin' here alone. I'm takin' you home."

"But I'm not finished here. I have a job to do, Buck, and I'm not going home until I've done it. And that's that." She had been going to tell him how happy she was to see him in one piece but decided against it. She didn't like it when he acted so heavy-handedly with her. This was the second time that night that he'd said jump and had expected everyone within hearing to ask how high. If she didn't nip this in the bud now, it would be even harder to break him of the habit later.

"Not New York. I'm takin' you home to my house."

"Oh, no you are not," she said, sitting down on the end of the bed and crossing her legs stubbornly.

He put his hands on his hips and glowered at

her for several long minutes. She sensed that he was very angry with her and that it didn't have a whole lot to do with her refusal to leave with him. When he spoke, his voice was softer than usual, his tone was controlled, and his brother was very nervous. "Okay. You stay here if you want to. Just don't say I didn't try to help you when Roy Shanks and his buddies come callin' tonight."

"Come callin'?"

"Oh, I don't think they'll hurt you," he said with very little reassurance. "But according to what they were sayin' down at the Steel Wheel, they seem to think that if they scare you a little bit, you'll go runnin' home to New York with your tail between your legs."

"Wha— what do you suppose they'll do?" she asked.

"Well, hell, Annie, how the hell should I know? All I do know is that I'm not plannin' to stick around here to find out. I'll be outside for five minutes in case you change your mind." And with that he slammed out of the room.

Anne and Bryce sat staring at each other. "Mr. Shanks," she said, "he isn't a good ol' boy, is he?"

Bryce shook his head very slightly. "You want help gettin' your stuff together?"

"No. I think I can do it in less than four minutes."

All Anne knew for sure was that they'd been traveling southeast and up hill for the past thirty minutes. Buck hadn't said a word since they'd left the motel. Bryce had opened the door of the truck for her, and she'd struggled to get in.

"You gotta pick her up and throw her in," he'd snapped at his brother. Bryce had done his best to be mannerly and had given her a watch-your-step look as he'd closed the door for her.

Since then, Buck had sat next to her in the cab

with his arm out the window in a permanent right-turn signal and had stared straight ahead at the road. The night air was growing cooler, and she was getting cold with the window open, but she hadn't dared mention it yet. She was still trying to figure out why he was so angry with her.

It wasn't because of Roy Shanks. She had a feeling that Mr. Shanks lived to stir up trouble and that it wouldn't have mattered what she'd done at the meeting, he'd have found something to get everyone upset about.

That left the employee-ownership thing. If Buck was mad about that, he should have left her at the motel. He knew from the beginning that they were to be on opposite sides of the mill issue. Being furious with her wasn't going to change that. Nothing could.

She looked back through the rear window to see that Bryce was still following them at a distance. Maybe a neutral subject would break the ice.

"Bryce is very nice. I like him," she said.

Buck's expression was rocklike as he glanced in her direction and then in the rearview mirror at his brother's headlights. He nodded but he didn't say anything. Anne got the distinct impression that she would be getting none of Buck's toe-curling, gut-gripping grins in the near future. But that didn't stop her.

"Why didn't you tell him that we'd met before today?"

"None of his business."

Okay.

"What's the Steel Wheel?" she asked. "A bar? Is that where you were all that time?"

He just nodded.

She couldn't stand it anymore. "Are you mad because I didn't agree with your employee-ownership idea?"

"Annie, I don't think we should talk about that right now."

"Why not?"

"Cuz I'm madder than hell, and I might wring your neck."

"Why? Because I think it's impossible?"

"Because you wouldn't give it a chance. You wouldn't even listen to what we had to say tonight."

Anne sighed and fell silent. Bryce had mentioned the same thing. Maybe she hadn't been fair. But how much of a bad plan did she have to listen to before knowing it wouldn't work? Joel Harriman would never sell Webster Textiles to anyone. They would be in direct competition with Harriman Industries, and Joel wouldn't allow that. If she took an employee-ownership proposal to Calvin Schwab, he'd laugh in her face, and then he'd fire her. Besides, what did a bunch of textile workers know about running anything? They'd go under in less than a year. She was saving them a lot of time, trouble, and pain by refusing to let them get their hopes up.

They'd turned off the paved road. She could hear gravel crunching as the truck's tires rolled over it. There were trees everywhere, but all she could see were their trunks and an occasional low-hanging limb in the headlights.

"I heard all I needed to to know it was a dumb idea. And if you think that rescuing me from Roy Shanks and his buddies is going to change my mind, you're sadly mistaken. I'm here to shut the mill down, not sell it. You knew how things would be between us yesterday," she said defensively.

"Well, I sure as hell didn't think they'd be like this."

"Me either," she said, feeling a little sick inside. All the caution she'd tried to show in dealing with him was overridden by her deep desire to please him. She wanted him to approve of her, wanted him to like her. She wasn't sure why, she just did. But there didn't seem to be much of a chance of that happening now.

At long last a house came into view, but even then it was hard to tell what it looked like when it wasn't covered in darkness. Her general impression was that it was an old house. It was bigger than she'd expected, but then she was beginning to realize that nothing in Kentucky was as she had expected it to be.

Buck parked at the bottom of a low hill in front of the house. It was then that something else occurred to her and sent her spirits spiraling upward once again.

"Okay now," she said, turning in her seat to face him, her voice loud in the silence that came when he turned off the motor. "Let me see if I've got this straight. You're super annoyed at me, but you want to protect me from Roy Shanks, but you're not going to talk to me, because you're mad enough to kill me yourself. Is that right?"

Buck's hands froze on the steering wheel. He turned his head and looked at her but was thoughtfully quiet. When he spoke, she didn't have to stretch her imagination to hear the barest trace of humor in his voice. "That's right."

"Good. I just wanted to clarify that before you stopped talking to me again," she said, feeling a little more sure of herself. "Now I have only one more question."

There was a suspicious silence, and then he asked, "What is it?"

"Should I say thank you?"

In the dark shadows of the cab she couldn't make out his facial expression, but she saw him turn his head and look away from her for a moment, and then she saw his profile. She could feel her heart pulsating heavily in her chest as she waited anxiously to see what he was going to do.

The noises of insects in the woods around them seemed to rise in stereophonic volume in the quiet.

Suddenly Buck threw up his hands and let loose a throaty growl of defeat. He turned to her. "Yes. You should say thank you. But not to me. Thank your lucky stars that I'm having such a hard time staying mad at you."

"I do, I do," she said in mock earnest, although she wasn't pretending in her heart. "I don't mind being with quiet people, but getting the silent treatment drives me nuts."

"I figured that," he said, his voice soft and sly. She could see the lightness of his teeth when he smiled, and her mind developed pictures of that cheeky grin he used all too frequently for the good of her libido. "Course, if you'd rather, we can always get down on the ground and wrestle it out."

All at once she wasn't cold anymore. She felt flushed and hot and in need of some air. Still facing him, she grappled with the door handle, saying, "I don't think you really want to do that. I had three older brothers, remember. I know every dirty trick in the book."

The door came open and she scrambled out, but not before she heard him say, "Oh, yeah? And who do you think taught all them Yankee boys how to fight dirty in the first place, huh?" He was still bragging when he came around the end of the truck and reached into the bed for her suitcases. "I bet I could still teach you a trick or two that didn't get passed on."

A trick or two or ten, she thought, noticing that even in the darkness his body seemed to cast a huge shadow over hers. She could feel his closeness and knew that he was near enough to touch, if she dared. Her fingers itched to do just that. They were actually tingling. She rubbed them together while she spoke.

"Just show me where you want me to sleep."

Buck laughed out loud. "I'll give you a two-second chance to rephrase that, Annie."

She used most of her time trying to recall what she'd said, and then rushed to say, "Okay. Show me a place where I can *get* some sleep then."

Buck laughed again and began to lead the way up to the house. There was a stone path that led to a big wraparound porch. The house was clean and painted white with dark green trim around the front door.

Buck stepped inside first, to turn on the porch light for Bryce and a table lamp for Anne. The interior wasn't anything one would see in a magazine. It had the distinctive marks of male-only territory, with newspapers and beer cans scattered about and books piled high in the corners. But it was basically clean, fairly well tended, and very homey. The furniture was old, heavy, and comfortable looking. Again, it wasn't what she had expected.

"You hungry?" Buck asked as he put her bags down at the bottom of the stairs across from the front door.

"No. Thanks."

"Tired?"

Not as tired as she was jittery and strangely timid all of a sudden. She nodded.

Buck leaned over and took up her bags again. At the top of the stairs he turned on a hall light that revealed four doors leading off the main corridor.

"My room." He indicated the one at the top of the stairs to the right with a nod of his head. "You could eventually get some sleep there," he said, grinning at her. The teasing twinkle in his eyes gentled his remark to something playful, so Anne cast him a droll stare. "Okay. This is Bryce's room," he went on, undaunted.

"You can have this one," he said when he reached a third doorway. He ushered her into a room on the right at the rear of the house. When the light came on Anne saw that the decor was at odds with that of the rest of the house. This room had pink-and-blue flowered wallpaper and frilly white curtains; it was very feminine. At the questioning look on Anne's face, Buck simply stated, "This was my sister's room."

"I didn't know you had a sister," she said, amazed. And then it occurred to her that with all the revelations in the past twenty-four hours of everything he wasn't, she really didn't know much about who he really was. She felt an acute need to know. She wanted to know. "Where is she?"

"She and her husband live in Covington," he said. She glanced up to find him looking at her, watching her. And when he spoke again, she felt as if he'd read her mind. "There's a lot we don't know about each other, Annie. But there's already a couple of things we're pretty sure about."

"Such as?" She knew she was going to hate herself in the morning for asking that question.

Putting his hands on her shoulders, he turned her to face him more squarely. With one index finger, he pushed her hair behind her ear, and then gently played with her lobe while he spoke. "Well, we know we'll probably never agree on the future of the mill."

Her heart was hammering in her throat, choking her when she tried to speak. "That's true."

"And we know our lives and backgrounds are totally different."

"That's true too." There seemed to be less and less air in the room, and his face seemed to be getting closer and closer.

"We know that there might not be a whole lot of time for us."

She nodded slightly. Speech was too difficult.

"You know I want you."

Half a nod this time.

"And I know you want me."

"I know," she uttered. Unable to stand the suspense any longer, she closed the distance between their lips. Buck met her greedily. His mouth warm, wet, and demanding. Without a thought in her head or a warning in her heart, she leaned into the strong, lean contours of his body. She hadn't realized how much she'd wanted him to kiss her until that moment. It was as if she had been hungry and thirsty and didn't know it. He aroused needs in her that she didn't even know she had.

He may not have gone to college. He may not have seen much of the world. He wasn't the slickest, most debonair person she'd ever met, but the man knew how to kiss. He was a master at tantalizing sensitive nerve endings, drawing them into a frantic, frenzied state of excitement. His hands traveled her body, seeking out erogenous places, launching Anne's senses on a voyage of expectancy and hope. He teased and charmed her in turn, sweeping the ground from under her feet. The good ol' boy lavished her with kisses slowly, thoroughly, and to Anne's way of thinking, exquisitely.

She felt her blouse being pulled away from the band of her skirt, and she tensed, waiting, waiting for the touch of his hands on her skin. When it came, her tension only increased. She yearned for a deeper, more intimate touch, and moaned her desire. Buck deepened their kisses, his fingers trailing gooseflesh over her back and up the sides of her body. But to Anne, it was as if he were only giving out samples. She wanted all of him.

Buck heard the footsteps before she did and reluctantly raised his face from hers. Her eyes were heavy and slow to open, but her efforts were rewarded with a quick, sweet kiss.

"He didn't learn his timing from me," Buck said, speaking of his brother, as the two of them listened to the bedroom door close down the hall.

Anne had forgotten all about Bryce. She was still breathing too heavily, her heart was still hammering too rapidly, and her bones were almost the consistency of pudding. She smiled at the stern, disapproving look on Buck's face, and said, "Maybe it's just as well."

He pulled back a little to get a better look at her. He searched her face with gentle, intuitive green eyes. Something inside of him beckoned her. And again it occurred to her how easy it would be to let herself slip into Buck's soul and lose herself there, forever. It seemed as though it would be the simplest thing in the world for her to do, and yet it frightened her.

"Scary, huh?" he asked, his voice hardly a whisper but reassuring at the same time. He appeared to understand the enormity of what they had found in each other. He seemed to know what it was, where it came from, and how it was going to change them. But he didn't give her the impression of being particularly frightened by it.

Anne nodded self-consciously and smiled. "I felt safer when you were angry with me."

He placed a kiss on her forehead, then held it there with his own. "Don't be afraid, Annie. We've got time. And I'm right here with you."

Oddly enough, his comment was comforting. She liked the idea of having him around in times of danger or when she was fearful. In a world full of things that were instant, disposable, and temporary, Buck was as solid as a rock. He made her feel safe, and she trusted him.

"Bathroom's downstairs, next to the kitchen," he said, pulling her close and holding her tightly.

He released her, kissed her good night, and turned to go. "If you need anything, holler."

"Thanks." She watched him edge toward the door, and for a moment she thought he might say something else.

"Good night."

"Good night, Buck."

Five

At least spring was as inconsistent in Kentucky as it was in New York. When morning came the sky was gray and cloudy, and a cool breeze ruffled the curtains in Anne's room as she stood looking out of the second-story window at Buck's back-yard. There was a deer standing in the middle of it.

Anne had never seen a deer out of captivity before. It awed her that the wild animal would actually amble out of the woods, only two hundred feet from Buck's back door, to eat the grass from his lawn. "You'd never see anything like that in the city," she told herself aloud, a wry smile on her lips.

In fact she'd probably never see anything like this part of the country again. There were *so* many trees. Different kinds of trees. Without the benefit of a degree in botany, she knew the names of only a few, such as the maples and oaks. But it seemed to Anne that someone had done a fine job of mixing and sculpting the trees to the hills and valleys they grew on. If she angled her head just right, she had a breathtaking view of a valley that looked as if it were carpeted with the new green leaves of springtime.

Buck's house was much older than it had ap-

peared the night before. From the buildings and
fencing that surrounded it, Anne gathered that it
had once been a farm. There were no animals,
but there was a small, newly planted garden to
the right of the back door. And the house itself
wasn't white, as she had thought, but a faded
yellow. The outside was in good condition but could
use some fresh paint.

She'd been awake for over an hour, waiting for
a sound that would indicate the brothers were up
and she could go downstairs to take a shower.
When it came, it was the roar of an engine from
the other side of the house. The deer heard it too
and bounded back into the woods. Anne listened
as one of the trucks went down the gravel road,
and she wondered how the driver had gotten up,
dressed, and done whatever else he'd done before
driving away, without her hearing him.

She found Buck alone in the kitchen. His back
was to her, his shoulders broad and powerful under a blue denim work shirt. His long lean legs
were stretched out under the table before him. He
was holding up the corner of a newspaper with
one hand, in the other was a cup of something
steaming hot that smelled incredibly like coffee.
She'd spent so much time in her room that she
could have wrestled him to the floor for his morning brew. Recalling his willingness to get down
and dirty with her the night before, she decided
against it.

"Good morning," she said sweetly, hoping he'd
be a good ol' boy and offer her a cup of coffee. "I
just saw Bambi in your backyard."

He turned in his chair to smile at her, and the
sun broke through the rain clouds to shine brightly
in the sky. She wasn't sure if that actually happened, but it seemed like it for a moment.

"I hope you invited him back for the huntin'
season," he said, laughing at the horrified gri-

mace on Anne's face when she realized what that meant.

"You'd shoot Bambi?"

"Only if he walked out in front of my gun." He laughed again at her moans of disgust as he got up and opened a cupboard to show her where the coffee mugs were kept. "How'd you sleep?"

"Like a log. You and Bryce are very quiet people. I've been upstairs waiting for you to make some noise so I could come down." She held her mug out and let Buck fill it for her.

He nodded and grinned. "We heard ya. Couldn't figure out what the hell you were doin' up there."

They laughed, a little uncomfortable with the intimacy of their circumstances as they moved back over to the table to drink their coffee.

Anne didn't miss the covert inspection he gave her nightwear, nor was she unaware of the way her body quickened when she knew Buck was looking at her. Part of her wanted to put a little extra sway in her hips and look more seductive, while another part of her just wanted to get her hips back to New York and out of harm's way. She pulled her robe more tightly around her and reminded herself not to get too deeply involved with Buck. Their worlds were galaxies apart, their time together would be short. It could never work out between them . . . or so she'd been telling herself throughout the night and early morning hours.

"I was looking out the window. I can't get over how beautiful it is here. I think I'm falling in love with Kentucky," she said whimsically, forcing herself to think of other things."

"So stay," he said, as if it were as easy as that. "You wouldn't be the first Yankee transplant we've had."

"No, probably not. But I bet I'd be the most unpopular," she said, thinking of the night before.

"Hmm," he said thoughtfully. "That's probably

true. Unless of course you'd like to reconsider your position on the mill closin' down."

"It's not my position. It's Harriman's," she said as she sat down at the table.

"But you're his representative here. You could talk to him for us."

"Buck." She let the tone of her voice tell him that it was too early in the morning to have a reenactment of the workers' meeting with him. He seemed to understand.

"Okay. Okay," he said, his gaze skimming down over the upper half of the satin robe and tailored pajamas she was wearing. The arm he had propped on the table fell toward her, his fingers catching themselves on the collar of her nightshirt. "What is this? Silk?"

All she could do was nod as his hand moved down the lapel, slipping inside to test the quality of the fabric between his fingers. She held her breath as his knuckles gently grazed the top of her breast. She thought for a moment that her heart might have stopped except that there was something throbbing in her throat.

She looked up and met his stare. It was knowing, confident, and satisfied. His voice was, too, when he said, "Nice fabric. Fine weave."

"I—I've never known a man to be interested in—in cloth before," she stammered, all too aware that *he* was aware of what he was doing to her.

"It's my business, remember? I make cloth," he said, as he slowly withdrew his fingers, gathering the front of her shirt in his fist. With a light tug he pulled her closer and closer until she could feel his breath on her lips. "As a matter of fact, in my business, we call this a *material come on.*"

She groaned over his silly joke, but that was all she got out before his mouth closed over hers for a deep lingering kiss. He hadn't lost his touch since the night before. Within seconds Anne felt like a weightless mass of charged energy. Her whole body seemed to pulsate, and yet at the same time she felt as if she weren't really there.

She heard Buck sigh his enjoyment and felt his lips move lower, along her jaw and upper neck. The temptation to slide off her chair to the floor and to make wild, desperate love then and there was almost overwhelming. Lord, the things he did to her. . . . She was weak with wanting, but something was very wrong.

It seemed strange to her that Buck's attention could swing so swiftly between her, the mill, and back again. It wasn't a complete thought or a whole feeling, only a niggling uneasiness in her that kept her teetering on the brink of total surrender.

"Buck," she said, her voice husky with emotion as she tried to capture his attention. With her hands over his, she managed to loosen his hold on her nightshirt and pull away a little. "Buck. We need to talk."

" 'Bout what?" he asked, trying to silence her with his mouth.

"About the mill. About us."

"Later."

"No. Now. I don't want any misunderstandings between us."

He stopped his attempts at distracting her and looked her square in the eye. He seemed to be considering her words, considering her, and then finally appeared to agree. "Okay. But later. I mean, I wouldn't mind discussin' the us part now, but I never talk shop with a woman who isn't wearin' any underwear. It keeps me at a distinct disadvantage."

"Yes, well talking about the two of us, dressed as I am, would have *me* at a disadvantage. So I think I'll get dressed," she said, standing self-consciously, more aware than ever of her lack of underwear and the thinness of her nightclothes.

"Well, if you feel you have to . . . ," he said, disappointed. "When you're ready we can go for a walk, if you want. We'll talk then."

"But what if it rains?" she asked, glancing out the window at the dark clouds.

"Then we'll get wet." His gaze lowered once again to take in the outline of her breasts under the soft clinging silk. All over again, her stomach started jumping up and down, and her heart began to throb in her throat. Deep inside her, she admitted defeat and acknowledged a wish for rain.

She should have gone to the mill and started her audit on the financial records, but Buck and his offer were too tempting. Besides, who worked on Saturdays if they could find an excuse not to? She planned to tell Calvin that Lily didn't work weekends and that she couldn't find anything without her. He'd understand this, since he was unable to find the executive washroom without directions from his secretary.

When she'd packed her bags in New York three days earlier, a nature walk in the wilds of Kentucky hadn't even crossed her mind. The best she could muster on such short notice was a lavender cotton sweater, a full floral skirt, and espadrilles, the lowest heels she had with her.

At first their "walk" consisted of ambling around the LaSalle property. Apparently, Buck's grandfather had "bought the land from the bank" when the original owners had moved away in search of better times during the Great Depression. Since then, it had stayed in the family through good times and bad because, as he put it, "you can't grow roots in land that doesn't belong to you."

"My dad was sort of a wanderer," Anne told Buck, absently making conversation. "He'd get restless in one place, at one job, and pack us all up and move us to someplace new." She laughed softly. "I was in college before I realized that some people actually spent their whole life in the same place."

"That must'a' been tough," he said, surprising Anne with the sympathy in his voice. "Making new friends all the time, new schools, new towns."

Anne had to pause and think. She'd hated it at the time. She'd never really felt comfortable anywhere because she knew that as soon as she did, she'd move away again. She could remember the pain of having to leave people she loved and things she knew. And she could recall the fear and the loneliness of being the new kid and getting lost on the way home from school. But that's the way it had been all her life, and since she'd never really thought it could be any different, she accepted it, until that very moment, when a pang of acute envy for Buck's sense of belonging passed through her.

"It wasn't so bad," she said, too proud to admit her true feelings. "My dad always made a great adventure out of it. And if nothing else, it drew my brothers and me closer together. Because lots of times the five of us were all we had."

Buck didn't look at all convinced that a nomadic life was in any way acceptable, but he didn't press the point. Instead, he went on to explain how his land had been a working farm at one time. But since neither he nor Bryce had the time or inclination to be farmers, it now consisted mostly of the garden and a few animals that were slaughtered to supplement the meat they got by hunting and fishing. Anne thought butcher shops were a lot less trouble and not nearly as grisly.

Soon they began to travel into the woods. Of course where Anne came from, this sort of walking was called hiking, but who was she to quibble? The scenery was as pleasant to look at as her guide, and she was enjoying them both very much.

She asked about the different trees and flowers, and he pointed out the hickory, beech, and poplar; the rhododendrons, magnolias, and mountain laurels. He even stopped to show her a huge Kentucky coffee tree.

Still, what may have seemed like a major expedition had a strong undercurrent of sensuality. There were accidental touches, chance eye contact, and other subliminal messages of their mutual attraction. Anne wasn't sure which electrical storm was more imposing or which would break first, the one gathering in the sky above or the one between them below.

They came to a stream that eventually widened into a long, broad pond. Trees, bushes, and vines grew wild at its edges, as if the forest had grudgingly stopped where the water began, only because it didn't want to drown in its depths.

"This is incredible," Anne uttered, almost breathless in her awe as they walked out over the water on a small, rickety old dock. "Except for this thing," she looked down with a great deal of trepidation at the planking under her feet, "it doesn't look as if man has ever stepped foot here."

"Pretty, isn't it?" Buck was clever at understating the obvious.

"It's incredible," she repeated, her voice a whisper. She had this strange notion that she was standing on the edge of God's summer resort.

"Tomorrow mornin', if it's nice, I'll take you fishin'. You'll love it," he said, grinning at her. "We'll stand barefoot on the riverbank and wiggle our toes in the mud. There's no other feelin' like it—'cept maybe catchin' something."

"Sounds delightful." Somehow, spending Sunday morning in church had more appeal to Anne than it ever had before.

When the land began to tilt upward, Anne knew she was now hiking for sure. They went higher and higher into the isolated woods until she came to a halt on a small plateau that overlooked a green, wooded valley below.

"I don't suppose there's an escalator around anywhere," she questioned as she stood looking up at the huge jagged rocks and cliffs above her, trying to catch her breath at the same time. Higher still, the clouds grew darker and more threatening.

"Tired?"

Again the understatement, Anne thought. "Just a trifle. This isn't exactly my idea of a walk, Buck. This is more like mountain climbing, trail blazing, wilderness forging."

"Annie!" he cried in mock dismay. "I'm disappointed. I grew up on stories about how tough and unrelenting Yankee women were. Don't tell me I got the only weak one in the bunch."

"Cute, Buck." She grimaced at him and then motioned for him to lead the way. She was as patriotic as the next woman, after all—and she never had been able to resist a dare.

The climb wasn't as bad as Anne had anticipated. They didn't actually go over the rocks; they went around them or between them, staying well away from the edges of the mountain. They finally stopped their journey on a small grassy knoll covered with knee-high grass and sprinkled with goldenrod and bluebells.

It was a glorious setting. Very romantic. But as Anne walked over to look at the vista below, she had a sneaking suspicion that he had handpicked it for a more specific reason that had nothing to do with romance.

The town of Webster lay sprawled against the hillsides and along the valley floor. There were thousands of houses, apartment buildings, and businesses. At its center, between the river and the railroad tracks that ran from east to west, sat Webster Textiles, white smoke swelling up from its chimneys.

Without words, Buck was again trying to make his point, to explain his resistance to the directive to shut the mill down. The mill was the backbone of Webster, Kentucky. Located in a plush green valley between the Appalachians and the Cumberland plateau, the people for miles around had made their living for over a hundred years weaving threads into fabric. Only in the past seventy years had they included the printing and treating of the material, drawing more and more people out of the mountains and into Webster and the smaller towns nearby as employment increased.

He wanted her to know that Webster, indeed the entire valley, faced mass unemployment, which would eventually strangle the economy, drive the population away, and leave it looking like a ghost of its present existence.

"Doesn't look like much from up here, does it?" he asked, coming to stand beside her. She looked up at him but didn't speak, only waited for him to finish what he'd gone to so much trouble to say. "It's old. The mill's old. The buildin's and houses are old. Even most of the people are old, because the younger ones are leavin' as fast as they can for bigger, newer cities. When the mill closes, everyone under sixty will have to leave too, so they can make a livin' someplace else. And when the people who stay die off, this place won't exist anymore."

He was painting a gruesome picture in a lifeless tone of voice. But she knew better than to believe he was giving in to the company's way of thinking. She could see the devotion he had for the land in his eyes. In the straightness of his shoulders she saw the pride he had in his people. And there was no missing the stubborn set of his jaw when he looked down at her and began to speak again.

"But from up here you can't really see the town, Annie. It's not the buildin's or the mill that make Webster a town, it's the people who live there. They have roots here, deeper than most of the trees. The people who stay here have chosen to stay because they love it. Their families are here. They have hopes and dreams and memories here. Who they are is part of this place, and no one has the right just to wipe it off the face of the earth, like it never existed. Like they don't exist."

There was no denying the strength of his feelings on this subject. Not only did he have more to say about this than he did about anything else they'd talked about, but she could feel how emotional was his attachment and how much he wanted her to understand. Her frustration escalated.

"Dammit, Buck. What do you want from me? Do you think I'm enjoying this? Do you think this is the way I get my kicks? You're dead wrong, if you do. The decision wasn't and isn't mine. Closing the mill is just my job. It doesn't have anything to do with the way I feel."

"How do you feel?"

"I told you. I think it stinks."

"Then why won't you help us?"

"Help you do what? Invest every penny, every drop of blood you have left into that damn mill, only to lose it in the end anyway?"

"How do you know that'll happen? Why can't we make it work?" His gaze was so intense, so confused, so frantic.

"Harriman won't let you," she shouted at him in a sudden fit of hopelessness. Why couldn't he have accepted her word for it? Why couldn't he have accepted the closing as inevitable and let it go at that? She knew as well as she knew her name that Buck wouldn't give up without a fight. Maybe now that he knew what he was up against, he wouldn't keep trying to run himself into the ground with it. "The competition is bad enough already, with foreign trade and other companies, without adding you to the list. He can't afford to keep you open, and he can't afford to let you go it alone. Either way, he'd be cutting his own throat."

Buck seemed to consider her statement. His gaze was on her face, but she couldn't tell if he was really looking at her or if he was seeing something else. Suddenly he frowned.

"How big a threat could we ever be to him?" he asked. "The market's not all that small. We don't want to make millions. We just want to make a livin'."

Anne turned away. She'd said too much already. She had her own means of making a living to consider.

"Annie." With gentle hands, he guided her back around to face him. "Try to understand. If we don't try to keep the mill open, we'll lose everything. Not only our jobs and our homes and everything that goes with them, but we'll lose our pride and self-respect as well. If it doesn't work, if we fall on our face, at least we'll have the satisfaction of knowin' that we tried. It's the tryin' that counts. Can't you see that?"

She saw it and she understood. It could have been her own father saying the exact same thing. That didn't mean that it would be any easier to watch. She began to see another reason for his dragging her into the dingle bushes to tell her all of this. She could see how much it was costing him to talk about his pride and his self-respect. They obviously weren't topics normally open for discussion. But clearly he'd been willing to make the sacrifice, if it would help her to understand.

"I can't stop you, Buck. Send in a bid for the

mill if you want to," she said, defeated. At least he knew the name of the game he was playing now. "I hope you get it, and I hope it works out for you. But I want something else to be perfectly clear between us."

"What?"

"Don't ask me for any help. I can't give it to you. I have my own job, my own pride and self-respect to take care of here. And until I get word to the contrary, I'm going ahead with all the things I have to do to close the mill down."

"Sounds fair to me," he said, nodding his agreement. Then a slow grin spread across his face, and his eyes twinkled happily. "Now that we have a professional understandin', there's one other thing I brought you up here to discuss."

It was apparent that he didn't want to talk about the mill anymore, but he still looked as if he meant business.

"This isn't going to make me mad or get me into more trouble, is it?" she asked playfully, eager to have all their serious talking over with.

"I hope not."

"Okay. What else did you want to talk about?" It was getting cold, and she hoped that Buck would say what he had to before the storm struck and they got hit by lightning. How would she explain that to Calvin? How was she going to explain any of this to Calvin?

She looked up at Buck and patiently waited for him to begin. His smile had diminished by half, and there was an uncertainty about him, an uncharacteristic shyness that had her spellbound before it got the better of her curiosity.

"What is it?" she asked again, her tone coaxing.

For a very long moment he just stared at her. He was asking her questions, but she couldn't hear them and didn't know how to answer. She wanted to look away and break his penetrating gaze, but something in him compelled her not to. Silence wrapped itself around them.

At long last he shifted his weight uncomfortably, and in one fluid motion he took off his hat and rubbed the back of his neck with his hand, saying, "Maybe this isn't such a good time."

"A good time for what?"

"Nothin', forget it. Let's just go."

"No, Buck. You were going to say something. What was it. I want to know."

"Annie, it's not important. Let's go before the storm hits," he said.

"Is there a stream or something up here? I'm thirsty," she said, stalling for time, hoping he'd change his mind and tell her whatever it was that was making him so uncomfortable.

"No. You'll have to wait till we get back to the house." Again he reached out a hand for her.

"Then just let me sit a while longer. I'm beat."

"For cryin' out loud, Annie." He grabbed at her this time, and catching her by the arm, brought her to her feet in front of him. "If you're thirsty and tired, let's go. You can drink all you want and take a nap when we get back."

"I don't want to go. I want to hear what you were going to say," she said, refusing to budge.

Frowning at her in frustration and exasperation, he seemed to be debating what to do. Then he suddenly snatched her up into his arms and pressed a kiss to her lips. It was hard, hungry, and full of pent-up emotion.

The suddenness wore off rapidly. She felt his tongue slide across her lips, tasting, testing, demanding entrance. Readily she opened herself to him and, with great ardor, set about her own explorations, discovering thrills and sensations never before charted in her senses.

A thought about the size of a gnat buzzed her

consciousness and was no less pesky in telling her that getting too involved with Buck was a bad idea. But her body didn't give it time to settle on her brain. It smacked it dead as she leaned into Buck's strong arms, wanting him to devour her. Her breasts grew hard and tight against his chest, her senses whirled, and still she squeezed closer to him.

He pulled away slowly, gauging her reaction, seeing her through eyes he didn't seem accustomed to using. His right hand came up to touch her face, palm flat against her cheek, his thumb stroking. His disquiet was gone, leaving only his longing and wonderment for her to see. He lowered his head once more.

Tiny sipping kisses on her forehead and cheekbones, along her jaw and down her neck, set a zillion quivering tingles zinging through her body. Her eyes closed, and her knees grew weak as her head lolled to one side, exposing more of her flesh to his gentle kisses.

"Annie." She heard his whisper in the wind and gradually forced her eyes to open. The desire in his eyes should have frightened her. It was consuming and possessive, as if he wanted to own her soul. But all she felt was the immense tenderness with which he regarded her.

They stood gasping and staring at each other, wondering if they should simply enjoy the moment or take it one step further, into a realm they had yet to discover together.

Buck came around first, looking up at the menacing sky and then back down at Anne with that tickling grin on his lips and a twinkle in his eyes. "Are you happy now?" he asked, teasing.

"Very. But I'd still like to know what you were going to say."

Buck laughed and shook his head. "Weren't you listenin' to anythin' I just told you? I've been thinkin' about that kiss since the last time I had you this close and all to myself. Sometimes it's just easier to show somebody what you're thinkin' instead of tryin' to explain it."

"A man of action, huh?" she said, smiling her pleasure at his words and pushing away the caution that warned her not to invest anything in this man that she couldn't afford to lose. "Should I warn Harriman about you?"

He released her as he considered the question. With her hand firmly clasped in his, he began to walk back in the direction from which they had just come. "Nah. Let's let him find that out on his own. It was more of a warnin' for you, anyway."

"For me? My, that sounds ominous." She tried to sound duly impressed and keep a straight face.

"Believe it," he said, turning to help her down to a small path between two huge boulders. He didn't remove his hands from her waist once she was on firm ground. Instead, he pulled her close again and laid a promissory kiss on her lips. He smiled and tweaked her nose as he said, "I got plans for you, sugar." Then he turned and led the way back down the path.

Oh, be still my heart, she mumbled to herself, watching his posterior as he moved. *No wonder the guys in the office never let me have any of the fun jobs.*

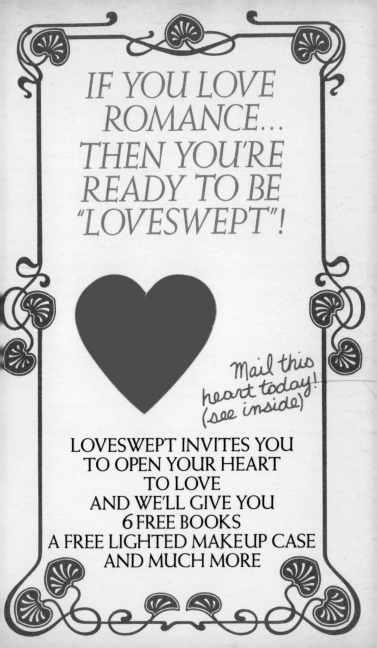

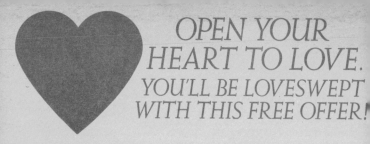
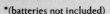

FREE – LIGHTED MAKEUP CASE!
FREE – 6 LOVESWEPT NOVELS!

- NO OBLIGATION
- NO PURCHASE NECESSARY

(DETACH AND MAIL CARD TODAY.)

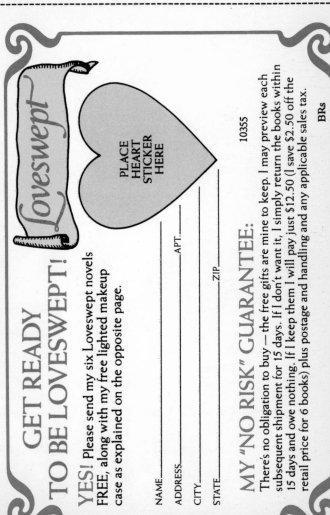

GET READY TO BE LOVESWEPT!

YES! Please send my six Loveswept novels FREE, along with my free lighted makeup case as explained on the opposite page.

Loveswept

PLACE HEART STICKER HERE

10355

NAME _____

ADDRESS._____

CITY_____ APT._____

STATE_____ ZIP._____

MY "NO RISK" GUARANTEE:

There's no obligation to buy — the free gifts are mine to keep. I may preview each subsequent shipment for 15 days. If I don't want it, I simply return the books within 15 days and owe nothing. If I keep them I will pay just $12.50 (I save $2.50 off the retail price for 6 books) plus postage and handling and any applicable sales tax.

BRs

REMEMBER!

- The free books and gift are mine to keep!
- There is no obligation!
- I may preview each shipment for 15 days!
- I can cancel anytime!

(DETACH AND MAIL CARD TODAY.)

BUSINESS REPLY MAIL
FIRST-CLASS MAIL PERMIT NO. 2456 HICKSVILLE, N.Y.

POSTAGE WILL BE PAID BY ADDRESSEE

Loveswept

Bantam Books
P.O. Box 985
Hicksville, NY 11802-9827

NO POSTAGE
NECESSARY
IF MAILED
IN THE
UNITED STATES

Six

"You wanna meet Bry at the Steel Wheel, or would you rather go home?" Buck asked as they finished their coffee in a small homey restaurant in town. It was the end of a lovely spring day, and their mood was mellow and light.

The skies had remained dark and threatening throughout the afternoon, and when finally the storm broke, Buck set logs ablaze in the fireplace. While thunder and lightening boomed and flashed outside, they had curled up in front of the fire to share stories, secrets, and dreams.

Anne couldn't remember ever being so relaxed or open with anyone of such short acquaintance before. She had long-time female friends who didn't know some of the things she found it so easy to tell Buck about. He was a good listener for someone who appeared to be so full of himself.

He sat close to her, watching her face as she spoke. Somehow, he always seemed to be touching her. It didn't appear to be something conscious on his part, nor was it anything that generated uneasiness or annoyance in her. She would simply look down and see his fingers entwined in hers or feel them on her neck and arm or against her thigh. Oddly enough, she took comfort from it. She liked this closeness between them, this warmth. And always there was an underlying energy, a force between them that was strong and powerful but not urgent in its need to show its strength.

It did occur to her that perhaps Buck wasn't the person she should be telling her whole life story to. He was an enemy of sorts, after all. But it seemed the easiest and most natural thing in the world for her to while away their time together from the rest of the world. When they were alone, one on one, there was no mill, no barrier of difference between their hometowns and backgrounds. They were simply Anne and Buck. She felt as if she'd known him forever. She trusted him, and she didn't give a tinker's damn about anything but the moments they were sharing.

The rains had subsided to a drizzle when they decided they were hungry. Anne had offered to cook to repay him for his hospitality. Readily, he'd agreed and promised her the best piece of apple pie in three states for dessert. She'd merely laughed when he'd informed her that they'd have to go into Webster to get it.

"How do you know that Bryce is at the Steel Wheel?" she asked, licking the last crumb of the best apple pie she'd ever tasted off her fork.

"He called."

"When?"

"After we got back from our walk this mornin'." Anne laid her fork on her plate and then looked at him. She sensed he wasn't telling her something. From the guarded look on his face, she guessed what it was.

"What happened at McKee's last night?"

"Not much," he said with a too-casual shrug. When she made it clear that she didn't believe him, he told the rest of the story. "A couple of bricks went through the windows of the room you were supposed to be staying in. Jimmy heard 'em

pull in but didn't get there in time to stop them.
He saw them though and plans to send them the
repair bill—after he pads it a little for all the grief
they caused."

"Was it Roy Shanks?"

He shook his head. Anne couldn't tell if he didn't
know if it was Shanks or if he didn't want to tell
her. On a more cheerful note, he asked, "How
about it? What do you say to meetin' Bry for a
beer at the Steel Wheel?"

"Oh. Well, I don't know. Is it a good idea for you
to be seen with me? I don't want you getting
caught in the cross fire if someone decides to take
a couple of potshots at me."

He grinned and shook his head. "Bryce has
spent most of the afternoon puttin' bugs in all the
right ears. He got the message around."

"What message?"

"That you've reconsidered your position."

"But I haven't," she said emphatically, worried
that he'd misunderstood her that morning.

"But you're not goin' to stand in our way either.
All folks want is a chance, Annie. You've given 'em
that, at least."

In the end they agreed to go to the Steel Wheel.

During the drive through town, Anne was on
the edge of her seat—literally and figuratively. Occasionally Buck would comment on what he thought
might be a point of interest to her: a church that
was over a hundred years old, the youth center,
an interstate highway and what cities could be
found on either end of it. But at one point he
stopped the truck in the middle of the road to talk
to a friend who was heading in the opposite direction. He introduced Anne to his friend, who smiled
at her amicably. She smiled back, trying not to
show how nervous she was getting about the traffic pulling up behind them.

Granted, it wasn't exactly rush hour in Manhattan, but even for Webster, the drivers in the cars behind them were showing incredible tolerance for Buck and his friend. When they finally waved good bye and started moving again, Anne sank back in her seat and sighed with relief.

"You know," she said informatively, "if you were to pull a stunt like that in New York, someone would have gotten out of their car and shot you both dead."

Buck chuckled, and then holding out his hand as if to say it was a very simple matter, he said, "But that's the beauty of it, Annie. We ain't in New York."

Anne just nodded.

If you've seen one Steel Wheel, you've seen 'em all, she thought as they pulled up in front of the single-story brick structure, with its neon signs and beer displays shining through the windows. It looked very much like some of the bars in New York, Philadelphia, or Boston. It was a relaxed, cozy, let-your-hair-down sort of place that every faction of the working class seemed to adopt as its own. This one just happened to belong to the textile workers of Webster, Kentucky.

Inside the Steel Wheel the air was cloudy with cigarette smoke and smelled of beer and bodies. It took several seconds for Anne's eyes to adjust to the dim lighting. She felt, before she could see, that their arrival was not going unnoticed.

Gradually a hush fell over the crowd, leaving only the loud whining of some female country singer on the jukebox to fill up the silence. Only a few of the faces were familiar to Anne. The only conclusion she could come to from their expressions was that Bryce had carried out his mission well. The hostility in the crowd had diminished to suspicion and a wary dislike for her. There was some relief in knowing that they weren't going to jump her if she walked by their tables. She couldn't really blame them for not taking a liking to her. To her way of thinking, aloof tolerance of her presence in their bar was a grand gesture indeed.

"Hey, you all," Buck called out in a friendly manner, slicing the air with his hand in greeting. "Looks like most of you know who this pretty little lady here is. We're out tonight socializin', just like the rest of you. So if you got anythin' to say to her that isn't of a social nature, we'd be happy if you'd keep it for another time. But if you'd care to come over and show her what right fine people you are . . . well, hell, I'll buy the drinks."

Anne wanted to sink through the floor. Slinking off to a secluded table in one of the corners would have pleased her very much. Buck's announcement to a roomful of people that if they didn't have anything nice to say, to say nothing at all, which drew even more attention to her position in the middle of enemy territory, made her feel exceedingly vulnerable. And yet, in the back of her mind, she registered that Buck was addressing not strangers but his friends, neighbors, and allies. She couldn't help but wonder if she knew any other man who would do the same on her behalf.

The reaction of the crowd was hard to judge. Expressions were mixed and varied, but within seconds the incident was over. Gradually people went back to doing whatever they'd been doing before Anne's invasion.

Country music blared as she followed Buck around the bar while he sought out his brother. She was trying very hard not to look as conspicuous as she felt. It didn't work. Buck was well liked—no matter who he associated with—and greeted frequently. He kept trying to hold her hand and draw her into the brief conversations he was having as he passed from table to table, but her discomfort made her back away.

It wasn't until after she'd spotted Bryce in the crowd that she realized the uneasiness she was feeling was of her own making. She looked back at the older gentlemen to whom Buck was speaking and saw for the first time that his timid glances toward her weren't filled with displeasure. He was naturally curious, but his demeanor was well disposed and accessible. The man seemed willing to give her the benefit of the doubt, presuming she was a halfway decent person despite her position with Harriman Industries.

Instantly she warmed to the man and smiled at him. She looked back over the crowd, at the people Buck had spoken to previously, and saw the same willingness to accept her in most of their faces. She marveled at the strangeness of these Kentucky people. These were the same people who had given birth to the legendary Hatfields and McCoys. They knew how to hold a grudge. Still, they were willing to give her a fair chance and judge her on her own merits as a person. Somewhere deep down inside her she hoped she wouldn't disappoint them.

When they finally sat down at the table Bryce had been guarding for them, Anne was almost relaxed. A barmaid came to take their order. The bar looked well stocked, but Anne knew better than to call more attention to herself by ordering anything other than a cold beer. Actually she liked beer, but it wasn't something she normally ordered in the chic New York lounges and nightclubs she occasionally went to.

Bryce got up to put more money in the jukebox and Buck moved his chair closer to Anne's, looping one arm across the back of hers and leaning so he could be heard over the music already playing.

"See. That wasn't so bad, now was it?" His face was so close, she could feel every word he spoke as his breath tickled across her cheek. She turned her head slightly, brushing his nose with hers. Then she smiled and shook her head slightly. His gaze was as intense as hers even when he continued to speak. "Most of these folks are good people. The best. Given half a chance, they could be the best friends you ever had in your life."

Anne could only nod her agreement. Buck's face was so close, his eyes so intense, his body so warm and big, all she could do was stare back at him. For a moment she thought he might kiss her again. For that same moment she hoped he would. She'd been waiting all afternoon. He'd said he had plans for her, and she had assumed they were similar to the plans her heart and body had for him. But so far he hadn't done a whole lot to reveal that they were on the same wavelength. And frankly she wasn't sure how much more touching and looking she could take from him before she gave in to the tiny tingles and excited muscle spasms and just flat out attacked him.

He wanted to kiss her. She could tell by the look on his face. And she certainly wasn't doing anything to prevent him. In fact the opposite was true. She did everything in her power, aside from screaming at him, to let him know that she wouldn't object to another one of his kisses.

She inched herself closer to him. When his glance moved down to take in her lips, she purposefully moistened them with the tip of her tongue, trying to make the simple gesture as erotic as she possibly could. She'd seen the same ploy work a thousand times in the movies. But all Buck did was reach up with his hand, his elbow resting on the table, to play with a thick shaft of her hair.

"You're about the prettiest thing I've ever seen," he uttered all of a sudden. This was good news to Anne, and she was very flattered, but she truly liked it much better when he was a quiet man of action.

"You wanna dance, Anne?"

It was Buck's scowl that tipped her off to the fact that he hadn't asked the question. She looked over her shoulder at Bryce and saw him looking from his brother to her and back again in confusion.

"Unless *you* wanna dance with her?" he said, addressing his brother uncertainly.

"Be my guest," Buck said, opening his arms wide as an invitation but still frowning at his brother. That the final choice was hers alone didn't seem to enter into their picture, and under other circumstances, Anne might have reminded them. But it didn't seem necessary as she'd have danced with Bryce anyway, just because she rather liked the unhappy glower on Buck's face.

She smiled at both gentlemen, and then let Bryce lead her to the small dance floor in the center of the bar between the sitting area and the pool tables in the rear. Multicolored lights dimly lit the space, on which only four or five other couples were dancing.

Western music was another thing Anne wasn't altogether familiar with. She'd heard it before, of course, but dancing to it was foreign to her. Bryce started out with a bouncy, rhythmic step that caused Anne great pain when she couldn't move her feet fast enough to keep them out of his way. He quickly realized the problem and grinned at her.

"Jeez, you Yankees don't know nothin,' do ya?" he said, teasing.

"I guess not. So teach me," she said, leaning close to his ear and shouting to be heard over the music.

"Everybody has their own two-step. There's the Texas two-step, the Tennessee two-step—in Virginia they call it a reel. They're all pretty much the same thing, only ours is more fun."

"Of course."

Slowly he took her through a series of stomps and small kicks, a step-close-step, then a hop and foot-brushing thing that was hard to get the hang of. She felt clumsy and awkward at first, but wound up in hysterics as her feet continually refused to do as they were told.

"Okay. Let's do it," Bryce finally said, taking her left hand in his and placing her right hand on his shoulder.

At first, she was stumbling over his feet and her own as well. But eventually everything seemed to slip into sync, and she gained enough confidence to look up and grin triumphantly at Bryce. He laughed at her. She was so proud of herself that she wanted to make sure that Buck was watching her.

The next time Bryce turned her in Buck's direction, she looked over at him. Not only wasn't he watching her, he had a woman in his lap.

"Oops. Sorry," she said to Bryce after she'd viciously trampled on his feet. She had to concentrate on her dance steps again to get back in rhythm but couldn't help stealing glances back at Buck.

He was smiling and talking to the woman, as if they were old and very good friends. Very good friends. She was wearing tight jeans and a halter top and had long dark hair that covered most of her face and his, as she leaned over to hear him and to talk into his ear. Buck's arms were around her waist, holding her in place, his hands splayed out across her abdomen.

Anne had to look away. She fought to control a rage she didn't even understand. She knew what it was. She'd felt jealous before. But she had no right or reason to feel jealous over Buck. Something had clicked between them, and they were friends. It was a tentative relationship at best, she told herself. It only made sense that he'd have other friends, other female friends, who'd known him longer and far better than she ever would.

This all should have made sense to Anne, but feelings didn't always make sense.

The music ended, and Bryce was about to take her back to the table. Flustered and angry with Buck, herself, and the woman in the tight jeans, Anne excused herself to go to the ladies room to regain some control over her emotions. She was in no condition to face Buck and his girlfriend.

Once she was sure she was alone, she began to sort out her thoughts aloud.

"Anne Hunnicut. You stop this right now," she told herself, staring straight into her own blue eyes through the mirror over the sink. "You're acting crazy. You have absolutely no claim on that man out there. You're going to be here a few days, two weeks tops. His whole life is here. He's bound to have a bimbo like that on every corner around here," she said, wishing she'd thought to bring along her own pair of too-tight jeans.

"Are you out of your mind? Do you have any idea what you're asking for?" She gave herself a blank stare. "Trouble. That's what. You'll get involved with this guy, lose your heart to him, and then have to leave. Is that what you want?"

She looked away as she thought about it. "I can handle it," she said, facing her image once again. "Buck and I are mature adults with—with needs. I'll only love him a little bit. That's all. And when I go back to New York, I won't have any regrets. I promise. It'll be a beautiful affair to remember."

She stopped suddenly and gave herself a droll stare. "You're certifiably insane. You know that, don't you? You don't have it in you. The only place you'll ever find a beautiful affair to remember is late at night after the David Letterman show. You'll fall—"

There was a noise in the hallway outside the restroom door. Anne didn't want to get caught standing in front of the mirror, so she quickly slipped into one of the toilet stalls.

"See, there's no one here," she heard a woman's voice say, "Come in here and settle down before you blow a gasket."

"Well, can you believe that hussy? Who the hell does she think she is anyway?" said a second woman, her angry words reverberating off the tile walls. "She waltzes in here like she owns the place, tries to shut down the mill, and then moves in on Buck. I wanna scratch her eyes out."

"Settle down, Georgia. You don't own him. And it probably isn't anything serious anyway."

"Oh, yeah? I told him that when he got tired of playin' with her, that he could always come over to my place. And you know what he said?" The other woman didn't have an answer. She was apparently waiting to get one from her friend. "He said that he thought his nights were going to be pretty well occupied from now on, but thanks anyway." She growled and released a squeaky little scream of rage.

The first woman laughed. "Oh, he probably just said that to get your brassy little bottom off his lap. You know how he likes to tease." There was a short pause. "You know what I think?"

When the other woman didn't answer, Anne mouthed, "What? What?"

"I think he's just usin' her. He got her to reconsider lettin' us buy the mill, didn't he?"

"Yeah."

"Well, maybe now he's workin' on gettin' her to help him with them negotiations."

"Think so?"

"Yes. Now you come on out here and act as if

nothin's wrong. You'll see. In a couple weeks, when Her Majesty goes back to wherever she came from, everything'll be all right and tight again."

"You really think so? Her clothes *are* pretty tacky and she . . ." The voice trailed off as the two women left the rest room, closing the door behind them.

Slowly, Anne opened the door and walked out. The first thing she saw was her reflection in the mirror. The answer to her previous dilemma was clear in the hurt and disappointment in her face. Was that the plan Buck had talked about? Was all his charm, all those smiles and kisses just bait to get her to help him with his doomed employee-ownership scheme? Was she so gullible that she actually fell for it? Would any one of the men back at the office have been so stupid? If they had been, she certainly hadn't heard about it.

No one was going to hear about this either. She'd come close, but she hadn't fallen into Buck's clever little trap. She hadn't screwed things up completely yet, and all her mistakes could be easily rectified.

Buck and Bryce both looked up and smiled as she approached their table. There was a warm appreciative glimmer in Buck's eyes, but it didn't phase her the way it normally would have. The only flush of heat it generated in her came from the anger it fanned.

"I'd like to leave now," she announced to the men's obvious surprise.

They exchanged looks of confusion, and then Buck got to his feet. "Is somethin' wrong?" he asked.

"Not anymore."

He nodded and motioned for her to precede him, watching her closely. Over her shoulder he asked, "Did somebody say somethin'?"

"About what?"

"About anything. Did somebody say somethin' to upset you?"

"No," she said flatly, closing the subject to further discussion.

The ride back to Buck's house was much like the one the previous night. Very quiet. Except that this time it was Buck's turn to be uncomfortable while she was boiling mad, and when she got cold from driving with his window open, she didn't hesitate to tell him. "Close that damn window before I freeze to death."

Buck hadn't even turned off the engine before Anne was slipping out of the truck on the passenger's side.

"Annie, aren't you goin' to talk to me at all? Tell me what this is all about?" he asked, sounding perplexed and frustrated.

"Just please keep the motor running, will you? I'll be right back," she said, before she slammed the truck door closed and turned to march straight up to the house.

Seven

The moon was full and bright, the sky clear. A zillion stars twinkled like diamonds on black velvet, and Anne could have cared less. In record time, she was back at the truck with her packed bags in tow. The only use she had for a romantically glowing moon was to light her way down the front path and away from Buck's home.

"What's this?" Buck asked, having come around to her side of the truck. His frown deepened with his added confusion.

"Would you please take me back to McKee's."

"Yes. But why? Why are you leavin'?"

"The danger's over. I should have gone back this morning."

"Annie, tell me what happened."

"Nothing happened."

"That's a lie. Something happened, or you wouldn't be actin' like this," he said in total frustration.

He had a point. And he'd most likely use it until he got an answer he believed, she reasoned.

"All right. Let's just say . . . that I learned a good lesson."

"About what?"

"About . . . good ol' boys."

"Good ol' boys?"

"Yeah. Are you going to help me with these bags or not?" she asked, shifting under their weight.

"Not. I don't want you to leave. I want you to tell me about this lesson you learned," he replied, leaning against the truck as if he were settling in for the night.

"Fine. Then I'll walk," she said. Then as it occurred to her, she added, "How come I don't have my car? I could have followed you here last night, or we could have picked it up today. How come we didn't do that?"

The question sounded strange even to her, but her pain and outrage had compounded itself to a point where she could hardly see straight. She wanted to cry but didn't want to give Buck the satisfaction. She wanted to hit him but wasn't too sure whether or not he'd hit her back. All she knew for sure was that she had trusted him almost from the moment they'd met, she cared for him, and he had been deceiving her all along. All she wanted now was the privacy of her hotel room, bricks or no bricks, where she could cry and punch pillows as much as she liked.

"We left it as a decoy, so they'd think you were still there. I'm not sure why you didn't think of going to pick it up today, but when I thought about going after it, I decided I wanted to keep you completely dependent on me for as long as possible, so I didn't mention it," he told her point-blank. His expression was passive, his stance was relaxed to the point of being limp, but his eyes told her it was all a facade. He was wound up inside, tighter than a cheap clock. Was he afraid that she'd found out his secret?

"Ha. That figures. You don't say much, but you're thinking all the time, aren't you?" It wasn't meant to sound like a compliment. His answer had been very honest, coming from such a snake in the grass, she thought. She also thought he'd picked a rather peculiar time to start being so blunt and forthright with her.

"Is that why you're mad, then? Because we didn't go get your car?"

It was becoming more and more apparent that he wasn't going to guess the real reason for her anger. He probably thought he'd been so clever in deceiving her that no one would ever guess what he was up to, she speculated. And she sure as hell wasn't going to leave while he was feeling smug.

"No, that is not why I'm angry," she shouted at him. She dropped the heavy suitcases at her feet as she wasn't sure how long this was going to take. She didn't want to wear herself out in case she did have to walk back to Webster. "I'll tell you why I'm angry. I'm angry because you used me. Oh, I let you, and that's part of why I'm so mad. But you tricked me. All that good ol' boy garbage and those stupid smiles and your granny's pansies. It was all a game, and I fell for it. Well, I couldn't have stopped you from bidding on the mill, so all that hooopla about your pride and self-respect was a waste of time. But I'm sure as hell not going to stand around and let you try to charm me into helping you with your damned proposal and negotiations. That was the plan you told me about this morning, wasn't it? It was your plan all along, right from that moment on the road, when you realized who I was. Well, I'd rather die than—"

Suddenly, Buck lunged at her. She took a step back only to discover that he hadn't been reaching for her but for the suitcases that sat near her feet. He picked them up as if they were filled with feathers and threw them into the back of the truck. Then he reached over and flung the door of the cab open for her.

"If you really believe all that, then get in. I'll be more than happy to take you back to Jimmy's place," he said, his voice still soft, his green eyes blazing with fire.

She simply stood there, staring at him. He was more outraged than she was, thoroughly insulted by her accusations. It was as if he'd cut off all the wind to her sails. She lost all momentum and went dead in a sea of calm logic. It was very bewildering, but she knew in her heart that he hadn't tricked her, no matter what she'd heard.

All her rage churned inside her with no place to go, no way to vent itself. Her eyes began to sting and grow blurry with tears.

"I don't want to believe it," she said, sniffing loudly. "But it sounded so logical when I heard it. I—I didn't know what else to think."

"Who told you that I was using you like that?"

"No one. I mean, I overheard two women talking about it in the ladies' room." She took the large white handkerchief he'd anticipated the need for and shook out the folds before wiping the corners of her eyes with it.

"In the ladies' room?"

Anne nodded a; wiped her nose. "One of them was upset because—because I was there tonight, and the other one told her that you were only being nice to me so I'd help you get the mill."

"And I suppose you believe everything you hear in a ladies' room." This wasn't a question.

"Well, men believe everything they hear in locker rooms, don't they?" she accused in return, hating the tears that were weakening her ability to fight back.

"Only stupid men who don't know any better."

"Oh, yeah? Well one of them had been sitting in your lap, so I figured she knew what she was talking about."

Everything was jumbled. Her heart trusted him, but her mind was full of conjectures and fear. She turned her back on him, hoping everything would clear up if she didn't have to look at him.

A long silence followed. Anne was just about to turn around to see if Buck was still there, when he spoke in a soft voice full of speculation. "You know what this sounds like to me?"

"No. What?" she asked, turning to face him.

He cocked his head to one side and watched her with the same thoughtfulness that he had in his voice.

"Sounds to me like you're not nearly as upset about being tricked, as you are about the woman being in my lap."

"Don't be ridiculous," she said, not quite able to look him in the eye. "That's the dumbest thing I've ever heard."

"Is it?"

"Yes. Of course." A small nervous laugh escaped her. "I have no claim on you. It's your lap. You can let anyone you want sit on it, for Pete's sake."

Again, he was thoughtful for a moment, and then he said, "Would you like to have a claim on me, Annie."

"No. Absolutely not." She was vehement about this. "I'm just passing through."

"Are you sure?" he asked, leaning away from the truck and taking several steps toward her. He held his hands out at his sides. "I'm free and easy. I've got no ties. I'm real claimable at the moment."

He was teasing her with his voice.

"Will you stop? I'm serious."

"So am I, Annie. I want you to stake your claim on me. Right here." He swung his hand up and placed it on his chest, over his heart.

"Oh." She gasped. "You're such a jerk."

"Why?" he asked, undaunted. "Because I like the idea of you and me claimin' each other."

"Each other?"

"Sure," he said, humor creeping into his words like ants into a picnic basket. "This claiming business goes both ways, you know."

His grin was Anne's undoing. Suddenly she wanted nothing more than to claim Buck as her own. She wanted sole title to his long, sinewy body. She wanted dibs on those lips that drove her wild. She wanted tenure of his thoughts and a petition on his soul. She wanted the deed to his heart.

"Is that right?" she asked, smiling. "How exactly does it work?"

There was a gleam in his< ye that Anne was becoming very familiar with. He wasn't a foot away from her, but he crooked his finger at her. Her heart went wild, flopping and twisting in her chest in a fit of excitement. On rubber legs, she stepped forward, leaving a hand's breadth between them.

He just looked at her. She saw a desire that matched her own in his eyes. "It's easy. Just reach out and claim me, Annie, and I'll do the same."

"Easy." It didn't feel easy. Her arms felt like lead weights. Her whole body was trembling. But she'd never wanted anything more than she wanted Buck at that moment. Determinedly and with shaking fingers, she reached for the buttons on the front of his shirt. He watched her fingers loosen the first two buttons before he looked at her. His eyes glimmered with fire and passion. Her fingers faltered momentarily when she sensed the raw urges and ungovernable emotions he had freed within himself. She focused her attention on the third button, trying not to think how reckless she felt.

Had she really thought it a chilly night? She felt feverish, flushed with a heat that made her skin damp and sticky under her clothes.

Her concentration failed when Buck's hands moved to the hem of her sweater. He leaned forward as he pulled it up over her head, looping his arms around her and pulling her close in one continuous motion. Tiny wet kisses along her shoulder sent spasms of shivers rippling through her body. She felt his tongue make slow, swirling circles on her neck and hardly noticed that he was moving her backward toward the house.

His callused hands snagged the silk of her slip but felt bold and powerful, soft and gentle as they moved across her skin. Suddenly, she felt him lowering her to the ground. Cool, dew-damp grass tickled her back and soothed her fiery flesh. His weight, as he eased down on top of her, squelched the flighty, impetuous impulses that hung onto the fringes of her emotions.

There was no turning back now. Nothing else mattered at this moment. Not the past, the mill, the people of Webster, Kentucky . . . not even the future held any influence over her. Only Buck mattered, as he drew thin silken straps down from her shoulder to clear a path for his lips. She gave of herself with all her heart and soul, wanting to pleasure him more than anyone else he'd ever known before. Deep inside she knew she didn't want any brassy bottom but hers to sit on his lap ever again. She had every intention of making such sweet love to Buck that any other woman, past or future, would pale in his memory.

Cloying kisses and searching hands soon created an impatience in both of them for higher excitement and deeper satisfaction. They grew intolerant of such obstacles as clothing and madly began to remove them, flinging them off indiscriminately. Bare flesh met bare flesh and they both sighed, savoring their gratification.

His mouth, wet and hot, covered the peak of her breast as he sucked gently and raked the hard, sensitive tip with his tongue. The moon and stars receded into the sky. Anne closed her eyes when there was nothing left to see. Her fingers tangled in his thick dark hair, and she drew him closer, held him to her breast, never wanting him to stop giving her such exquisite pleasure. She arched her back and released a soft moan of ecstacy that seemed to trigger something deep and savage in him. Instantly he was more aggressive, more possessive, and much more demanding.

He used his teeth to drive her to the brink of madness. His hand slid slowly, tortuously over her abdomen to the apex of her legs, slipping between her thighs to spread them farther apart. Instinctively, her hips rose up to meet his probing fingers. She was aching with emptiness and needed to be filled.

Her hands were frantic, reaching out to touch all of him. She experienced a rush of trepidation as she rediscovered the solid sinew and strength in his shoulders and chest. Her impelling emotions quickly overshadowed her caution. They pushed her to seek out what she needed. She felt the muscles in his back, tight and trembling under her finger tips. Her heart sang with joy in knowing that she had driven him as far beyond control as he had taken her. She maneuvered a hand in between his thighs and thrilled to his moan of anguish as she wrapped her fingers around him.

"Annie," he groaned, his voice hoarse and guttural. His fingers became more aggressive in a calculated act to drive her wildly insane. She cried out, but the sound was muffled by his mouth. He insinuated his knees between her legs and, placing her legs around his waist, pulled her hips toward him. He took her with a quick, eager thrust that made her feel as if she were exploding inside, over and over and over again.

The stars and the moon were back. Bigger and brighter and closer than she'd ever known them to be. Their light was blinding, but she knew if she reached out, she could touch one. She did reach, and her body rose up off the ground toward the stars. She touched one, then another. She held them in her hand for a long precious moment, then she opened her fingers wide to set them free again.

Slowly, Anne returned to the earth. For a while she seemed to float, unaware of her surroundings. Gradually she felt the wet, prickly grass beneath her. It was cold, and she shivered. Strong arms gathered her up off the ground and held her in a warm cradling embrace.

"Buck." She didn't need to open her eyes to know she was in his arms. She had no fear of being dropped, because she knew no other arms that made her feel as safe. She wrapped her own around his neck and put her trust in him.

She kept her eyes closed and let her head rest on his shoulder even when she was aware that they were entering the house. Not so long ago she'd hoped never to see the place again. Now she never wanted to leave it. She didn't make a sound as she realized that they were moving up the stairs. And when she felt crisp sheets and the warmth of a blanket being tucked in around her, she snuggled close to Buck to steal more heat from his body.

"You're a greedy woman, Anne Hunnicut," he said, taking her loosely into his arms and letting her cuddle up as close as she wanted.

"I thought you said you liked fast women and slow sex?" she mumbled against his chest, wiggling her nose as the hair there tickled it.

"That wasn't an invitation to try and blow my brains out. You coulda killed me out there."

"Ha. You southerners just can't take it. No wonder we won the war." She giggled.

"Why, you little hussy, you," he said, taking her whole jaw into his hand and drawing her face up to meet his. "I was tryin' to be a gentleman our first time out. Everybody knows how prissy Yankee women are. I didn't want to scare you."

"Prissy? Did I act prissy or scared?"

He grinned with delight. "No, ma'am, you didn't." He pressed his lips to hers gently, nibbled on her bottom lip, and then kissed her again. Her body quickening and eager, Anne pressed closer, nestling her breasts in the thick, coarse hair of his chest.

Rolling toward her, Buck laid her flat on her back and eased a leg up over hers, before he disentangled her arms from around his neck and pinned them to the pillow on either side of her face. Taking his time, he kissed the soft hollow at the base of her neck, making a necklace of sweet sensations across her throat to the other side. She wallowed, luxuriated in his tender, tingling touches.

When he stopped, Anne opened her eyes, moaning her disappointment. She met his gaze in the moonlight.

The soft, silver light cast his face in shadows outlining the high cheekbones, the full chiseled lips, and the angle of his jaw. In fascination she watched as only the very tips of his dark eyelashes picked up the light, as if each one were dipped in magic fairy dust.

"Before we get all hot and bothered again, I think we should settle a coupla things," he said, his drawl thicker than usual in his effort to maintain his control. "I don't want there to be any more misunderstandin's between us."

Anne's heart flinched instinctively. She had a feeling that she'd had this conversation before. She had hoped that since they were both aware their relationship was to be temporary, this conversation wouldn't be necessary. Apparently Buck thought otherwise.

"I'm not a stupid hillbilly," he said, surprising her with his choice of topics.

"I—I know," she said, faltering.

"And I don't want or need your help with the mill. Eight to four-thirty, you do your job, and I'll do mine. When we leave the mill, we don't discuss it. Deal?"

"Deal."

"From four-thirty to eight A.M., you're mine," he said, seeming to want this clarified as well.

"And you're mine."

"All yours," he said, his soft lips and warm breath tickling the sensitive skin of her neck.

"And the woman in the tight jeans?" She was glad to hear her voice sounding playful, when she was so far from teasing in her heart.

His head came up, and the moonlight reflected off his white teeth as he grinned down at her. Then, purposefully misconstruing her words, he said, "Annie, you don't need any help. You keep my lap plenty warm enough all by yourself, sugar."

Eight

Anne slept late into the lazy spring morning that followed. With everything she owned still packed in the back of Buck's truck, she slipped into the large flannel shirt he'd worn the night before. The soft material felt warm and fuzzy against her skin, as erotic as a bearskin rug. She was feeling sensual and aroused as she made her way downstairs.

She found Buck at the kitchen table once again. Only this time he wasn't reading the Sunday funnies but was up to his chin in books, files, and papers.

"A-hem," she cleared her throat loudly.

"Mornin'," he said absently without turning. He finished whatever he was working on with an elaborate period. Then he turned and smiled at her, dissolving her insides into a churning wad of goo. "I gotta tell you, Annie. I much prefer this to what you were wearing yesterday."

"This ol' thing?" With a hand in the air and one on her hip, she pivoted for his approval.

"That ol' thing never looked so good," he said in a deep throaty voice. He held out his arms invitingly and asked, "Can you spare me a Yankee dime this mornin'?"

Anne grinned at him. For some strange reason, there still seemed to be a lot of Yankee jokes in the South, even though the war they'd spawned from had ended over a hundred years before. A *Yankee dime*, as she had been informed sometime during the wee hours of the morning, was a kiss.

Before that, Buck had gone to great lengths to explain a *Yankee shot* as well. It seemed that when a child was too young to understand the concept of an umbilical cord, his mother would tell him that his belly button was where he'd been shot by a Yankee. It was his Yankee shot. Anne felt that Buck had developed a strong fondness for hers, even though it was from the wrong side of the Mason-Dixon.

She had giggled at the story and squirmed with delight when he'd laved hers with his tongue. With her fingers in his soft, thick dark hair, she had pulled his face up to meet hers. They had kissed slowly, thoroughly, until they had to break for air. With Buck at her neck, her body aquiver at his every touch, her mind an eddy of sensations, she'd heard him say her name as if it were a prayer.

Looking at him now, with his arms outstretched, his embrace so enticing, she knew he was remembering those breath-stopping moments they'd shared before the sun came up, before it cast a golden glow across their naked bodies and they'd slept.

"Gee, mister, I'm not sure. If I give you a dime, what will I get in return?" she asked playfully as she walked slowly across the kitchen toward him.

"Anything you want." His voice was like a physical caress, as real as a touch. His green eyes twinkled with desire and delight.

She took the last step into his arms and let him draw her between his legs and down onto his lap. One of his hands slipped smoothly up under the tail of his shirt to cup her bottom, as if it had done so a thousand times before.

"Tell me what you want," he urged in a husky voice, when she made no demands. How could she? she wondered. There wasn't anything in the world she wanted except . . .

"Just one more day with you," she said. "Just you and me and no mill business."

Buck's smile broadened, and he looked as if he were in hog heaven at her answer. "You got a deal. Now gimme my dime."

It was Anne's joyful opinion that a Yankee dime was the only currency in the world whose value hadn't deflated in the last one hundred years. And Buck knew how to make every penny of it count.

His hand moved gently up her back and across her ribs until he could cradle her breast in his palm. The fire he'd stoked throughout the night now surged with hot flames once more. A bonfire went wild inside her, consumed her, and left her burning with passion.

"Buck?" The front door slammed at the same time they heard Bryce calling out. He yoo-hooed up the stairwell and called his brother's name again, before his steps started coming their way.

"I'm gonna kill him," Buck muttered under his breath as Anne scrambled off his lap and into a chair behind the table, trying desperately to cover her nakedness.

"Mornin'." The doomed brother greeted them with a bright, cheerful smile. Anne's cheeks flushed hot with embarrassment as he briefly scanned the scene before him. He then turned nonchalantly to help himself to a cup of coffee, as if everything was as he'd expected it to be. Without looking up from his coffee pouring, he added, "Nice day for a yard sale."

Buck, who had been openly frowning at his

brother, now looked confused. He shrugged at
Anne when they exchanged curious glances and
asked, "Who's havin' a yard sale?"

"Well, I thought we were," he said, doing a poor
job of looking perplexed. "There's clothes all over
the front yard and—"

"You wanna live to see thirty?" Buck stood and
gave his brother a threatening glare. Anne had
forgotten all about the clothes they'd tossed off in
the throes of their passion the night before. Her
flaming cheeks got even hotter.

Bryce was so intimidated by his brother that he
dissolved into laughter. "You want me to bring
down some of my old stuff and throw it out in the
yard with yours?"

"That does it." Buck and Bryce made a blurred
exit. Anne couldn't help laughing.

"I was only tryin' to be helpful," she heard Bryce
say plaintively as the front door slammed open
and the screen door echoed with a squeak. "What
will the neighbors think?"

"We don't have any neighbors, you fool."

Anne soon heard a truck engine start, a sound
she'd missed before when Bryce had arrived. Buck
returned with a grim look on his face, but he
didn't look like a murderer.

"I was just thinking," Anne said, calmer now
that they were alone again, but still a little off
center with the whole situation. "What if Bryce
had come home last night? I mean, while we were
still outside or—or even later."

"Then I *would* have killed him," he said. He
handed Anne a cup of coffee and went back to the
pot with his own. "But I was pretty sure he
wouldn't."

"Why?"

He grinned at her then. "Cuz I told him what
would happen if he did."

"You mean you—you told him not to come home because you knew—you knew we'd . . ."

Buck laughed. "I hoped is all. And then when you started actin' so strange, well, I sure as hell didn't want him around then."

"Well, where was he all night?"

Buck's grin took on a sly angle. "You remember Liddy Evans?"

She shook her head.

"The one with the boy who's diabetic. You met her at the mill on Friday, remember?"

"Yes. Yes, I do," she said, recalling her promise to the young woman.

"Bryce is sweet on her." He confided this with a great deal of satisfaction. "He stayed with her last night."

"With all those children around?" She vaguely remembered the mention of two besides the one the woman was most concerned about.

"He manages to get to the couch before they get up, and to tell the truth, I've never been able to figure out who he cares about more, her or her kids."

Anne suddenly had a whole new respect for Bryce. It was one thing to dally with the mother of three children. To care for her children as well was very special.

"He came home for clean clothes, then," she decided out loud.

"Nope. He took clothes with him yesterday mornin'."

"Buck!" She couldn't believe the man's presumptuousness.

"I was only hopin'. Can't blame a man for that."

She sent him a disapproving glare before she asked, "Then why did he come home this morning?"

"Stopped at Jimmy's to see if you had any messages. You had three from Calvin Schwab."

"He stopped—well, you thought of everything, didn't you?" she said, marveling at Buck's determination.

"Just about."

She gasped dramatically. "Well, what on earth *didn't* you think of?"

"How to keep Schwab from ruining our day together. He is going to ruin it, isn't he?" he asked glumly.

Stopping to think about it, Anne couldn't help but agree. She had a sick feeling in the pit of her stomach that she knew exactly how their conversation would proceed.

"Well, it's about time you called," Calvin Schwab bellowed over the phone an hour or so later. "Where the hell have you been?"

"Out." Anne didn't keep an account of her time for her father anymore; she certainly wasn't going to account for it with Calvin.

"Don't tell me you were out sight-seeing. Anne, you could look till your eyes fall out and never see anything. I've been there, remember? There's nothing to see in those mountains."

She wanted to tell him how wrong he was and how beautiful the mountains were. She wanted to tell him about some of the people, about their courage, generosity, and kindness. She wanted to tell him about good ol' boys, but instead she asked, "Do you want to hear how the employee meeting went or not?"

She didn't mean to sound angry and abrupt with him. He didn't know that he'd spoiled her day with Buck. He could never guess that she'd been so happy with Buck, she'd wished she wouldn't ever have to think about New York, Harriman Industries, or him again. It simply wouldn't have occurred to him that in less than a week,

Anne was ready to dig a deep hole in the rich Kentucky soil, climb in, and grow roots. How could he? She'd only just realized it herself.

How did she feel about that, she wondered, as she gave a robotlike accounting of the union meeting. She felt good about it and yet knew it was all wrong and didn't make sense at the same time. It seemed like the most natural thing in the world to do, but it scared her to death. Her heart grew heavy when she wondered what Buck would say to the idea.

After all, he was assuming that their relationship was a temporary thing. Would he feel put upon or obligated if she stayed longer than she was supposed to?

She shook her head and pushed the thought out of her mind. It was a crazy idea.

"Well, at least they know we mean business now," Calvin was saying. "Sounds to me as if they wanted to eat you alive, but you gave them the old what-for and held your ground. I'm proud of you, Anne."

Oops. She must have forgotten to tell him about the mob scene and her rescue by the LaSalle's.

"There's one other thing, Cal. I don't see it as a big problem, but I think I ought to mention it to you," she said, bracing herself for his reaction. His silence was her cue to proceed. "They're planning to make a bid for the mill. They want employee ownership."

Silence.

"I told them they could try it."

Silence.

"Cal?"

"And you don't see this as a problem?" he asked, his voice quivering under the strain it took to control his temper.

"Well, you're the one who called them a bunch of stupid hillbillies, remember? And personally, I don't think they'll be able to come up with the resources. Economically or professionally. What harm can come from their trying?" She paused before adding, "Besides, it'll keep them busy and off my back, while I finish up what has to be done. They'll never make the sixty-day deadline."

"They'd better not, Anne."

"Even if they do," she said, thinking of Buck, "all you have to do is turn them down when they make the bid."

"Let's hope for your sake that it doesn't get that far. The last thing we need is a bunch of bog-stompers clogging up the works."

Anne's chest grew stiff with anger and resentment at his disparaging remark. Something in her heart half-wished that Buck and the other workers would pull it off in spite of all the obstacles before them. It would be worth it, just to see the look on Calvin Schwab's face.

Since they hadn't known what Calvin wanted or how long her discussion with him would take, they had agreed that Buck would take Anne to town so she could pick up her car, make her call from the office at the mill, and go back to Buck's whenever she was finished.

Apparently Jimmy McKee was a very understanding fellow. He'd agreed to continue taking messages for Anne at the motel, as a favor to Buck, so that nothing would look untoward. She had insisted on paying for the room she wasn't staying in, but Jimmy McKee had said that was crazy. "Round here we look out for each other's . . . best interests," he'd said, a wry smile on his lips and a decided twinkle in his eye. "Right now, you seem to be what Buck's most interested in."

Anne had been grateful, but she couldn't help speculating on how long "right now" would last.

She managed to do some work at the office, to justify her presence in Webster and to appease the guilty conscience she'd developed after talking with Calvin Schwab. It wouldn't be fair to anyone, she'd decided, to let her crescive feelings for Buck deter her from her purpose.

It was late afternoon by the time she returned to the LaSalle home. The trees cast long, lazy shadows across the gravel road as she approached the house. Nestled in the small clearing, with nature growing up around it on all sides, the house had a very safe look about it. It was big and old and it had withstood the test of time. As a matter of fact, the house looked as if it had been there forever, as if it belonged there.

It was a strange notion—belonging. Anne hadn't ever felt she truly belonged anywhere. And yet Buck's house belonged. Buck belonged. The trees and the mountains seemed to fit right in; they looked as if they belonged where they were. Was there a secret to belonging? How long did people have to stay in one place before they became part of the scenery, before the things around them became a part of them? two years? ten years? a lifetime?

Anne wasn't sure. All she knew was that she'd never felt more comfortable than she did at that moment. Sitting on the front steps of Buck's house, she breathed in the clean air, listened to the wind as it fluttered the leaves in the trees, and knew a sense of peace she hadn't ever experienced before.

Hustle, bustle, and tussle didn't live here, Anne realized, as she felt herself unwind. Quiet, simple, and peaceful resided in these mountains, and Anne had the oddest feeling they were bidding her welcome.

She laughed at herself. She didn't usually get so carried away. It was time to get back to something solid and real, she decided. She went in search of Buck, who was very solid and very real.

She found the note on the kitchen table, in a big black frying pan with a can opener holding it in place.

Gone fishing. If you remember
the way, join me. If you don't,
start dinner. I'll be back.

Buck

"Start dinner? Start dinner? Just like that? Start dinner?" she repeated, irked beyond belief. Buck was taking this claim-staking business a little too seriously. If he thought he'd claimed her *and* her servitude, he was about to be informed otherwise. She not only thought that she might remember the way to the pond, but she was more than willing to die wandering the forest looking for it. She didn't even care if she had to battle lions, tigers, and bears to get there. But she sure as hell wasn't going to start dinner on his order.

In a snit she marched upstairs to change her shoes, only to discover that her bags had been put in Buck's room. She also found a box of old clothes and another note on the bed waiting for her.

These are some of my sister's old
things. If you can use them, feel free.
Here's a map, in case you get lost.

He'd drawn a prominent-points map to the pond that made Anne giggle. And then she growled. "Buck LaSalle, you're enough to drive a perfectly sane woman nuts," she told him, not caring that he couldn't hear her.

• • •

He looked carefree and a little bit like Huck Finn when she found him. Out on the end of the old jetty, slumped against one of the pilings, he sat alone and at ease—with himself and everything around him. He had his bare back to her, his folded shirt and his boots on the ground beside him, and his fishing pole was propped between his crossed legs, balanced between his toes on the other end. His head was bent as he read from a book in his lap. She almost hated to disturb him. Almost.

"Start dinner?" she asked, her hands on her hips as she stood on the land end of the dock.

He turned his head and smiled at her. He wasn't the least bit surprised to see her. "It got ya here, didn't it?"

"It was a dirty trick, but I thank you for the clothes." Cautiously she began her walk out to join him. She tried not to think of the planking disintegrating under her feet, as she was sure it was about to do, and concentrated on getting closer and closer to Buck. She knew he'd keep her safe.

"Oh, no. *I* thank *you*," he said, his eyes taking in the white sleeveless shirt she had knotted at her waist and the jeans, cut off well above the knees, that hugged her hips. Anne thought they gave her a decided Daisy May look and was pleased to see that he liked the effect. "Now I know there is a God and He does listen to our prayers."

"You really shouldn't talk like that out here," she cautioned him, letting her smile and her eyes tell him just how glad she was to be with him again. "She might decide to let this thing fall apart, after all," she said glancing at the dock. "And then we'd both drown for your disrespect."

"She might, huh?" He grinned, extending his hand to her. "Well, if you're afraid that She's so easily ticked off, you can always come down here and hold on to me. I'll tell you a different story."

"What. About God?" she asked, sitting down beside him, in much the same fashion as he was sitting. Again she thought that this quiet place could very well be His summer place, as she got comfortable and thoughtfully took in her surroundings. "Don't tell me you talk to God here."

"All the time." He handed her an open can of cold beer that he'd taken from the cooler beside him, then he took a long gulp from his own can.

"Recently?" She took her first and best sip of the cold brew and set it down beside her. Then she leaned back on her elbows.

"Not ten minutes ago." He moved her can out of his way before he leaned toward her and sipped the taste of the beer off her bottom lip. "*He* told me I'd be spendin' the rest of this day makin' love to a beautiful woman who goes by the name of Annie."

"I don't go by that name," she told him a bit breathlessly, as his lips skittered down her neck and into the V of her shirt. "You're the only person in the world who calls me Annie."

"Good," he muttered. He'd been leaning on one arm, but when he reached over with his other hand to loosen the button that was getting in his way, the book on his lap fell off. "It's just me and God then."

Anne laughed despite the way her stomach was tying itself in knots. "You're very conceited," she said, feeling she should point this out to him for his own good.

He looked up at her, surprised. "I told you, it's part of my charm."

"I remember." She angled her head and kissed him sweetly. "You're also very hard-working, aren't you?"

He frowned, and she glanced down at the book on office management that had fallen from his lap. He shrugged then and said, "When you work, I work. When we're together, we make love. Wasn't that our deal?"

"Sort of," she said, smiling her agreement with his rewording of their bargain. "But I thought you were supposed to be fishin'."

He looked shocked that she thought he wasn't. "I got my pole in the water." He bent and placed a warm wet kiss on her belly, which exposed itself just below the knot in her shirt. Absently he picked up her beer can and unerringly dribbled several drops of the liquid into her navel. "It doesn't matter what else you're doin' at the time, as long as you got a pole in the water, it's still fishin'."

He lowered his head and sucked the beer from her navel, his arms curled around her as he rolled his body over the lower half of hers. He nibbled gently on the sensitive skin of her abdomen. Anne's arms grew weary as she wallowed in the fine sensations crawling across her. She lowered her head to the dock and closed her eyes. When the knot in her shirt fell away, she reached out and let her fingers tangle in Buck's hair. It was warm from the sun, thick and soft.

The dock swayed and bobbed on the water. Time stood still. Buck's mouth closed around the throbbing tip of one breast and Anne's whole world disappeared. Her mind was empty, except for the sound of the water beneath the old planks and the feel of Buck's mouth and hands as he made slow, agonizing love to her.

They could have been Adam and Eve in God's garden, discovering all the wonders and joys of being his creations. Did He have any idea of the power Buck had over her heart, her soul, and her body? Anne guessed He did. Otherwise He wouldn't have designed such a miracle. A miracle that would last from the beginning to the end of His reign. An act so good and simple, so beautiful and glorious that it reflected His own genius.

Yes, there was indeed a God, she reflected in her love-hazed mind, and He had heard her prayers, she concluded as Buck's damp body pressed close to hers and she held his head near her breast. And then another thought occurred to her.

"Buck?"

"Hmm?"

"If a southerner drinks beer from your naval, is your belly button still a Yankee shot? Or does it then become a Dixie cup?"

"UGH!"

Nine

The next few days drifted by in a mist of pleasure, confusion, and pain for Anne. And it wasn't as though there were specific instances in which each emotion was evoked individually. It was as if they came to Anne in all things, in the form of an inextricable, self-contained package deal.

On one hand, there was her job and the mill. She'd gotten a head start on the employees with the work she'd done on Sunday. But when she showed up on Monday and discovered that she was going to have to share the conference room she'd been using as an office, she was very taken back.

"Do you mean to tell me that there isn't another room in this place for you people to meet?" she asked in disbelief.

"Yes, ma'am, there is. But we've divided into groups—budgeting, marketing, production, and management, you see?" a wiry little man in his middle fifties told her.

"No. I'm sorry. I don't understand what that has to do with my office space."

"Well, the other committees are meeting in the other rooms, you see." The man could probably tell that this didn't mean much to Anne. "We're the smallest group, ma'am. Production. We thought you might not mind if we used one corner of this room. We'll try not to disturb . . . what you're doin'."

Anne looked around the large room, and except for the small table on the far side that she was using as her desk, the place was empty. How could she say no?

"All right. But don't anyone talk to me," she said, her pride making her sound self-inflated and immature. "I'm going to be very busy here."

The workers didn't talk to her, but they talked among themselves, and she repeatedly found herself listening to them.

Buck had told her the truth when he'd said that they weren't going into this project with their eyes closed. And it was beginning to sound as though they'd been thinking about taking this step for self-control long before Harriman decided to close them down.

Something in Anne was very pleased with the way they were thinking and making their plans. Things were discussed in slow, methodical steps—nothing rash or outrageous. She marveled at their knowledge of the textile industry, until it occurred to her to wonder who would know the textile industry better than textile workers?

That was on one hand. On the other, there was Buck. They were both very careful not to work later than four-thirty, which was when most of the other mill workers went home. They were very careful not to discuss the mill once they were alone together. And once they were alone together . . .

Well, Anne thought she'd discovered the meaning of the words *pure unadulterated bliss*. She truly couldn't recall being happier or more content. She felt wanted, desirable, and understood. They had long serious talks, they teased each other, they made love. Better yet, Buck became more than just a lover, he was her friend. She'd never had both in one person before, but she found that it made everything so much better.

Buck seemed to know things about her that could never be put into words. For instance he sensed that on the days she talked to Calvin Schwab it was best to leave her alone until she settled the turmoil the man stirred up in her. He knew that when she was calm again, she would come looking for him. He knew where to rub the kinks from her neck and where to touch to excite her the most. He felt her need to be loved madly and when she wanted to be cherished. There were many words exchanged between them, but there were also times when words weren't enough and when words weren't necessary.

Which reminded Anne of something else: where the three conflicting emotions of pleasure, confusion, and pain came into play. This part of her life was as intangible as tomorrow, as oblique as right and wrong, and as formidable as pride and self-respect. They churned within her constantly, like bat wings and lizard tongues in a witch's caldron.

Anne may have thought she was as tough as nails when her plane landed in Kentucky. She may have thought that closing down a mill and putting thousands of people out of work was men's play when she'd rented the car and started driving toward Webster. But everything had changed for her since then.

With each passing day a layer of corporate blindness was removed from her eyes, and she saw the people of Webster, Kentucky, for who they really were: simple, hard-working people who asked for nothing more than to keep their homes and make a decent living. She felt sure that someone in authority would call them the backbone of America. And yet, there she was, Anne Hunnicut, in a position to break that back? Somehow, it just didn't seem right.

She liked these people. They were a close-knit community of kind, generous men and women. She couldn't make her heart do what it had to do to destroy them.

Day after day she listened to the production committee toil over the question of which fabrics to specialize in. This was an important dilemma because the mill couldn't produce enough material for a large, varied market, but it could produce plenty of yardage for a small, specific one.

Eventually it became necessary for the marketing and the production committees to join forces, and, of course, the larger group needed the larger room—Anne's. Buck, who had been working with budgeting and management, joined the group to lend a hand.

"I was halfway hopin' something like this would crop up," he whispered to her under the pretext of saying a friendly good morning beside her desk. "Now we can see each other all day long."

"I'm Harriman's from eight to four-thirty," she whispered back, a strained smile on her lips, her gaze darting around the room to see if anyone was watching them.

"We've been through this before, Annie. There's no law in Kentucky against lookin' at a pretty woman." He grinned at her. "And you don't have to be so nervous. Everybody knows we're livin' together."

Anne gasped and looked mortified.

"Well, hell, Annie. Wha'd'ya think? This is a small town. And Bryce hasn't been home for days."

"Buck. What if Calvin or Harriman get wind of it?"

He was silent as a strange look crossed his face and then disappeared without a trace. "They won't get wind of it, Annie. It's none of their business."

That had hurt. She'd known instantly that she'd shamed Buck and sullied their relationship by fearing it would be discovered. But all she'd really been worried about was keeping her job. And that was confusing. Because she hated her job. She hadn't been particularly fond of it in the first place. She'd stayed on with Harriman to prove a point. And now that point seemed superfluous when compared to what she had to do to accomplish it, which was close down the mill. It sure was confusing.

But that was only the half of it. Anne knew as well as she knew her own name that it would take only four small words from Buck to get her to quit her job flat. The words were: Stay. I love you. Not one of them was over five letters long.

It was crazy. It was foolhardy. It was irresponsible. It was very, very risky. But with all her heart, it was what she wanted.

The trouble was, Buck had never once said he loved her. And aside from that one morning when, in jest, he had suggested she stay in Kentucky, he never spoke of the future. How could she tell him she didn't want to go home, that she never wanted to see New York again? How could she tell him that she wanted to stay with him, where she was happy and safe and life made sense. How could she tell him that she needed him to point out the simple, important things in life for her, that she wanted him close to her always or that . . . she loved him.

Lord, she *did* love him. From the very first, she'd loved him. She knew that things like this never happened in real life, that she was cruising for a bruising, but she couldn't help herself. She was in love with Buck.

But if he didn't have any plans for her in his future, what then? Back to New York and Harriman, she decided. It was the only way she could save face. Hence, the pleasure of the time she spent with the man who was fast becoming the most important person in the world to her and the confusion and pain of what would come of it. And there would be pleasure in going back to the office and thumbing her nose at the men, showing them that Anne Hunnicut *could* do anything she set her mind to, except fix her own car. But would it be worth the confusion and pain of having to live with what she'd done to the people of the town of Webster?

It was a week to the day when Anne's kettle of turmoil finally boiled over. She made a decision.

"May I get you a cup of coffee or a soda from the machine, Ms. Hunnicut?" Buck asked in an overloud and obvious voice as he came to stand beside her desk.

In a like manner, she replied, "Why, thank you, Mr. LaSalle. A soda would be nice."

As was their custom, she would offer to pay for the drink, and he would refuse her money. She would pretend to go back to work, and he would leave the room. She would wait until she could stand it no longer, and then she'd look up to see him standing in the hallway. Out of sight of the others in the room he would mouth the words, "Let's go home. I want you." Or he'd tap the imaginary watch on his wrist and silently say, "Thirty minutes and you're mine." On this particular day, it was "Wanna go fishin'?" and then that grin of his.

Anne's cheeks never failed to grow warm, and she'd want to giggle like a teenager. This particular day was no exception. Her heart danced a jig, her body quickened in anticipation, and she quickly looked down at the papers in front of her, trying to regain some control of herself.

"Who's gonna tell him?" someone in the group of employees was asking the others. The tone was deadly serious. *Tell who what?* Anne wanted to know as she tuned back in to their conversation.

She hadn't missed much of the workers' strategy planning over the past few days. She knew they had whittled their production market down to four or five possibilities and that they had been debating over the best options. They had two good ones that she was mutely rooting for, but they hadn't yet voiced an opinion on her personal favorite, the one she would have chosen if it were up to her.

"Not me," another man said. "I don't think he's wrong. If we stick to a local distribution, we'll cut the cost of transportation, and that'll make up for our limited sales."

This was true, Anne concurred.

"But with a cutback on our overhead, we can cover the cost of shipping the stuff to New York and sell twice as much," someone else offered.

This was true but risky, she told them in her mind, as she shuffled through the papers on her desk, looking for a specific contract.

"Not one of these is gonna work," the first man said. "Harriman can get twice as much to all of 'em twice as fast and at half the cost. We don't stand a chance. It's time to fold."

No! No, don't fold, her brain called in disbelief and alarm. *You can do it.*

"Buck thinks we still have a chance. I'll stand by him."

Good for you.

"I can't waste any more time. I gotta start lookin' for a job. I got kids to feed."

"We all do," a woman agreed. "I'm just not sure what to do anymore. I want to believe Buck, but I'm scared."

That was understandable to Anne. She was scared too. But in her hands she held the solution to their problems: a long-term, multimillion-dollar government contract for the fire-retardant material that the Webster mill specialized in. It would be a good foundation to keep the company open with and to build on later. Add to that the likelihood of loyal, local trade, which Buck was sure of, and . . . anything was possible.

The question now was should she, could she betray Harriman Industries? If anyone ever found out, it would mean her job. If it was the last link needed for the employees to pull the chain on the closure, she'd have to go home in disgrace. She'd have to swallow her pride and admit that she hadn't been able to close the mill down. She debated with herself right down to the wire, but when all was said and done, could she live with herself for the rest of her life, knowing that she could have helped these people to save the mill but didn't?

There were definitely times when having three older brothers had proved to be convenient. Anne knew six different ways to make a paper airplane. The cover letter attached to the government contract was of crisp military paper and folded into a fine fighter jet at Anne's insistence.

Without batting an eye or giving it yet another thought, she checked her target area to make sure no one saw her, then she lifted the plane into the air and sent it sailing. It touched down on the table, a four-point landing, gliding smack into the center of the perplexed committee.

A hush fell over the room. Using only her peripheral vision, Anne stared at her desk while the employees turned to stare at her. *Read it,* she shouted at them, even though her lips never moved. *Read it and please, please trust me.*

One by one she saw them turn their heads to the paper airplane. One of them reached out and picked it up. *Don't send it back to me. Read it.* She heard the sound of paper unfolding and breathed a sigh of relief. With a sense of a job well done, she went back to reviewing the retirement and disability benefits she'd been working on.

She gave Buck a distracted, half-smile of thanks for the soda when he returned several minutes later. She didn't want him to know what she'd done. Too late, she figured that he'd find out anyway from the workers, but she didn't want it to look as if she wanted his appreciation. Because she didn't. What she'd done, she'd done for herself, to ease her own mind by doing what she felt was the right thing to do, not because of her feelings for Buck.

"Where'd this come from?" she heard him ask minutes later. "How come we haven't seen this before?"

Anne wasn't sure if the committee shrugged in unison or if they all turned to stare at her pointedly. She kept her nose pointed at her desk and hardly breathed until she heard Buck speak again.

"Well, let's find the rest of this contract and get busy on it," Buck said. "This'll do it, but we've still got a lot of work ahead."

Someone left the room, and a few minutes later, Lily came to Anne looking for a particular file, one that contained a government contract for their flame-retardant fabric. Did Anne, by any chance, have it?

In all her life, Anne had never been so glad to see a Friday night roll around. All day long the committee members had gnawed and chewed on their government contract like sharks in a feeding frenzy. By the end of the day they all seemed well satisfied, but just watching them had worn Anne out.

She'd also done some very good work of her own. There were but a few final details left to take care of, and her job would be finished, she could go home. The thought was extremely depressing. Confusing too. And the only solution her weary, overworked mind had been able to come up with was going to sleep. It wanted to shut down and close out her disheveled thoughts and the chaos of her emotions. Like a survival mechanism, it wanted to block out the war going on within her, until the crisis was over.

Buck, however, made even something as simple as sleep seem impossible.

"I can't believe you exist with only one TV channel," she said, her expression revealing that she thought it was almost uncivilized. Admittedly she was feeling a little testy and unsettled about everything in general, but she was accustomed to having a broader range of television entertainment to choose from than *I Love Lucy* reruns and static.

"I told you," he said, walking into the living room with a cola for her and a beer for him, "we don't pick up the other channels because the mountains interfere with the reception. And I'd have to sell Bryce to be able to afford runnin' cable clear around the mountain from town. Luckily, this is the station that has Monday-night football."

What more could you ask for, Anne wondered sarcastically, then asked, "What about movies? Why don't you buy a VCR?"

Buck frowned and shrugged. "If we rented movies and watched them all at home, where would we take our dates on Saturday night?" He paused to give his own question some consideration. "Bowlin', I suppose, but it's not nearly as . . . romantic. Know what I mean?"

Dear Lord. She hadn't even left town and he was already talking about the dates he'd be having with other women. Anne's heart sank into her stomach and throbbed so hard, it made her sick. "Yes. I know what you mean. I'm going to bed."

She stood and looked down at him. He was

staring back at her, concern and speculation etched in his expression. "What's the matter, Annie? I asked you to go to a movie with me earlier, but you wanted to stay in." A small, wistful smile crossed his lips. "I even tried to get you to turn in early—with me—but you wanted to watch TV. Now you want to go bed. But I have a feelin' you don't want me to come with you. Am I right?"

Anne shrugged one shoulder indecisively but didn't answer him. She could hardly look at him.

"What's the matter, Annie? What have I done?"

"Nothing. You haven't done anything and nothing's wrong." She could tell by the look in his eyes that he wasn't buying this. "It's been a long week, Buck. I'm just tired."

He seemed reluctant to accept this, too, but didn't push it.

"I heard somethin' real interestin' today," he said. He was watching *Lucy* on TV, but his tone was baiting her to ask about it.

"What?" She never could pass up perfectly good bait.

"Liddy Evans was tellin' everybody at the mill how this nice lady from Philadelphia called and asked her a bunch of questions about her middle boy, Teddy. The one that has diabetes?"

"Yes."

"Well, I guess this lady said that she thought little Teddy was eligible for some special funding from the Diabetes Foundation. Liddy was pretty excited."

"That's wonderful. I'm glad for them both."

"You want to hear the interestin' part?" he asked, turning to look at her.

"No." She turned and took the first step up the stairs. She could feel him watching her and couldn't stop the warm, self-conscious flush that crept into her cheeks. This just wasn't her day.

"The woman from the foundation was named Grace Hunnicut."

"Dammit all to hell," Anne muttered under her breath, her shoulders sagging fatalistically. Aunt Gracie had promised to have someone else call so that there would be no link to Anne. Now the cat was out of the bag.

"You're gettin' quite a reputation down at the mill, you know, Annie. First the government contract and now this. People are startin' to think you're pretty terrific for a Yankee-type management person."

She sighed. "They told you about the contract." It was a statement not a question. Anne always hated this part about doing something nice for someone. She wasn't sure why, but it embarrassed her to death to have someone thank her for something she thought to be basic and human. But they invariably felt it had to be done. "My aunt wasn't supposed to reveal herself," she said in a soft voice.

Buck got up and walked across the room to her.

"Why do you feel so badly that I know the truth about you? Huh?" He bent to look into her face. "Is it so hard to have people knowin' that you're not as tough as you let on to be?"

"No. I just don't want them to think that they owe me anything in return."

"Why?"

She shrugged. "It wasn't any big deal. Calling my aunt was a simple thing to do. It was a shot in the dark that paid off. If she hadn't been on the board of directors, I wouldn't have thought of doing it."

"And the contract?"

"It's only a chance, Buck. It doesn't mean you'll succeed." She looked up at him then and shook her head over the praise she saw in his face. "I'm no saint, Buck."

He grinned at her. "No. You're not. But you're one hell of a woman, Annie."

Again she shook her head at him and said good night.

If he thought she was so wonderful, why didn't he ask her to stay with him, she asked herself, as she crawled into his sister's bed a long time later. It wasn't the first time the question had crossed her mind.

She'd stood in front of the window for a long time, already mourning the loses she was about to incur. She tried to tell herself that Kentucky was ugly, that Buck was a stupid hick, and that the people of Webster weren't much better, but she'd failed miserably. In a week's time, all three had come to mean more to her than anything else.

Buck had knocked on the door on his way to bed and had again asked if she was all right. She'd told him she was fine, but the truth was, she was far from it. She'd never felt so wretched or heartbroken. She'd taken her leave of a dozen places and hundreds of people in her lifetime, but it hadn't hurt like this. This time only part of her was leaving. She knew the rest of her would remain with Buck and in Kentucky for all of her days.

Already she felt lost and lonely. She let go of the hope of ever feeling as if she belonged. She would survive because it was her nature to do so. But from her present point of view her life looked like a hollow shell. Tears stung her eyes, and her throat constricted with pain. Her heart cried out for Buck; her body ached to be in his arms. All she heard was her heart's echo. All she felt was cold.

"You were only supposed to love him a little bit," she cried bitterly into her pillow. "You never were any good at having nice little affairs, you fool," she admonished herself.

So. Something inside her sighed haughtily. *You're giving up. You still have three or four days before you have to leave, but you're cut-*

*ting Buck out of your life early because you
know how it's going to end. Is that it?*

Well, what would you do? she asked her better half, the half that had encouraged her to love
him in the first place.

*Sweetie, I'd lap up every drop of honey in the
pot before I left. I sure as hell wouldn't leave
any for someone else.*

With a new resolve, Anne tiptoed down the hall
to Buck's room. The door was open, and she
stepped noiselessly into the room. Sheets rustled,
and she caught a flash of white as they were
thrown back from the bed.

Buck was waiting for her. His arms closed
around her readily and held her close, desperately
close for several seconds. Then his muscles relaxed a little. He pressed a tender kiss to her
temple and murmured, "Wanna talk?"

"No. I just want you to hold me for a while."

"I'm fixin' to."

Anne refused to allow another sad thought or
remorseful moment get the better of her. The rest
of the weekend belonged to her and Buck. She
wanted to cram it full of happy memories. She
wanted to make glorious, rapturous love with Buck
a thousand times. She wanted to know every little
thing there was to know about him, so that she
could cherish it over and over again when they
were no longer together.

Their mutual delight was uncontainable, spilling over into the workweek when they walked into
the conference room Monday morning. All eyes
turned to stare at them expectantly.

"Sorry we're late," Buck said, as a general greeting. Their tardiness might have been passed over
lightly or been excused without any notice at all,
except that neither of them looked particularly

remorseful, and they were both having an exceptionally hard time keeping a straight face. "We—" he looked to Anne for assistance and got a giggle, "we had car trouble."

Doubt settled into each and every face in the room. Buck made a halfhearted plea for mercy, then threw up his hands in resignation. "Okay. I admit it. I can't get enough of her. What can I say?"

By reflex, Anne gasped at his truthfulness and was frantically searching for some way to extricate herself from the situation, when she noticed that the workers had been quickly pacified by Buck's excuse. They acted as if it were far more believable that she and Buck had stopped by the side of the road to make passionate love in the front seat of his truck, than that they'd had car trouble. What's more, they didn't seem to think it was the least bit out of the ordinary. They didn't say a word about it; they simply smiled benevolently and moved on to the day's business.

She looked at Buck. He grinned at her and winked wickedly. "Ya see." He whispered his words so the others wouldn't hear. "I told ya it would be easier if you let me take the blame. They never would have believed us if we'd told them that *you* were the one who insisted we pull over."

"I was proving a point." She hissed back with great dignity.

Buck frowned. "I think I missed it."

"You said that you thought I should have more of an appetite in the morning. I was trying to prove to you that I have a very good appetite in the morning."

Buck stared at her, dumbfounded, for just a second, and then he gave her a crafty smile. "I meant for breakfast."

She gave him a craftier smile. "I know."

At noon that day, they agreed that they were

ready to call Joel Harriman, make a bid, and begin negotiations for the purchase of the mill. When
the small delegation of employees, including Buck,
went off to Drake Edward's office to make the call,
Anne began to watch the clock.

Twenty minutes past. Then thirty. She counted
every second and knew that the longer it took, the
harder Buck was fighting and the more disappointed and heartsick he'd be when he got the
inevitable answer. And the answer *was* unquestionable. It always had been. She felt like a traitor, knowing all along that the bid would be flatly
refused. She knew she was doing her job, being
loyal to the people who paid her wages. But in her
heart she felt she ought to be flogged for letting
the employees work so hard and for getting their
hopes up, when she had known from the start
how it would turn out for them.

All they had wanted was a chance, a fair chance
at trying to save the only life they knew, but they
hadn't really gotten one. The cards had been
stacked against them long before Anne had come
to Kentucky. They had never had a chance.

After nearly an hour of battling for a hopeless
cause, the workers returned, grim lines on their
faces. Anne wasn't surprised, but that didn't lessen
the sorrow she felt for them. Buck trailed in last,
looking beaten and dejected. Anne could actually
feel her heart cracking and tearing as it took on
the pain she saw in his eyes.

When he walked past her chair, he didn't say anything and didn't act as if he were truly seeing her.
But his hand skimmed across her back and gently
gripped the back of her neck in an intimate acknowledgment. It was as if he were wordlessly thanking her for the help she'd given them and apologizing
because her efforts had been wasted, as if he'd failed
her somehow. Then he joined the other employees
at the big conference table in the middle of the room.

"We gave it our best shot. We tried," Buck told his friends, trying to buoy their spirits and replenish some of their dignity. "I still think it could have worked, but it just . . . wasn't meant to be, I guess."

"What'll we do now?" someone asked. The destitution in the voice burned like acid in Anne's soul.

"What we would have had to do, anyway. Find new jobs," he answered fatalistically.

Anne could almost picture Buck's thoughts. He was already mentally selling his land and moving away from his home. He was digging up his roots and slowly dying inside.

She began to tremble from the inside out, reacting to the melee her emotions were in. She felt anguish and anger. She was sorry and indignant. She was frightened and feeling strangely courageous. Oddly enough, it was her courage that won out . . . or was it insanity she wondered briefly as she glanced over at the table of woebegone workers.

Maybe she was delirious, she speculated. She'd lose her job for sure if her employers ever heard what she was about to do. Still, using a perverse sense of logic, Anne felt very *right* about it. She wouldn't go home the superwoman she'd set out to prove herself to be, but she would go home with something better—a smile in her heart.

She leaned over and removed the morning newspaper from the trash can beside her desk. All three of her brothers had had jobs delivering newspapers at one time or another. And so, with the expertise of one who had often been called upon to help deliver those papers, Anne folded this one into a tight loglike object and pitched it over her shoulder with enough precision to have it plunk down in the center of the table.

By now she was very good at using her peripheral vision to watch the workers. They turned. They stared at her in confusion for several seconds, and then they went back to mumbling and grumbling among themselves.

Damn. They weren't picking up on her clue to their solution. She glanced around the room hastily, looking for something else she could use to get her point across. Granted, it would have been easier if she had simply blurted out the answer to their problem verbally. But she felt as if she still owed something to the Harriman corporation. She could hint, but she couldn't tell them.

She was greatly relieved when her gaze fell across a small electric clock radio that someone had brought to work the week before, because there had been no other way of telling the time in the conference room.

Slowly she scooted her chair away from her desk, stood, and walked over to the radio. She pulled the cord from the electrical socket, and then carried the radio over to the big table, setting it down beside the newspaper.

She had their attention at least. She looked from face to face to face . . . and saw nothing. They all looked stupefied by her weird behavior. Even Buck was frowning at her.

She snatched up a piece of paper from the desk, flipped it over to the clean side, and then grabbed a pen away from the man sitting beside her. She drew a square on the paper, and in each of the bottom corners she drew a small circle. Across the square she wrote *television*—instead of *TV*—so they couldn't possibly confuse it with anything else. Then she put her artwork in the center of the table, along with the radio and the newspaper, and stood there feeling mighty pleased with herself.

They all read the word out loud, putting their own little question mark behind it. There was no flash of realization, no flicker of inspiration in the

expressions she saw. There *was* some obvious
concern for *her* thought processes, however.

"Oh, for crying out loud! What is this?" she
shouted, pointing to the newspaper and addressing herself to Buck, who was the only person in
the room she knew well enough to take out her
frustrations on.

"A newspaper," he said kindly, humoring her
dementia.

"And this? What is this?"

"A radio."

"Now this. What is it?"

"A television."

"That's right. Now think about it." She stood
with her arms akimbo, staring at him, daring
him to be brilliant enough to figure out her riddle.

A light flashed, then faded, then reappeared
with some degree of certainty in his eyes. His
mouth fell open, then curved upward at the corners as it all became clear to him.

"The press," he murmured, as if it were a highly
classified secret weapon. "Harriman wouldn't want
this in the news. He wouldn't look like a very nice
person if he destroyed a whole town by refusin' to
let us buy the mill, now would he?"

Anne was pleased to see how one little spark of
smarts could spread like wildfire. She was elated
on a nonnarcotic high to see hope and enthusiasm back in their eyes. She freely admitted to
being addicted to this look on people's faces. And
it was for that reason, not their gratitude, that
she sometimes did the things she did for them.

Judiciously she began to back away from the
jubilation at the table, to go back across the line
of demarcation that separated them. But before
she could get there, one of the women stopped her.

"Ms. Hunnicut, ma'am. I—we'd like to—"

"Joyce, isn't it?" Anne asked, hoping her smile
would made up for her rudeness in cutting the

woman off. She walked back to the woman and
extended a hand to her. When Joyce nodded and
took her hand, she said, "I have to tell you, I have
to tell all of you," she added, turning to the group
as a whole, "that I have been very impressed with
your work this past week. I confess that I thought
this was a hairbrained idea at first, but you've
made it very clear to me that no one knows the
textile industry better than textile workers.

"I probably shouldn't have eavesdropped on your
meetings as much as I did," she continued, un-
abashed. "But I'm glad I did. My work here is
finished, and I'll"—she purposefully looked back
at Joyce to avoid Buck's reaction—"be leaving tomorrow. So I'd like to take this opportunity to tell
you all that I think you're going to do just fine as
an employee-owned company and to wish you the
very best of luck."

She waved and nodded through the varied and
generally incoherent remarks from the workers as
she went back to her desk. She had avoided an
out-and-out thank-you and told Buck she was leaving at the same time. She knew she should be
feeling very clever, but she wasn't. Setting a departure date made her feel heavy and sick inside.

Clearing off her desk didn't take long. It was
midafternoon by the time she delivered the last of
the files she'd been using back into Lily's capable
hands.

"Thank you for your help, Lily," she told the
kind-faced secretary. "I'm glad we met."

"You're pure wool and a yard wide, Anne Hunnicut," she said. "I'm mighty proud to know ya."

Anne sensed that being compared to fine cloth
was as good as being thanked and felt highly
complimented. She blushed and murmured a
thank-you, then backed out of the office.

"Hey, sugar."

She let out a startled squeal and spun around

to face Buck in the hallway. "You startled me," she uttered, gasping.

"And here I thought you'd be tickled pink to see me."

"I'm always tickled pink to see you. Can't you tell?"

He went to an extreme to check her out thoroughly, in a way that sent her heart soaring and brought a heated flush back into her cheeks. "Well, I guess you do look a little rosy and excited, at that," he said, pleased. He bent and placed a slow, warm kiss on her lips. His hands curled around her upper arms and pressed gently before he pulled away.

For a long moment he said nothing, expressing his thoughts only in the way he was looking at her and in the tender manner in which his hands caressed her arms. He wasn't happy that she was leaving.

She wasn't happy about it either. *Tell me you're as crazy as I am,* her heart pleaded with him. *Tell me that in one short week you've fallen hopelessly in love with me, and then ask me to stay. Please.*

"I'm on a break. Can I buy you a cup of coffee?" he asked, giving her a slow sweet smile.

"Something cold, maybe? I'm a little rosy and excited right now.'"

He grinned at her then, and said, "You'll have to drink it out of a can. The machine doesn't provide Dixie cups, you know."

"That's okay. I already have one."

Ten

Anne was very proud of the way she was handling the situation. She'd left work early, had a good cry, and looked fairly normal by the time Buck got home a few hours later. She was determined that nothing was going to spoil their last night together.

She made sure that there was no way of telling how shattered she felt, as she played and laughed with Buck while they cooked dinner. She was careful to keep her head turned away from him when her eyes became blurred with tears as they took one last walk through the woods to the pond. But there was no pretense in the ardor she displayed when they kissed or in the contentment she felt in his arms.

They sat out on the little jetty until the sun was almost gone. Buck's back rested against the piling, and she sat between his legs, savoring the warmth and strength of his body next to hers.

"How did your second call to Harriman go this afternoon?" Anne asked, after a long peaceful silence. She couldn't help but wonder, although she was a bit surprised that she hadn't wondered until now.

"I thought we weren't going to talk shop after business hours," he said, his lips tickling her ear.

"I'm done. The deal is over. And besides, I'm curious."

"We didn't make the second call."

"But why not?" she asked, turning in his arms to look at him.

"We decided we could just as easily wait until Wednesday or Thursday to blackmail them with the media."

Anne sighed and knew a warm, swelling sensation in her chest. Her heart felt full to the brim with gladness and gratification as she snuggled back into Buck's embrace. She had put her trust in the workers, and they were repaying her by waiting until she was far from Webster before using the information she'd given them. It had been a good decision on her part, all the way around.

"Why didn't you tell me you were plannin' to leave tomorrow?" he asked, his voice barely disturbing the quiet of the night. Lord how she did love to listen to him talk. When his voice was soft, each word was like a sensual massage, relaxing and invigorating at once.

"I didn't know for sure until today," she said, closing her eyes, soaking up the sounds of the night and the resonance of Buck's voice.

"I don't suppose there's any way you could put it off for a few more days?"

She smiled gently and pressed his arms tighter around her. She knew what he was feeling. She felt it far more intensely, of course, but she wouldn't insult him, or herself, by thinking that he didn't care and wasn't hurting. He did care about her. He simply didn't care to the extent or with the intensity that she did.

"That wouldn't make it any easier, Buck. I have to leave eventually. And besides, I had Lily fax the last of my work to the office this afternoon, along with my arrival time."

"I was hoping for more time," he said sadly. She felt his chest rise and fall with a deep sigh. "What about vacation time? You could—"

"Buck. Let's not do this," she said, as she turned in his arms. She framed the face she loved so dearly with her hands and pressed her lips to his tenderly. "Let's enjoy our last night together."

She didn't have to coax him. He tangled his fingers in her hair and kissed her with a passion that seemed to have no boundaries. It was as if he were trying to put a lifetime of kisses into one. Anne felt it and recognized it, because she was trying to do it too.

Buck broke off suddenly and slapped himself violently on the leg. "Dammit. Come on," he said, standing and pulling her to her feet. "I wanna make love to you somethin' awful, but if we do it here, you'll wind up with 'skeeter bites all over your cute little butt."

Anne laughed. "And wouldn't that make for an interesting plane ride tomorrow."

Hand in hand they walked back through the woods. The sky was darkening quickly. Already Anne could see the stars beginning to twinkle. She was amazed that Buck's steps seemed so confident, when she couldn't see as far as three feet in front of her.

The long silences between them had never bothered Anne. She had accepted from the start that even though he was sharp witted and well informed, Buck didn't initiate conversations just to hear himself talk. He kept his own council and appeared to enjoy the stillness around him. However, he seemed particularly talkative on this night.

"I suppose Webster's pretty dull compared to what you're used to," he said out of the blue.

"It's quieter, but I certainly haven't been bored," she said, intimating that he was the reason things hadn't been dull in Webster.

"Well, what if we hadn't met. What would you think of Webster then?"

"I don't know." It was a truthful answer.

"We live simple, ordinary lives here. We grow up, get jobs, get married, raise kids, and die. Along the way we laugh a little, cry a little, struggle a lot, and do what we can to be proud of ourselves. All in all, our lives are good, but they're not a thrill a minute. Do you think you could ever live like that? I mean, without all the lights, the fancy stores, and the city hubbub."

Anne's heart had begun to race about the time he mentioned marriage. Now it was chugging full steam. What was he trying to ask her? Was this it? The moment she had all but given up on?

She took a deep breath and tried to answer him as honestly as possible. "This is all on the speculation that I hadn't met you, right?"

"Right. I don't really enter in to this. This is just you, alone."

Her heart was still hammering, but it was up in her throat now. She had a sick feeling this wasn't going to be what she thought it was. She tried to clear her throat before answering. "Well, I do love Kentucky, but I don't think I'd be very good at staying home with the kids and keeping the kitchen sink clean, like some of the women do here. I don't have that kind of patience. I like the kind of work I do. I wouldn't mind having the kind of life you talked about, but I'd need an outside job too."

She couldn't see his face, but he seemed to be considering her answer. Then he said, "You told me before that you liked it here. You could still move here. We could use a controller at the mill. I can't see you havin' any trouble gettin' a job there."

"Thanks," she said meekly. For the mill, he could ask her to stay. But not for himself. "I'll keep it in mind . . . if I ever want to change jobs."

Swallowing her pride had never come easy to her. Even as they emerged from the woods and began to cut across the small field to the house, her dignity was stuck tightly in her craw.

Still, she wanted to be fair. Buck hadn't meant to hurt her. She instinctively knew that. At the moment he was as much against ending their affair as she was. And there was no denying that if she came back to Webster and took a job at the mill, their liaison would go on. She would be happy. But for how long? She knew herself well enough to know that she was an all-or-nothing person. She wanted Kentucky, the mill, and Buck, but not necessarily in that order. If she were going to make a new commitment, she'd make it to all three or not at all.

"Annie?" Buck's voice gently called her from her reverie. "You got somethin' on your mind? You're awful quiet."

"I was just thinking about tomorrow."

"What about it?"

She stopped in the middle of Buck's backyard and turned to face him. One hand was already locked in his, the other automatically reached out to touch his chest. "I want you to go to work in the morning before I wake up."

"I want to stay until you have to leave for the airport."

"I'd rather you didn't. I—I'm not very good at good-byes," she said, thinking of what an ironic lie that was. She'd been saying good-bye all her life. She just couldn't say it this time. With slightly more enthusiasm she added, "You know what I'd really like to do?"

"What?"

His voice was so soft, it was hardly more than a whisper. So she whispered too, very seductively, "I want to go to bed with you right now." Both of her hands came up to work on the buttons of his shirt. "I want to make love with you all night long." She pressed her lips to the underside of his

chin as she pushed his shirt aside and pulled
upward on his white T-shirt. She slide her hands
across smooth, taut abdominal muscles and murmured, "I want to fall asleep in your arms at
dawn, and when I wake up, I— "

She'd had Buck all primed to kiss her when his
head bobbed up as if he were an animal sensing
danger. "What the hell is that?"

"What?" she asked, and then she heard it too.
Laughter. Children's laughter. And it was coming
from the other side of the house.

The flash of light from the bulb hanging over
the back door blinded her, but it didn't impair
her hearing.

"See. I told you they'd be back soon, if we waited,"
she heard Bryce saying to someone Anne couldn't
see.

"He *is* going to die this time," Buck muttered,
as he took Anne by the arm and led her to the
back door. "What the hell are you doing here?"

"I used to live here. Remember?" Anne could
see Bryce's teasing smile as her eyes began to
clear. Buck opened the door and let her pass
through into the kitchen. "Not that I'm complain-
ing about my present living arrangements, mind
you. But now I have a woman of my own to deal
with, big brother. And *she* wanted to come callin'."

There was some muttering about "controlling
women" and "look who was talking," but Anne
missed most of it as Liddy Evans entered the
room with all three of her children trailing behind
her. Anne hadn't realized that her "middle boy"
was only about five, while the other two were
probably six and four. They looked so much alike,
they could have been triplets.

"Hello, ma'am. Ms. Hunnicut," the young woman
said in a nervous voice. She kept reaching out to
touch her children, pulling them close to her, as
if keeping them corralled. "I'm sorry if we're

disturbin' ya, but I made Bry bring me over here as soon as we found out you was leavin' tomorrow. I wanted—"

"Oh, please, call me Anne," she broke in to avoid what was about to become a very awkward moment. "And you're not disturbing us. Why, do you know that I had no idea your boys were so young . . . or so handsome," she said, turning her attention to the boys.

She stooped down to get their names, and that was all it took. For the next two hours the boys ran wild in the yard or came into the house to add life to the adult conversation in the living room, where Buck had finally broken down and offered coffee to their guests.

Liddy Evans slowly relaxed enough so that Anne could finally get a glimpse of the girl Bryce was so interested in. She was really very charming in a shy, sweet way that no doubt appealed to Bryce's protective instincts. She obviously was under a great deal of pressure and suffered from stress, but Anne could tell from the boys' behavior that she was handling things very well. She simply didn't look or act as if it were possible. There was a lot more to Liddy Evans than met the eye.

"Gutsy girl," Anne said, thinking out loud as she and Buck stood on the front porch watching the tail lights of Bryce's truck fade in and out of the night shadows.

"Yep." Buck loudly filled his lungs with fresh, clean air and just as loudly released it before pushing himself out of his slouch position against the railing. His arms circled her from behind, and he nuzzled her neck. "But I've got one of my own to deal with now. And she was just about to tell me what she wanted. Remember?"

"Yep. I do," she said, turning in his arms, locking her own around his neck and smiling up into his face. "Lordy," she said, affecting a poor imitation of a southern drawl and rolling her eyes. "Aw thought they was never gonna leave."

"You makin' fun a me, lady?" he asked, his eyes narrowing dramatically. He grinned at her in his own special way, that way that made her stomach flip over and try to turn itself inside out.

"Why, Awd never dream of doin' such a thing, Mr. Buck. Least ways not with you bein' so big and strong and all."

"I'm gonna big and strong you, if you don't stop that," he said, swatting her bottom playfully. Anne's hand instantly went to the same place to scratch vigorously. He grinned. "What's the matter? Got an itch?"

"Why, Aw do declare. Aw do believe one of those varmints bit me, clean through mah dungarees."

Always the gentleman, he placed his hand where hers had been doing the scratching. "I'm gonna bite you clean through your dungarees if you don't stop talkin' like that. I like your snooty twang better, and I want to get down to some serious business here."

His hands cupped her bottom and held her pelvis close to his. Anne gave him a sly, knowing smile. "Why, Aw do believe you've already fallen upon the best way of shutin' me up, Mr. Buck. And, Aw swear, if you don't do it pretty soon, Awm gonna say something right nasty about your general Robert E. Lee."

Buck was not a man to take a threat lightly. His mouth swooped down on hers like an owl on a field mouse. In no time at all he'd kissed her senseless, her body yearned and clamored for his most intimate touches. She grew hot and wet and feverish until she felt her fingernails digging into her palms, even through the wads of Buck's shirt she had fisted in her hands.

"What was that you were saying about biting

me through my jeans?" she murmured weakly on a quick gasp of air, her Southern drawl forgotten.

Buck laughed but not in his normal, robust way. "Come on," he said, scooping up her limp body into his arms. "I've got a better idea."

And that he had, indeed. In their lovemaking before this he had taken her to visit the stars and the moon. He'd sent her soaring to Jupiter and Mars. He'd loved her gently; he'd taken her fiercely. He'd shivered at her touch and surrendered to her unconditionally. But on this night, their last night, their love was like nothing that had taken place before.

They left the planet Pluto in their wake, as they suffused eternity with their passion. It was their epoch, their moment in time. They filled light-years with their ecstasy. They injected a lifetime of need with their exhilaration and joy. Their contentment spanned a generation of boundless desires; an age of seasons knew of their emotion, and the universe was their home as they lay in each other's arms.

And when at last reality overpowered their rampant splendor, and they began to count time in seconds and minutes once more, Anne's heart broke. Under the weight of Buck's head, as it rested peacefully on her breast, her heart shattered into a thousand unmendable pieces. She brushed her hand across his back, trying to memorize the feel of his skin, the strength of his body, and knew that she'd never be able to recall the exact same texture in her mind.

Time was her enemy. It was moving swiftly toward dawn. Time was also sadistic, she knew from past experience. It would fade her memory of the past week. It would blur Buck's face until she could barely remember what he looked like. But it wouldn't change the love she had for Buck. It wouldn't ease the pain of leaving him or alter the emptiness his absence would create.

She held him close and relished him. She couldn't bear the thought of saying good-bye to him.

"Buck?" she said, her whispering voice sounding loud and harsh in the darkness.

"Mmm?"

"Please don't be here when I wake up," she blurted out, afraid she wouldn't be able to say it, afraid she was going to start to cry.

His body tensed. "Annie . . ."

"Please," she pleaded when he sounded as if he were going to argue with her. "I want this to be my last memory of you. Holding you like this."

He released a sharp breath, but he didn't say anything. Anne thought he was going to give her this one last wish, but as his body began to relax against hers, he also began to shudder. His arms tightened around her possessively. Concerned, she intensified her own embrace. She closed her eyes and allowed her tears to run freely from their corners as she realized that he, too, was weeping, softly and quietly against her breast.

She held him in her arms, loving him more than he'd ever know, until the sun changed the black of night to the gray of early dawn. She listened to his deep, rhythmic breathing, feeling drained and numb. Tired eyes, stinging and dry, closed. When next they opened, Buck was gone.

Eleven

Gray. A mixture of all colors and no color. A very dull color, to be sure. Anne didn't think she'd ever seen so much gray in all her life. Everywhere she looked, everything she saw was gray. The New York sky was overcast, smoggy and gray, not at all like the blue skies of Kentucky. The buildings were gray. Men in elevators were wearing gray suits and women's summer fashions seemed to be predominantly gray this season. The world's hue was just as it should be to suit her disposition. Gray.

She stood in a throng of pedestrians waiting for the lights to change. She tried to recall exiting the subway and walking the three blocks it took to get her to this particular corner every morning. But as was the case so frequently these days, she feared she was doomed to spend another day wandering around in a dim, mindless fog. Not in hopeless despair, mind you, just a nothingness, a numbness that filled her heart and body. A dispiritedness in her soul.

She couldn't bring herself to feel happy about being home and once again in familiar surroundings. Nor could she still feel the acute pain and wretchedness she'd been submerged in a month before, when she'd first returned from Kentucky.

Sustaining that kind of agony for a prolonged period took up too much of her energy, a commodity she found little enough of these days. And so her life was neither black nor white, happy nor sad. Her life had become empty, void. It was gray. Not a pretty color, but one she could exist with without expending too much effort.

Still, as accomplished as she had become at not thinking, avoiding memories, and suppressing her feelings, some things did manage to filter through to her consciousness.

She stepped off the curb and looked up at the towering blue-gray building on the other side of the street. The Harriman Building. She'd looked up at it in the exact same way her first morning back. She had felt *everything* that morning. She'd felt beaten and haggard. She'd looked up at the building with intense hatred, despising everyone inside and everything it stood for. She'd been angry with Buck for not telling her that he loved her and begging her to stay. She'd missed him grievously.

"So. You're back." Calvin Schwab had said, leaning against her office door, a superior look on his long, clean-shaven face, his gaze knowing.

"Yep. I'm back," she'd said, using one of Buck's words. She'd kept her glance quick and otherwise hidden from his as she'd shuffled through the papers on her desk. She'd been afraid of what he might see in her eyes.

"Did you hear what happened when they called and tried to make their bid?" he'd asked, a gloating sound heavy in his voice. Anne bit her tongue. She'd wanted to stand up and call him a pig. Had he any idea how much he'd hurt and disappointed those people?

Instead, she'd slit open a letter a little too zealously, then leaned back in her chair to consider it. "I heard."

"Well, your plan worked perfectly, Anne. Letting them play at being businessmen for a while to keep them quiet and then slapping them down hard worked like a charm. We haven't heard a peep out of them since Monday. Ya done good, kid."

"Thanks." She hadn't realized that had been *her* plan, but she'd plastered what she hoped would look like a grateful smile on her face and looked up at him. He nodded his pleasure several times, and then strolled back to his own office.

However, the next time she'd looked up to see him standing in her doorway had been much more gratifying to Anne. She had set out to win his approval and respect, and she had apparently done that. But to see him glowering and angry was much, much better.

"Those damn hillbillies are at it again!" he'd announced later that afternoon. "They've given us until tomorrow morning to reconsider our decision to sell, before they go to the press."

"No," she'd said, her face a study of disbelief. "Well, which one of those dummies do you suppose thought of that?"

"LaSalle. He's the one who called Harriman." She'd half-suspected that being bypassed by Buck, who had gone directly to the top with his threat, was why Calvin was so angry. He believed in the chain of command, especially since he was so near the top of it. "That guy irks the hell out of me."

Anne had nodded sympathetically. "He does have a way of getting to you." She knew better than anyone. "What'll happen now?"

He'd shrugged restlessly. "Harriman doesn't want the publicity." He'd stopped to reconsider the problem for a moment. "Hell, I say give 'em plenty of rope. Let them hang themselves with it. They won't last six months."

Anne knew better, but she had let her head sway back and forth as if she agreed, as if to say he was probably right. Inside, her heart was smiling.

In that moment she had felt connected to Buck. Miles separated them, but they'd touched. And she'd known, as well as she'd known the pain in her heart, that he'd been feeling the same closeness at that moment. Their spirits had embraced, caressed and become one.

That was the last warm feeling Anne had had in almost a month. It had lasted well into the evening, and she had cherished it. She was happy for Buck and for the people of Webster. The mill would continue to nurture the town. Little would change, and that made Anne happy too. She liked to think that Webster, Kentucky, would always be as she remembered it. Beautiful, peaceful, and safe.

The phone rang. She was stretched out on the sofa, thinking of Webster and missing Buck. The phone was less than two feet away from her. She could have answered it, but she didn't want to exert that much effort. Her machine answered for her.

"Annie? This is Buck. I . . . well, I miss you. I just wanted to hear your voice. Call me sometime. We can still talk sometimes, huh?" There was a pause, as if he were going to say more, then the line went dead.

Call him sometime? Why hadn't he simply suggested that she commit emotional suicide every night? Calling him and saying good-bye over and over again would amount to the same thing. She'd never call him. She knew that. Clean cuts healed faster than long jagged wounds. He should have known that and left her alone, she thought bitterly. Racked with sobs, her chest painfully tight, she cried his name and ached for him to answer.

That scenario was repeated night after night for nearly a week before Buck gave up on her. She'd waited for the phone to ring again. When it didn't, she cried once more as she pictured Buck at the Steel Wheel, a girl in very tight jeans sitting on his lap.

Shortly after that, everything in her life just seemed to shut down and go insensate. Gray. Getting up in the morning was an ordeal. Going into work was worse. If she'd had the energy, she might have gone out looking for a new job. She had proven her point at Harriman. Maybe not the way she had intended in the beginning, but well enough at the office—and certainly to herself. She'd done the right thing for all the right reasons, and she was proud of that at least.

She stepped up on the curb and around the people heading for the double chrome-and-glass doors leading into the Harriman Building. Without looking she automatically pushed the elevator button and stood in a limp stance, waiting for it to arrive.

"Young people." A woman behind Anne spoke the words with great disparagement. "They give up so quickly nowadays. If they don't get the six-figure salaries their first year out of college, they think life isn't worth living. They turn to drugs and become street people. Whatever happened to the good old American work ethic?"

"Sylvia," the woman's companion said in a hushed tone of voice, "calm down please. Trevor will find his way."

"No. He thinks one try is plenty at anything. He failed as an investment counselor, so now he wants to go back to school to become a doctor. I swear, Milly, Marvin and I'll be paying that boy's tuition until the day we die if he doesn't figure out that nothing worthwhile comes easy. Everything takes work."

The elevator doors opened and Anne walked in, followed by the two women. One of the women, obviously Sylvia, gave her a "young person" stare with a raised brow. Anne smiled weakly in return and watched the numbers above the door light up as they began their ascent.

"My mother used to tell me that water could wear down a mountain if it kept moving in one direction," Sylvia said, leaning toward Milly and keeping her husky voice a little lower, excluding Anne from their conversation. "Do you know what Trevor said when I told *him* this?" Milly shook her head. "He said, 'I don't want to wear down a mountain, Ma. I want to be a doctor.' I tell you, Milly, young people have no sense of perseverance anymore. They try it, if it doesn't work like magic, they give up. No backbones."

Regrettably, Anne's floor came before Sylvia's, but not before the woman had struck a chord deep within Anne. The lift stopped, the doors opened, and the two women stared at Anne for several seconds before she realized she was supposed to get off.

Water *could* wear down a mountain! So could the wind. So, too, could Anne Hunnicut, she hypothesized, a brilliant smile forming on her lips as her life blossomed before her eyes.

"Oh, sorry," she muttered to Sylvia and Milly as she moved to get off the elevator. Impulsively she held the door open and turned to Sylvia, grinning. "Thank you," she said. "Find a way to make Trevor listen to you. You're a very wise woman, Sylvia."

The woman looked aghast that Anne had been eavesdropping, but for the life of her Anne couldn't feel sorry that she had been. Everything seemed so clear now.

A giggle bubbled up inside of her, and she didn't try to suppress it. She marched down the main hall with a spring in her step that drew the attention of several secretaries along the way. All the way to the end of the hall, to where the great window offices were located, her path to happiness grew clearer and clearer. So that by the time she reached Calvin's outer office, she knew exactly what had to be done.

"Mornin'," she said cheerfully. "Cal in?" Before the woman could answer, Anne was halfway to the door. She wasn't normally so pushy, but her life had been on hold too long. She felt superenergized, revved up, and ready to go. "I'll just go on in. This'll only take a second." Then she stopped and turned back to the somewhat flabbergasted woman. "Say," she marveled, "your blouse isn't gray at all, is it? It's teal."

"Y—yes," the woman stammered, stunned.

"What a relief," she said, grinning as she opened Calvin Schwab's office door.

"Anne," he said, looking up from the work on his desk, puzzled. "Were we supposed to meet this morning?"

"I believe we were, Cal," she said, placing herself in the hands of fate.

He frowned. "When was it scheduled?"

"A million years ago. In the stars." She was way beyond caring how she sounded. *She* knew where she was going and what she wanted, and *that's* all that really mattered.

"What?"

"Never mind, Cal. I just came in to tell you that I quit."

"What?"

"My job. I quit."

"What?"

"I'm sorry, but I don't want to give you two week's notice. In fact, I quit as of yesterday, because I have a zillion things to take care of today. And you needn't tell me that this is very irresponsible of me, because I know that. Actually, I don't think I've *ever* been so irresponsible in my whole life. But I just can't help it Cal. I gotta go."

"Where, for Pete's sake?"

"Kentucky, Cal."

"What?"

"I have to keep moving forward, or I'll never wear down the mountain. And I don't care if it takes me the rest of my life to do it, I'm going to wear him down."

"What?"

"Thanks . . . for everything, Cal. Have a wonderful life," she said sincerely, as she backed up toward the door.

"Anne. Are you out of your mind?" he screeched, appalled by her behavior.

She grinned and another silly giggle escaped her. "Yep. And it feels great."

She had ducked into her office, took what she wanted, left what she didn't, and was back at the elevator doors inside fifteen minutes. With the skill of the practiced, she had half her apartment packed, an appointment with a realtor for the next day, and a moving company lined up for the day after that, all by five o'clock. She hadn't felt so alive in weeks. Why hadn't this occurred to her before?

She'd never been a quitter, never . . . well, except for that very morning at Harriman's. And that had been a long time coming. And yet, she'd given up on Buck without so much as a good old American heave-ho. She had gone into their relationship thinking of it as a temporary thing. Buck had too. Her feelings had changed. She wanted Buck forever, but she'd been too proud to tell him. What if, just what if Buck's pride was getting in his way too? What if he did love her?

Ha! It didn't matter if he did or not. At this point, if there was the slightest possibility of a future with Buck, she was going to take it. She'd make him love her. If the move to Kentucky didn't work, she'd try something else, and she'd never give up. Not ever.

She loved Buck and she loved Kentucky and she was going to have it all. And everyone who knew Anne Hunnicut knew that there wasn't anything she couldn't do. Once she set her mind to it.

"I'll call when I have a new address and number to give you," she said, speaking excitedly into the phone as she shoved the last of the packed boxes into her bedroom with her foot and closed the door. "The movers'll be here tomorrow, and I'll leave after they do, so I'll probably have something definite for you by Friday or Saturday."

"Are you sure this is wise, honey?" her father asked, worry and concern clear in his voice. "It's all so sudden. You don't usually make your mind up about this sort of thing quite so quickly."

"It's the wisest thing I've ever done."

"Well, you've got a good head on your shoulders, and you've always known what you wanted. So, I suppose you'll do just fine," he said, trying to convince himself that Anne's odd behavior was still based on the good sound judgment she'd used all her life.

"I'm going to do better than fine," she told him. They exchanged news about her brothers and finally said good-bye.

Anne stood with her hands on her hips, wondering what else was left to do. All but the bare essentials were packed and stacked neatly in her bedroom, out of sight, so the realtor could get a good look at the apartment. She'd left the furniture in place, because even as excited as she was about this particular move, she still hated the "moving" look a place got when the furniture was out of place, set about haphazardly.

With nothing but last minute things to do, she walked over to the window and looked down at the busy street below. Two months earlier she'd been so content with her life. She never would have dreamed of giving up her cute little apartment in the family neighborhood she'd grown so fond of. She looked down at the shops and stoops and admitted that she'd miss them. A little bit.

There were people she wanted to say good-bye to, sights and tastes she wanted to experience once more before she left. The idea of throwing her own farewell party took root just as the phone began to ring.

"Annie? Is that you?" Only one person in the whole world called her Annie. She was too surprised to speak. It was as if her thoughts had conjured him up into reality—an extremely weird phenomenon. "Damn machine," she heard him mutter.

"No, no," she said hastily, her heart seeming to come to an abrupt halt. "Buck, it's me. I'm here."

"Oh, Annie. Thank God," he said, relieved.

"Buck? Are you all right. Is something wrong?"

"Well, not now. But I was beginnin' to think I'd never find you. I guess I should have taken a cab, but I figured that I might as well go ahead and jump in with both feet, so I took the subway. It's not exactly like a bus, is it?" His soft laugh kicked her pulse rate into a barreling speed.

"No. It isn't," she said a bit breathlessly, afraid to ask the question uppermost in her mind, fearing she'd be disappointed.

"I broke down and finally asked a man for directions, but I think I took one too many blocks to the right and turned left when I should have turned right. But to make this long story a little shorter, I'm lost."

Now she had to ask. "You're in New York?"

"It's real hard to get lost in Webster, Annie."

She laughed, as much at his discomfort as in pure joy. "Where are you, do you know?"

"Some I-talian place. I can't even pronounce it."

"Spell it for me." He did. "Stay right there, Buck. I'll be there in twenty minutes. Don't move."

She spent the first two minutes screaming and flitting about her apartment, bouncing off the walls as if she were a bird escaped from its cage. In the next few minutes she pulled herself together and freshened up, trying to look as presentable as possible under the circumstances. She still made it to the restaurant, which was two blocks away, with three minutes to spare.

She stood in the doorway while her eyes adjusted to the dim lighting. His deep, intimate voice caught her attention before she could clearly make him out. There were only a few tables occupied in the main room. *He* was sitting in the lounge with a beer in his hand, regaling two very enthralled young women with his good looks and soft southern accent. He looked as contented as . . . as a goat in a can factory.

"I swear. I caught one as fat as ol' Mario's arm there, last summer. Course—" He looked up then and saw Anne. He grinned that belly-twisting grin of his and got slowly to his feet. "Annie," he said. Well, she thought he said it. His lips moved, but there was no sound.

They walked across the room, weaving through tables and strangers, until they met in the middle. For a long awkward moment they stood staring at each other, gauging reactions, questioning, silently wondering. He didn't seem to be aware that his hands had reached out and taken hers, as if he were testing to see if she were real.

"Hi," she murmured stupidly, when the silence began to tear at her nerves, and she couldn't think of anything else to say.

"Hey." His voice was hardly more than a whisper.

They embraced. It was an uncomfortable gesture, a formality between two people who weren't at all sure what was happening.

Then Buck stood back and looked at her. Without blinking, he watched her, his eyes foretelling a thousand ways in which he wanted to kiss her. And then, looking suddenly self-conscious and out of place, Buck glanced around the restaurant as if he were trying to find something. Then he turned back to Anne.

"I . . . Is there someplace we can go? Someplace private. We need to talk," he said, his voice urgent.

"My apartment?"

He nodded, turning her back toward the door. He made a typically southern adieu to Mario and the girls that curled Anne's lips and warmed her heart. A month's time hadn't changed him. He was still the friendly, overly confident, kind, sweet, sensitive, adorable man she'd fallen in love with.

"Pictures and maps don't do this place justice, do they. Ya gotta see New York to believe it," he commented as they left the restaurant and entered the stream of pedestrians on the sidewalk.

Laughing softly, she took his hand and held it tightly. She was supremely eager to be alone with him. She refused to pinch herself. If she were dreaming, she certainly didn't want to wake herself up.

They filled their time walking with small talk. How were Bryce and Liddy? Jimmy McKee and Lily and a few other people? How was his trip? Did he drive or fly? How were things at the mill? What position did he hold now?

"Well, that's one of the things I wanted to talk to you about in private," he said, following her up

the second flight of stairs to her apartment door.
"But they'll be closin' the deal in another month
or so. Art Anderson, the attorney, and Lily and
Drake'll be comin' to town then, to sign all the
papers. Everyone's real excited. I think it's gonna
work out fine."

"But what about you? Are you keeping your old
job or taking a new one?" she asked, sensing that
he was deliberately leaving something out. She
had the key in the lock but was too busy looking
at him, trying to read his expression, to turn it.

He bussed her lips with his, and then smiled at
her. "Let's go inside. There's somethin' a lot more
important than the mill I want to talk to you
about."

She opened the door and turned on a lamp.
They both stood in the middle of the room, looking at the absence of anything personal or interesting in the room. Anne had completely forgotten
about her move. She had hoped to hear what he
had to say before springing her own surprise on
him, but he was bound to notice that something
was amiss.

He was frowning.

"What's wrong?" she asked, noticing his hesi-
tancy.

"I guess I didn't realize what a *clean* person you
were." He gave the room another glance and then
shrugged. "It doesn't matter, though, I . . ." He
turned back to her, took her by the shoulders,
and led her over to the couch, pressing down
gently until her knees bent and she sat. Then he
walked away from her, as if distancing himself
would make whatever he had to say a little easier.

He paced back and forth between the bedroom
and kitchen doors. His agitation made Anne
squirm uneasily and move to the edge of the couch.
She'd been nervous and jumpy to begin with; his

silence was exacerbating it. She was half-expecting him to tell her he was pregnant.

Suddenly, he gave a shaky laugh and ran his hand through his hair and down the back of his neck anxiously. "Jeez, Annie, I've been practicin' this speech for weeks, and now I can't remember how it starts."

She smiled at him encouragingly but didn't know how to help him. Besides, she had news that needed to be told too. She was busy searching for her own lead-in line.

"Do you remember the night you accused me of usin' you? The night you said that you thought I'd had things all planned out between us, right from the start? When we met on the road?"

"The first night we made love?" she asked with a sweet soft smile of remembrance. "Yes. Vividly."

"Well, you were right. I did have all sorts of plans laid out in my mind for you. Five minutes after we met. But none of 'em had anything to do with the mill."

She met his gaze straight on. He had that same look on his face that he'd had the day they'd met. That voodoo look that seemed to paralyze her and make her heart quake with fear at the same time. She didn't speak but waited for him to continue.

"You see, the minute I saw you standin' there on the road I wanted you. When you got ticked off and told me what an expensive piece of meat you were—" he smiled and chuckled then, remembering the moment, "I figured you might not just hop into bed for me, that I might have to court ya for a while."

"Court me?" She couldn't help giggling at the old-fashioned term. But only in her mind was she amused. In her heart, his words conjured up emotions of another nature. It surged with excitement and with such vigor that it seemed to energize every cell in her body.

"Woo you," he said, grinning. And then he gradually became thoughtful once again. "That was the initial plan. I've revised it since then. My goal was basically the same, but . . . it all changed. Everything is different."

"How is everything different?" she asked in a coaxing voice, wishing she could tell if he was feeling as supersensitized as she was, wondering if he was as anxious inside as she felt.

He looked at her for several long seconds. She saw uncertainty and a real live fear in his eyes that she never dreamed someone as bold and self-assured as he could feel. He turned away from her. Absently, he twisted his MADE IN AMERICA cap in his hands, then he turned back to face her a few seconds later.

"Annie. I . . . damn. This is so hard to explain," he said, concentrating on every word he let out of his mouth. "I feel things for you. You scare the holy livin' hell out of me, but . . . but it's worse when you're not with me. I want to hold you in my arms and make love to you till you scream, but . . . I'm afraid to touch you. You're different from the others."

"How am I different?" she asked, worried. She couldn't change who she was, but she did want his approval, she wanted him to like her as a person, love her as she was.

"You're more. You're more woman than any other female I've ever known. You're as smart and tough-willed as any man I know, and you're as gentle and tender-hearted as a momma with a brand new babe." He walked across the room to the window and stood looking down into the street.

Again Anne was struck by the difficulty this man had in expressing his feelings. Every word seemed to cost him dearly, yet he went on talking because he needed her to understand how he felt.

"It makes me crazy that you don't seem to need

a man in your life. I kind of admire your independence, but then . . . well, it makes me wonder what I have to offer you."

"Who said I didn't need a man in my life?" she asked, floored by his remark, wondering how she'd given him that impression. "I may not need one to support me financially, but I've often wished I could find one to support me emotionally. One who would meet me at home every night. One I could share a life with, raise children with, grow old with. There are different ways of needing someone, you know. I think financial need is probably the most insignificant of all."

First he glanced over his shoulder at her, then he turned around completely, leaning back against the windowsill. "All I know is that I sure have one helluva need for you," he said without a trace of humor in his voice. "Annie, I love you somethin' awful."

Anne was as restless as spit on a griddle. Already she was trembling with desire. She wanted Buck to touch her, to feel his lips on hers, and to know his hands on her bare skin again. She longed for the taste of him, for the heat of his body, and to hear him groan in misery and delight. If he wanted to kiss her again, now would be a good time, she thought. If he was going to act, this would be the moment to do it, she urged him mentally.

But quite obviously, Buck wasn't finished with his speech. He held up his hand and motioned her to be silent when her mouth opened to speak her heart's desire.

"No. Wait a second," he said gravely. "There's more. I need to get it all out and over with."

This was beginning to sound like the big *BUT* that all too often accompanied good news. She swallowed her words of love and devotion and sat half-thrilled, half-dreading whatever he was about to say.

"I quit my job."

"You what?"

"I quit my job at the mill."

"Why?" she asked in disbelief.

"Because I want to be with you!" he said, holding his hands out at his sides, as if the act explained itself. "I wanted you to stay with me. Stay in Kentucky, work at the mill and marry me. But the more I thought about it, the more I realized that I couldn't ask you to give up your life here. I didn't have anything *better* to offer you. So, I thought—" he looked down at the toes of his boots, "I thought I'd come to New York and live with you."

Everything and nothing flashed through Anne's mind and sent it spinning. She could hardly believe what she was hearing. He'd quit his job? He'd given up his beloved Kentucky just to be with her? It was a very good thing she couldn't think of anything to say. The lump in her throat would have choked her. Tears stung her eyes as she stood and crossed the few feet that separated them physically.

He looked up at her when her feet came into his view. She couldn't help smiling at the uncertainty in his expression. She'd probably never know what it had cost him to come to her like this, but she knew he had paid dearly.

She hadn't realized that she was crying until he reached out and tenderly wiped a tear from her cheek. She swallowed hard several times and finally managed to speak his name.

With both hands he cupped her face and feather-touched her cheeks with the pads of thumbs as he probed her soul through her eyes. With the same light touch, the same reverent awe, he pressed his lips to hers. He sipped at her bottom lip, and she leaned into his embrace, pressing herself close to his warmth and his strength, feeling anchored for the first time in her life.

There were no loose ends, no questions, no fear of never belonging in her life. Buck was her hearthstone. His arms were her home. It didn't matter where they were; as long as they were together she was sheltered, cherished, and bound deeply and eternally in one safe familiar place. Buck's heart.

Feverish kisses dulled the memories of the weeks spent in misery without him. She was exultant. She wanted to bellow from the rooftops that she was in love and that Buck belonged to her. His lips tickled down her neck, and she giggled her delight.

"Quitting your job was a stupid thing to do," she said, laughing. She took his face in her hands to draw him away from the cleavage of her cotton shirt. She wanted his full attention.

"I'll find somethin' else to do," he said, shrugging. "I'm pretty good with my hands. And I saw a help-wanted sign in Queenie's Massage Palace down the way a bit."

"Queenie's . . . do you know what that place is?" she asked, her eyes wide.

"Sure. Folks go in there to have their backs rubbed. I think a walk in the woods would take care of a lot more of their tension, but this bein' New York and all . . ." He shrugged. "Anyway, I thought I could give back rubs until somethin' better comes along."

"Back rubs? Buck—"

He broke out laughing then. He snatched Anne up into his arms and twirled her around once before kissing her soundly.

"You *do* love a country bumpkin, don't you?" he said, laughing at her gullibility, insinuating that she'd most likely never get over thinking she was more worldly than he. "I don't care what I do. I'll find something. I'll get used to New York. All I care about is being with you, my Annie."

He kissed her again, and she let him, but just once. Then she pushed him away. "I want to be with you, too, my love. But now that you've quit your job, we're both out of work. We won't be able to afford to feed each other. We'll be too weak to make love. We'll die in bed—"

"What?"

"We'll die in bed—"

"No. What do you mean, we're both out of work? You quit your job too?"

"Yep," she said, smiling and stepping away from him. "And I'm not all *this* clean." She gestured with her hands to the room in general. "This is how things look when I'm moving."

"Moving?"

She nodded once. "I had this great offer to be controller at this little textile mill in Kentucky. I've decided to take it."

Things she hadn't previously noticed in his facial expression began to melt away. Regret, sadness, some pain. A slow grin came to his lips. His green eyes twinkled with awareness. Tension slipped out of his shoulders, and his stance seemed to loosen all at once. The knowledge of what she'd done, of how she felt about him, returned the cockiness to the tilt of his head. It was like creating a macho monster, something no woman in her right mind would do, but she laughed anyway. He was her macho monster, and she was crazy about him.

"How come you didn't tell me you were in love with me?" he asked, a sly grin on his face. He took two easy strides forward and looked down at her face, taking in every detail with great care.

"How come you didn't tell me?" she countered.

He looked surprised. "I did, sugar. A hundred

different times. A hundred different ways. Don't you remember?"

All she could do was nod silently. She did remember. She'd felt his love. He'd told her every time he'd touched her or looked at her. It was in his kiss. It had shivered through his body every time they'd made love. He wasn't a talker; he was a shower, a doer.

"See where bein' too proud'll get you?" he went on, brushing a few stray hairs away from her face with the palm of one hand, while the other slid possessively over her hip to her bottom. "Up here pinin' away for me all that time, when we coulda been lovin' each other."

"Pining? Me?"

"Weren't you pinin'? I was pinin' for you somethin' awful, Annie," he murmured, moving closer.

"Then why didn't you stop me? Tell me not to go?" she asked, childishly resentful of the fact that he hadn't dramatically chased her all the way to the airport, begging her to stay with him.

"What? You think a good ol' boy like me would ever think of gettin' by with tellin' a modern Yankee lady like you what to do?"

"I think you've gotten by with it before," she said, refusing to fall for his dumb yokel act again.

He took a quick glance at her apartment, and then looked back at her, all the teasing light extinguished from his eyes. He looked exposed and in need of reassurance. "I'm real sorry, Annie. I thought this was what you wanted. I loved you so much, I thought letting you go was the only way I could make you happy."

"You're what I want, Buck. You make me happy."

"And I'm going to make you a whole lot happier in a minute here," he muttered, his mouth moving against her neck, his hands fumbling at the buttons on her blouse. "That is, if you haven't packed up the bed yet." After a minuscule pause, he tumbled her to the floor, and added, "Hell. Who needs a bed?"

Who, indeed, she wondered sometime later. They had rarely gotten to a bed in Kentucky. Why should anything be different in New York? Diamonds were diamonds. Men were men. Women were women. But there was nothing else in the world like lovin' a good ol' boy.

THE EDITOR'S CORNER

Those sultry June breezes will soon start to whisper through the trees, bringing with them the wonderful scents of summer. Imagine the unmistakable aroma of fresh-cut grass and the feeling of walking barefoot across a lush green lawn. Then look on your bookstore shelves for our striking jade-green LOVESWEPTs! The beautiful covers next month will put you right in the mood to welcome the summer season—and our authors will put you in the mood for romance.

Peggy Webb weaves her sensual magic once more in **UNTIL MORNING COMES,** LOVESWEPT #402. In this emotional story, Peggy captures the stark beauty of the Arizona desert and the fragile beauty of the love two very different people find together. In San Francisco he's known as Dr. Colter Gray, but in the land of his Apache ancestors, he's Gray Wolf. Reconciling the two aspects of his identity becomes a torment to Colter, but when he meets Jo Beth McGill, his life heads in a new direction. Jo Beth has brought her elderly parents along on her assignment to photograph the desert cacti. Concerned about her father's increasing senility, Jo Beth has vowed never to abandon her parents to the perils of old age. But when she meets Colter, she worries that she'll have to choose between them. When Colter appears on his stallion in the moonlight, ready to woo her with ancient Apache love rituals, Jo Beth trembles with excitement and gives herself up to the mysterious man in whose arms she finds her own security. This tender story deals with love on many levels and will leave you with a warm feeling in your heart.

In LOVESWEPT #403 by Linda Cajio, all it takes is **JUST ONE LOOK** for Remy St. Jacques to fall for the beguiling seductress Susan Kitteridge. Ordered to shadow the woman he believes to be a traitor, Remy comes to realize the lady who drives him to sweet obsession could not be what she seemed. Afraid of exposing those she loves to danger, Susan is caught up in the life of lies she'd live for so long. But she yearns to confess all to Remy the moment the bayou outlaw captures her lips with his. In her smooth, sophisticated style, Linda creates a winning love story you won't be able to put down. As an added treat, Linda brings back the lovable character of Lettice as her third and last granddaughter finds true happiness and love. Hint! Hint! This won't be the last you'll hear of Lettice, though. Stay tuned!

(continued)

With her debut book, **PERFECT MORNING,** published in April 1989, Marcia Evanick made quite a splash in the romance world. Next month Marcia returns to the LOVESWEPT lineup with **INDESCRIBABLY DELICIOUS,** LOVESWEPT #404. Marcia has a unique talent for blending the sensuality of a love story with the humorous trials and tribulations of single parenthood. When Dillon McKenzie follows a tantalizing scent to his neighbor's kitchen, he finds delicious temptation living next door! Elizabeth Lancaster is delighted that Dillon and his two sons have moved in; now her boy Aaron will have playmates. What she doesn't count on is becoming Dillon's playmate! He brings out all her hidden desires and makes her see there's so much more to life than just her son and the business she's built creating scrumptious cakes and candies. You'll be enthralled by these two genuine characters who must find a way to join their families as well as their dreams.

As promised, Tami Hoag returns with her second pot of pure gold in *The Rainbow Chasers* series, **KEEPING COMPANY,** LOVESWEPT #405. Alaina Montgomery just knew something would go wrong on her way to her friend Jayne's costume party dressed as a sexy comic-book princess. When her car konks out on a deserted stretch of road, she's more embarrassed by her costume than frightened of danger—until Dylan Harrison stops to help her. At first she believes he's an escaped lunatic, then he captivates her with his charm and incredible sex appeal—and Alaina actually learns to like him—even after he gets them arrested. A cool-headed realist, Alaina is unaccustomed to Dylan's care-free attitude toward life. So she surprises even herself when she accepts his silly proposal to "keep company" to curtail their matchmaking friends from interfering in their lives. Even more surprising is the way Dylan makes her feel, as if her mouth were made for long, slow kisses. Tami's flare for humor shines in this story of a reckless dreamer who teaches a lady lawyer to believe in magic.

In Judy Gill's **DESPERADO,** LOVESWEPT #406, hero Bruce Hagendorn carries the well-earned nickname of Stud. But there's much more to the former hockey star than his name implies—and he intends to convince his lovely neighbor, Mary Delaney, of that fact. After Mary saves him from a severe allergy attack that she had unintentionally caused, Bruce vows to coax his personal Florence Nightingale out to play. An intensely driven woman, Mary has set certain goals for herself that she's focused all her attention on attaining—doing so allows her to shut out the hurts from her past. But Bruce/Stud won't take no for an answer, and Mary finds herself caught under the spell of the most virile man she's ever met. She can't help wishing, though, that he'd tell her where he goes at night, what kind of business it is that he's so dedicated to. But Bruce knows once he tells Mary, he could lose her forever. This powerful story is sure to have an impact on the lives of many readers, as Judy deals with the ecstasy and the heartache true love can bring.

We're delighted as always to bring you another memorable romance from one of the ladies who's helped make LOVESWEPT so successful. Fayrene Preston's *SwanSea Place:* **DECEIT,** LOVESWEPT #407, is the *pièce de résistance* to a fabulous month of romantic reading awaiting you. Once again Fayrene transports you to Maine and the great estate of SwanSea Place, where Richard Zagen has come in search of Liana Marchall, the only woman he's ever loved. Richard has been haunted, tormented by memories of the legendary model he knows better as the heartless siren who'd left him to build her career in the arms of another. Liana knows only too well the desperate desire Richard is capable of making her feel. She's run once from the man who could give her astonishing pleasure and inflict shattering pain, but time has only deepened her hunger for him. Fayrene's characters create more elemental force than the waves crashing against the rocky coast. Let them sweep you up in their inferno of passion!

As always we invite you to write to us with your thoughts and comments. We hope your summer is off to a fabulous start! Sincerely,

Susann Brailey

Susann Brailey
Editor
LOVESWEPT
Bantam Books
666 Fifth Avenue
New York, NY 10103

FAN OF THE MONTH

Ricki L. Ebbs

I guess I started reading the LOVESWEPT series as soon as it hit the market. I had been looking for a different kind of romance novel, one that had humor, adventure, a little danger, some offbeat characters, and, of course, true love and a happy ending. When I read my first LOVESWEPT, I stopped looking.

Fayrene Preston, Kay Hooper, Iris Johansen, Joan Elliott Pickart, Sandra Brown, and Deborah Smith are some of my favorite authors. I love Kay Hooper's wonderful sense of humor. For pure sensuality, Sandra Brown's books are unsurpassed. Though their writing styles are different, Iris Johansen, Joan Elliott Pickart, and Fayrene Preston write humorous, touching, and wonderfully sentimental stories. Deborah Smith's books have a unique blend of adventure and romance, and she keeps bringing back those characters I always wonder about at the end of the story. (I'm nosy about my friends' lives too.)

I'm single, with a terrific but demanding job as an administrative assistant. When I get the chance, I always pick up a mystery or romance novel. I have taken some kidding from my family and friends for my favorite reading. My brother says I should have been Sherlock Holmes or Scarlett O'Hara. I don't care what they say. I may be one of the last romantics, but I think the world looks a little better with a slightly romantic tint, and LOVESWEPTs certainly help to keep it rosy.

60 Minutes to a Better, More Beautiful You!

Now it's easier than ever to awaken your sensuality, stay slim forever—even make yourself irresistible. With Bantam's bestselling subliminal audio tapes, you're only 60 minutes away from a better, more beautiful you!

__ 45004-2	**Slim Forever**	$8.95
__ 45112-X	**Awaken Your Sensuality**	$7.95
__ 45035-2	**Stop Smoking Forever**	$8.95
__ 45130-8	**Develop Your Intuition**	$7.95
__ 45022-0	**Positively Change Your Life** ...	$8.95
__ 45154-5	**Get What You Want**	$7.95
__ 45041-7	**Stress Free Forever**	$8.95
__ 45106-5	**Get a Good Night's Sleep**	$7.95
__ 45094-8	**Improve Your Concentration** .	$7.95
__ 45172-3	**Develop A Perfect Memory**	$8.95

THE DELANEY DYNASTY

THE SHAMROCK TRINITY

- ☐ 21975 RAFE, THE MAVERICK
  by Kay Hooper $2.95
- ☐ 21976 YORK, THE RENEGADE
  by Iris Johansen $2.95
- ☐ 21977 BURKE, THE KINGPIN
  by Fayrene Preston $2.95

THE DELANEYS OF KILLAROO

- ☐ 21872 ADELAIDE, THE ENCHANTRESS
  by Kay Hooper $2.75
- ☐ 21873 MATILDA, THE ADVENTURESS
  by Iris Johansen $2.75
- ☐ 21874 SYDNEY, THE TEMPTRESS
  by Fayrene Preston $2.75

THE DELANEYS: *The Untamed Years*

- ☐ 21899 GOLDEN FLAMES *by Kay Hooper* $3.50
- ☐ 21898 WILD SILVER *by Iris Johansen* $3.50
- ☐ 21897 COPPER FIRE *by Fayrene Preston* $3.50

THE DELANEYS II

- ☐ 21978 SATIN ICE *by Iris Johansen* $3.50
- ☐ 21979 SILKEN THUNDER *by Fayrene Preston* $3.50
- ☐ 21980 VELVET LIGHTNING *by Kay Hooper* $3.50

Bantam Books, Dept. SW7, 414 East Golf Road, Des Plaines, IL 60016

Please send me the items I have checked above. I am enclosing $_____ (please add $2.00 to cover postage and handling). Send check or money order, no cash or C.O.D.s please.

Mr/Ms _____

Address _____

City/State _____ Zip_____

SW7–4/90

Please allow four to six weeks for delivery.
Prices and availability subject to change without notice.